D0021722

THE
GHOST
SHIFT

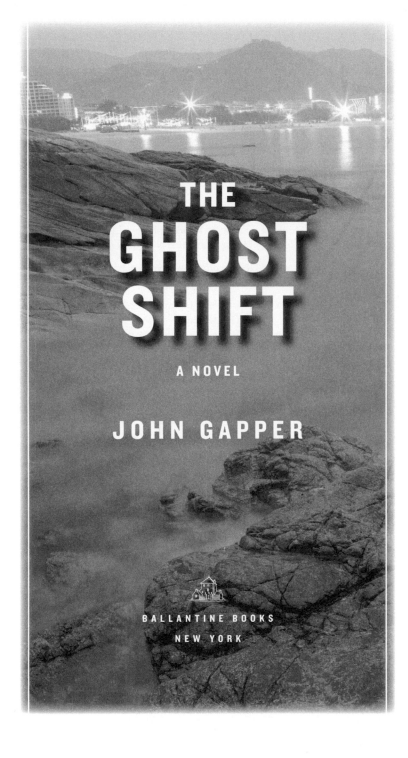

THE
GHOST
SHIFT

A NOVEL

JOHN GAPPER

BALLANTINE BOOKS

NEW YORK

The Ghost Shift is a work of fiction. Names, characters, places, and incidents either are the product of the author's imagination or are used fictitiously. Any resemblance to actual persons, living or dead, events, or locales is entirely coincidental.

Copyright © 2015 by John Gapper
Map copyright © 2015 by David Lindroth, Inc.

All rights reserved.

Published in the United States by Ballantine Books, an imprint of Random House, a division of Random House LLC, a Penguin Random House Company, New York.

BALLANTINE and the HOUSE colophon are registered trademarks of Random House LLC.

Library of Congress Cataloging-in-Publication Data
Gapper, John.
The ghost shift : a novel / John Gapper.
pages ; cm
ISBN 978-0-345-52792-9 (hardcover : acid-free paper)—
ISBN 978-0-345-52794-3 (ebook)
1. Political corruption—China—Fiction. 2. Corporations—Corrupt practices—China—Fiction. 3. China—Fiction. I. Title.
PS3607.A66G48 2015
813'.6—dc23   2014031964

Printed in the United States of America on acid-free paper

Title and part-title page images: copyright © iStock.com / © Kanmu

www.ballantinebooks.com

2 4 6 8 9 7 5 3 1

First Edition

Book design by Victoria Wong

In memory of my mother

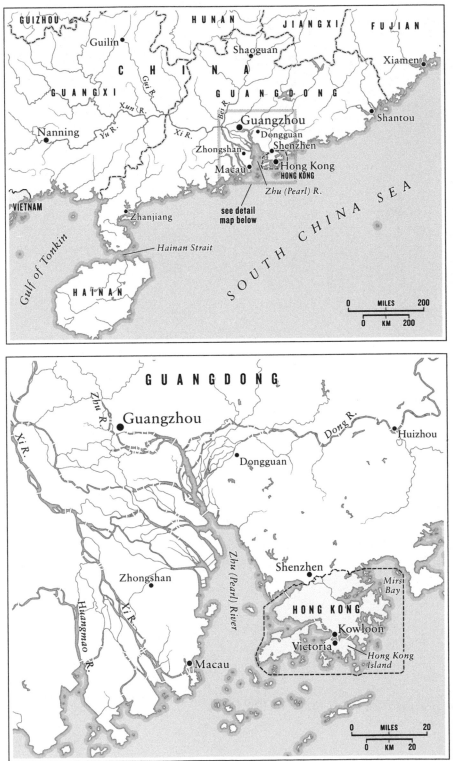

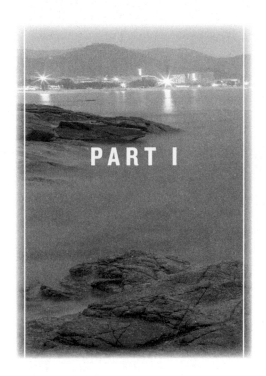

PART I

1

Guilin, 1989

*M*argot grips the armrest tightly as the Southern Airlines flight descends, hardly noticing the green hills and lakes below, the lush countryside so unlike Beijing's arid heat. She has suffered a terrifying journey in an Antonov turboprop that lumbered into the air in Shenzhen, propellers whining as it bounced westward. Only in the final, floating moments before the wheels bang onto the runway tarmac does she see the beauty of the place.

The airport is lined with fields and as the aging plane shudders toward the low-slung terminal, tooth-shaped limestone hills appear in the window. She pauses on the stairway as the other passengers leave, some staring at her western face, and breathes in the aroma of earth and humidity. This is the China that Margot loves, the one she will soon lose. She hasn't been outside of Beijing for a long time; it is like stepping into a steam bath that soothes her clenched muscles.

Walking through the terminal, she stiffens again. Two military vehicles are parked by the exit at a bus stop, and a line of soldiers from the People's Liberation Army stands by, rifles held at a diagonal. Their faces are blank under their green peaked caps with the red star encircled in gold braid. Margot avoids their gaze. Those weapons mean death—she had heard muffled sounds of gunshots echoing across Beijing two months earlier, like fireworks in Tiananmen Square. When she ventured out of their compound the next morning, the spring's excitement had vanished from the faces of passersby. They all kept their heads low, trying to be invisible.

The three-wheeled motorcycle taxi bumps along a potholed high-

way, past lines of pencil-trunked trees. As they reach the center of Guilin, bicyclists swarm them. Margot has never felt so lonely, on this journey that may change everything. He hasn't come, and she doesn't believe his excuse. It is his way: His was was to fix things and leave the details to others. He requires the freedom to walk away; she has seen him check the exits upon entering an unfamiliar building. Margot forces herself not to mind too much, even to laugh. But now, alone in this city, among three-wheelers piled with people and vegetables and crates of chickens, she feels betrayed.

She catches a glimpse, on one side of a boulevard, of two gilded pagodas in the morning sun, and cranes her neck to look back. The driver doesn't slow down, speeding past a cluster of bicyclists with a muttered oath of irritation in a dialect she doesn't understand. They must be close, she thinks, and pulls a clasp mirror from her bag and dusts her cheeks with powder, trying to spruce herself up. In the tiny bobbing circle, her face looks ashen and crumpled, hopeless, and she snaps the mirror shut.

It is farther than she had imagined. They emerge on the other side of the city center and wind through hills before plunging into a district with roads bristling with shacks and workshops. In their ill-lit interiors, stuffed with doors, pipes, and metalwork, men check stacks or haggle over a transaction. Then onward again, past a street market with stallholders squatting in the road and ducks poking their heads through cages to gape at the customers. A school, a playing field, before the houses fall away and they reenter the countryside. The driver swerves up a long dusty track surrounded by watery fields.

"Where are you taking me?" she calls to him in Mandarin. But he does not seem to hear.

Just as she is starting to panic, he turns a final bend, stamps on the brakes, and lights a cigarette. She opens the door and climbs out. They are in the middle of nowhere, the fields stretching to hills and sky on one side—deep, luminous greens and blues, as if she is seeing them through Polaroids. From behind, she hears the high-pitched chatter of children and turns to face a concertina barrier with a sentry hut to one side and a courtyard beyond. Steps lead up to a blocklike four-story building—a brutalist place whose builders lacked any sense of style. Six small children in muddy smocks watch wide-eyed, as if they have never seen anyone like her.

The doors open and a man strides down the stairs, scattering the children with a swat of his hand. He gives them a hard glance and turns to Margot with a broad, fixed smile, acting out a greeting. The expression stays in place as he walks across the yard, a young woman following a pace behind. The man is wearing a Mao tunic, his hair molded on his head as if glued down, making Margot feel even more disheveled. As they reach the barrier, a guard emerges to open it and the man bows to her.

"We were told about you. Follow me," he says. It sounds like an order, translated into poor, mumbled English by his companion. As they walk, she grimaces at his back like a naughty student and the translator stifles a smile.

They sit on hard chairs in his office, official photographs of Mao Zedong and Deng Xiaoping on the wall, and make small talk about her journey and his job. As they talk, she glances over his shoulder at the children walking down the hall of the Social Welfare Institute. Margot wonders how long this has been their home, why they are so quiet, and how they are punished if they misbehave. Holding her teacup on the saucer, her hand trembles as she waits for the protocol to finish. She already feels like running away from the place and she's been there only twenty minutes. When honor is satisfied and she has signed a form she does not bother to read and smiled and bowed again, she is taken into another room. By now she is shaking.

There, for the first time, she sees her, lying inside a wicker basket, covered with a thin blanket.

Friday will be Margot's thirty-fourth birthday, and this is every present she's ever gotten, all wrapped into one. She's read stories of orphanages being dumping grounds for the disabled and has tried to prepare herself for the bad side of this unexpected offer—it can't come without complication—but the baby is perfect. The basket rests on a table, and Margot brushes back a lock of hair on the girl's forehead as she sleeps. When she puts a finger under the baby's hand, the tiny fingers clasp it. As if she's been waiting for Margot to come.

A woman is close by. Margot had not noticed her yet because of *her intense focus on the child. The woman is fifty, she guesses, with a broad face split by a crooked smile that reveals a missing tooth. Reaching down, the woman fusses with the blanket, tucking it in tightly.*

"Hello," *Margot says in English. The woman smiles and clasps one of Margot's hands. Then she nods and waves at the child, as if to introduce her. She reaches into the basket before Margot can say,* "Please don't bother, let her sleep"—*not that the woman would understand, what is she thinking?—picks up the baby and puts her in Margot's arms. It is such joy, after everything, that she can't help crying. As she dabs at her face with a tissue, the older woman takes charge. The baby's cloth diaper is wet; the woman gestures inquiringly, prompting Margot to fetch the bag she's brought, stuffed with bottles and formula and baby clothes and Pampers from Hong Kong. She stumbles putting on the first diaper, and the woman helps her.*

They return to the courtyard, where the driver is standing next to his car smoking. Suddenly remembering her camera, Margot digs into her bag. She hands it to the translator and poses with a smile, one arm around the woman's shoulders and the other holding the gift she has received—a daughter.

2

Guangdong, 2012

The Wolf was waiting for her.

He stood in the far distance, on a ridge between two banana fields, facing Mei. The moonlight illuminated his pale face and the gray wedge of hair that marked him out from others in the fifth generation, with their black slicks of hair, red ties, and unlined faces. They looked as if the Party had granted them, along with all the other perks, eternal youth.

He was called Lang Xiaobo; his family name—狼—was the same character as "wolf." The Commission for Discipline Inspection cadres used it as a nickname, and Mei had complied without thinking. It was then, slipping into the mud as she climbed out of the Audi A8 and cursing at herself for not having worn boots, that she realized how apt it was. He was like an animal, snout to the sky, tensed for intruders. It was midnight and the clouds had cleared, cooling the air. She was relieved to be there, not wrestling with her sheets in bed.

Mei stood at the border of the old and the new: Guangdong's peasant past and the electronics factories of its future. In the distance she saw the lights of the giant Humen Bridge spanning the Pearl River. The glowing beads a mile or so away were trucks on the Jinggang'ao Expressway driving between Guangzhou and Shenzhen. A low coaster passed on a tributary, its backwash lapping over the shallow banks. Refineries and factories hummed on every side, separated by dark patches—the farms and rice paddies that had once covered the delta.

Farms lingered among the rail lines and freeways on messy patches of land that had not yet been ripped up for industry or grabbed for apartment blocks. Here, peasants still grew bananas, strawberries, and lychees, damming the mud in ridges to irrigate the crops. They built ponds, where they raised fish and eels caught at sea or in rivers until they were big enough for the tanks of seafood restaurants. A few huts perched at the water's edge. Inside one, a lantern flickered.

"Fuck it."

Her concentration broken, Mei looked across at the young man on the far side of the Audi. He was bending over in annoyance to scrape mud from his polished shoes, a lock of hair falling over one eye.

"What's wrong, Yao?"

"I'd rather be in bed."

"Having fun, were you?"

Mei stepped past a makeshift barrier erected by the uniformed personnel of the Dongguan Public Security Bureau to warn off intruders. There was no need—nothing had driven on the road since their arrival. But it gave the cops something to do, she supposed. One kid stood alert in his blue-and-white uniform—he'd found a job and wasn't about to give it up. He offered a white-gloved salute, snapping his fingers to his cap and staring ahead, not daring to demand Mei's card. She nodded, enjoying his subservience. He looked well suited to the job: high school diploma, not so bright. The kind who had once bullied her but wouldn't get that chance again.

Yao joined her. "Who's your boyfriend?" he said, gesturing with a thumb over his shoulder to the guard.

"Him?" She was half-listening to Yao, but her mind was on the scene in front of her. She didn't understand why they were there. Corruption among Party officials, backhanders, sweetheart deals, soft loans, stock transfers—these were the bread-and-butter work of the Commission. Trying to make the elite behave itself, in the face of all the temptation, but nothing that required a bunch of police in a marsh at night. The glow of the Wolf's cigarette lit his face briefly before he tossed it into the water. His brand was Chunghwa, the Shanghai tobacco with the scent of plums that had been favored by Mao himself.

"That boy was checking out your ass."

"He can dream."

"Why did that turtle's egg drag us out here?" Yao muttered as he gazed into the marsh at the dark shape of the Wolf.

"Dragged *me*. He didn't ask for you."

"Ouch." Yao grinned.

Mei frowned at him. His casual attitude toward the job got under her skin. Yao didn't care about anything but chasing skirts. His father was a PLA general, and he was a princeling, one of the Party's modern-day nobility whose grandparents and great-grandparents had fought alongside Mao in the 1949 Revolution. He was immune from trouble, and he knew it.

The call had come an hour before, breaking the silence in her apartment. She had clambered from her bed in a cotton shift and extricated her phone from the raincoat hanging on the door.

"Comrade Song?" The voice had been husky, unrecognizable; the formality of expression had thrilled her. The curtness meant business—something for which she was needed.

"Yes." She had gulped, repeated the word louder.

"This is Secretary Lang. I . . ." He had paused, and for the first time Mei had felt vulnerable. The Wolf was alone. He'd had a wife but she was dead, it was said. Nobody explained, and it was best not to probe that generation unless they invited it. "I need you. I'll send a car."

The ambiguity of his summons had made her panic. He couldn't mean *that*, could he? As she'd pulled on her clothes, she had thought of how to chaperone herself. She'd bring Yao, whose room was a floor below.

When she had knocked on his door, he had answered the door in a robe. "Hello, partner." He had worn a self-satisfied grin; she'd seen a shape moving in the room behind him.

Three cops waited in a huddle fifty feet down a shallow hill, under a floodlight. The flickering lantern had been shuttered, and the huts were dark. Dongguan loomed on the horizon, a city of eight million stuck between Guangzhou and Shenzhen, to which migrants had first come in the Qing dynasty. Now, it was a Las Vegas of hotels, clubs, and prostitutes that drew business people from across China and all over the world to trade during the day and to play at night.

The Wolf, noticing company, trudged back toward them along the ridge. The two little groups—Mei and Yao, and the Dongguan police—waited in silence. Dressed in a long overcoat, he walked up the hill, beckoning as he spoke.

"Inspector Wen, I have asked Comrade Song to help with my inquiry. You will permit us."

It was a statement, and the officer's chubby face stiffened before nodding. He knew that the Party took priority over the state authorities. The Wolf turned his attention to Yao, regarding him impassively, as if waiting for a good explanation of his presence. Yao brushed back his hair and straightened his back.

"Secretary," Mei said. "This is Comrade Zhang Yao. I thought he could assist." She waited for a rebuke, but the Wolf nodded, as if bored with the topic.

"Follow me," he said, turning toward the fields. Mei obeyed and Yao stepped forward with her.

"Not you," the Wolf said brusquely, walking away. "Her."

3

As they stepped onto the ridge that led through the fields, the earth sank underneath her shoes. The mud was bound together by scrubby plants and felt precarious, as if it might crumble at any moment. Mei reached instinctively for the Wolf's arm but pulled back before touching him. He strode a step ahead, the Tiger Head flashlight casting a dancing light. The night turned black as the glow of the floodlight receded, and the only sound was the tread of their shoes on the mud. The Wolf's nicotine breath rasped in the silence as he pointed the flashlight onto a clump of earth or knot of twigs she should avoid. His shoulder blocked her view forward, and she kept her eyes down so that she wouldn't slip.

They walked beside a banana field, the leaves brushing her shoulders. She tried not to stumble, but her height made it difficult to step precisely on the ridgeline. A leaf loomed out of the darkness and slapped her on the face before she could avoid it. She gasped, and the Wolf halted.

"I'm sorry, Secretary. It was nothing."

He did not reply, and Mei looked up at him, trying to gauge his mood. He kept his light down, and she saw the outline of his face above the rippled flesh of his neck. When he spoke, his voice was softer than before.

"Do you like your work, Comrade Song?"

"Yes, Secretary. I have learned a lot."

"It is not easy to investigate the Party. People will resent you and tell you to look the other way. Sometimes, they will threaten you."

"It must be done, to earn the people's trust." She repeated the rote phrase that they had learned.

"That's right. How old are you now?"

"Twenty-three."

He nodded.

She felt his eyes on her in the gloom and thought of the first time she had seen him, a month before. She had been pulled out of a lecture to take notes at a Party meeting. It was an honor, of course, and she had rushed to the building, shaking with nerves. A delegation was visiting from Chongqing, and they had needed to fill the seats. The armchairs, topped with lace antimacassars, had been arranged in two lines of eight facing each other, with a pair of armchairs at the head for the leaders of the delegations. Shown into the room as the meeting started, she scurried to the junior place. All formal meetings were like this—they started with the careful filling of teacups by young attendants and polite expressions of good wishes to the other side.

She had taken out a pen and listened as the Wolf had croaked his way through a welcome to the visitors before the business began. He had looked uneasy. Words did not come easily to him. That was why he hadn't risen further, they said—the honey tongue belonged to Chen Longwei, the Party secretary for Guangdong. After his set piece, the Wolf had remained silent, interjecting occasionally to correct an official. But once, when she looked up, she had seen him gazing at her as if she intrigued him. Even after she had caught his glance, he had kept looking. She had bowed her head, embarrassed.

The Wolf spoke again. "Song Mei, I've brought you here to show you something you have to see. It will be hard for you. It will require all of your strength. Do you understand?"

"I understand, Secretary Lang." She did not, but she felt the shock of being called by her name. She was alone, three months after she had been recruited, with an official so senior that many people who worked for the Commission served an entire career without ever speaking to him directly.

"You cannot talk about what you see to anyone else, not even that eager young man. Promise me that."

"I promise." She wondered at his casual dismissal of her partner, as if Yao's family meant nothing.

The Wolf gestured at her to follow, pulling another flashlight out of a pocket for her to use. As they walked, the leaves fell away, and they passed beyond the grove to a field that had been dammed at each side and flooded to form a fishpond. The Wolf turned right and tiptoed along the edge, his flashlight casting a glow on the water's surface. Then he halted and looked back, illuminated by her beam. His face was rigid, and he looked desolate.

Mei shone her light on the water where he was pointing. In the pool of white, she saw rushes and noticed a tubular shape a few feet from where she stood. She turned the beam on it.

It was a leg, the ankle poking above the surface. Dark shapes moved against the leg in the water and she could see mud carp trawling the body in search of food, their fleshy lips open. Their scales glinted in the light; a large fish nearly the length of the corpse's foot flicked its tail and swam off. It looked big enough to be harvested.

Mei shuddered at the sight of the fish swimming mutely around the body and then stilled herself, afraid of looking frail in front of the Wolf. He had told her to be strong, and she was going to prove herself.

She ran the light up the leg to the corpse's buttocks, twin moons against a watery sky. The width and roundness of the hips indicated that it was a woman—a young one, her skin smooth and full, still with a faint echo of sexuality. She was naked.

Mei had not breathed since directing her light on the water. Inhaling, she smelled, mingled with mud, the stench of ripe human.

A tattoo marked the small of the corpse's back, and Mei bent toward it. The blob was distended by the bloated skin, and she couldn't make out the shape or the lettering. The body beyond the hips lay below the surface, twisted so that only one shoulder and arm were in view. Her hair on the water spread out around her head like a black halo. The woman was facedown, staring blindly into the pool. Her fingers were long and delicate, like Mei's, and she was just as tall and slim. The wrist was marked with a welt, like a red bracelet.

The Wolf wedged his foot on the slope, holding a branch with a rough fork at the end. Leaning forward, he lodged the fork under the armpit, and lifted, the corpse's arm bending at the elbow as it twisted in the water. He executed the maneuver expertly, as if knowing exactly how to exert the minimum effort, and was already stepping back as the body rolled.

One breast came clear of the water as the arm flapped backward and fell with a splash behind the body, then the other. Mei was beginning to realize why the Wolf had brought her there. This wasn't just a body in a field. The corpse's shape was hers, she realized—the same length, the same curves. She gazed along it as it settled in the water, like a nymph rising from the deep, until she came to the face.

Then she understood, and everything else—the slap of the wave against the bank, the laughter of the cops across the water, the moon dimming as a cloud obscured it—receded to nothingness. All she could see was a woman with the same nose, the same eyes, and the same face.

Her twin.

A drop of water trickled off Mei's nose and splashed in the water by her feet, then another. She breathed normally, she did not weep, yet tears flowed out of her as if a pipe had burst. She stepped forward, descending the bank into the soft mud. The Wolf grunted, but she didn't halt.

She reached out, touching the cheek and stroking a lock of hair from across the girl's left eye. Close up, she saw a green iris surrounded by blood vessels. Her eyelashes were long and her eyebrows neatly shaped. The head turned and the mouth opened as if the corpse were about to speak, but only water spilled out.

The Wolf leaned forward with his branch and tapped Mei's shoulder. Her mind was in such turmoil that she hardly noticed, but after a few seconds she came to her senses and climbed out of the pool to stand by him.

"Do you see why I called you?" the Wolf asked.

"Yes, Secretary Lang, I understand."

"Did you know this woman?"

Mei gripped her palms to her ribs. "I didn't know I had a sister. Nobody told me."

"Not even your parents?"

"I never knew my parents."

The Wolf did not respond. Instead he threw the branch far into the darkness and rubbed his hands briskly to shed the dirt. Then he placed a hand on her shoulder to guide her back toward the police and Yao. He lit the way with his flashlight, while hers dangled at her side, and spoke over his shoulder.

"Something happened here, Comrade Song. You can't explain it and neither can I, but we will discover the truth. You see those people?"—the Wolf pointed at the cops in the arc light—"They don't care. If we weren't here, they'd have given up. Just a migrant girl lost in the city. Maybe a big man was involved, and they shouldn't provoke him. Case closed. Am I too cynical?"

"No, Secretary Lang."

"I've lived a long time. Too long, some people think. I'm an old head. I should retire. They say that, don't they?"

"They don't," Mei lied.

They were two hundred feet from the police when the Wolf stopped, facing Mei in the banana field, amid the drooping leaves.

"No one knows who she was. Not these fools, not those who did this. Remember that."

As they left the field and walked up the hill, Mei saw Yao laughing with a cop, having lost interest in where she had gone. The Wolf stopped by Inspector Wen, and pointed into the darkness.

"You can take her now."

4

Before dawn, Mei dreamed of the water ghost.

She was in a boat on the Li River, being drawn toward a cormorant fisher, with two of the birds perched on the bamboo pole that rested on his shoulders, his face hidden by his conical hat. The man frightened her, and she paddled as hard as she could to evade him. She would be safe around the bend, but the tide flowed against her, pulling her back. Her shoulders ached, the paddle twisting in the stream. Somehow she made it to the bend, then drifted to the far edge of the river, where the water was still and clear. The pebbles were green and yellow, and fish swam across them in shoals, flicking from side to side.

As Mei gazed at them, a woman floated under the boat and broke through the surface toward her. It was the spirit who lingered in rivers and lakes, waiting to seize the ankles of passersby and drag them down. The water ghost longed to be reborn, but she first needed a substitute to take her place. This story had scared Mei profoundly as a child. When the lights went out, she had imagined the ghost in the shadows.

The ghost's fingers were long and elegant, the nails painted a deep red. Mei pried them off her ankle, but the hand fastened on her wrist instead. The ghost was too strong to resist. It dragged her into the water, her body scraping the side of the vessel. The water was inky green, impenetrable. She held her breath as the ghost pulled her deeper, its long hair in her face. Her lungs felt like they would burst.

Mei awoke with a start. She was in her bed. Her coat was back on the door, her other garments scattered on the floor where she'd pulled them off only a few hours before. It was six-fifteen, and light was creeping past the edges of the blinds that were supposed to block it. Her shoes, spattered with mud, rested under the desk on the far side of the room. She flung an arm over her face, burying her eyes in the crook of her elbow, as much to block out reality as the dawn.

One child.

Until the moment she'd looked into her sister's eyes, Mei had never known a relative. No brother, no sister, no cousin. Not even a parent. Everyone in her generation felt an absence, living in a country where siblings were banned in case the population grew even more, from one billion to two or three. Deep down, late at night, each of them was alone. Yet she had been the loneliest. Until now.

It was a terrible discovery—that in the moment that she'd gained a twin, the woman had disappeared into the black water. Her companion, the sister who would have understood her the way that no one else did, was gone. She'd had to make her own way in life, with no background or family to give her the connections that Yao took for granted. Unknowingly, she had had a shadow.

Breakfast was in less than two hours, and she yearned to lose consciousness again, but it was time to rise. All her life she'd forced herself to get up, to learn, never to be stuck where she was. She'd come so far, and she couldn't give up now. As she swung her feet from the bed, she remembered her last sight of the Wolf, sitting stiffly in the back of the Audi A8 as it drove away, leaving the body behind. He'd looked older than when she'd first seen him in the marsh, half an hour before. His last act had been to bind her to secrecy. She wondered whether it was for her sake or his.

"How old are you now?"

That extra word—*now*—he'd used the night before had stuck in her head, unexplained. Not "how old," the question a stranger would ask, but *how old now*—the phrase of a relative or an old family friend. *Haven't you grown? Are you enjoying school? How old are you now?*

She put on a tracksuit and ran down the stairs from the fourth floor of her apartment block—the old elevator was too slow and unreliable, and the noise would wake others. Then she stepped onto Yuexiu Bei Road, turning right toward Yuexiu Park along the red-tiled sidewalk. The road was nearly empty—only a woman squatting under a banyan tree, a yellow bus hauling early commuters, and a lone PLA soldier standing to attention by the entrance to the compound on the far side of the street. The sun was starting to gleam through the gaps in the apartment blocks.

Crossing Xiaobei Road, she entered the park through the arched entrance and walked along the old city wall, which was covered by a scrambled mess of roots that had descended from the trees above, like upside-down climbing plants. Paddleboats lined the green lake on her right under the lattice cone of the old Television Tower, an ugly monument to the era when making steel had been an achievement in itself.

Thirty people stood in formation on a lawn by a playground. She hurried to join them, slipping into place between two women amid lines of black-uniformed men. The imbalance did not matter, for this was Wing Chun, the Cantonese martial art invented during the Qing dynasty by a woman. The story went that Ng Mui, the female Shaolin monk, based it on a fight between a snake and a crane—the darting punch of the cobra's strike and the soft blows of the crane's wings. Yao laughed at her—"You want to be a prizefighter, Mei?"—but she was devoted to her twice-weekly sessions, under the stern eye of her *sifu*.

They started with *siu nim tau*, the set of understated movements or "little ideas" that represented every kick and punch of full-blown combat as small, graceful wrist twists and knee bends. It was more like t'ai chi than kung fu, and she loved the elegant patterns the moves traced. It was a graceful discipline in which poise defeated strength. As you deflected a clumsy punch with one hand, you retaliated with a lightning thrust—defense and attack in one movement.

Mei drew her feet into the character two—heels splayed outward and toes pointed in. She'd felt stupid the first time she'd tried the stance, her knees bent in as if holding a goat, but it was second nature now—it rooted her to the ground like a tree, and when she hit someone, they felt it. She crossed her arms, palms up, and started the twists and turns of *siu nim tau* in unison with the others. As her palm angled around her wrist in *huen sau*, her tension faded. She was a Wing Chun disciple again.

They finished by boxing in pairs; one partner holding up a pad while the other launched a flurry of punches, throwing vertical fists forward with the full weight of arm and body. The *sifu* partnered with Mei; she tried to force him backward with punches, but he didn't move. He looked at her impassively, absorbing the force with ease as her face reddened. He was an old man, small and white-haired, but it was like trying to shift a tank.

"You're shooting a cannonball from a bow, Song Mei. What is wrong this morning? You must be relaxed, like water flowing, then the force is in the punch. Hold this."

She held the pad against her chest, and he stretched out his right arm, resting his fingers against it. Then he straightened his arm from the elbow, forming a fist that flowed forward as though she weren't there. She felt an explosion against her chest and found herself flattened on the grass.

"No tension," the *sifu* said.

Yao was in his usual seat in the commissary, eating with the appetite of a man who had not seen a corpse the night before. He was dipping deep-fried *youtiao* into a bowl of rice congee, and he grinned at Mei as he stuffed the golden stick of dough into his mouth. Bile rose in her throat as she watched, dehydrated from exercise and haunted by the night.

"Yao, you're disgusting."

"What's wrong?" His smile grew wider, and she looked away to avoid the sight of half-chewed dough.

She sat next to him with a glass of orange juice and a bowl of congee and picked at the white gruel with a spoon.

"Why so silent last night?" he said. "What's the Wolf's secret?" He sounded amused, but she knew it was killing him not to know.

"Nothing."

"The cops said there was a body out there. Wen told them to wait for a guy from the Party, then the Wolf turned up and took over. Who was she?"

Mei thought of the Wolf's last words in the marsh. *No one knows who she was. Remember that.*

"How should I know? Some girl who got herself into trouble. I didn't ask questions."

"But he wanted you to see. You're his special agent now?"

"Get lost."

She shoved a spoonful of congee into her mouth, then regretted it and tried to ease the slimy rice down her throat without gagging. Yao looked dissatisfied, but he didn't say any more. He always pushed as far as he could until she got angry and then backed off. That had been the pattern since they'd been matched as interns.

Mei had to fight the urge to be grateful for Yao's friendship. She was a nobody and he was a chosen one—fresh out of Tsinghua University in Beijing, lanky and good-looking, charm to spare. She hadn't known how to treat him at first because she'd never known anyone so privileged, anyone who took his status so much for granted. The cadres all laughed at his jokes, and the lecturers indulged him if he needed more time to complete an essay after a weekend home in Beijing. Yet without knowing why, she noticed that he was trying to please her—his eyes would rest on her as he told a story, waiting for her approval.

Mei didn't have a brother, but that was what he'd become. He asked for her help on assignments and she indulged him, feeling a glow of superiority. They wrangled over everything from how to handle cases to who would eat the last dumpling. For some reason, she caught his attention in a way others could not. Even if he had a girl-friend in tow, he would spend the evening talking mainly to Mei and neglecting the girl. He irritated Mei, often infuriated her, but his presence was reassuring.

As she gulped down the last bit of gruel, Yao scrambled to his feet, his eyes on someone behind her. She followed his gaze and then stood up herself. Standing at her shoulder was Pan Yue, the deputy secretary in charge of training.

"Comrade Song, come with me," Pan said, walking toward the exit that led to her office.

As Mei followed, the others watched out of the corners of their eyes, wondering if she was in trouble or being singled out for praise.

Pan had been the first official to address the twenty recruits three months before, and they needed to satisfy her to get permanent jobs at the Commission at the end of their training. She had no life other than the Party: none that anyone knew about, anyway. She was the first one to her desk in the morning and never seemed to leave—her office light gleamed constantly. Her only respite was to the gym in the compound; her clothes hung on her as if she had lost weight and had never bought new ones.

"I've examined your reports, Song Mei," Pan said as they walked. She gave a thin smile and nodded approvingly. "They are excellent. You are fulfilling our expectations when we recruited you."

"Thank you, Deputy Secretary. I try to do my best." Mei had seen Pan's mouth move and heard her words, but they felt disconnected. She always wondered how she'd been recruited to the Commission. It remained a mystery. A letter had come one day asking her to an interview, even though she hadn't applied. She had been "recommended," it stated.

"You performed excellently at Sun Yat-sen University."

"Yes, thank you."

"I am impressed by your achievements. You did not have an easy upbringing, but you show great character."

Mei nodded. It felt foolish to keep thanking the woman. Mei had worked insanely hard to ace her exams, spending long nights memorizing facts. From childhood, she'd been driven by the fear of not escaping Guilin, of spending her life in a backwater. She'd known she had to break out.

"Sit here with me," Pan said as they reached her office, indicating a leather chair in the corner. The springs sank uncomfortably under Mei when she sat, and she had to hitch herself upright.

Pan's office was featureless—ugly desk, steel cabinet that seemed to date from the 1949 Revolution, Party certificates on the walls, Party mementos on the shelves. There was a photograph of Pan with a Politburo member in the Great Hall of the People, and a pair of tiny flags commemorating a friendship event with the Democratic People's Republic of Korea. If she had any pleasures in life apart from doing the right thing, they were not visible.

"Secretary Lang asked you to help him last night."

Pan's eyes fastened on her and her smile dimmed, the pleasantries over. Mei came to attention with a jolt.

"Yes, Deputy Secretary."

"He clearly understands your potential and wishes to encourage you. Tell me what happened."

Mei picked her words carefully, trying to seem cooperative without giving too much away. "He asked me to attend a crime scene in Dongguan. A young woman had died, I'm not sure how."

"What an interesting mission." Pan's smile returned and she nodded, endorsing the Wolf's decision. "Who was the girl?"

"I don't know. I was not told."

"And now the police have closed the case. Ah well, nasty things can happen in Dongguan, I'm sad to say. Some girls do not do behave themselves in the city. You are not too shocked?"

"No, I am okay."

"Secretary Lang has had a distinguished career, serving the Party. I expect you know that," Pan said.

"I believe so."

"We can learn much from him. He had to overcome obstacles, as you did. There was an incident early in his career involving his wife. It could have set him back, but he regained the Party's trust."

Pan nodded significantly, and Mei nodded back. A lesson was being imparted, but she was mystified as to what.

"Even good men can be led astray. Their brains do not always guide them. Women hold up half the sky, Mao said. Sometimes, we carry more of the weight, don't we?"

"Yes, we do." Mei tried to smile in a complicit way, but Pan seemed to be talking to herself.

"Especially old men." The warmth was gone from Pan's face. "They often make fools of themselves." She paused. "I will give you a piece of advice, Song Mei. Do not permit yourself to be misled. It would be a shame."

"No, Deputy Secretary."

Mei felt a tremor of panic. Without doing anything but obey orders, she had been caught between the Wolf and his deputy. She had no idea what was going on. All she knew was that a body had appeared to her in the night and turned her life into a mystery.

"Now," Pan said, smiling. "I have a task for you."

5

The blue steel cranes stood to attention at Humen Port, saluting the sky. Far above Mei and Yao, a crane lifted a container toward a cargo vessel docked by the side of the Pearl River. She gazed upward as the operator, invisible in his cabin, swung the giant box through space and settled it in place on the pile of others, like giant Lego bricks.

It was a fine day for Guangdong. The smog had thinned sufficiently to allow the sun to gleam and for Mei and Yao to feel its glow. Yao had removed his jacket and walked with it slung over one shoulder, Dolce & Gabbana shades perched on his nose. He swung the other arm in rhythm to one of his father's old marching tunes, which he whistled to get on Mei's nerves. She still had a headache a day after her encounter with Pan, not helped by the tang of oil and chemicals in the air.

The ship was one of five sitting under the row of cranes. The vessels were leviathans—vast and fat underneath hundreds of containers piled so high that it seemed as if they might roll over at sea. As Mei and Yao walked, the ground trembled. A train moved slowly along tracks set into the dockside as cranes removed the load from one ship. The river looked muddy green in the sunshine. In the channel, an enormous number of boats—steamers, ferries, and cargo vessels—plied their way back and forth. Water lilies and weeds floated by the dock, feeding on the oily scum.

Dongguan sprawled to the east; a mile to the south, a line of trucks trailed across the Humen Bridge, high above the river. The

Pearl River was a trading place for the world, as in the nineteenth century. The iron cannons that had fired on British gunships in the Opium Wars of the 1840s still sat in their stone barricades by the bridge. The British had enfeebled the Canton population by trading opium from Indian poppies for Chinese commodities, so weak and compliant had been the Qing emperors. The Party was a far tougher negotiator with its trading partners—it took Treasury bonds instead.

"This is better than lectures. How did you get us the job?" Yao said.

"Treat me nicely and you get rewarded." But Mei wasn't as happy as Yao about their day out. She wondered if it wouldn't be simpler to be back in a stuffy classroom than doing Pan's bidding.

Two dockers stood smoking by the side of a truck a hundred or so feet ahead. One of them bent down and snorted, vacating phlegm onto the dockside. Then he looked up at Mei and grinned, showing the gap where a tooth was missing. He said something to his companion that Mei couldn't hear, and the other man laughed in response, gazing at her. As Yao drew his breath to speak, Mei put a hand out and touched his arm. She could handle it.

"Which one is the *Yunnan*?" she asked tooth man in Cantonese.

He looked blank, so she repeated the question in Mandarin. It was hard to tell before anyone spoke what language or dialect they used. Like a magnet, Guangdong drew people from all across China and beyond—dockers, workers, traders, and hucksters of all kinds. The local taxi drivers and market stallholders complained loudly in Cantonese about becoming a minority in their own province.

"You hitching a ride, baby? Where are you heading?" He had a northern accent Mei couldn't place—perhaps Heilongjiang?

She said nothing, reaching into her jacket to produce her identity card. He saw the five gold stars—the largest one representing the Party—stamped on a red circle and stiffened. He threw his cigarette aside, twisting a foot on it to crush the embers.

"That way." He pointed to the next vessel, two hundred yards beyond. It sat higher in the water than those around it as the last of its cargo was removed.

The *Yunnan* looked as if it had seen a good portion of the world.

It was black and red, its paintwork faded and battered where it rubbed against the dock. The deck was flat, with nothing to block the view of the ship's stack of cabins, topped by a navigation deck with its broad sweep of glass that glinted in the sun. A gangway slanted on the ship's side, and Mei saw a tiny figure walking up it. Her heartbeat quickened and her palms pricked as she realized that it was the way to board.

She'd spent her childhood in Guilin with her feet planted firmly on the ground, but Guangzhou was full of skyscrapers. Two years earlier, when they'd finished the new Canton TV Tower, which rose above the Pearl River like a twisted bundle of firewood molded in white steel, a college friend from Sun Yat-sen had insisted on ascending what was then the world's tallest building. Mei felt a vague sense of dread but lacked the nerve to refuse. She knew she was in trouble when they were shown into the elevator at the foot of the tower. After one glance through the steel girders as they rose, she closed her eyes and pushed against the rear of the elevator.

When they stepped onto the 107th floor observation deck, she'd felt a new kind of terror, like nothing she'd ever experienced. The black tiles stretching to triangular windows at the edge seemed to melt before her, tipping her toward the river, nearly fifteen hundred feet below. Luli, her girlfriend, had clattered to a glass-floored wedge protruding into space and cried at Mei to take her photograph. It was unthinkable. Crushed by vertigo, she knelt on the cold floor with her eyes gripped shut. She could not bear to watch the jagged rows of apartment blocks and office towers melting into the misty distance beyond the curve of the river.

Safely on the ground again, she'd sat shivering at a café table while her friend had gone off to get a glass of water. She'd felt like a country girl unable to cope with the scale of the city. It defied her sense of logic—that even when she was in no danger of falling, it felt as if she were falling into a void. Afterward, she'd vowed to train herself out of it, but she'd not had the time. She could not bear to show weakness to Yao. She'd lose all authority over him.

Mei placed a hand on the rail of the stairway, feeling it slip between her fingers as the ship shifted against the dock. She started the climb a couple of paces in front of Yao, holding the rail on each side to steady herself while trying to look as if she wanted to get on board quicker. From behind, Yao could not see her fix her gaze on the steel steps, frightened to raise her eyes to the dark cliff above her.

"Son of a dog. Look at that motherfucker." Yao halted behind her, pointing upriver.

Mei had no choice but to obey. She twisted in the direction he was gazing, into space across the port. When she opened her eyes, her stomach lurched. They were high between sea and sky, only the ship's bulk orienting them in space, and the ground felt lost below them. Yao indicated a fully laden container ship edging its way into the Pearl from the East River, looking barely afloat.

Mei tried to hide her fear with a tone of disdain. "It's just a boat, Yao." She felt the blood drain from her head as she gripped the rail— she had to get moving again or she'd be rooted to the spot.

"That should keep the foreign devils happy."

"Not for long." She faked a laugh, trying not to sound hysterical, and dragged herself forward. As they neared the ship's entrance, she could not hold back her panic and she rushed up the last few steps blindly, stumbling through the bulwark to safety.

6

They waited by the door to the ship's navigation deck, listening. It was bolted shut; a man was shouting angrily on the other side.

"It happens every time I dock. The crew in this port are thieves and cocksuckers."

The voice that replied was softer—conciliatory, almost jovial.

"These things happen. I know you've got it right, but check the manifest again, will you? There has to be an explanation."

Mei's knuckled fist, poised to rap on the door, was suspended in midair. She heard someone cross the deck, stomping urgently on the wooden floor, and she waited to hear what would happen next.

"Look. Two thousand and twenty-four. Maybe one went astray in Taiwan. Are you sure you counted right?"

"I know, all right. I've had this shit here before." The man's voice was still exasperated, but there was now a hint of doubt.

Mei pulled the bolt and swung the door open. The deck was filled with light from sun streaming through the navigation deck that ran from one side of the deck to the other. There was a stunning view of the river and the channel to the sea. Below, she saw the length of the ship and its dark belly, from which all of the containers had been scooped. Crew scurried around far beneath them, like ants in red helmets. She felt queasy, but it would be manageable if she just kept away from the windows. Two men stood by a desk—the ship's captain and a thick-necked customs superintendent. The official ran a finger down a checklist, rubbing his jaw with his other hand.

"You're right. How can we fix this? What can I do for you?" As he spoke, he turned to look at Mei and Yao and threw an arm around the captain's shoulders. "What's all this? Two fresh crew for you, Xilai? They look young and eager."

Mei felt herself blush, and Yao seemed to lose his usual insouciance under the official's gaze. The man watched cheerfully as he stumbled over his introduction.

"Superintendent Hou. . . . We're with the Discipline Commission. We need to speak with you, if we may."

Mention of the Commission was usually enough to ensure cooperation, as the card gave them the authority to cause trouble for any Party member. But this one was tough. His eyes stayed blank and hard even as his smile widened.

Yao put his bag on the floor next to Mei's ankle, leaning the wedge of official papers up against her calf. He walked over to their target and presented a card, both sides of which the man examined. One side showed Yao's title in the Ministry of Inspection, the other his Party affiliation. Officially, every Discipline Commission official had two jobs—one in the government and one in the Party. The Party was the master, though. The man nodded, tucking it in his top pocket.

"So, young man. You're here to take me away for unspecified crimes, are you? Do I face a spell of *shuanggui*?" He guffawed, slapping his companion on the back, as if he'd made a great joke.

Mei stared, abashed. He was laughing at *shuanggui,* their most fearsome power, the right to arrest a Party member on suspicion and detain him in secret for months or years. No lawyer, no *habeas corpus,* no record. The suspect might eventually reappear, spat into the courts in a distant province for the judges to sentence him to a prison term or even death. It was treated as a given that the Party's verdict was correct. Yet here was a middle-rank official in a cheap suit acting as if he didn't care.

"We want to talk to you. In private." Mei's voice was curt, but she heard it waver. It was hard for her to order middle-aged men around, even with a Party official's card—too many treated it as flirtation.

"I know what this is about." He turned to talk to the captain, presenting his back to Mei. "The boss is being posted to Fujian and I've applied for his job. He said the Party would check on me and they've sent these kids, so there's obviously no problem. Don't worry, you're not mixing with antisocial elements."

"Please, sir. We have a job to do." Yao's halting voice sounded pathetic to Mei. Whatever questions she had about the assignment, she didn't want to be humiliated. If Pan found out they'd been treated this way by some customs official she had sent them to investigate, she wouldn't be happy.

"Listen, son. Don't make a big deal of this. I know important people in Guangzhou."

As she stared at the man's complacent face, Mei's temper flared. She was exhausted and distressed, and she could not bear to be pushed around any longer. Bending down, she reached into the bag at her feet. She felt the thick file inside and turned it so that Hou could see the embossed cover as she drew it out and held it to her chest.

"We don't need to talk to anyone in Guangzhou. We have all the information that we need."

His smile faded, and he ran a fleshy thumb along his jaw, gazing at the file. He'd never seen it before and might never see it again. It was the script of his adult life, the document that determined whether he got a promotion and what happened after that, and then after that—how far he would rise in his career, how he might fall. Inside was a record of every assessment and infraction for the past thirty years, every incident of disloyalty.

Mei was holding his Party file.

She'd read it in the car on their way to the port, absorbing their target's unspectacular ascent within the Customs Ministry. He dealt rough justice to the dubious characters who hung around the place, his managers noted, driving out smugglers of cargo, human and otherwise. He starred in the Party's periodic public campaigns to clean up the docks—a hopeless mission that it addressed with sunny confidence. There was little to stand in the way of him being promoted—a few complaints of petty abuse and one incident of a few cartons of cigarettes being found in his office just before the New Year. If only others had such modest appetites.

On paper, he was a model Party member, but that wasn't how she'd heard him behave. Her fingers flicked the top corner of the pages, and he stepped forward to intervene.

"Captain," the man said. "Could we have the use of a room for a while? I want to assist these *guan yuan* in their inquiries." For the first time, he had used the formal term for an official.

In a small cabin off the navigation deck, she dropped the file onto the desk. Then, seating herself behind the desk, she leafed through it. Following her lead, Yao sat next to her and observed the official, some of his usual nerve coming back.

"Sorry about that before. I was just fooling around a bit." Hou plumped himself on a faded green couch under a porthole and spread his arms, submitting to their authority.

As Hou watched, Mei worked her way carefully through the pages of the file.

"So you've always worked in customs," she said. "A lot of people would like your job—that or being a tax official. It was the top choice in my graduating class at university. Why is that?"

Hou shrugged. "Variety. Everything in the world gets carried on the Pearl River. Jeans, cell phones. Opium, in the old days. You see amazing things here, I'll tell you."

"So they want to see the world, do they? Nothing to do with the opportunity to take bribes?"

The man sat up warily. "I've never taken money. I get given things sometimes, but that's the same wherever you go. Petty stuff. You can't stop people doing it. There's nothing in the file that says different, is there?" He pointed to it. "Is there?"

"You tell me."

"There isn't." She turned the pages in search of something to catch him with, but there was nothing. As he looked on, his confidence returned, inflating him like a balloon. She had tried to unnerve him, but it had not worked. He could tell she was bluffing—Pan had sent her there with nothing.

Mei ran through some routine questions about his family and his
sessions at the Party school; after a few minutes, she closed the file
and replaced it in the bag, defeated. She was here for a purpose but it
was hidden from her, like the Wolf's invitation to the marsh.

"We're finished, are we?" Hou said, thrusting himself off the sofa.

"For now."

Mei felt like a failure—as they rode the elevator from the deck to
the ship's bulkhead, Yao watched her doubtfully, as if he'd mistakenly
believed her to be charmed, now that Pan and the Wolf favored her.
Confused and miserable, she stepped out of the bulkhead into the
haze before she was fully prepared for it and was blinded by the vista
of Dongguan. Losing her footing, she tripped forward, feeling as if
she were falling into a void. She gripped the rails, trying to block the
sensation.

"What's wrong?" Yao asked from behind, but she held on tight
and kept walking without replying until she saw through squinted
eyes that they were close to the ground. She stood on the dockside,
breathing rapidly and letting the faintness in her head fade.

"Are you all right?" For once, Yao had dropped his bantering tone
and sounded worried.

Mei was on the edge of tears, but she forced a smile. "I'm fine. I
didn't eat enough breakfast. Looking at you put me off."

High above, at the edge of her vision, she saw Hou emerge from
the bulkhead and make his way down the stairway that they had just
descended. He took his time as she and Yao waited, gazing out at the
port that he controlled.

"Hold on, I've got something for you," he called once he was close
enough. He flourished an envelope; she could see the blue seal of
Guangdong Customs on its flap.

"Will you deliver this to Secretary Lang for me? It's a note of appreciation for the way you handled things. No hard feelings, I hope.
You show promise. I'd like to help you if I can."

"Have you met Lang Xiaobo?" Mei asked.

"I know him well. Very well." Hou smiled broadly.

He offered the envelope, one end between his finger and thumb, and suddenly Mei realized what this expedition was all about. This was the reason Pan had sent her—to witness it, to involve her in it. *Old men often make fools of themselves,* she had said. The whole thing—the Party file, the interrogation, the transaction—now made sense. Mei turned away, leaving Yao to take the envelope.

7

The scene was scrubbed by daylight, the landscape less sinister. It looked ordinary, the kind of place people drove by at speed. Mei pulled up about where the Audi had brought her two nights before and, stopping the engine, surveyed the marsh. Wind gusted; a flock of birds scattered from a broken tree.

There was nothing left—the barrier was gone, along with all traces of the Dongguan cops. They'd packed up and disappeared, not bothering to track where the woman had come from. She could imagine what Inspector Wen had done as soon as the Wolf had dismissed him. His job was finished, and his boys had fled with the dawn, forgetting the night as soon as it was over. Her admirer was probably directing traffic with white gloves on Yuanling Road.

Mei climbed out of the car, a Chery Cowin allocated to junior officials. This time, she'd brought boots to shield her from the mud, but they weren't needed—the sun had dried the top layer of mud into a crust. It had preserved a jumble of footprints—the boots of the officers and her own heels punching holes into the ground. She saw the ridge along which she'd walked with the Wolf, between the banana fields. Somewhere—perhaps just visible, she couldn't tell—was the pool in which the body had lain.

She turned left and marched across the muddy ground toward the cabin where she'd glimpsed a lantern. As she closed in, she saw how flimsy the structure was, although it had been there for a long time. The walls were crumbling, the wooden frames parched by years of exposure to the wind and sun, and a rusty metal patch had been nailed over part of the tin roof to keep it watertight. Two buckets and an old broom were propped in one corner of the low porch, where a dog slept contentedly in the shade. Mei walked to the rear to find two scraggy-necked chickens pecking for corn in a square of dirt. It was as small and unwelcoming a hovel as she'd seen outside of Guilin.

It was then she saw the woman squatting in a patch of rust-colored ground a few hundred feet away. Her head was covered in a conical hat, fastened under her chin with a frayed silk ribbon, which was the most colorful thing about her. Her blouse and slacks blended into the gray and green like camouflage, and she sat back on her haunches, prodding the earth with wiry fingers. She had a broad, impassive face, and it was hard to tell her age—surely over seventy. She looked as if she'd been occupying that position for many years.

"Is this your farm?" Mei called, walking toward her.

The woman swiveled and raised one arm to gesture behind Mei with her finger. Then she turned away, the hat hiding her head.

Mei didn't know what she meant. Was she saying it was hers, giving Mei directions, or telling her to go away? Whichever it was, the conversation was over. There wasn't anything to do short of ordering in the riot police—she'd met enough peasant matriarchs to know how hard they were to shift. So she reversed, stepping onto the porch by the slumbering dog and peering through a loose slat on the door. It was dark inside, one rod of sunlight falling across the floor from a crack in the roof. The light was blurred by smoke, and she could just make out in one corner a clay pipe hovering in the darkness.

She rapped twice but the pipe didn't move, so she pushed at the door. It opened with a creak, admitting a flood of light. The pipe's owner, a round-faced man with a wispy gray beard, grimaced at her and spat into a brown bowl. He sat on a rickety chair in a largely empty room, containing only a low table and a grate in which rested the blackened bones of a roasted bird.

"You're back?" His voice rasped.

"There was a lantern in this house two nights ago. Did you see me?"

The man cackled. "I can't tell the difference, girl. You're all the same to me. You try to frighten me, but it won't work. I've seen a lot worse and the answer's still no."

"I don't understand. What's your name?"

"They didn't tell you? Just another body to clear?" He laughed again and took a hit from his pipe, tamping the tobacco with a finger.

"I don't mean you harm." She gave him her card and he traced the characters warily with the long stem of his pipe.

"The Party, eh? My bit of land must be valuable, if they get you down from Guangzhou. More than they've offered."

Recognition dawned on her. It was a shakedown to acquire land. A Hong Kong real estate developer who wanted him out, maybe a local Party official who'd been offered stock to smooth the way. It sounded like a two-bit scheme—what apartments would even stand upright on this marsh?—and she didn't want to waste time.

"I'm not here to take your land. I just want to know about the body. The woman who died."

"I don't know about a woman."

"Did you see anything? You must have."

"I wasn't here. We were at home."

"This isn't your home?"

"This?" The man looked up at the roof and burst out laughing. "Why would I live in this shithole?"

Mei gave up and walked out. Her foray had come to nothing, except uncovering a scandal that hardly deserved the name. Hundreds of such complaints flooded the office every day; this one wouldn't have merited getting into a car to investigate if she hadn't stumbled across it.

Looking into the fields, she tried to see where she'd been standing with the Wolf. She set off to retrace her steps and then halted again, unable to face entering the marsh. The body wasn't there anymore, but even the thought of seeing the fish in the pond was dreadful. She breathed deeply and sat on her haunches to gather her nerves.

She walked to where the crops began, then stopped to stare out at the banana fields and fishponds. Closer to hand was a jigsaw of small fields, some filled with rice, some with tomatoes, others with wheat.

They were bordered by an intricate pattern of ditches to keep them moist. The peasant woman had wandered into the middle to hack at a mud wall and let the water flow. The fields gleamed in the sun, young rice plants poking above a field like hair implants.

Then, from the corner of her eye she caught a glimpse of something in the marsh—a flash of blue. By the time she looked around, it had vanished into the landscape, and she ran back up the hill to her car, her boots like weights around her ankles. When she got there, she leaned across to unlatch the passenger-side cabinet and pulled out a leather case. She flipped open its buckle and drew out a pair of HiOptic binoculars. Mei had been lent the PLA device—black and stubby with nitrogen-filled chambers—one night to spy on a smuggler in Shenzhen. She had gazed into his apartment from a nearby block but seen nothing.

Mei rested her elbows on the car's roof to steady the binoculars and scan the landscape. The sun was in the west, casting an intense light across the fields that dazzled her. In the distance she saw the expressway and banana fields, grainy and foreshortened by the magnification. Following the ridges until she came to a thicket of bushes in a dry patch, she paused. After thirty seconds, the wind lifted the branches, showing a patch of blue.

Holding the HiOptics in one hand, she walked steadily down the hill. She trained her eyes in front as she went, checking the thicket to make sure that the occupant didn't slip away. As she approached, she saw through the gaps in the leaves a blue shirt and a pair of eyes.

"Come out," she called in Cantonese.

The leaves shuffled and there a small boy stood, barefoot and wearing a Chelsea football shirt with a Samsung logo. He clutched a bundle of sticks in one fist, and his legs were streaked with mud. She remembered playing in the fields at his age, while the adults planted rice. The local kids used to play chicken, rushing around for cover in the bushes. She squatted to be at his eye level.

"Are your friends here?"

The boy shook his head, his foot scoring the dirt nervously.

"Who's looking after you?"

He raised a slender arm and pointed to the shack where she'd met the pipe smoker and the old woman. His grandparents, she thought—they were too old to be his mother and father.

"I didn't want to scare you. I'm going now."

She rose to her feet and headed toward her car, with the setting sun casting her shadow in front of her. She'd been walking for a minute or so when she heard the sound of the boy chasing after her, his feet scuffling on the mud. As he ran up, she took the object he held out. It was a green-bordered rectangle with a metal clip—an employee identity card. The woman in the photograph, staring blankly in a red factory tunic, was the body in the pond.

8

"Where did you find this?"

The boy's eyes widened. Mei had raised her voice, not thinking. Leaning down, she placed a hand on the silky material of his shirt, feeling it crease between her fingers. She spoke softly.

"You're not in trouble. You're clever to have found it. I'd lost it and I was trying to find it. You understand?"

He nodded, then reached out and took her hand in his. It was small, his slender fingers wrapped around her index finger. Her heart settled a little.

The boy moved and she followed, slinging the binoculars over one shoulder. They reached the bush where had been hiding, and he dropped to all fours and scuttled inside like a marsh animal. She heard him scrabbling in the earth and could see his head bowed at the task. Then he wriggled back out and stood beside her, holding a piece of red material. He gestured for her to take it. She held it up to the sky.

It was a tunic, open-necked and short-sleeved with a line of four buttons at the front and black piping on the collar. The fabric was covered with dust and ripped on one side. Mei tucked two fingers inside its front pocket to check that it was empty and felt a groove in the cloth. She placed the badge against it, noting how the line matched the clip. It was the dead woman's uniform, the one she'd worn in the photo. Mei held it to her chest as the boy watched. It fit exactly, as the body in the water had matched hers. She raised it to her nose to detect a scent, but it smelled only of musky earth.

"This is where you keep things?"

The boy nodded.

"Where did you find this?"

He seemed eager, now that his cache was revealed. He took her hand again and led her eastward, out beyond the banana fields and into some scrubland beyond. She was pulled forward and had to break into a trot to keep up. The motion twisted his arm behind him, but he didn't seem to feel pain—the cartilage had not stiffened yet and it moved in ways that no adult's could. He had taken on the mission she'd given him, like a dog chasing a stick.

At the far end of the field, a line of bushes marked some sort of boundary. He pulled her to a gap and scrambled through, hardly touching the branches. She bent and shuffled after, falling to her knees and crawling with her hands in the earth. Her knees hurt and a twig scratched her face as she pushed through, then she emerged near a canal. It was deep enough to take a small steamer or a fishing vessel—anything that could pass under the bridge half a mile down toward the Pearl River—but there was no activity. Two boats were moored nearby, empty.

The boy led her through clumps of grass toward the riverbank. As they neared, she saw a jetty by the water's edge. Six wooden stakes had been driven into the wet ground, planks fastened on top. A frayed nylon rope hung from a steel ring fixed to the wood, awaiting a vessel. Mei climbed on top to look around. Water flowed past, leaving muddy rivulets and swirls on the surface of the canal. Apart from the hum of traffic in the distance, it was silent. She looked for the boy, expecting to find him at her side, but he'd vanished from sight. Hearing splashing, she gazed down through the gaps in the planks to see him stamping in the mud at the edge of the bank, thumping the structure.

Mei jumped into the soft mud and clambered under the platform to join him. The space was not high enough for her to stand upright, so she squatted, trying not to fall over.

"There." The boy pointed to the foot of one of the stakes, where it merged with the mud and water.

"You found these here?" She held out the jacket and the badge. "When?"

"Before."

"Do your parents know where you are?"

The boy shrugged.

"Where's your mother?"

He reached out and tapped the badge she held, by the body's photograph. *Had she been his mother?* Mei wondered, but he didn't look upset. He moved his finger to the woman's photo. She held it up to her and, wiping it with a thumb, read the words: "Long Tan Technology."

"Your mother works here?"

He nodded, then led her from under the jetty, hopping on board to where she had stood. Mei climbed up next to him.

The light was fading, the brown of the water darkening and losing its luster. It was turning black and impenetrable, as it had been in the night. Clouds drifted near the horizon, lit up orange by the dying sun. Mei felt protective toward the boy. How could his parents leave him to play? How could they abandon something so precious? Anger swelled in her.

She felt his hands grasping the binoculars at her side, pushing them upward, and she raised them to her eyes.

At first, she saw nothing on the marsh but a flock of birds settled on a patch of water. Then she lifted the sights and saw the first buildings on the outskirts of the city—a scramble of apartment blocks and roads crossing the landscape. The chaos of squares and lines was broken by a long ribbon, a high wall stretching for miles by the side of a waterway, like the border to another country. Beyond it were rows of factory buildings broken up by apartment blocks and what looked like foundries, with chimneys poking into the sky.

Mei scanned the wall, trying to measure it. It had to be three or four miles—it held a city, not just a factory.

"Does she work there?"

"She comes home every month." The boy's resigned acceptance made her eyes water, blurring the image.

It was a long way from the jetty to Long Tan—a mile, maybe two. No road joined them, just a network of tributaries and streams. How could the body have gotten here, stripped of its uniform and left in a fishpond? How had she died in a marsh where no one but peasants and real estate developers ventured? She could easily have vanished altogether if the Wolf hadn't taken an interest. For some reason, he'd risked himself to summon Mei and show her that she wasn't alone.

9

The god of fortune was the only one that Lockhart believed in. He kept a figurine of the fat Buddha at home and rubbed its belly as he left his apartment whenever he was in need of luck. The little idol laughed back reassuringly, holding its golden ingots and promising wealth. Lockhart had always trusted fortune and, until now, it had worked for him. His gambles had paid off, or they hadn't hurt too much when they had failed. *Don't waste your life,* his mother had urged him when he was a child. *Take a chance.*

By the temple, he rubbed his own belly. He was still in shape, only fifteen pounds heavier than when he'd left Yale. Few of his classmates could say that. Lockhart had seen them at a recent reunion, hair graying, stomachs bulging, content to lapse into middle age. He'd fingered his collar during the speeches, suffocated by the company. Once, he had caught the eye of a woman he'd tried to sleep with— now married with two children at college—and she'd smiled, as if it might not be too late. His spirits had lifted but, recalling it now, he cursed his stupid pride.

Once a resting place for Qing nobles, the temple had been abandoned for decades. It was still handsome, the entrance topped with red tiles that were arrayed in curves like an emperor's boat. Mao's destruction of temples and works of art during the Cultural Revolution was long finished; these days, the Party preferred to let temples decay. A guard waved him into the courtyard, past a eucalyptus tree strung with red lanterns. He walked by a bell tower and approached the main building. Tiles were missing from its roof, but its wood panels shone with gold and blue lacquer. Stone lions guarded the steps, each with a foot resting on a ball. The yard was empty except for a middle-aged couple standing by an incense-burning brick oven.

The man placed a stack of fake paper bills in the oven, the red and gold sheets of joss tightly rolled and arranged in circular stacks, like a wedding cake. He struck a match and lit the pyre, sending smoke in spirals up the chimney. It was an offering of money to the ghosts of dead relatives, Lockhart knew, to make them comfortable in the afterlife. The woman pulled out a bundle from her bag—copper money for the recently deceased. She gave them to him to throw on the flames, and they watched the fire in silence, their heads bowed.

When the fire died out, they walked up the steps into the temple, Lockhart following. He had to bend his head to pass through the entrance, and he stood by a rear wall, feeling confined. The windows were low and the passages narrow. The space was crammed with four Buddhas, their heads in the temple eaves. They rested on a dais behind clusters of candles in glass jars, which emitted a watery light, offerings of fruit strewn in front of them. A smaller idol of the god of fortune sat to one side. The woman knelt, lighting candles and incense sticks.

Lockhart bowed his head; by the time he looked up, the man was staring at him. He left again, finding a place on a wall under the eucalyptus tree where he could wait in the shade. When the couple emerged, they walked across to where he sat, looking like strangers to the city. The woman wore a tunic and cotton pants, good for farm labor, and the man had cheap jeans and a zip-up jacket. Lockhart saw stoicism in their faces: they'd known bad times before.

Lockhart stood. "Mr. and Mrs. Wu. I'm very sorry for your loss. You have my condolences."

"You speak Chinese." Mr. Wu looked surprised.

"Not *Sichuanhua,* I'm afraid. Only Mandarin, and I need to practice. I learned it years ago."

"What do you want with us?" The woman's eyes were narrow. She was used to being misled by officials and did not expect any different from him.

"Please, let me explain." He indicated the chairs he'd set by the tree. He'd given the sentry twenty yuan to fetch them from a store-room and to dust them off—it was ages since they'd been used. "May I ask you something first? Have you heard anything from Long Tan?"

"They told us nothing," she said, bitterly. "We were sent a letter. They haven't even sent back her things."

"I'm sorry to hear it. I sympathize," Lockhart said. He felt terrible, not only because of his task but also because of their story. Everything they said heightened his sense of anxiety. The man nodded once, embarrassed by the sympathy. Lockhart pressed on.

"That is why I am here. Poppy wants to treat you fairly. It is a matter of honor, although—" He hesitated in shame at the next words of the script. "Although the company bears no legal responsibility."

The couple looked at him blankly.

"You understand? It is not responsible under the law."

Lockhart felt physically sick. He was trying to force a waiver from a bereaved couple. What kind of man was he? Had he always been like this but had never noticed? Had never cared? Drops of sweat trickled down his forehead. Two nights before, the moon had broken from behind the clouds above Victoria Harbor, and its beam had shone through the blinds, searing his eyes as he lay awake, cursing his recklessness. He'd lost something so precious that his brain kept returning to the blunder he'd made, tormenting him. He waited desperately for the phone to ring or the ping of an email to break the deathly silence, but nothing came. All he needed, the thing that could restore his sanity, had vanished.

"She loved her Poppy phone," Mrs. Wu said, smiling sadly. "She was happy to make them."

"Tell me about her," Lockhart said, gratefully.

"Ning was a good girl. She sent us money. She didn't waste it, like some of them. She wanted to come back to Sichuan when she could—she said she'd find a husband here."

"She looked forward to that?"

"She was always happy and laughing. She talked about the New Year holiday when we last spoke."

"When was that?"

"A month ago."

"That is a long time, Mrs. Wu. Why didn't she contact you again?"

Mr. Wu broke in. "It wasn't her fault. She was assigned a new job, and she said she might not be able to call."

"I see." Lockhart looked over the temple wall toward an apartment block on the far side of the canal, and his throat went dry. It was as if Mr. Wu were telling him his own story.

"Your wife says that Ning was happy, Mr. Wu. I must ask: Do you know why she killed herself?"

"Ning did not kill herself." Mrs. Wu stared at him fiercely. "We taught her how to work hard, and she wanted us to be proud. She would not have made us suffer like this."

A few days before, he wouldn't have believed them—he would have smiled and dismissed it as parental blindness. *Of course* it was suicide. Twenty of them—sixteen women and four men—had thrown themselves off roofs. What other explanation could there be but self-harm? Now, after his own nights of hell, he felt differently. However Ning had died, it wasn't her doing. He knew it, and it scared him sick.

He lifted his briefcase and took out an envelope, putting it on the wall between them.

"I am sure you're right, Mr. Wu. She sounds like a wonderful young woman, and this is a tragedy. Poppy is doing all it can to ensure nobody else suffers in that way. You have heard of Henry Martin?"

Mr. Wu nodded. Even a Chinese farmer without a mobile phone knew of Poppy's founder.

"Mr. Martin trusts in Long Tan to manufacture his products responsibly and to keep all of the workers safe. He is very upset by what has happened. That is why he sent me to see you."

Another lie. Lockhart doubted whether Martin gave the life of Wu Ning a single thought, except that it was trouble for his company. The Chinese media was filled with stories of the deaths and the price that migrant workers paid to build his devices.

He picked up the envelope. "Mr. Martin wants to offer you this. The sum of money Wu Ning would have earned in a year, with overtime. We hope you will accept a token of our respect."

Mr. Wu glanced at his wife and, after a second's pause, she closed her eyes and nodded.

"I am glad. There is just one thing to sign." Lockhart's hand trembled as he took a document from the envelope. It wasn't possible to feel lower, dirtier. In the night, he'd imagined the dark tunnels of the Shenzhen subway, the trains shooting into stations, their lights blazing. *What would it be like to jump? How painful would it be?*

"It is English, but let me explain. There is a lot of legal language, and I hardly understand it myself." He smiled, his charm switching on automatically. He'd always been good at this. "It says you will accept this settlement and you will not take legal action."

Mr. Wu looked at his wife again, and she nodded her consent.

"One other thing. You will not talk about it with anyone. Not to the media or others. You will be silent."

This time, the man did not bother to check but reached forward and scratched his name on the paper, where Lockhart had indicated.

Lockhart left the couple under the tree and went back through the courtyard to the gate. The sentry had taped a rope across the entrance in a halfhearted effort to dissuade others from coming inside. In the evening light, he stepped down to the bank of the canal, where two barges were moored. He lit a cigarette, his hands shaking, and tried to calm himself by imagining the scene as it had been centuries before. The temple, the shacks lining the water, a boy fishing with a rod. No towers, no six-lane highway.

Taking a piece of paper from a pocket, he examined the characters with a frown. His calligraphy had deteriorated, the feathered strokes becoming crude lines. He folded it between his fingers and set off down the towpath, around a curve to where a bridge crossed a canal. Three families sat on the deck of a restaurant, under glowing lanterns. A waiter passed out dishes at one table—pork and marrow soup, goose with sour cherry sauce, *lai niao xia* shrimp.

Lockhart crossed a passage at the side of the restaurant and into a courtyard at the rear. Two waiters smoked on a bench and one called to him.

"Not here. The other side."

He ignored them, walking through the kitchen door. It was filled with steam, cooks rattling pans over open flames. Every surface and tile was coated with grime. If he'd been an inspector, he'd have wanted a bribe to ignore it. He passed a tank of lethargic eels, eyes bulging, as he made his way to the chef.

"We spoke," he said.

The man looked up from the book he was reading. He leaned back in his chair, lifting the front legs from the floor, and grabbed a set of keys from a hook on the wall behind him. Then he walked into the dining room and unlocked a door under the stairs.

At the rear of the cellar, Lockhart stooped so that his head would not knock against a stone arch. The chef swung a sack of rice to one side and reached behind it to a pile of smaller ones. He pulled a sack from halfway down and delved into his pocket for a knife, slicing the cloth so that fat grains of rice burst out. The man let a portion spill onto the floor, then lifted the bag up onto a crate. Plunging a hand inside, he pulled out a package wrapped in two Ziploc bags.

As Lockhart unsealed them, he smelled the oil that had been rubbed over the object to keep it from rusting. It was a Sig Sauer P238, dark and squat, with a fluted polymer grip. Its six-bullet magazine lay next to the weapon. Lockhart raised the weapon and pulled back the Nitron slide. Then he squeezed the trigger, releasing the pin against the chamber. The German parts clicked together smoothly, despite their time at sea.

10

The badge was a mystery. Mei sat at her desk at dawn trying to understand it, but she kept running into the same problem—the number on it was wrong. She had examined it painstakingly the previous evening and thought she must be making a mistake, but a night's sleep had changed nothing. The eighteen-digit identity code printed under the girl's image made no sense.

She gazed at the photo again. The face was so like her own, it was almost identical. The eyes were hers, the way her brow dipped to meet the top of her nose, the flow of her lips. It was more than a mirror image, for Mei's face would be reversed in a mirror, and this was the right way around. She could have accepted that it was mistaken identity, just someone uncannily like her, but she'd seen the body in the pond. She had touched her face. This hadn't just been her sister—it was her twin.

The number told a different story. Aside from the photo, the laminated card held three pieces of data—the woman's name, her workplace in the Long Tan complex, and her number: TANG LIU, BUILDING P-2, 430104199304074425. Her name was not a surprise; it might have been anything. Nor did the workplace mean much—it must be one of the buildings she'd observed through her binoculars. But the long number, that was full of information.

This was the woman's national identity number, and Long Tan had adopted it. Eighteen numbers, starting with the administrative code for her place of birth—province, city, and district—then birthdate; then three digits to distinguish her from China's other Tang Lius. Last, a checksum number to prevent forgery.

Mei could reel off her own number. 450300198905072264. The first six digits represented a district in Guilin in the autonomous region of Guangxi. Then her birthdate: May 7, 1989. If this were her sister, the first fourteen numbers on the card ought to have been identical, but they were utterly different. The woman had been born in a village outside Changsha in Hunan province and had been nineteen. Mei could explain away the first discrepancy—a baby could be taken to another city to be registered—but not the second. The girl had been allocated a number at birth; *that* could not be faked.

Whoever she had been, she wasn't Mei's twin.

Near the end of ideology class, everyone relaxed. Most of the cadres perched on benches shut their notebooks and stopped writing. The lecturer didn't notice. He'd acquired the habit of epic speech making from the Party leadership, measuring his output by how long he talked, not by what his students learned.

The lecture was on Deng Xiaoping Thought, which meant taking some bits from Mao and dropping the most brutal parts. Mao was out of favor, although his portrait still hung at the Gate of Heavenly Peace. He had been "seventy percent good, thirty percent bad"—this was the official mantra. The "thirty percent" was the Great Famine and the Cultural Revolution.

After the disaster of Tiananmen Square, Deng had rescued his place in history on his southern tour to Guangdong, prodding those back in Beijing into reform. His image still adorned billboards, exhorting political loyalty to the Party, but he'd dropped Mao's state economic control for "socialism with Chinese characteristics." Twenty years later, the characteristics were evident in the Pearl River. People lived good lives here, building new apartments and renting them to migrants, eating well, not working too hard.

The lecture over, Mei shuffled to the exit. She found Yao under a banyan tree by the nursery. He was smoking a cigarette and grinning at the small kids as they ran around in circles.

"Where did you go yesterday?" he asked. "Big date?"

"Oh, that. It was a waste of time."

"Never mind. Let's get this over with."

Yao led the way across the courtyard, amid apartment and office buildings. The compound had grown into a kind of campus, with every kind of department and function fighting for space. The Guangdong branch of the Ministry of State Security, where they were headed, was in the middle. Taking Hou's envelope there, as Pan had instructed them to do, was serious—like a combination of the CIA and the FBI, the ministry had sprawling powers. Mei was worried about the Wolf. She'd heard nothing from him for two days.

The ministry had lost the property lottery—it was housed in a squat building with rusty windows that did not open, behind the education wing. It took a while to find the right office, which was stuck along a corridor with no Party title on the door, just a name: Lai Feng.

Lai Feng wasn't what Mei expected of a spy. She looked no older than the pair of them, and her black hair was drawn back in a band above a white moon face. Her eyelashes were coated in mascara, and her nails were painted gunmetal. She looked more like a Goth from the streets of Shenzhen than a Party official, and she stared at them as they entered. Although she had her own office, she did not appear to occupy most of it. She huddled by a window, holding a Poppy tablet, while the oak desk in the middle was empty.

As she stood, the tablet gave an electronic squawk and she glanced down. "Ah, I'd forgotten. Come in. Except that you're already in."

Yao stepped forward, grinning amiably. "Lai Feng, I am Zhang Yao, of the Discipline Commission. Deputy Secretary Pan sent us. I believe you know about our mission."

"Your mission?" Feng raised an eyebrow in a perfect triangle and whistled. "So you're secret agents." She stepped past Yao and held a hand out to Mei. "You're not his girlfriend, I hope."

"My name is Song Mei. I'm his partner."

The woman wrinkled her nose. "Well, any sacrifice for the Party." She shot Yao a glance. "You two have something for me?"

Yao reached into his pocket and put the envelope on the desk's stitched leather surface.

Feng picked it up and rocked it between her fingers, weighing the contents, then turned her gaze to Yao.

"An envelope, eh? This will test my expertise. Have you tried one of these?" She pulled a letter opener from a drawer.

"I think it's secret." Yao sounded like a small boy.

The woman sniffed. "*Top secret?* Okay, so you want me to open it up and seal it again. Well, this is exciting. Is it a letter in invisible ink? Maybe a microdot hidden in a character?"

"Can you do it or not?" Mei interjected. She was tired of Feng messing with Yao's dignity. He irritated her too, but she had earned the right to give him a hard time. This woman hadn't.

Feng looked at Mei. "I'm just saying, our work is less analog these days. Physical objects are so last century."

Mei pointed toward Feng's tablet, which she'd left by the window, with its Poppy logo on the back. "That's an object, isn't it? You think the Chinese economy is stuck in the last century?"

Feng raised an amused eyebrow.

"Okay, you've got a point. Anyway, they taught us this stuff. There isn't much call for it now, like making molds of keys in clay. I need to revise the method a little."

She walked to a bookshelf, from which she took a leather-bound volume.

"Here are the old potions. Lovely binding. I'd collect these if I didn't have the set already."

She rubbed a thumb, with its dark nail, over the leather and flicked through the pages. Then she giggled.

"It's like Harry Potter. Come on, let's try it."

In a basement laboratory, the strip lights flickered to life. The room was white-tiled, with desks spaced throughout bearing flasks filled with chemicals. One wall was covered with shelves behind glass panels. Feng slid a panel aside and took a box from one shelf, then tipped its contents into a thin-necked flask. White crystals flowed out, forming a pile, and Feng poured two slugs of clear liquid into the vessel.

"Magicians measure by instinct. Here, give me that envelope." She put it on a table, twiddled the flask between finger and thumb, and made a spell-casting gesture with the other hand. "Aparecium!" Then she frowned, her eyebrows knitting together. "It's supposed to reveal invisible ink. It worked on Tom Riddle's diary. Oh, fuck this. The Party knows best."

She brought down a cork and some glass tubing, which she stuck in the top of the flask. Then she lit a burner. After a minute, white fumes rose off the crystals and floated along the pipe. She waited until it streamed and then held the envelope to it. Thirty seconds later, the flap sprung open.

"And the Americans say we can't innovate," she said, handing it to Mei. "Have a look inside."

"Am I supposed to?"

"Supposed to?" said Feng mockingly. "Go on, I won't look."

Mei took the envelope to a corner, feeling a flat, hard rectangle inside it. She didn't want to know what it was. But as she hesitated, Yao moved.

"Let me see." He put a hand on her shoulder, pulling her body back against his to gain a better view.

Taking the envelope, he pulled out a packet of green-and-purple bills bound in a white band. Each bore a cross and the image of a bald man in a high white collar, and next to it the words "Schweizerische Nationalbank." They were crisp, unused one thousand Swiss franc notes.

"Fuck." Yao pushed the packet back into the envelope and tried to close the flap, but it lifted open. He hurried across the room to Feng, who was sitting on a bench, gazing at the ceiling.

"Close it, please."

She bent over the envelope, stroking gum from a nail polish-sized bottle onto the paper. "You know what a guy I knew told me? The most important quality in a spy is the ability to forget."

Feng held out the envelope to Mei, and she took it reluctantly. No matter how hard she tried to shun it, the evidence kept seeking her out.

11

Yao opened the door and beckoned Mei inside. He wore pajamas under a silk nightgown, sash tied lightly at the waist, displaying a wedge of bare chest. The silk was embroidered with a red dragon, on fabric finer than anything she owned.

"Don't let anyone spot you. It might spoil your reputation."

Mei lacked the energy for a retort. It was late, and she was tense. Even Yao didn't look at ease.

Yao's room was like hers—a bedroom with a small bathroom attached to a tiny kitchenette, a study with a desk, and a two-person sofa. Their lives as cadres were the same too. They ate every meal in the commissary, except for a few excursions—nights in Guangzhou, shopping in Shenzhen, a walk in the park. The Party made sure that they didn't have much time for recreation. Yet there was a gulf between them in the room's small touches—the fabrics draped across his sofa and the photographs on his desk. He had so many cousins, it was unimaginable to her. There he was with his mother and aunt in Tiananmen Square, there with his father next to a rocket launcher at an Army parade.

Yao's pedigree was impeccable. His family tree had army officers and high-level officials. One line led back to a great-granduncle who'd been among the Eight Immortals—Deng and the seven Party officials who'd followed Mao. That alone gave him an exalted stature—he was destined for high office. Which didn't escape the attention of the girls who fell into his bed, she thought.

She sat on Yao's sofa while he paced around the room in his slippers. "What do we do?" she asked.

The envelope with its customs seal was still in her pocket, the stack of Swiss franc notes shifting inside when she moved. Mei knew that if she gave it to the Wolf it would be the end of him, and knew that she'd been chosen for the task.

"You heard Feng. Give it to him, walk away, forget it. The Wolf's at the end of his career, and we're at the start. I bet he's been on the take for years."

"I don't believe that." It was too neat, this affair. Pan had been onto her as soon as she'd returned from Dongguan, with a mission to bring him down.

"What don't you believe?" He was exasperated, as if Mei were being deliberately obstructive.

"That he's corrupt. This is a setup, Yao, can't you see? Why were we sent to the docks? Why did Hou produce the envelope? Why did Feng open it and tell us to take a look? It's all fixed."

Yao clenched his jaw and groaned. "Do you really believe that? What's in the envelope, anyway? Ten or twenty notes, fifteen thousand francs. That's nothing for a man in his position. Do you think he's been clean for all these years and that this is his first sweetener?"

"So why were we chosen to catch him?"

"Isn't that supposed to be our job?"

Mei laughed. "Of course—two cadres in training at the Discipline Commission. Just the people you send to trap the boss of the organization. They must do that all the time, we just haven't heard of it."

"Okay then, so why?" He stood in front of her, waving an arm in frustration. "You're so much smarter than I am. I'd just a dumb princeling, that's what you really think."

"I don't."

"Yes, you do." He was shouting, angrier than she'd ever seen him. "You do. So, why us?"

Mei's fingers dug into her knees. "Not us. *Me.*"

"Right. *You.* Because you're special."

"No, because of what he showed me."

Yao exhaled and reached for a chair. He sat and leaned toward her, his face close to hers.

"What did he show you?" he asked quietly.

"The woman in the marsh."

"Who was she? I asked you before."

Mei grimaced apologetically. She had tried to keep the Wolf's secret but it was no good—she needed Yao's help.

"She worked at Long Tan."

"A factory girl, was she? The people who manage that place work them to death. They've been falling off the buildings for months. Did you see the photos? They've put up nets to catch them."

"This one didn't jump. She drowned."

"What difference does that make?"

"She's the reason for all this. I want to know who she was."

"How are you going to find that out?"

"By going to the factory. You have to help me."

Yao frowned. "If I do, you'll stop making trouble for us? You'll do what you're told?"

Mei nodded. Yao rose with a smile, looking more like his old self.

They drove to Dongguan the next day, after lectures were over. The sun was setting by the time they arrived, and uniformed workers poured out of the high-walled complex, filling the street. Yao edged the car forward through the rush and stopped by the gate. A line of vehicles was waiting to get in, but the guards were not in any hurry to let them through. Two studied the truck at the front of the line slowly, as its driver grumbled. The other drivers stood in a huddle, passing around a packet of seeds to chew and spitting dark juice on the ground.

"You go in. I'll wait."

Yao looked startled. "Why? You're the one who brought us here."

"A woman poking around attracts attention. It's better this way."

He sighed. "I don't even know why I'm here. You owe me, okay? So what do you know?"

"Tang Liu. Nineteen, from Changsha, Hunan. I'll write her identity number for you." Mei took a pen and scrawled it on a pad.

"Good memory. Got a photo?"

"That should be enough."

Mei saw the guard stiffen as he scanned Yao's card, then wave him through. She relaxed a little: With Yao asking the questions, nobody would spot the resemblance between the dead girl and her. She climbed out of the car to stretch her legs and wandered across the road toward an Internet café.

Inside, kids in tunics sat in rows, yellow headphones clamped to their ears, eyes locked to screens, posting on Weibo and scouring the Internet. She was one of them—the post-1985 generation that had flooded out of Guangxi, Sichuan, and Hunan, following their parents to jobs in factories on the coast. But they weren't content to work for a few years and return with the cash to build a house and raise one child. They wanted to earn a resident's permit. They dreamed of buying apartments, despite the high prices. There wasn't room for them, despite the noise of construction. People talked of the Pearl River's cities being filled in with concrete and the delta becoming a metropolis of fifty million. Even that wouldn't be space enough.

Mei walked along an alley, where a tattered old *Hui Chun* poster from the New Year was taped in the dingy entrance to an apartment block to bring the dwellers good luck. The alley, lit by the glow of storefronts, was like a gorge between buildings rising a dozen stories on each side, so close that it looked possible to leap the gap from one balcony to its opposite. A wedge of evening sky was visible high above.

It took Yao an hour to reappear. By the time he did, she'd drunk all the tea she could take and was back in the car.

"There you are. That's all they had on her. The cops took the file a couple of days ago."

The recruitment notice yielded only brief details—her date of birth, identity number, and address in Shenzhen. She had walked into Long Tan two months before—as long as Mei had been at the Commission.

"So she joined in July? And she killed herself *last week*?" Nothing in this affair made sense.

Yao shrugged. "Maybe she didn't like the job."

12

For the mid-autumn festival, paper lanterns were lit all over Guangdong. Mei watched them drifting at night along Fazheng Road,
near the Commission's offices. She loved the story of Chang'e, who
ascended to heaven and lived in the moon after her husband was
killed by a villain. Every year, Mei ate a moon cake on the night of the
festival and remembered how she'd gazed into the sky as a child, trying to see the goddess.

The festival was an excuse for Guangzhou to eat, which it did
with relish. Mei was amazed at the appetites of its citizens. They
happily swallowed things that revolted her even to look at. Street
stalls lined the gates to Revolutionary Martyrs Park, their lamps pale
in the sunlight. They were piled with sea horse, abalone, alligators,
chicken's feet, pig livers—every organ imaginable.

"Ugh, get it away." Mei ducked and held her nose as her friend
waved the legs of an octopus in her face.

"Coward." Luli said. "You've got to learn to eat."

The stallholder cursed at them as Luli dropped the slimy creature
on the ground. Mei paid for a bag of star fruit to placate the grouchy
vendor, and they walked through the red gates, past characters in
Zhou Enlai's handwriting on a white granite pedestal, topped by red
and yellow tiles. Every bush was neatly clipped, and the granite stones
were scrubbed. The pair was soon engulfed in a crowd heading for
the rally.

"This had better be fun," Luli said, sucking on a fruit.

"You'll learn something."

Luli groaned. She wasn't dressed for school—she strode along the avenue in heels, white jeans, and red T-shirt with "Lucky 69" stitched in English on the front. The authorities had erected a wide stage in front of the memorial to the 1927 Communist uprising—a huge hand grasping a rifle that pointed to the sky—and a troupe of dancers in silk costumes filled it. Luli took Mei's arm, leading her to an advantageous spot on the lawn, where she spread a blanket. She took a box of moon cakes from a bag and placed it by the fruit.

"Eat, Mei. And wake me up if anything happens." Luli put on a pair of Gucci sunglasses and lay down on the grass.

"Thanks for coming," said Mei.

"I don't know why you asked me. I'm not even a member. What about that Party boy of yours?"

"Who?"

"Don't play ignorant. Yao. He's got a nice smile. I bet he's got a good body too. That's what you need—a distraction."

Mei blushed. "Don't be stupid."

Luli propped herself on one elbow and looked at Mei over her sunglasses.

"It would do you good to have a bit of fun. It's like you're married to the job. Where do you bring me on your day off? A Party rally. Ooh, exciting." She shut her eyes and lay down again.

"I'm sorry. It's been crazy at work."

"What's going on?"

Mei looked at Luli, half-dozing on the ground, happily oblivious. There was so much to tell her, but none of it made sense. Mei didn't know who she was anymore—she'd never had much information, but even the precious scraps she'd gathered were suspect now. She had no family, only a fantasy. It would make no sense to Luli, who went home to her village every New Year's holiday and sent her parents gifts from the city. All Mei had was a ghost in a pond. Even if she'd wanted to confess to Luli, how could she? Even thinking about the body made her shiver.

"I can't say," she said. "I'm sorry."

"You'll go far, my dear."

The dancers finished. A poster in the commissary had urged

everyone to attend the rally, billing it as a cultural celebration of Guangdong. Chen Longwei, the Party secretary himself, would lead it. Mei hadn't seen him except from afar, striding across the compound in a wedge of officials. He had charisma, even in the distance—tall and good-looking, with a ruddy face and a small, heart-shaped mouth.

People said that Chen had changed. When he'd come to Guangzhou from a military post elsewhere, he'd been happy with Guangdong's informal, business-friendly ways. The Party shouldn't stand in the way of enterprise, he'd said. But over time his tone had changed. He made speeches, held rallies. He'd started to invoke Mao's name alongside Deng's, complaining that old virtues were being lost, that corruption had led the Party astray. Peasant wisdom, he now said, was needed to restore discipline.

In Zhongnanhai, the Party compound near Tiananmen Square from where the government operated, it gave them heartburn. There was talk of him burnishing his image for the Party Congress in November, vying for a seat on the Politburo Standing Committee. But the people loved him. He'd pledged to help migrants by letting their children into schools and improving their living conditions. His rallies were full of them, cheering his speeches and singing the old Party songs that he said expressed the pure spirit of the country's past.

As the dancers left, they were replaced by a choir of women in red tunics and officials in military uniform. Chen walked on as the orchestra tuned up, and he waved to the crowd.

The band played the tune to "March of the Volunteers," the Party's anthem, but the choir sang the words to the 1978 version—the one venerating Mao that had been dropped long ago.

> *Raise high Mao Zedong's banner, march on!*
> *Raise high Mao Zedong's banner, march on!*
> *March on! March on!*

Luli sat up. "What the fuck?" She put a hand to her mouth and laughed. "My dad would love this." She held up her phone and took a video.

As the anthem ended, the crowd roared, and the choir went

straight into "Spring Story," a patriotic song praising Deng. Chen beamed, waving a red flag in time to the music. They sang three more—"Spring Comes Early in the Commune," "A New Look Has Come to Our Mountain Village," and "The East Is Red"—and Chen stepped to a microphone as they filed off.

"Wasn't that refreshing?" he began. "To hear songs that tell of honest labor and building the country for the people? Not of fighting for profit or officials putting themselves before the Party? It reminds me of happier days."

People at the front of the crowd cheered.

"This guy even sounds like my dad," Luli said. "He's always moaning about how life was simpler. They could go on a long march together."

"Guangdong is thriving," said Chen. "It has become the engine of China. We've gathered at this festival to celebrate it. This is the Year of the Dragon, the year of good fortune and prosperity. There is nothing we cannot do. We are hardworking, ambitious, and lucky. We have an appetite for success—a big appetite!"

Chen grinned and held up a moon cake to the crowd before taking a bite out of it. There were more cheers, and Chen clapped along, laughing. Then he motioned to the crowd for quiet.

"There is much to admire in our society, but some things worry me. I see wealth, entitlement, and fraud—things that are concealed from the people. There are officials who let you down, who use their privileges for their own advantage instead of helping others. We've all suffered."

Luli scoffed. "You don't look like you've suffered too badly."

"Shush." Mei waved at her friend, wanting to hear what Chen would say. She knew that his words would be quoted back to them on Monday, with approving comments. Perhaps they would be the basis of a new campaign. The Party constantly announced campaigns to make things better, although one seemed to pass into the other without much effect.

"We've dealt with the little ones—officials who take a bribe to house a family or to get them a job. They deserved the people's justice. But it's time for us to go higher, to hunt for tigers and not just flies. The village boss who tries to hold back progress, the senior Party official whose job is to impose discipline but who wants a red envelope himself."

Mei stood. People near the stage were shouting angrily and booing, as if they wanted to march through the city and drag away those whom Chen had condemned. They waved banners that had come from somewhere—Hunt the Tigers, Set the People Free Again. Chen raised a clenched fist, as if standing in solidarity. The mood had turned ugly.

Mei gazed at him, her heart racing with fright. *The Party official who takes a red envelope.* She felt the packet of banknotes hidden inside her jacket, resting near her heart.

13

The Wolf lived in a white-walled villa in the Party compound. As Mei approached, a full moon threw silver light on the building, making it glow like a cottage in a fairy tale. Two guards stood at the gate, and one wrote her name in a leather-bound book.

"You found me," said the Wolf, upon answering the door. He was in a suit, a red tie loosened around his neck, as if recently returned from a formal dinner.

"They let me in." Mei nodded her head in the direction of the guards, who were watching.

"That pair arrived yesterday. The Party thinks I need protecting. Or others must be protected from me. Come in."

She followed him into a living room, with cream sofas set around a black lacquer table. It was more comfortable than she'd expected. She thought of Chen's speech and wondered if this was the sanctum of a corrupt official, whose private life was richer than his public image. There was wealth here, but it looked like old money—objects he'd saved for, ornaments he'd kept for a long time. A baby grand piano sat in one corner, the score to a Schubert sonata on its stand. A Poppy tablet, still in its box, was the only hint of modernity.

There was a set of four photographs on the piano in matching frames. They revealed the same woman, a solemn-faced beauty. She was pictured as a girl in a Mao tunic, with university friends, as a young bride, and with her husband by one of the stone *huabiao* columns at the Gate of Heavenly Peace. She looked happier in age, as her face lost its roundness and lines crept under her eyes. The man next to her was the Wolf, his hair black instead of gray.

"My wife," he said, walking over to pick up the bridal portrait. He examined it, then handed it to Mei.

"She was beautiful."

"All of her life."

"When did she—" Mei stopped, embarrassed by her boldness. His wife's death felt like common gossip, given a nasty edge by Pan.

"The year you were born. It's hard to imagine now." He took the photograph back and replaced it gently on the same spot.

"How do you know when I was born?" she asked.

He stared at her. She thought he might lose his temper at being challenged, but instead he walked over to a sofa and sat, tapping a document on the lacquer table with one finger.

"Your file, Mei. It's not a mystery. Sit. Tell me why you're here."

Mei steeled herself. She took out the envelope and, sitting opposite him on the sofa, put it on the table. The Wolf looked at the blue customs seal and frowned, then leaned forward and picked it up. He squeezed it between finger and thumb, feeling the notes inside, and shook his head.

"Who is this from?"

"Superintendent Hou of Humen Customs. He asked me to bring it to you." She felt herself falter under the Wolf's gaze. "He said he knows you."

"Was there a message?"

"He said it was a note of appreciation."

"Very kind. Tell me, who instructed you to visit Superintendent Hou? It wasn't your idea, was it?"

She shook her head. "I was sent by Deputy Secretary Pan, the morning after I saw you in Dongguan."

The Wolf shook his head again. "She worked fast, didn't she? I expected this, but not delivered by you. An old surveillance tactic— employ one suspect to trap another. I taught her well."

He raised the envelope to his nose and sniffed.

"You know what's inside, don't you?"

Mei looked down in shame at the Persian rug between their feet. It was lustrous, despite its frayed threads.

"That's in the book, too. Make the suspect a witness. Use one to crush the other. I've done it myself many times. Mao taught us to strengthen the Party through self-criticism. Let's open it and take a look."

Slitting the envelope with a steel opener, he let the packet of Swiss notes fall onto the table.

"I'm sorry. They made me do this." Mei flushed with shame.

"If it hadn't been you, there would have been someone else at my door with this"—he paused, uttering the word contemptuously—"*evidence.* Perhaps your princeling. Forget it now."

"I can't."

"We don't have much time."

Mei had clenched her eyes, unable to look at the Wolf, but his tone made her open them. He extracted a red pack of Chunghwa cigarettes, with its embossed emblem of the Gate of Heavenly Peace, tucked one in his pocket, and rose. Unlocking a glass door at one end of the room, he stepped onto a narrow lawn with a birdcage at the end. A blue cockatoo watched them from a branch.

"I thought it would take longer, but they're at my gate already. I need you to do something."

"Of course."

"You must find the dead girl's father."

"I think I have."

"Have you? Where?" It was the first time she'd surprised the Wolf, and it gratified her.

"Look—"

She pulled the Long Tan badge from her pocket and gave it to him. The Wolf examined it with the flame of his lighter, as she explained how she'd found it in the marsh.

"This is good," he said. "You've turned up something significant. I knew you could. The badge is useful."

"But this girl came from Changsha and she was—"

"Nineteen, yes." The Wolf moved away to the cage, checking the water. "That's not the point. There aren't many people who could have fixed it. It's clever. I told you: Find her father."

"Is he in Hunan?"

"In Guangdong. He must be close."

"Tell me." Mei shook with frustration at the Wolf's elliptical clues. "We don't have much time, you said. If you want me to help, you have to guide me. Tell me where he is."

"I don't know, but you'll find him. You found the badge. Why would I have called you if I didn't believe in you?"

As he spoke, a phone rang inside the house, an insistent sound. The Wolf stepped away from the bird and crossed the lawn in a few steps, passing into the living room. By the time she had caught up, he was already ending the call, and she only heard his final words.

"Wait. I'm coming."

14

Mei lingered as the Wolf's car passed under the barrier from Dengying Road onto Yuexiu Bei Road. She'd retrieved the Chery Cowin and parked at the curb, waiting for him with her headlights dimmed. Her former self—the Mei of two days earlier—would never have taken such a risk, but her life had changed. There was nothing safe for her anymore.

An Army car trailed the Audi A8, and the Wolf stared past her as the convoy hit the street, lights flashing. His overcoat collar was lifted, and his eyes were blank. She followed them, feeling the g-force as they tore around the bend onto the Donghaoyong Elevated Road and pulled onto the Inner Ring Road. The cars weaved among lanes, loud and bright, making a spectacle.

I'm coming, he'd said, and from the hesitation she'd heard in his voice she knew where. She had revealed the evidence against him, and he had given up hiding. They took the Guangyuan Expressway, with White Cloud Mountain looming in the dark, a shooting star above the delta. Approaching Dongguan forty minutes later, they took the exit over the flatlands to Long Tan.

The barrier was raised to allow the convoy through, and the guards stood at alert. A group of Dongguan police stood nearby, and she thought she saw the one who had looked at her card in the marsh. She looped around the apartment block and parked in the back, then walked up the alley to the Internet café. It was as full as before, warmed by the bodies hunched over the screens. Mei paid for some

Internet time and sat among them uncertainly. She had trailed the Wolf this far, but now she was blocked.

As she hesitated, a man near her took off his headphones and stood, stretching before stepping outside. He wore jeans, sneakers, and a purple tunic, like the red one that the boy had found in the fields. She glanced at the card on his chest as the man passed; it also had his photo and the usual details, including his identity number. She watched as he walked along the alley and, ignoring the police, toward the gate. As he disappeared inside the complex, she felt in her pocket.

The victim's card was right there. All she needed was the tunic.

Mei walked to the car and opened the trunk, delving inside a bag she'd left there. Then she trotted back to the café and went into the toilet. The stall smelled foul and she averted her eyes, pinching her nostrils and trying not to inhale. She unbuttoned her blouse and pulled on the red tunic. The tear in the fabric was visible, and she tucked it into her pants before clipping on the badge. Then she turned to check her appearance in the mirror.

It felt wrong. The disguise shouldn't have been so perfect, the badge so seamlessly hers. It was as if the woman had risen from the dead.

Hanging the bag on a hook, she set out along the alley, imagining herself a migrant who'd slipped out to call her family. The police ignored her as she quickened her step to catch up to a pair of factory girls who were standing at the barrier.

"Stop! Wait for us!" one of them shouted at an electric vehicle that had halted by the gate.

They were back from a night out, in short skirts and sequined T-shirts. The guard's face stiffened and Mei shuffled forward. He let her through and she followed them to the eight-seat electric vehicle, which was like a golf cart.

"Where to?" The driver didn't look around.

"N-5," the giggling woman said.

Mei nodded and the driver didn't seem to care. The buggy jerked forward with a whine, rocking her back in her seat, and she grabbed a handle to stop herself from falling out. They sped along the road, passing couples walking hand in hand. It was like driving through a small city. Mei looked at a line of stores to her right—a barber, a fortune-teller, a neon-lit unit in which fish and turtles swam in tanks, ready to be snatched up in plastic bags. A supermarket stood next to a plaza, its shoppers bent forward, peering at shelves and prodding vegetables. It could have been any town, but its citizens were all in their twenties and wore tunics in white, green, and purple. Mei was the only one in red, she noticed.

The driver accelerated along a narrow road beyond the shops, then halted by an apartment block twenty stories high, shaped like a T and striped with walkways along each side. Each walkway was caged with mesh: it looked more like a jail than a home, a place that kept its dwellers imprisoned. Fixed near the roof, where the walkways intersected, were two English characters on a white background: N-3.

"This is it." The driver sat back, pulling a pack of cigarettes from his top pocket and tapping one on the back of his hand.

"I can't walk." One woman thrust out a leg into the gap next to him. She had four-inch heels, the leather covered with golden glitter.

"Nothing I can do." He pointed ahead. A few hundred feet away, the road was closed and a crowd of workers stood silently, their backs to her, looking at something.

"Another food bird thought she could fly, huh?"

"Don't talk that way, Yin." The taller woman poked her friend in the ribs, but she laughed, wiping her fists under her eyes as if she was crying.

"Poor me, I'm so sad. They don't pay me enough to go and see my daddy. I know, I'll take a jump."

"Shush." The woman gestured back at Mei with a flick of her head, as if warning her friend of danger.

Mei pushed along the seat and reached for the door before anyone could ask who she was.

"I'll walk," she said, stepping out.

15

There were fifty in the crowd, standing in place, those at the back stretching on their toes to get a better view. Mei threaded through the bodies, whispering apologies as she bumped elbows and hips and ignoring the murmurs of protest at her intrusion. Near the front, she thrust forward to see the spectacle.

It was what she had known it would be—a dead body. It was slumped on the ground, left leg backward and right arm snapped at the elbow, stuck out the wrong way. A man in his twenties, with the shaggy haircut—the first thing the kids got when they made it to the city—puffed out in electric spikes. It looked as if he'd been running vertically at high speed, his attention distracted by something to his left, when he'd smacked into the concrete. A trickle of black blood oozing from his head was the only sign of the collision; otherwise, he'd left hardly a mark. He wore a red tunic and skinny jeans.

She looked up, trying to trace his path through the air. He was about twenty feet from the building, as if he'd launched himself into flight from a balcony or perhaps from the roof. *Food bird,* the party girl had called him, believing it was a woman. Anger surged in Mei. She wished that she could drag that girl over to see what death meant—the ugly surprise of it. She gripped her nails into her palm, the way she'd been taught as a kid. *Breathe in, breathe out.*

Blue lights shined at the barrier, and lamps illuminated the body. Two guards in black-and-white uniforms and peaked caps stared intently at the crowd, looking for unrest. Their job was simply to be there, to occupy the space and be counted in the records. Mei felt like stepping out and taking charge, but her badge wouldn't allow it. Instead she tried to melt into the crowd. The corpse wore Anta sneakers, unmarked apart from a black scuff running the length of the right one.

As she stared, she saw a shape moving jerkily on the outside of her vision and glanced to her left. A man was making his way toward the crowd in some haste. There was something wrong with his right leg, so he hobbled along with a lacquered bamboo walking stick. It had a silver handle that he squeezed into his hip each time his weak leg twisted. He was dressed in black pants and a crisp white shirt—not a uniform—and was suppressing a smile.

Mei returned her gaze to the body, trying to follow the man out of the corner of her eye as he got within a few yards and then curved his path to the right, walking to the rear of the crowd. She could sense him a little ways behind her, the click of his cane approaching as if the throng was parting for him. The ripple of the human wave reached her a moment or two before he did, the last layer of onlookers behind her shifting aside to accommodate him.

The man stood to her left, the cane planted in front of her foot, not quite grazing it. He was significantly shorter than she was; the top of his head was level with her eyes. She flashed a look sideways, catching sight of a shallow nose with broad nostrils and long, black eyelashes. He stared ahead, ignoring her.

"You made it out. Why didn't you tell me?"

He whispered, his light voice quavering with nerves. Behind the reproach, he sounded happy.

Mei realized that she had never heard the dead woman's voice. Her face was identical, but Mei didn't know if, just by speaking, she would give herself away. It flashed through her mind to stay silent but she heard the sentence emerge from her mouth before she'd made a decision. She spoke in a stolid country accent, like a factory girl, rationing the words.

"I tried to find you."

"You're so brave. I must know everything." He rested the handle of his cane on her arm, and she felt its chill.

"Not here." Two more words, this time deliberately chosen. He hadn't noticed any difference.

"You're right. Come to my room in an hour."

His instruction was interrupted by a shout.

"You in red!"

A guard stared in their direction, one finger pointing. His partner held a walkie-talkie that crackled with the sound of voices, making the Cantonese vowels harder. She felt the man shift on his leg as if considering; a moment later he had melted back into the crowd with a few clicks of his cane.

The guard marched toward her. Her Party card, her best protection, was out of her reach beyond the gates. She'd always taken risks to get her own way, relying on talking her way out of trouble. Now, she realized, she could not save herself.

She felt a change in the crowd around her, an organism facing danger. Whatever faint sounds of breathing that had been present were now gone, replaced by a frozen silence. The girl to her right expelled a hiss between her teeth, audible only to those next to her; it sounded like she wanted to spit. The guard arrived at Mei and stared at her, then reached for her badge without speaking. His fingers were as rough as a farmer's, one thumbnail split. He looked unblinkingly at the card, lips moving as he read it.

"Come." He grabbed her by the arm and dug his nails into her flesh.

She grunted in pain but he didn't stop, pulling her with him out of the crowd toward the building.

"Let me go," she cried, but she felt his fingers punish her arm with even more force. She had turned from an official with authority over this dolt into a factory girl who had no power to stop him. She could feel the nervous energy behind his aggression; he was scared to let her go.

They came to the building's entrance. Moths were crashing against the sodium lights as off-duty workers sprawled in front of a large television set tuned to a dance show. None looked up as the guard pulled her to a stairwell and pushed her up the first stairs, prodding her to keep moving.

"Where are you taking me?" she said.

She spoke in clipped Mandarin, but it had no effect—he grunted and shoved again. They were on a dark stairwell that led up one side of the dormitory building, with only dim lamps to show the way. At each landing, the space opened up to a view of a walkway—the sky on one side and a row of dormitory doors on the other. Some doors were open and groups of workers lounged outside, smoking and chatting or hanging clothes from the wire mesh. It was a vast cage, holding them inside the building like chickens.

A woman with weathered skin, clutching a mop, gave a half-glance as they passed a landing. Mei grimaced at her, hoping for an intervention, but it was useless. They were on the eighth level, passing another row of doors along another identical balcony. She could cry out for help, but the kids on the balconies would freeze and withdraw.

"Tell me," she gasped, her breath short.

His only response was a further push against her back, his fingers straying toward her hips. Her anger was overridden by fear—she had to escape, but there was nothing she could do. On the top floor, they stepped onto a pitch-black landing, with a floor that smelled of urine. The guard stepped closer, and she flinched, fearing what he might do to her in the dark, but he reached across to a steel door. He pulled it open, thrust Mei through, and bolted it behind her.

16

ei swayed, trying to find her balance. Her senses were on alert as she tried to feel for a wall or a door—her eyes were adjusting to the dark and she couldn't see anything. Then she felt a gust on her face and knew she was in the open, not locked in a cupboard or a prison. A dark rectangle stretched a thousand feet in front of her, ringed by reflected light. It was like an inverted pool—solid in the middle, with gravity controlling the outside. She was on the roof. Mei breathed slowly to reassure herself—she was far from the edge, provided she didn't stray.

The roof was flat and uncluttered, the surface pebbled. Two lines of pipes, supported two feet or so from the surface by metal brackets, ran along its length to a water tank in the middle. There were no air-conditioning units; she thought of the workers sprawled watching television or gossiping outside their rooms in the sultry air. It must be hot in those dormitories. She looked at the edge of the roof, moving her head back to ward off vertigo. She was a couple hundred feet from either side, but she felt tremors at the idea of getting closer.

Suddenly she realized that she was not alone.

The Wolf stood in the middle of the expanse. Before she could react, he walked toward her, his eyes glittering as he approached.

"Why are you here?" he demanded.

"I followed you."

He reached out to touch the badge on her tunic, rubbing a thumb on Tang Liu's photo.

"You look like her. Do you want to die like her, too?"

Mei shook her head.

"Unless you're careful, you will."

"Why are they falling?"

"You don't think they're so miserable in this place that they throw themselves from roofs, like that boy?" The Wolf pointed to the side of the roof under which the body had been found. "You don't believe the official story?"

"Do you?"

"When you're my age, you'll know it's rarely true. The first one, I mean. It's drafted by a committee to play for time. They'll say he jumped, of course. Let me show you something."

He turned and walked in the direction he'd pointed. Mei's shoes crunched on the pebbles as she followed, her eyes down to ensure that she stayed on solid ground. It reminded her of trailing him through the banana fields, into the night. Glancing up, she saw him on the edge of the roof, etched against the sky. She was fifty feet away, nearly frozen with fright.

"Come here," he said.

"I can't."

"Why not?"

Her shame was overwhelmed by terror. "I'm scared of falling."

"You won't fall. Quickly now."

"I can't." It was unthinkable. She felt her knees sink beneath her, talking to him. "I have—"

"Wait." The Wolf paced along the edge of the roof like a tight-rope walker, and she emitted a low yelp of fear. He halted and looked down, his cigarette marking the border of roof and sky.

"Stay," he commanded.

He twisted and ran past her, with a surprising turn of speed, toward the door that the guard had locked behind her. Still on her knees, Mei heard him striking it with both fists, calling out loudly.

"Open it! Now!"

There was no response and he struck it more heavily, sending a dull echo into stairwell voice.

"Now, you fool! That is a command."

Nothing.

The Wolf placed his palms flat against the unyielding metal, muttering an obscenity, and then ran over to her.

"You've brought the snake out of its lair," he said.

He shook his head and scanned the roof from one side to the other. He remained silent for a long moment, then took hold of her wrist. He began to walk, pulling her behind him.

It struck Mei that she was about to die.

"No, no. Please," she called to him, "Please let me go."

Her body started to shake, and she dug her heels into the pebbly ground, but he kept on pulling. He was far stronger than she'd imagined; she couldn't even slow him down. She trembled, her vision dimming. The edge was twenty feet away when she dropped down to her knees.

"Get up."

She moaned in panic. "No. No."

He dragged her again, her body twisting in the dirt and pebbles scraping her hips as she writhed. When he let go of her wrist, she curled into a fetus on the ground, her eyes clamped shut.

"Stand up." His tone was stony, colder than any she'd ever known. She'd made a terrible error in trusting him. She knew then that she should have taken Pan's advice and kept her distance from him. She should have had faith in the Party.

Mei rolled onto her knees and raised herself to a standing position with her eyes clenched shut. She felt him take her shoulder and position her body at attention, seizing control of her.

"Open your eyes."

She obeyed, a crack at first and then a squint, and saw his face, grave and impassive. Her feet were at the edge of the roof, the border between solidity and nothingness behind her. She felt the suction of the void.

"Turn around," said the Wolf, taking her by the shoulders.

"I can't." It was unthinkable to face the sky and look down. Her feet were fixed, her muscles locked. She scanned his black eyes and weathered face in search of some compassion, but there was none to be found.

"Goodbye, Song Mei," he said, and pushed.

17

With the first lurch, Mei's center of gravity was thrust into empty space. She didn't breathe as she hung there, holding her arms desperately toward the Wolf for him to pull her back. Her mouth opened, but nothing came out. Her body was a watch's hand, halted for a split second at midnight. Then her hips buckled, her arms splayed out, and gravity took her.

Mei dropped into space, hands spread wide, back and hips flattening. She blinked and saw sky above her, as if she were lying in a field—stars, clouds, soft blackness. Her life would soon be finished. It was like drowning, sinking into the depths after a final, liquid breath—almost peaceful. The air rushed past as she picked up speed, plunging downward.

Something clutched her.

Wires bit into her back and closed around her legs and shoulders. Her head jerked, wrenching her neck to the side, and the breath was knocked out of her. Her fall slowed, stopped, then reversed itself—all within the smallest instant. She rebounded, then lay gasping, unable to make sense of what had happened. When she opened her eyes, she was hanging in a wire net, twenty feet beneath the roof. The Wolf was standing above, looking down at her.

Her heart was racing, and she shook uncontrollably with the rush of it all, but she was alive. As she watched him, he brought one finger to his lips, beckoning for her to be silent. Then he passed from view. She tilted her face to the side in tiny increments and examined the net, gripping the cables tightly in each hand. The line reached all along the side of the building, strung between poles about thirty feet apart, strung there to catch wayward objects. Yao's words came back to her: *They've been falling off the buildings for months. They've put up nets to catch them.* She could sense the ground looming far below her and she stiffened, the terror returning.

Above her, she could hear a bolt slide and the door push open so forcefully that it slammed up against the wall. She heard a drumbeat of steps—it had to be a dozen men—scrambling across the roof, with one shouting commands.

"Check there! And there! The tank!"

A man's face poked over the edge. He wore a green helmet, and she caught a glimpse of PLA fatigues. She shut her eyes, waiting for a shout of alarm, but none was forthcoming. When she looked again, he was gone.

"Clear!" The man in command shouted and stamped his feet at attention, then the unit ran across the roof in unison. She could hear their footfalls, like a herd of cattle, as they disappeared down the stairs.

There was silence, and then she heard the door creak again, slowly this time, and someone stepped onto the roof. He had an unhurried gait, and his shoes crunched gently for a few steps. When he spoke, his voice was as gentle as his walk—it had a rich timbre.

"So, old comrade. What brings you here?"

"I could ask the same." The Wolf's voice was closer, not far from where she lay. In the moment when he'd pushed her off the roof—a few minutes ago, although it already felt like hours—she'd believed he was her murderer. Now he had become her guardian again.

"I heard you were here, and we haven't spoken in so long. Not the two of us alone. Not like the old days."

"And you always liked a view."

"You don't forget anything, do you? I've always envied your memory." The voice turned sharp. "Where is the girl?"

"What girl?"

"The one you had fetched here. That one, Comrade Lang. Perhaps your memory's fading, after all."

"Her? I sent her away. I wanted someone to tell me about the boy who fell. She didn't know him."

"That is a pity." The voice was soft. "One thing puzzles me, though. Why are you so interested? It's not any of your business, is it? Some kid in a factory takes his own life. The Party's got bigger things to worry about. Tramping around the marshes last night? It sounds like one of your obsessions."

The Wolf laughed, the gurgle of phlegm in his throat.

"That's my life. Chasing after stray incidents, trying to make them add up. Most of it comes to nothing. I don't know why you're interested."

"A couple of sad kids, far from home? That's trivial. It's for the security bureau, if anyone. You've got more urgent matters to address—criminals and capitalist roaders. Eliminating antisocial elements in our society. The standing committee has warned of the threat to the Party. There are temptations in this world—not a simple life, like when we were young. You've always been loyal, but someone who didn't know you might wonder if you've lost your way. Maybe it's deliberate—vested interests have blinded you. That would be serious. We don't mind you taking a red envelope here or there, but perhaps you've gone too far."

"You needn't worry. I do my job."

"Oh, I trust you. I'm just worried in case others misunderstand your behavior. I've heard disturbing stories. Come, let's take a walk."

The two sets of footsteps receded. Mei heard a few more words and then an indistinguishable mumble, getting softer.

Without them to distract her, her senses focused again on her plight. Her hands tightened, fingering the tight threads wrapped and bound into squares. As the wind blew, they whistled softly. She felt paralyzed, afraid to let go in case she rolled over and fell. She had an image of the corpse far beneath, limbs twisted against hard earth. Where had he jumped from? How could he have evaded the net? Either he'd been hell-bent on dying, or someone had helped him into the air.

The voices returned, at first faintly and then louder. Eventually the murmurings turned back into words.

"Come. Let me take you back."

"There's no need. I can find my way," the Wolf said.

"I insist."

"Very well."

"Come along." The stranger's tone of voice was somewhere between an invitation and a command.

The Wolf's boots scraped on the gravel, and a burst of dust and stones tumbled over the roof onto Mei. She flinched as debris scattered on her face, one pebble bouncing against the ropes as it fell, making it hum like the string of an instrument. She listened to his steps—heavy, bearing the weight of age—follow the other man's toward the door. The last thing she heard was the shuffle of boots and the scrape of the bolt.

18

lone, Mei looked at the stars and calculated her chance of escape. It felt close to zero. She could not climb onto the roof. It was twenty feet above her, and the wall was smooth. She'd first have to clamber to her feet and try to stand on the cable mesh, an intolerable thought. There was no way down—she could not even dare to look.

For the time being, the darkness made her invisible. Nobody could see her from the ground; from below, she hadn't spotted the net, even though it ran the length of the building. Come dawn she would be obvious. She was doomed, not just by where she was but by her status—a young woman with no connections. The Wolf had tried to shield her, but he couldn't now. She lay in the web, waiting for the spider.

Lying there, she thought about what she'd overheard. It frightened her how easily the Wolf had submitted. She had thought of him as all-powerful, with the privileges that high Party rank brought. Yet he had followed meekly, as if he lacked the power to resist. Time passed slowly. She gripped the cables, holding tightly as the wind sent shivers through the net.

Above her, the bolt scraped and the door opened. Someone came through it and called out in a high voice.

"Liu! Liu! Are you here?"

She soon realized who was calling her. It was the man who'd stood excitedly by her in the crowd and then melted away at the guard's approach. As if to confirm it, she could hear the click of his cane striking the roof as he walked toward the edge. She wondered whether to give herself away and realized there was no choice.

"I'm here," she called, quietly at first and then louder. "I'm over here. Beneath the ledge."

The cane clicked more rapidly than the other men had walked, and the man's face peered down.

"Shit, girl. You jumped?"

"Of course I didn't."

"What happened, then?"

"Just help me." She no longer bothered to disguise her accent.

"As easy as that?" He laughed suddenly, as if tension had been released from him. "You're the same, even down there. Push me around, dangle me from your finger. You know I'm your puppet."

The head vanished and she heard him clicking away, then an echo on the stairwell. Mei lay back, her fingers slackening a notch. There was something about his laugh that reassured her. She heard the bang of a door and the tap of his cane from beneath her position. As she twisted to look down, a rush of vertigo made her head snap back again.

"Look this way. Crawl toward me." His voice sounded from somewhere below, but at least a hundred feet distant, at a diagonal. It appeared to be coming from midair, as if he were a sprite.

"I can't do it," she cried. "I'm scared."

"Scared? Not the woman I know. Come on, we don't have time to mess around. They'll be back from the overtime shift soon."

Mei took a deep breath and calmed herself: She would do this if it killed her, and indeed, she felt as if it might. Clenching her eyes, she lifted her arm and rolled onto her stomach, making the cables sway. Then, counting to three, she forced her eyes open. The lights of the city and the vision of the delta spilling toward the Pearl River disoriented her, but she peered across to see him standing below the net. A line of balconies was punched into the side of the building, hung with laundry. He gripped the rail with one hand and waved his cane.

She had to obey. Pushing her arms, she got herself up on all fours and crawled, climbing the incline toward one of the poles. That part was bearable, but she now faced the drop on the other side. She grunted to block her thoughts, placed her palm on the downward slope, and slithered her hips over the pole. Her left hand went down, missing the cable and plunging through the gap into space, making her cry out in terror.

The young man laughed, closer now. "God, girl. You're making a mess."

"You try it," she called out in pain, making him laugh again.

She inched her way slowly across until she was suspended about ten feet above him, with a view of his upturned face from the balcony. He climbed on a tattered chair and reached out with his cane, rattling the small gap between the building and the net.

"Through here."

"I can't do that."

"You said you couldn't do *this*. Pull yourself over and twist."

Mei obeyed, letting her legs slide until her butt hit the wall. Then she thrust herself into the gap, feet first. She slowly wiggled her hips past the cable and squeezed it over her breasts, then hung there, trying to calculate a soft way down. Finding no way to do so, she twisted her face sideways and let go of the wires, falling into his arms. She landed with a painful crack on one ankle and sprawled on the balcony.

Hopping off the chair, he bent down and kissed her, then clapped his palms, hands upright.

"Baby, you made it."

Mei pulled herself to her haunches, with her arms wrapped around her knees for comfort. She was on a solid surface—still a dozen stories up, on a balcony that she'd never have ventured onto by choice, but safe. She felt faint with the shock of what she'd achieved.

"Thanks," she croaked. Her voice wasn't working properly.

"So?" The young man's face was still lit up with excitement at the escapade, as if it had been a game he'd invented.

"So?"

"You've got a lot to tell me. Remember the last time we saw each other before you went? What I said?"

"How could I forget?"

"Let's get out of here."

He grabbed her hand and pulled her up so that she was standing in front of him, his face tilted. Then he pulled her through the door to the balcony, into a dimly lit room. It was a women's dormitory, in which a lamp glowed softly from behind a pink and white sheet veiling a bottom bunk. There were eight bunks, crammed top to bottom in the room, lining the walls on both sides and leaving a narrow path through the middle. As they passed, a row of teddy bears stared at them.

He didn't pause, pulling open the door and emerging onto a long corridor, empty apart from two green-uniformed workers gossiping at its end. He trotted toward them, tugging Mei in his wake. Despite his cane and three-legged walk, she had trouble keeping up. Her wounded ankle made her limp, and the scrape in her cheek was starting to burn—she was beginning to feel sensations other than terror. The two women turned, staring at her red tunic, then turned away, sensing trouble and not wanting to get involved. The young man nodded to them as he pushed the elevator button.

She stood at the back of the elevator until the doors opened on the first floor and her companion peered out. Satisfied, he took her hand and they limped hurriedly past the same array of workers in front of the same television show, as if nothing of interest had happened, and emerged onto the road, where normality had resumed. The crowd and the guards had dispersed, and the corpse had been taken away. Mei saw the flickering headlights of an electric cart in the distance.

"Stop." She pulled her hand from his.

"What, baby?"

"I can't talk now."

"We must. You made me sick with worry."

She grasped his soft, downy cheek.

"We'll chat tomorrow. Look at me, I'm a mess, and I need a shower. I have to clean up. I'm a woman, silly."

He nodded and she seized the opening, limping across the road as the cart stopped for passengers on its path to the exit.

19

Mei's head ached and her ankle throbbed. She squinted at her alarm clock, which she had set to seven o'clock after returning to the compound in the early hours. Nodding to the guard, she had tried to look like she'd been out on a job. She figured it was true, in a way.

Pipes shuddered as a hundred taps were turned on at the same time and the water spurted out unpredictably, first icy, then burning. You had to be ready to jump to avoid being frozen or scalded. She let the jets strike the back of her neck, appreciating the force this time, and examined her body as the water ran down it in rivulets. A scrape on one wrist and bruises on her hips, others down her back where she had been trapped by the mesh. She tested her ankle as she stepped out. It made her wince, but the bones were intact. She'd have to bear it for a couple of days.

Sitting in the hall after breakfast, she pretended to listen to lectures on China's courts, techniques of surveillance, and land rights. In her mind, she replayed scenes from the night again and again—the brutality of the guard as he'd hustled her up the stairs, the Wolf's cold stare as he'd pushed her, as if her life were of no value, the sound of the door when the other man arrived.

It had been Chen, of course. The soft voice was different from his public tone, more subtle and pliant, but it was unmistakable. From her place in the net, she'd heard high politics at work. *We don't mind you taking a red envelope here or there.* It was gentle, far from the pledge he made at Revolutionary Martyrs Park to root out the corrupt officials. But it came to the same thing—the end of the Wolf's inquiry. She was terrified, yet Chen's role made ghastly sense. It explained why the Wolf had sneaked out into the fields alone. He could chase after anyone he wanted in Guangdong, just not the person senior to him. It was the Party's ultimate protection for its elite. The Commission had to clear any investigation into an official with a higher official, and Chen was the highest in Guangdong. He was beyond justice.

The thought stayed in her mind all day, especially on the drive south to Shenzhen after class. She hardly said a word to Yao and he sat stiffly at the wheel, staring at the highway like a chauffeur who was following orders.

They parked in the courtyard of an apartment block, between a Mercedes and a Buick. Someone here had a scam going—the block was run-down but the cars were all expensive. The spaces were clearly being rented to owners who needed a parking space in Shenzhen, and the block's Party committee was either turning a blind eye or taking a cut. Each time Mei came to Shenzhen, another mall or development had sprung up. Towers blocked the sky, and the city's streets buzzed with migrant accents and the roar of construction.

"This is stupid." Yao finally spoke, staring at the lines of balconies surrounding the courtyard.

"One evening's work. That's all."

"You're crazy, Mei. The Wolf is on the way out. You should keep your distance from this."

"He's the boss, remember? Nothing's changed yet." She hoped her words did not sound as empty to him as they did to her. The Wolf had saved her from being caught by Chen, but he could not save himself.

Yao snorted. "He took the envelope, yeah?"

"He took it."

"Okay, ten minutes." He opened the door.

"I'll stay here while you go up."

"What?" Yao was already halfway out but he sat down again, frowning. "Are you timid, suddenly? It's not like you to hide."

"You don't need me. I'll keep watch."

She glanced down at her feet, embarrassed by the deception, and Yao took her chin and pulled her face to his.

"Is this a setup? You're scaring me."

"No—honestly. Just get it over with, and we'll leave."

"Fuck." Yao muttered and climbed out of the car. "This is the last favor I'm going to do for you."

He crossed the courtyard and took the stairs up to the third landing, where Tang Liu had lived. Mei saw him from the waist up, walking along a balcony, then stopping at a door to knock. Light flooded from inside the apartment as the door opened, but she couldn't see the other person. After a moment, Yao went inside.

A group of uniformed waitresses walked by Mei's car, laughing, but the courtyard was otherwise empty. The block was eight stories high and was overlooked by towers on two sides. It was old and faded, almost swallowed up by Shenzhen's growth. Soon, it would be demolished, replaced by a flashy tower. A developer would come, cash would change hands, the residents would be evicted.

After ten minutes the door opened and Yao appeared. Mei watched him retrace his steps, looking as irritated as before.

"They don't know much. Tang Liu arrived a couple of years ago from Hunan and got a job as a waitress. Two of them still work at the same restaurant. There's a woman there, a motherly type. She says the girl's father got sick two months ago and she went home to help take care of him. They haven't seen her since."

"She didn't mention Long Tan?"

"Didn't know anything about it."

"Does she have a contact for her?"

"She had a mobile number, but it's dead. No address. Village girls pass through here all the time. It's not unusual."

"That's all they know?"

"Oh, she had a photo. Now can we go?"

Mei's heart jumped, but Yao handed her the photo without interest. He started the car as she examined it. There were four women in the frame——three in their twenties, hugging and laughing, an older woman behind them. None of them was the girl on the badge.

"Tang Liu's on the right, they said." He put the car in gear and started to back out of the space.

"Wait! Stop!"

"What *now*?" Yao jerked the car to a halt, exasperated.

Mei scrutinized the photo more closely. The girl on the right was pretty, with pale skin, wide eyes, and perfect teeth. She smiled, showing no sign of distress. There was no doubt. She might have been the Tang Liu who was born near Changsha nineteen years earlier, but she wasn't the dead woman and her face wasn't the one on the badge. The badge was a forgery.

"I need to ask her something." Mei opened her door and started to jog across the courtyard.

"Where are you going now?" Yao opened his window and shouted at her but she ignored him.

Mei climbed up the stairs two at a time. As she reached the third-floor balcony, she smoothed her skirt and walked to the door. Below her, she heard Yao revving the engine threateningly.

The woman who answered had a gentle face. She wore a green tunic and pants, and her hair was shorn at the neck, as if she'd given up trying to make the most of her looks.

"I'm sorry to disturb you. I work with my colleague." Mei showed the woman her card. "I have a few questions."

Inside, a bucket rested in a tiled shower, and the kitchen was piled with pots and plates. There was no living room, just a single bedroom with four beds crammed up against each other, and a balcony at the back. The girls on the lower bunks had draped fabrics for privacy. One of them was sleeping; two fluffy toys were propped by her pillow. The only place to sit was on a bunk, and Mei took one, with the woman opposite.

Mei pointed at the photo. "My colleague said this is Tang Liu—the girl on the right. That's correct?"

The woman smiled fondly. "Yes, that's Liu. She was a sweet girl. She went home to help her father. Not many of these girls are so dutiful to their parents. They do bad things."

"How long have you been here?"

"Ten years. My husband's at home in Sichuan. He's been sick for a long time. I must keep working. My son wants to join the army. We have to find the money for his place. He's a good boy."

"I believe Liu went to work at Long Tan after she left here. You didn't know? She didn't say anything?"

The woman shook her head.

"She wouldn't do that. These girls don't want to work in factories. It's better to be a waitress, they have more freedom. Liu had a good job and the men liked her—she got plenty of tips."

"She looks pretty in the photo."

"It's not even a good shot. She had lots of admirers."

"But she went to take care of her father?"

"That's right."

Mei looked over the balcony when she emerged—Yao was still parked below. The woman sounded genuine. She had liked Liu and she had not known about the factory or the disappearance. But her story didn't hang together. Why would the girl go home to care for her father when her mother was there? She had been making good money by the sound of it, and she didn't look tired of Shenzhen in her photo.

The gaggle of young women she'd seen by the car emerged onto the balcony, laughing and screaming. One of them playfully slapped another on the shoulder. As they approached, Mei stood in their path.

"Do any of you know Tang Liu?"

The laughter broke off. The five women stared at her, trying to work out who she was. One glanced away; Mei wondered if her papers were in order. She gave her card to the tallest one and they all shuffled closer to gaze at it, looking solemn.

"Don't worry. She's not in trouble. We're checking on some of the restaurants. They've taken money and not declared it—tips that ought to go to staff. Maybe you're owed money."

One girl nodded. "I am. My boss has no quality."

"I can make trouble for him. I just need some help. The woman inside said that she was a waitress."

Two of the women exchanged glances and smiled.

"What's funny?"

"Liu didn't tell her everything. She worked at a restaurant for a while and then got bored. The men liked her. She moved to the karaoke bar in the Golden Dragon Hotel. She made more money."

"Is it well-paid work?"

"It depends on how you treat the customers. Liu was nice to them. She didn't just sing. She played the bamboo flute."

The group dissolved into laughter.

"She said that Tang Liu went home to take care of her father."

"She's easy to fool. Her husband eats soft-boiled rice."

A girl at the back of the group who hadn't yet said anything suddenly spoke up. "Liu told me she'd met a western guy—a diamond bachelor. He didn't want her to keep on working."

"Did she tell you about him?"

"She wouldn't say. He wanted to be discreet."

"Thank you," Mei started walking to the stairs, her pace quickening as she went.

"What about my boss?" shouted the first girl who'd spoken.

"We'll talk to him," she called back.

20

The Golden Dragon Hotel was perched by a canal next to a six-lane highway that cut through the Luohu district. She'd had trouble directing a sullen Yao to the right place, but the hotel was impossible to miss. It was ten stories high, shaped like a flag waving in the breeze and tiled in glittering neon. A neon dragon was draped from the roof, its jaws enclosing a pink and blue banner: Karaoke—12 floors of VIP rooms—Shenzhen's best KTV.

As they pulled up, a couple emerged from the foyer. A girl in her twenties, wearing a miniskirt and a fur vest, was clutching a balding man, trying to keep him upright. He was pitching from side to side like a ship in a storm. Russian, Mei thought, or Kazakh. His suit and tie were brown, his face sweaty. The girl was struggling to stop him tumbling down the slope into the canal. She wore a determined smile as she whispered in his ear.

"I'm done with this," said Yao. It was the first time he had spoken since she gave him directions.

"Don't worry. Leave it to me."

There were a dozen nationalities in the reception area, lining up to check in with suitcases or drinking in groups in the bar. They were traders passing along the New Silk Road—Americans, Europeans, Africans in long robes. The woman at the desk pointed Mei to an elevator with glossy black doors—the entrance to the KTV club. As she emerged six stories up, there was a second lobby with a podium to welcome visitors. Beyond, the lights dimmed into a dark hallway.

Nobody was around, so Mei walked past the podium along a line of doors with porthole windows. Hearing a thumping beat, she peered into a cabin that pulsed with yellow light. Five men lounged on chairs inside. Four were Chinese and one western. The westerner, no longer wearing his jacket and tie, was bouncing a young woman on his knee. Another woman in her twenties was swaying in front of a karaoke screen, crooning an Eason Chan ballad. The man was singing along with the melody, staring drunkenly at her.

"You want work?"

Mei turned. A woman in a satin blue dress embroidered in silver braid looked at her inquiringly. She was glossily made up, with black hair, blue mascara, and a slash of lipstick—she could have been a karaoke girl herself in the past. She had the eyes of a survivor.

"I'm interested, yes."

"Are you working now?"

"In an office. It's boring."

"Okay. Come with me."

The woman led her into another of the hallway rooms, this one smaller, with only three chairs. A video was playing with the mute on, the lyrics passing across the screen. The woman sat down and twirled her index finger. Mei obliged by turning in a slow circle, showing off her body.

"You're a tall girl. That's good. My name's Madame Zhou. That's what you call me. Where are you from?"

"Guilin."

"Take your jacket off."

The woman stood and examined her, running a finger down the front of her blouse and squeezing one breast appraisingly. Mei flinched but then pushed herself forward again.

"Your clothes are dull."

"I came from work. I like to dress up."

"You know how to make men happy?"

"I make my boss happy."

"What special things do you do for him?"

Mei reached into her jacket and showed her card.

"I eliminate antisocial behavior. Criminality, prostitution."

"Fuck. I should have known it from that terrible suit." The woman sat down again. "Listen, honey. There's nothing to interest you here. The cops know us well—they're our friends."

"I bet they are."

"The Party bosses too. They like to relax. They don't want us to be shut down. Don't make trouble for yourself."

Madame Zhou smiled tightly. She looked as if she had plenty of contacts she could call in an emergency. Mei guessed she was right— she ran a brothel with flashing neon lights in the middle of Shenzhen, and nobody had closed it down yet.

"You help me and it won't happen. A girl called Tang Liu used to work here, didn't she?"

"The men liked Tang Liu. She got plenty of calls."

"Why did she leave?"

"They all leave. I guess she got bored."

Mei sat opposite. "I heard she found herself a boyfriend."

Madame Zhou shrugged. "Maybe."

"A westerner? In town for business?"

"Maybe."

"What happens when your girls find a special man? Do you let them go and wave goodbye?"

Madame Zhou grimaced. "Young girl, you're crazy. I take good care of them. I tell them, don't give a man your number. Don't get trapped in a hotel where no one can see. Some men think they can do what they want with you. Don't want to get into trouble? Better be careful. If he wants to visit you, he can call Madame Zhou and make an appointment. I'm your chaperone."

"And you take the money."

As if on cue, there was a bang and a scream from the hallway. Madame Zhou was at the door in an instant. Mei followed her into the hallway. The businessman she had seen in the VIP room with a girl on his lap was splayed on the ground, held down by a youth in a black T-shirt.

Madame Zhou chuckled icily. "Who's been a silly boy? It's time to drink water. Enough fun for the night."

She turned to Mei. "See? I care for them. I cared for Tang Liu."

Mei nodded. "So you've got her boyfriend's number."

Madame Zhou regarded her carefully, weighing her best strategy, and then she nodded.

Lockhart was standing by the window when the phone rang. He was on the sixteenth floor of the Peninsula Hotel in Kowloon, watching the Star Ferry plow its way across Victoria Harbor to Hong Kong Island. A southern wind was blowing, pushing the smog toward the mainland.

Hong Kong's skyscrapers gleamed in the dark—the lattice of the Bank of China and the white-tipped International Financial Center tower. The water was covered with ferries, lit with neon colors. When he'd come to China, Hong Kong had been an island of wealth in a sea of poverty. Now Kowloon was rich and Shenzhen's skyline had erupted to the north. The money had moved across the water.

The mobile phone on the bed pealed with the Nokia ringtone, and he turned in hope. Hardly anyone knew this number, and only one person was likely to be calling him. He strode across the room and threw himself on the bed, fumbling with the buttons. The terrible weight of anxiety and guilt lifted as he answered, longing for relief.

Even in desperation, Lockhart did not say his name, nor utter hers—he was better than that. He waited for her voice.

"Mr. Davies, how are you? It is Madame Zhou calling."

The voice was unbearably bright and polished, and he felt a crushing sense of misery as his hope died. He spoke instinctively, not knowing what he was saying but desperate to finish the call, to close the blinds and to lie there in darkness, shutting out reality.

"Hello, Madame Zhou."

She did not appear to hear. "Can you hear me, Mr. Davies?" she repeated loudly. "It is Madame Zhou. We haven't seen you for a long time. My girls wish to entertain you again."

"That's kind, but—"

"Would you like to visit? When can I make an appointment for you?"

"I'm afraid I have business here."

"Mr. Davies, I have a message for you from Tang Liu. She is here and wants to spend more time with you."

Lockhart shut his eyes, unable to cope. He had believed that he had seen Liu for the last time. She would disappear back home and stay there until the job was done. He had tried to find the most stable of Madame Zhou's brood, had thought the deal would stick. It was her namesake he longed to see again.

"I thought she had gone home."

"She has returned. We are so happy to see her again."

"Please tell Liu I hope she is well. But it will be difficult to meet with her. I'm sorry."

There was a pause on the other end of the line. Lockhart thought he heard a whisper in the background.

"Liu says you must come. She will not be able to keep her secret unless you help her."

His instinct was to shut the phone off, go down in the elevator, and throw it into Victoria Harbor. He didn't want anything to do with the Golden Dragon or Tang Liu or this tawdry blackmail. But he couldn't do that—the device was his only lifeline. He crafted a reply, trying to calculate how much trouble they could cause. He imagined that Madame Zhou had done this before.

"Could I speak to her, Madame Zhou?"

"It is impossible, I'm afraid. Liu is not here at the moment, but she wants me to arrange a meeting."

He sighed. "Is it money? Can I help in that way?"

"Oh, Mr. Lockhart." She sounded shocked, as if he were rude to suggest that cash was her motive, rather than engineering a touching reunion. "Liu wants to see you. Please don't disappoint her."

"Very well. I will come tomorrow," he said and terminated the call.

Lockhart put the phone back on the bed. He'd known this kind of thing before—a fool thinking that, because Lockhart had paid a bribe, he could be blackmailed for more. He wondered if it was Liu's idea or a racket by Madame Zhou. Either way, they would discover they were wrong.

21

The news broke overnight. Two women caught Mei as she stepped out of her room to ask if she'd heard.

"I can't believe it," she said, and they nodded with wide eyes and solemn faces, excited at passing on the gossip but aware that they should not look like they relished it too much. She did believe it, of course: She'd been dreading it for days.

They had come to arrest the Wolf at four in the morning—a matter of show since guards were posted outside his house and he'd been asleep, alone. The police could have walked across the compound after breakfast just as easily. But that wasn't how the Party behaved when it wanted to make a public example of someone. After all, the official in charge of preventing corruption had been caught taking a bribe.

Mei composed her expression into shocked surprise and kept it that way as she listened to the others. He'd tried to escape through his garden when they came, they'd found a stash of foreign currency beneath the frame of his piano, he had an apartment in Hong Kong. One cadre, the daughter of a village mayor who seemed perpetually on the edge of tears, denounced the Wolf in sorrow. *How can the people believe what their leaders say? It is a terrible day for the Party.*

"What do you think, Mei?" she asked, her eyes glistening.

"It's shocking," Mei agreed.

She had known it was coming because he'd told her. *Goodbye, Song Mei,* had been his last words to her; later, he had put a finger to his lips as he looked down from the roof. *Don't say anything.* Amid her fear at what would happen and her sense of isolation, she was angry. He'd led her into a maze and abandoned her, shattering her life with only a hint as to why. *Find her father.* But if the girl was her sister, wasn't her father Mei's father too? *Her* father, the Wolf had said, and he used words deliberately.

She was used to isolation. She'd felt it from her first moment of consciousness, the knowledge that her parents had left her behind. As a toddler, it hadn't worried her because her playmates were the same. But as she had grown, she had eventually realized that they weren't average children. Others had mothers and fathers, if not siblings. They were born to two people who loved each other and together made a child to care for. She was not. It was a tantalizing, depressing unknown—a void that couldn't be filled. Had they never loved her? Had she disappointed them?

Lectures were canceled, investigations put on hold. Everyone was told to gather in the auditorium at ten o'clock. When she arrived, the room was full of people awaiting fresh gossip. Mei scanned the space for Yao. He was sitting seven rows down, by himself. She walked around the rear circle and down the same aisle, taking a place two rows in front of Yao. When she glanced back at him to signal her presence, his expression didn't change.

A single podium stood on the stage, the red national flag draped behind it. The audience waited in silence. After fifteen minutes, a door opened and a line of officials filed in, taking seats on the front row. Another five minutes passed. Then Pan Yue walked onto the stage. Her expression was like the cadres Mei had encountered first— solemn, yet filled with excitement. Her face was flushed, and she looked as if she had just won a prize.

"Young comrades, thank you for being here this morning. I know how busy you are," she said, ignoring the fact that they'd been given no choice. "Remember this day, for it will be your most important lesson. All those who fulfill their duties with honesty and vigor need fear nothing. Only those who betray the Party will suffer. I know some will have doubts and may feel uncertain about the future. I cannot lift your spirits alone, and our leaders wish to encourage you. It is my honor to introduce Secretary Chen Longwei."

Mei's heart thudded and two cadres in the row in front of her glanced at each other in awe at how the Wolf's arrest had so quickly overturned the old order. Chen had never intruded on the Commission's business before—he had left the Wolf to run his empire. She felt sick at their eager innocence.

As Chen emerged from the side of the stage, the line of officials at the front stood up, and the cadres in the row behind them followed, the wave rippling past Mei to the rear. Mei studied Chen's walk. He placed his feet as gently as he'd done on the roof of the Long Tan building.

Chen waved both hands downward to make his listeners sit. Microphone in hand, he walked forward until he was at the front of the stage and looked out at the faces.

"No need to be formal." He smiled, and the officials laughed, the tension easing. "I wanted to come here today to talk to you and to reassure you. You know why that is important to me? Because you're the future of this Party, its sixth generation, and you will determine whether it thrives past this generation, as it has thrived until now, in the service of the Guangdong people. That's quite a responsibility, but I know you're up to it."

He passed a hand over his jaw and wiped away his smile.

"Yours is an enormous responsibility because the Commission ensures that the Party earns the people's loyalty. There are many temptations and even those we least expect to succumb can fall into the trap. Even your leader—the man you most trusted—has let you down. It is an awful day when that happens. A moment of confusion and danger."

He bowed his head, walking to the edge of the stage and then down some steps onto the floor. Then he leaned against the stage and raised the microphone. The room remained silent, but the silence had turned from expectant nervousness to rapt attention.

"I'm older than you. I've witnessed what can happen when the people lose faith. You've read your history books. Maybe your parents have told you things. Mistakes were made because the people lost trust in the Party. I was one of those who suffered. It won't happen again." He paused for effect, then emphasized each word with stabbing gestures. "It—will—not—happen."

Chen smiled, as if he'd been caught in terrible memories but had shaken them off. Then he slowly ascended an aisle of the auditorium as he spoke, like a talk show host moving through his audience. Mei realized with alarm that he was heading in her direction.

"We have a task. It's simple, but tough. It demands effort from you all. You must be honest and willing to criticize yourselves. When something of this nature happens, we must ask ourselves searching questions. Did I compromise myself? Did I take part in wrongdoing? Did I hold my tongue when my duty was to speak?"

Chen's eyes were on her. He was four steps away, then three. She could hardly hear. He halted one step below her and smiled at the cadres in her row.

"You're young. I wish I had your energy and your ambition." His gaze settled on the cadre next to Mei, and he spoke at her. His eyes were copper, his pupils narrow. "You can learn from this and move on. But if you lie to us, the Party will know."

Mei's fingers gripped her knee and she felt words rising in her throat. In that moment, she wanted to confess, to clear herself of whatever crime the Party thought she had committed—to cast aside the past few days. Chen walked on, his gaze switching off like a searchlight being extinguished. He took three steps forward and turned to the stage, his hand falling on Yao's shoulder.

"Those who are open have nothing to fear, and I know that you will be honest and support Comrade Pan in her task. Then our Party's leaders in Beijing will know we are loyal and true."

He raised his hands, starting to clap. The sound of his palms echoed around the hall like a shot, then another one. As the third clap sounded, Pan rose and joined him, followed by the other officials and then the cadres, until the room echoed with applause. It died down only when Chen had left the stage and Pan had signaled for them to leave the auditorium.

"Say nothing," Yao said, from behind Mei. "Follow me."

He overtook her, skipping down the stairs lightly as if he had nothing to fear, his hips twisting easily. Mei walked behind him, drawn in his wake. When they reached the exit, he crossed the courtyard, delving into his shirt pocket for a cigarette. He stood by the wall, ignoring the others who were already chattering excitedly. Expelling a stream of smoke through pursed lips, he delivered his verdict.

"It's over, Mei. The Wolf is finished. We did our job. You don't need to worry anymore."

Mei shook her head, lips pursed like an obstinate child's. It would be wisest to heed Yao, but she couldn't. She thought about what Feng said: *The most important quality in a spy is the ability to forget.* That would mean leaving the Wolf to prison and abandoning her sister. They had stood together in the fields, with the laughter of the Dongguan cops sounding in the dark and the body floating in the pond nearby. She couldn't erase that from her mind.

22

At the border, Lockhart filled in the entry form from memory. He was traveling under his own name, so he didn't need to check his passport. A Canadian diplomat, a French businessman, a British executive. He'd lived all of those lives in the past and shredded them.

He passed the Hong Kong checkpoint and walked with the crowd over the bridge. Apartments towered over the border from the mainland, where once there'd only been farmland. Every square inch of Shenzhen was occupied, although green hills and paddy fields remained in the New Territories on the Hong Kong side. He peered through the windows to the waterway that divided the two Chinas. It still looked scary, with high walls and boats patrolling the water to stop anyone swimming across. But it wasn't the old days—it was easy now to get a visa to visit relatives or to go shopping in Central. On the mainland, a blue-shirted border official compared Lockhart's face to his passport and took his photo. Then he tore the entry form in two, slotting one of the sections back into his passport. As he moved on, the man raised one hand and pointed to a panel by the cubicle, asking him to rate the service. Lockhart pressed the "Excellent" button with the smiley face.

By the time he reached the Golden Dragon, its neon emblem was glowing. As he walked by, heading for the elevator, the receptionist smiled at him. On the sixth floor, Madame Zhou was at the podium. She smiled brightly, her lips parting to show a smudge of lipstick on one tooth, like blood. He felt like locking her head in one arm and twisting, so he'd never hear from her again, but he smiled at her instead. It wasn't difficult: he had years of experience at hiding his feelings.

"Hello, Madame Zhou."

"It's a pleasure to welcome you back, Mr. Davies. You are one of our best customers." She took his arm and tried to lead him down the hallway into the club, but he stood his ground.

"Is Tang Liu here?"

"She will arrive soon, don't worry. We have refreshments. Maybe you'd like to be entertained by another girl?"

"I'll wait for her."

"Of course."

He had no choice but to follow her to a room that was lined in yellow silk, with two tasseled lanterns hanging from the ceiling, like a cowboy bordello. A set of chairs faced a low stage with a karaoke screen and two microphones for duets. A hostess brought in a porcelain teapot and two cups, placing them in front of the sofa where Lockhart was sitting, then bowed and left. The strains of a Lady Gaga song wafted in from another room down the hallway.

This was where he'd met Liu the first time. She had clumsily tried to make him sing, but he'd refused and insisted that she sit with him to talk. Unusual among clients of the Golden Dragon, it hadn't been a euphemism—conversation really was all he'd wanted. And so she'd talked, of her village in Hunan and how she wanted to be a fashion designer and open a shop on Donglong Fashion Street in Shenzhen. She'd taken out her phone and showed him photographs of herself, dressed in some of the clothes she'd made. Lockhart had listened. She was a sweet kid, he had thought. She ought not stay much longer in the city and be corrupted entirely. He had a plan that would take her home for a while, and maybe she'd meet a young man and stay. No need to confess what she'd gotten up to in the city. He offered a better bargain than most of the visitors—more cash for less shame. She'd turned down his first offer, but her eyes had widened, and she had accepted the second one a few days later.

There was a knock on the door, and Lockhart stood up. It was Madame Zhou, with her ghastly smile.

"Mr. Davies, you have a visitor."

"Madame Zhou, I told you—"

His words faltered as she ushered a young woman into the room. Madame Zhou shut the door behind her, but by that time Lockhart no longer noticed. He was gazing in wonder.

"Lizzie," he said. The words came out of him in a rush. "Oh, thank God. I thought I'd lost you."

He took two steps toward her, arms held out. He wanted to hold her, for it to be over, and to leave the Golden Dragon—to get out of China and not to return for a long time. It was like the euphoria of waking from a nightmare, and he would never make this mistake again. She was several feet away from him and when he reached her, he would get his life back.

Lockhart stopped.

Something was wrong. His heart was swelling, but his instincts told him that something was wrong. Lizzie hadn't moved. She hadn't reacted at all—he might have been a stranger to her. She stood in a cheap suit and blouse, frowning. It wasn't the way she dressed. Her face was different somehow.

Then she spoke.

"Who are you?" she said in Mandarin.

He took a step back. The more he stared at her, the more the image faded, like a jigsaw torn apart. Her skin was paler, her eyes set differently. She was almost Lizzie, but not quite. Who was she?

"Sit down," the woman said.

"Tell me who you are."

"Only when you sit."

Lockhart obeyed. The woman handed him one of her cards and sat down, letting him read.

GUANGDONG COMMISSION FOR DISCIPLINE INSPECTION
CADRE SONG MEI

Then, in a flood of anguish, it came to him. He knew who this woman was. She would not remember him, but he had met her once. One afternoon in Beijing twenty-three years earlier.

"Yes?" he said, composing his face into bland indifference.

"I have some questions about Tang Liu."

"I'm happy to assist you if I can." His heart beat rapidly.

"When did you last see her?"

"Two months ago. Madame Zhou would know the last date I visited, I expect. Has something happened to her?"

"She was your mistress?"

"I wouldn't say that. We liked being with each other." He grinned. "You know how it is, when you're away on business."

"I'm not a man, Mr. Lockhart, so I don't know. You come to Shenzhen for your work?"

"Often, yes. I work as a consultant."

"Your Chinese is very good."

"Thank you."

"I'm surprised you learned so well on your visits."

"I lived in Beijing once."

"You were a consultant?"

"In business. Ms.—" He glanced at the card again. "Ms. Song. I would like to help you, but I don't think I can. I don't know much about Tang Liu. We met a few times, that's all."

She was good, he thought. The Chinese cops he'd known came through the front door, in a mob. She was smarter than that, more devious. She tricked him. But she was far from her base, without a partner. She looked, he thought, vulnerable.

"Passport."

He reached into his jacket and handed it over.

"Mr. Lockhart," she said, leafing through the pages.

"Your English is very good."

"You're not called Davies?" she said, ignoring him.

He smiled. "Not many of Madame Zhou's western visitors give their real names, do they?"

"You don't know where Tang Liu is, Mr. Lockhart?"

"I have no idea, I'm afraid."

"Then why did you come when Madame Zhou called?"

"Madame Zhou said she wanted to see me."

"No other reason?"

"No."

"All right, Mr. Lockhart." She closed his passport and gave it back. "I see that you entered the mainland from Hong Kong this afternoon. Where are you staying, in case we need to talk?"

"I'm at the Peninsula Hotel in Kowloon. Please do call."

She rose and walked to the door. Then, as she grasped the handle, she turned to him again.

"Why did you call me Lizzie?"

"Lizzie?" Lockhart framed his face in puzzlement. "You misheard me."

"No. You called me Lizzie, like the American girl's name. Who's Lizzie, Mr. Lockhart?"

They gazed at each other for what felt like a long time. Her eyes were just the same—soft, determined. Never giving up, never willing to be defeated. He hadn't been able to fool her, even when she was little. Her eyes would regard him coolly—*You're lying to me.*

"You're her father," said Mei.

23

It was obvious from the way he looked at her, from the way his eyes softened. He was thinking of another girl, the one whose name he'd blurted out when she'd entered. *I thought I'd lost you,* he'd said, with desolation in his voice. He didn't know the truth yet.

He was a handsome man, although the flesh around his jaw had slackened and his peppery gray hair was thinning at the crown. He had a presence, even sitting on the sofa, legs crossed, watching. She felt an urge to please him, to make him approve of her. His blue eyes were set in deep sockets, above round cheeks that gave him a boyish air. He looked like an adventurer, at home in a foreign land but watchful. On paper, she was in charge. Yet he behaved as if he were in control.

The girl's father and not hers—the Wolf's words made sense. It came to her in a tumble why he was there, and why the number was wrong. The dead girl's name wasn't Tang Liu, and she hadn't come from Hunan. Liu was the decoy he had found in a KTV Club. She recalled the Wolf's tone of admiration as he'd held the badge. *There aren't many people who could have fixed it. It's clever.*

Then she realized. She was a beacon, signaling to Lockhart across the province, drawing him closer. The Wolf had wanted to alert him, and Mei was the method he had chosen.

"Where is she?"

"Who am I?" she replied.

"Her sister." He made it sound so obvious that it wasn't worth dwelling upon. "Tell me where she is."

Lockhart sat with his chin forward, his eyes locked on her, barely holding himself together. He wrapped his left hand in his right and squeezed it, like the leather bit in the mouth of a man who was about to be lashed. Mei wished she didn't have to hurt him so, but she had no choice.

"She's dead."

Lockhart shuddered and put his face in his hands, while Mei stood uselessly, wanting to help him, unable to. It was the first time in her life she'd broken such news to anyone, and it pained her. Tears dripped through the gaps between his fingers and splashed on the floor. His shoulders shook with grief. After a minute, he lifted his face. He looked ravaged, a vessel that had run aground.

"How did she die?"

"I'm sorry, Mr. Lockhart."

"Please tell me."

Mei wondered if she could make it sound less brutal, but it looked like he wanted it straight—he needed to hear the worst.

"We found her in a pond, near Humen Port, about a mile from the river. It looked as if she had drowned, but there were marks on the body that suggested violence. She was not clothed, but I later found a badge from Long Tan with her photograph. Here—"

Mei removed the badge from her pocket and gave it to him. Lockhart gazed at it, then nodded.

"You said, 'We found her.' Who is 'we'?"

"The police, the Discipline Commission."

"Secretary Lang?"

Of course, she thought.

This man knew the Wolf, and the Wolf knew him. The Wolf had sent Mei to find him, had given her this mission, all the while knowing that Lockhart lay at the end of it. The two of them, it came to Mei, were similar. They were alike in their aloneness, their secrets, how they worked. They were a pair, like her and Lizzie.

"Yes."

"It had to be." He looked blank, recalling something, and then his face folded up again.

This time, Mei reacted without thinking, stepping forward to comfort him. But as she knelt, placing a hand on his knee, she found herself staring into the barrel of a gun. He'd brought it out in one swift movement and pointed it at her head, his hands perfectly still.

"Step back." It sounded like a polite request, not a command backed by a semiautomatic pistol. "We have to go now."

She obeyed him, and he led the way. Madame Zhou was waiting as they came out, Lockhart's arm linked in Mei's. They seemed to be walking casually, but his body was guiding her.

"Is everything well, Mr. Davies? You two have made friends, I see," Madame Zhou called out.

Lockhart nudged Mei to prompt her. "Everything is fine. Mr. Davies is coming to help us," she said.

"Wonderful. I'm so happy."

He held her arm all the way to the first floor. They walked together through the lobby, smiling at the receptionist, and across the parking lot. He went to the passenger side; by the time she'd sat behind the wheel, he was cradling the gun in his lap.

"Take me there," he said.

She pulled onto Fuzhong Road, heading for the Jinggang'ao Expressway. The traffic was bad, and they chugged along slowly, waiting for the glow of taillights to ease and the path to the city's outskirts to clear. Out of the corner of her eye, she saw him gazing at her, the way he'd done when he thought she was his daughter, before he knew. He said nothing on the way. It took them half an hour to get to the Expressway and another forty minutes on it, passing a line of apartment blocks, industrial estates, and then the blankness of rivers and marshes. Mei felt as if she ought to panic, as an armed man directed her to an isolated place, but she didn't.

She stopped where she'd first parked, with a view down to the marshes and the cabins. Lockhart sat looking through the windshield at the waterlogged landscape, then buttoned his overcoat and stepped out, standing in the mist. As she joined him, he bent over a phone, thumbing a message.

"It was there," she said, pointing through the mist. She could smell decay rising from the fields, the stench of chemicals or human waste.

"Show me." He placed the gun on the car's roof, holding it flat with the eye of the barrel staring at her.

She bent inside the Chery and pulled out a flashlight before starting down the slope to the fields. They struck out in single file along the ridge, in the same direction she'd gone with the Wolf. This time she led, hearing Lockhart's breath behind her. The moon was hidden behind the clouds and darkness enfolded them. The leaves slapped her body. Mei felt the first twinge of worry that she might not survive—that he wouldn't let her return to tell others about him. For a moment, she imagined herself with Lizzie, lying in the water. She'd seen him at his most vulnerable, but he'd pulled a gun on her faster than she could think.

"Why are you doing this?" she asked.

The only sound was their feet falling on the earth in rhythm. Then, when she thought he wouldn't, he replied. "You're just like Lizzie," he said.

"Tell me about her." She wanted to keep talking so that he would not kill her, but she also wanted to know.

"I can't." His voice trembled.

They had walked through the banana fields, and she saw the glint of light on the ponds. She halted. "It was near here."

"I'm going to remember her." She glanced sideways and saw that he'd bowed his head, putting his hands together. His face was hardly visible, just a tiny glint of light from his eyes and the luster of the gun's handle. She could have knocked it out of his hands, but it would be sacrilege.

She bowed her head and stood next to him, until he spoke. "Goodbye, Song Mei. Don't follow me."

His command was so strange that she almost laughed—where could he be going in the delta at this hour? But, as she opened her mouth to respond, Lockhart walked off. Within seconds, he was thirty feet along the dike, disappearing from sight. She waited until he'd vanished, then ignored his warning and followed. There was no light or sound. She walked invisibly, by herself, her flashlight turned off so that he wouldn't see her. As she darted between ponds, wind rippled the surface.

The sound of a diesel motor broke the silence five hundred feet ahead, and a beam struck the jetty where she had stood with the boy, looking across the fields at Long Tan. Lockhart was in the same position, bathed in light. Then a fishing boat pulled in beside him, he took one step forward from the jetty onto its deck, and it carried him into the night.

24

Mei turned and ran, cursing Lockhart. She had let him escape to the Pearl River, toward Hong Kong and the sea. He hadn't needed a guide to where her sister had died—he had known already. This had been his rendezvous with Lizzie, but it had failed that evening. Tonight, the boat had waited in the delta, in case of emergency, and he had fooled her into driving him there. *How stupid could she be?*

She raced back toward her car, sliding in the mud. On the edge of one field, she stopped briefly to pull her phone from her jacket and checked the signal: nothing. She ran on, leaping over a pool onto a ridge, defying the ghosts to grab her. Twice she felt her shoes sliding into the liquid and once missed her footing entirely, stumbling forward and only just keeping her balance.

Then she was out the other side and grasping for her phone. She saw a single bar and stopped, panting and stabbing at the device. Through hissing interference, it rang.

"Lai Feng? It's Song Mei."

"I remember." The voice sounded low and relaxed, almost drugged. "How can I help? You need a shoulder to cry on?"

"I need your help tonight."

"That sounds like fun." Her voice lightened. "Where are you?"

"In Dongguan. I can pick you up."

"I'll get dressed."

Mei halted by the Party compound on Dongfeng East Road forty minutes later. She had raced along the Expressway, banging a fist on the wheel in frustration at having to drive in the opposite direction from Lockhart. Feng stood by a guard, who was cupping his hands around a flame to light her cigarette. She wore a leather skirt and red tights. Her hair was plaited, and she had a suitcase with her.

"Hey, wild thing. I got the stuff." Her eyes widened as she looked at Mei. "Whoa. What happened to you?"

"What do you mean?"

"Looks like you've been mud-wrestling." She pointed to patches of dirt on Mei's clothes and, licking her thumb, rubbed Mei's cheek.

"It's a long story."

"Save it. I brought some clothes. I just want to say something. This is a crazy idea. Now of all times."

"I know. I—"

"Okay, I said it. Let's go."

It was ninety minutes to the border, with the accelerator crammed down all the way. As they rounded the curve to the customs point, Feng pointed her to a slip road. They passed the checkpoint with a wave of their cards and came to a stop on the Hong Kong side. A young official with a shadow of a mustache sauntered over to the car and thrust out his hand for their papers. He peered at them for a long moment and returned to his cabin, still holding them.

"Bureaucrats," Feng muttered. She took her phone and selected a Hong Kong number. "It's me. I'm at Futian. I'm stuck. What? I was in a hurry." She giggled. "No, we can't have drinks tonight. I've got plans. None of your business. Okay, next time. Yes, I promise." She lowered her window and shouted at the cabin, "Hey, come here."

The young man lumbered back without their papers, looking as if he would enjoy punishing her for causing trouble with an even longer wait. "Tell him," she said into the phone, and handed it to him.

He put it to his ear and listened for thirty seconds, then handed it back to her. Then he went back to the cabin and retrieved their papers.

"My apologies for the misunderstanding," he said.

"Remember next time. Don't piss me off," Feng said.

"How did you manage that?" Mei asked as she drove through.

Feng shrugged. "Connections."

They passed through the New Territories in silence. After a while they came to a turn in the highway where Hong Kong Island appeared, its peak rising from the sea, and sped down the highway toward the harbor. Mei drove to Salisbury Road and stopped at the Peninsula Hotel, where a green-jacketed valet took the keys and handed her a ticket. It was midnight when they walked into the foyer, Feng wheeling the suitcase she'd brought from the compound.

"This way," she said.

She led Mei across the lobby to the bathroom. Inside, she knelt and brought out a set of clothes. She handed them to Mei, together with a pair of high heels.

"I guessed your size. You won't need them long."

Mei took the package into a stall and laid it on the seat, then stripped off her things. Feng had brought stockings, a white blouse with pearl buttons, a leather skirt like hers, and a yellow jacket, with high heels that pinched Mei's toes as she put them on. In the mirror, she still looked terrible. There was a muddy streak on her face where Feng had rubbed her thumb, and her hair was all mussed. The shadows under her eyes stood out against her pale face.

"Give me those," Feng said. She took Mei's clothes and folded them into the suitcase. Then she brought out a hairbrush and some clips.

"Put your hair up," she said.

Feng pinned a purple flower into it and made Mei lean down so that she could apply mascara and a dab of red lipstick.

"You can be my escort," Feng said.

Another woman gazed back at Mei in the mirror. They looked like two Shenzhen girls out for the night, with pouting lips and tight skirts. Mei towered above Feng in her heels and tottered as they walked into the lobby together, Feng pulling her suitcase like an off-duty air steward.

The man behind the desk gazed at them without warmth, as if politeness was more than they deserved.

"Can I help?"

Feng gave him a wide smile.

"We're here to visit Mr. Lockhart. He's a guest."

"I see."

"He wants company tonight."

The man looked them up and down sternly. His gaze lingered on the pearl buttons of Mei's blouse.

"It's embarrassing," Feng added, looking unashamed. "We've forgotten his room number. We want to know where to go."

"Who should I say is calling?" he said, picking up a phone.

"It's a surprise." Feng said, leaning forward and clasping notes into his hand. "We need his number. That's all."

He glanced around and then scribbled a number on a slip of paper and handed it to her.

"Mr. Lockhart is a valued guest. We want him to have everything he desires. But don't come back."

They took the elevator to the twenty-third floor and walked along the thickly carpeted hallway. The only sound was the squeak of Feng's suitcase. When they got to the room, Mei pressed the bell and rapped on the door. They waited for a long while, but there was no response.

"Watch out," Feng said. She placed the case on the floor and brought out a plastic card attached by a strip of wires to a small box. She inserted the card in a slit by the door and pressed a button. After twenty seconds, there was a click as the lock released.

They looked at each other and laughed, the tension of the escapade releasing. Mei walked into Lockhart's suite, tugging the suitcase. It was large and lavishly furnished in pale fabrics and lacquered wood, with a pattern of cotton tree branches painted on one wall. The windows reached to the floor, with a glittering view of the harbor. Mei stood and gazed, open-mouthed.

At the end of the lounge, a walk-through closet led to the bedroom and bathroom. The suite was so tidy that it might have been uninhabited. The bed was made, and all of the cushions were smooth. There were hardly any objects lying around—only a pad on the table with a few doodles and a couple of numbers. Mei copied them down.

In the bedroom, Feng opened drawers. Lockhart's shirts and socks were neatly stacked, and she felt underneath for objects. There were two jackets and pants hanging in the wardrobe and little else. On the bedside table sat a thick biography of Deng Xiaoping, with a bookmark halfway through.

"Where's his laptop?" Feng said. She took out another device with a fan-shaped scanner and walked through the suite, stopping whenever it beeped to open a drawer or cupboard. "Nothing," she said, entering the bathroom, where Mei was looking at the toiletries. "He's taken anything that could be useful. They're not always this smart. I wonder where he learned?"

"Is that it? Nothing?"

"Nothing tells us something. He's a professional."

"So what do we do?"

"We leave. After we've finished."

"I thought we had."

"Not if he's a professional. Go through the clothes. Take all the drawers out. Look under everything."

Feng took a stick with a mirror on the end from her bag and twisted it. It expanded to several feet long, and she held the mirror up to examine the top of the cupboards and then went back into the lounge. Mei got down on her knees and looked under the bed, then started pulling out drawers, as she'd been told.

"Come here," Feng called.

Mei heard a high-pitched whine from the lounge. When she walked in, Feng was perched on a chair with an electric screwdriver, trying to reach the air conditioning panel above one door.

"I can't make it. You try."

Mei climbed on the chair and reached up to the four small screws at the edge of the plate. The paint had chipped off one of them, as if it had recently been unfastened. She inserted the head and it twisted free easily, dropping to the carpet below. Then she released the others with three squeezes of the trigger and removed the panel.

She reached inside the ventilation shaft. There was nothing there at first but then, as she pushed her hand to the left, she touched the edge of an object. She twisted her fingers and pulled it out.

It was an envelope with something inside—a blue passport with an eagle on the front, and "United States of America" embossed in silver.

"I knew it!" Feng clapped in delight.

Still standing, Mei opened the passport to the picture page. Beneath the bald eagle and the "We the People" declaration was a photograph of the woman whom Lockhart had mourned.

SURNAME: Lockhart
GIVEN NAMES: Elizabeth Song Ping
NATIONALITY: United States of America
DATE OF BIRTH: 7 May 1989
PLACE OF BIRTH: Guilin, China

25

By the time they got back to Guangzhou, it was two o'clock in the morning and Mei was exhausted from the drive. Feng waved goodbye as she crossed the compound, leaving Mei to drag herself upstairs. She undressed, put on a T-shirt, and took a pill to block her thoughts, then fell asleep, hugging the pillow.

They came for her thirty minutes later.

Mei was so deeply unconscious that she didn't hear the knock on the door at first. Then the pounding started, like thuds against her head. She rose groggily and pulled on sweatpants. She still couldn't figure out what was going on—was the building on fire? When she opened the door, blinking in the light, she saw others ajar down the hallway. There were three people at her threshold—two PLA guards and Pan Yue. The official's eyes were bright, as if exhilarated by her mission.

"Get dressed, Song Mei. We're leaving."

A woman soldier came into the room and watched as she dressed. Then they filed along the corridor, as the other cadres pulled their doors shut, trying not to be caught spying.

Two Audis were parked outside with their engines running and drivers at the ready. One soldier took a seat in the front of one car, and the other opened the rear door for Mei to climb in. Pan leaned forward to adjust the heating as they pulled away, passing through the compound gates on to Yuexiu Bei Road. The city's lights looked pale and ghostly, and Mei wondered when she would see them again.

She summoned the nerve to speak. "Where are we going?"

"You'll find out."

"Have I done something wrong?"

"Do you think you have?"

Mei didn't answer—it was a rhetorical question and Pan had not turned to look at her. The lights of a police car shone in the mirror as they hurtled along Baiyun South Avenue, heading toward the mountains. The car pulled ahead to form a three-vehicle convoy going 95 miles per hour, then 110. Nobody wore a seat belt, and Mei was terrified.

As they drove on into the countryside, the passing lights pulsed hypnotically, and the warmth made her sleepy. Despite her fear, she was terribly tired. Her head rolled forward and snapped back painfully and she dug her fingernails into her palms to remain conscious. The convoy started winding along a long, curving road, and she drifted off.

She woke abruptly in a parked car, just in time to stop herself tumbling out as a guard opened the door from outside. Pan already stood at the entrance to a low building with a corrugated roof. It felt high up, in cleaner air than the city, with a splash of stars overhead. Two helicopters rested by a row of green hangars on the far side of a runway. She glanced at her watch. It was nearly four o'clock—they'd driven for more than an hour and a half.

"Go through." Pan pointed at the door, and one of the soldiers nudged Mei forward.

She had to bend to step past the door into a narrow corridor lit with barred lamps. It was lined with metal doors on each side, one of which was open, displaying a small cell with no window and padded walls. The facility looked half-abandoned, as if it had been a military prison but now had another use. The smell of confinement made Mei's chest tighten, but she kept on walking to the end of the hallway. They passed through another door to a landing, with stairs down to a cellar.

As they reached it, Mei heard the slap of flesh and the guttural cry of an animal in a trap.

There were three men in the cellar. One sat by a table, holding a cigarette that sent spirals into the cramped room. The other had a

close-shaven head and wore an apron over a blue shirt. His sleeves
were rolled up, and he wore latex gloves. He stood by the third man
wearing an inquisitive expression, as if interested to discover how
long he could last.

The third man was the Wolf.

The Wolf wore only a pair of cotton pants, tied at the waist. He
was sitting on a narrow iron bench, six inches off the ground, bound
at the ankles and knees. His hands were cuffed behind his back, and
he strained to keep himself from falling backward into a lying position. Blood trickled down the white hairs on his chest from a gash on
his neck, and his face was gray.

"Release him," Pan said.

The interrogator scowled. He gestured at the Wolf, and the other
man stubbed out his cigarette, walked over, and undid the handcuffs,
then unwound the straps around his legs. The Wolf sprawled sideways onto the floor, gasping in relief.

"Get up."

The Wolf rubbed his legs to make the blood flow and tried to
obey, but he couldn't rise.

"Bring him here. And fetch a shirt. Have you no respect?"

"Not for traitors," said the interrogator.

He bent and grasped the Wolf under both arms, hauling him up
in one motion. Then he pulled him to a chair by the table, the Wolf's
legs dragging across the floor like those of a puppet. Walking to the
corner of the room, he picked up a sweat-stained shirt and threw it at
Mei.

"You dress him. I'm not his little sister."

The Wolf had slumped on the table. As she offered the shirt to
him, he raised his body and threaded his arms through the sleeves,
then buttoned it. He brushed back his hair and stared at Pan.

"Song Mei is here," the woman said.

"I can see."

"So let us ask you the question again. What was in the envelope
she brought you?"

"I don't know."

"How can you not know?"

"I burned it." He looked at Mei, and a light came back into his eyes for the first time.

"Why did you do that?"

The Wolf sighed. "Because it was a trap, set by you. When you've been around as long as I have, you can spot them."

Pan's eyes narrowed. "Have you lost your senses, Lang Xiaobo? You burned the evidence of a crime? No court will take that seriously."

The Wolf laughed, phlegm rattling in his throat. "Now *you've* gone crazy, Pan Yue. No court will treat it seriously because it won't be a serious court. The Party will decide on this after a few months of *shuanggui*. We know that. You seem to have your verdict already." He pointed to the bench on the floor, to which he'd been lashed. "The tiger bench is the only judge."

"It will not help to criticize Party justice. This isn't my imagination. We have a witness." She turned to Mei. "Tell us what was in the envelope, since the culprit won't admit it."

Both pairs of eyes were on her, the woman's expectant and the Wolf's curious. It felt like she'd been brought to play a part in a play. She knew the truth, and they did too, but Pan needed her to say it. The Wolf had been discredited and discarded. He would end up in a distant province, under house arrest for the rest of his life. He'd never be spoken of again, after this.

"I don't know," she said.

Pan's face froze, and the Wolf looked at her with concern, as if she were a child in danger.

The woman's voice softened. "Song Mei, tell us honestly and don't be confused by old loyalties. What did it contain?"

Mei gazed at the Wolf, blood-spattered and degraded before her. She could stay blindly loyal to the Party or protect the man who cared enough about her sister's death that he'd risked his career to stop her from being forgotten. Days ago, she couldn't have imagined this choice; now she didn't hesitate.

"I don't know."

Pan stared, pulling her head back as if seeing Mei for the first time as a threat. She turned to the Wolf's inquisitor, who was in the corner, chewing areca husk and watching the show. He'd hung his apron from a hook while he took a break.

"Take her to the car."

"She can find it herself."

"I want you to take her."

He smiled, his upper lip pulling back to show a row of yellow-stained teeth, and spat into a metal pail. Gesturing at Mei to climb the stairs, he walked so closely behind that she could feel his breath on her neck. They passed along the corridor between the cells, with him tracking her.

The driver had the engine running and the headlights on as they reached the car. Mai opened the door and climbed in, then tried to close it behind her. The man reached forward and held the door open. He leaned in close and whispered.

"I'd like to have you on my bench."

"Screw yourself." She pulled the door shut and turned away so that she wouldn't have to hear him, but her hand trembled as she pressed the lock. He cursed and spat, leaving a glob of saliva trickling down the glass, then backed away, staring.

Mei shifted to the far side of the seat and looked out at the stars. The Wolf was in *shuanggui* and Lockhart had abandoned her—strange, but that was how it felt. She had betrayed the Party; she was alone.

It was half an hour before Pan opened the door and sat beside her.

"Why did you lie?"

"It's the truth. I—"

"Stop."

Pan reached over and placed a hand on hers.

"You know who you remind me of? My daughter. Clever, head-strong, and willful, but loyal. She felt uncertainty but, with guidance, she triumphed. You hate to contradict your mentor. I understand. But hard choices must be made. Remember the words of Deng Xiaoping? We cross the river by groping stones. When we go astray, we must change our direction. You will be suspended for a week, and your error will be noted in your file. You will take time to reflect. Then your reeducation will start."

26

Mei was on the K36 night train from Guangzhou. She'd paid 320 yuan for the soft sleeper with only four bunks, and she lay on her mattress as the train pulled out of the city at sunset. An old couple lay in the upper bunks, legs entwined in baskets of food and clothes. The man was already snoring so loudly that Mei had to stick her fingers in her ears.

She was going home.

She'd been given an hour to pack, and then a guard had come to escort her off the compound. Nobody asked where she was going—it was enough that she'd be absent for a while. The news was out, and other cadres had whispered as she passed them in the hallway. Yao was nowhere to be found, and she hadn't called Feng, not wanting to implicate her further. Now, as the train throbbed around the curves, she tried to sleep.

When she woke again, the shades were down, and the man was still snoring. She tried to let the steady rhythm of the train lull her but was disturbed by a woman speaking English nearby. She drew back the cover and took a shawl from her bag, draping it around her shoulders. It was two o'clock, and the train was passing through Hunan, Tang Liu's province. She saw scrubby hillside and a lake, bare in the starlight.

The English speaker stood three cabins down, dressed in a down jacket and jeans. She was about Mei's age, and her hands were thrust in her pockets as she described the landscape to a friend inside the cabin. Mei knew she was American from the way she talked blithely in the corridor, unworried at being overheard. She was a tourist who could visit the Guilin hills, take a scenic boat trip on the Li River, and return home with her snapshots of rural China.

Mei felt like a tourist herself now—a stranger who didn't know the place. She had thought she did, but now she carried the evidence of her ignorance in her pocket—Lizzie Lockhart's passport, with her birthplace marked there: Guilin, China. They had been born together on the same day, in the same place, yet she'd never known that Lizzie existed. Nobody had ever told her, until too late.

She looked at her watch: one-thirty in the morning. They would be in Qidong soon, then a climb toward Yongzhou, and homeward. She got back into her bunk and slept fitfully until she felt a weight pressing on her foot. The snoring man had climbed from his bunk and was sitting on it, eating noodles.

The osmanthus trees rustled in the breeze as she hauled her bag from the train at Guilin in the morning light. This was what she missed most in Guangdong—the green lakes and hills, the clean air. It was a city of five million now, far bigger than in her childhood. But it had a sweet, provincial air—women with parasols smiled at her from motorcycles, and the streets were divided with flower displays beneath decorative streetlamps. After the terror of Dongguan, she was relieved to be back. Pushing her way through the crowd, she found a driver leaning on his taxi.

They took the second ring road past Xishan Park, then through tunnels into the city's northern districts. Mei felt herself regressing to childhood as they drove, past her elementary school, along Fulu Road by Guilin Railway Middle School, where she'd trudged, day after day. Finally, he swung along the curving lane at Aishantangcun to her destination. Here, behind a barred gate, by green fields and ponds that stretched down to the Li River, under the wavy outline of the karst hills, was the closest thing she had to family.

She walked into the courtyard and stood, looking at the four-story block of the Social Welfare Institute. It smelled the same as ever when she put her head through the front door—an aroma of boiled food and bleach. A toddler rushed along the hallway, kicking a ball.

"Where are you going?" She squatted next to him.

"I want food."

"It is back there." She took his hand and they walked toward the babble of high-pitched voices, entering a breakfast room full of adults and kids.

"Come, Tian." An assistant hurried him away to a table where toddlers sat, eating noodles. She glanced blankly at Mei as she reached to prevent one of the bowls falling off the table.

"I've come to see Zhu Wing."

"You know the way?"

The handrail to the stairs felt low. She remembered being not much older than the boy, shrieking with laughter as she chased another girl up the stairs, hardly able to reach the rail. She wondered what had happened to those kids who'd been her gang, the closest thing she'd had to siblings until she'd discovered her sister, too late. Some of them had been adopted. Others must still be here, stranded in the adult home. One boy she'd played with had Down syndrome and had been left for adoption as a baby by the gates. She'd been relieved to escape, but now she felt guilty for abandoning them.

On the fourth floor, she walked along the hallway to the last door to the east, with a jade number eight pinned on the outside for luck and a nameplate: Zhu Wing. She dropped her bag and knocked.

After several moments, an old woman in a cotton tunic and pants opened the door. Her face was unlined, but her eyes were cloudy and she breathed shallowly. She stared at Mei, trying to figure out what she was seeing and then a smile spread across her face, like sunrise. She held her arms wide and Mei bent down for her embrace, crying at the feeling of comfort.

"Hello, my child."

"Hello, Auntie."

"Are you well, Mei?"

Mei nodded, unable to speak.

"Come in, come in."

The woman guided her into a study with a small kitchen and a bedroom to one side. Mei stood for a while, with the light on her face. Wing bustled in the corner, heating water for tea and hunting for cake.

"What a pleasure for an old woman to have you back here. I don't see many of my children now." She carried a teapot to a table and set it down, waving for Mei to kneel by it.

"I'm sorry I haven't visited for so long."

"Hush, hush. You're here now. That's all that matters. And you brought a bag. Are you staying?"

"Only for a day or two."

"You will have my bed. I prefer the mat on the floor anyway. It's better for my joints." She clapped her hands, and then her face turned serious. "There's nothing wrong, is there?"

"Not serious. I'll tell you later, Auntie."

"Why have you come to see me now?"

Mei sipped her tea and bowed her head. She couldn't look at the old woman as she spoke.

"I found something. I have it with me. I don't understand it and you're the only one who might."

She reached into her pocket for the passport. The old woman looked at it carefully, holding it lightly in her hands. Then she walked to a table and reached into a drawer for a pair of spectacles. She knelt opposite Mei and leafed through to the identity page.

Wing looked at the photo for a long time and then traced her finger slowly across the image.

"Read this to me, will you. Mei? It's all in English."

Her voice was light, as if she knew the truth already but was trying to delay it. Mei read the lines slowly, letting the vowels of the dead girl's name roll slowly off her tongue. When she came to the birthplace, Wing nodded and reached across to hold it again.

"Where is this girl now?"

"She died, Auntie."

Wing placed the passport on the table and rose, walking into the bedroom stiffly. When she came out, she held three incense sticks and a figure of Buddha; she knelt and put it by the passport, then lit the sticks. There were tears on her face as she looked at Mei.

"Did you come all this way just to bring me sorrow?"

Mei flushed with anger at being blamed for a secret she should have known long before. Throughout her life, she'd had substitutes for sisters, playmates who had come and gone. No one had mentioned the real one.

"Why did you never tell me?"

"I didn't think it would be right."

"Who was she, Auntie?"

"Later, child. It is a long story. First, you rest."

"I'm not tired."

"I knew you as a baby. You never admitted it, even when you screamed and stamped your feet. I would sing to make you stop. Do you need a lullaby, or have you grown up?"

Wing picked up Mei's bag before she could protest any more and carried it into the bedroom, lowering the shade. When Mei lay down on the bed, she found that the old woman was right.

27

"I had night sweats. The change was coming. I'd wake at two o'clock every morning, my pajamas soaked. And it was a difficult summer, a terrible heat that year. I kept an electric fan on at night, and I would get out of bed and sit by the window, looking at the hills. Sometimes I'd cry. I knew my hope was gone. I was surrounded by children, but I'd never have my own."

The light had gone by the time Mei woke up—she'd slept all day in a dazed, exhausted bundle. Wing had fussed over her after she got up, bringing her tea and water. Then she'd made them rice noodles with beef, and they had knelt by the table to eat. When Wing had cleared the bowls and lit candles in the room, she stood by the window and talked.

"That night, there was a noise in the courtyard. Nobody had told me of visitors. Do you remember Bai Gang? He retired when you were five, went back to his village. He came from Longshen—he ate pickled cabbage every evening, I remember. He was a nasty man. They must have sent him here as a joke, because he hated kids. We had to keep them out of his way.

"I looked out and there was Bai. He was out there, wearing a suit and a big grin. I remember because it was so unusual—he never smiled. He was standing by a Hongqi with a big square grille and Beijing plates. It had driven all the way, twelve hundred miles! I couldn't believe it. The roads weren't good, and this place was very poor then. I wondered if they'd come for Bai, but he looked like he had won at baccarat. It was a man and a woman. I couldn't see them well. They talked, and the woman opened the rear door and brought out two baskets, each with a baby in it. One of the babies was you, sweet thing. Bai took them inside, very chatty, lots of bowing. Five minutes later, they came out, and drove away. They never returned."

"A couple brought me here?"

"Yes, Mei. You came in that car."

"I'm from Guilin."

"From Beijing."

"But you told me I was from Guangxi—that my mother was a local woman."

A sob rose in her throat as she spoke. She was like a child again, the teenager she had been when Wing had been the closest thing she had to a parent. *Not fair, not fair, not fair.*

Wing knelt by her and held her hand.

"If I'd told you the truth, you'd only have told someone else. I thought it was better not to fill your heads with dreams. At breakfast, they said that Bai wanted to see me in his office. I was scared that he had seen me at the window, but he had a job for me. Twins had been left in the night, and they had to be cared for. I was to make sure they were well fed. I should tell him if they needed anything. I thought, *You think these two are special because they come from Beijing.*

"I went to the nursery and you were there in your cots, sleeping. So pretty, both of you, with your dark hair, pink cheeks, and perfect fingers. I thought: How could anyone give them up? Not one, but two. To be blessed with twins. To be permitted two and then just to throw them away. It didn't make sense. But I thought you were a gift— that you'd come when I needed you. You were the first to wake, Mei. You looked at me with those eyes and smiled. I slept better after you came.

"Whenever anyone asked, Bai would say you'd come in the night, and that was it. Many girls were left by the gates by mothers who wanted a boy. But there was nothing wrong with you. I was the only one who knew."

One of the candles in the corner of the room started to flicker and smoke as the wick got close to the wax, and Wing rose to snuff it out.

Her voice had calmed and she had shed her self-consciousness at tell-ing Mei things that she had hidden for years. Mei gazed at her as she shuffled around, spilling her old secrets.

"I told you you'd come here with a name but it wasn't true either. I named you. I called you Song Mei because you were so beautiful—a beautiful plum on a tree. Your sister I called Song Ping, for peace. She would lie quietly and listen to you, bawling. I'd sit in the garden, gaz-ing at you both, so happy to have you. This place wasn't civilized, back then. Some of the staff were cruel, and the kids were left dirty. It was shameful. I protected you, as Bai told me to. But I didn't have Ping for long."

"Where did she go?"

"Bai called me to his office again, a month after you'd come. He wanted to know if all was well. He didn't care about you. It was like he was raising a crop and he didn't want it to spoil before he sold it. He told me a western woman was coming to take one of you. It was painful, like a knife through my heart. I'd thought I'd have you both for longer. I didn't reveal my sorrow—I just asked him which one she would take. He hadn't thought of that. 'You choose,' he said. Then he talked sternly. 'She will not be told there are two babies. She has been granted one child. When she comes here, you will bring one baby to the hall for her. She will not go to the nursery, and she will not talk to any of the staff except for you. You will remain silent during the visit.' I went to see you both in the nursery, knowing I had to make a choice. Which would I lose? You'd been the first to open your eyes, the first to smile at me. I held Ping tightly, but I knew it would be her.

"The woman came that week. She was young enough to bear her own child, but she cried when she saw Ping. I gave her the baby to hold, and I had to show her how to change a diaper. I could sense that she was kind. 'She'll be a loving mother,' I thought. They took a photo of us together, and she sent me a copy. I still have it."

Wing walked into the bedroom and reached under her bed for a box. She put it on the table, lifting the lid to reveal a bundle of papers. An old letter with a checked border lay near the bottom. It had a French Revolution airmail stamp with the goddesses of liberty, equality, and fraternity in red, white, and blue. The woman's name and address had been inscribed in Chinese characters, with a return address in English at the top left:

Margot Lockhart
16 Perth Street
Chevy Chase MD 20815
United States

The photograph was inside. Wing pulled it out and handed it to Mei like a precious object. It was as she had described. The woman stood in a blue skirt and jacket with wide lapels, with an exultant grin on her face. She had one arm gripped around Wing's shoulders. The baby was in the woman's other arm, a glimpse of her face visible. The younger Wing smiled for the camera. Mei held it close to her face, straining to see her baby sister.

"What happened to her, Mei?" The old woman looked at her as if she had done her penance.

"She died, Auntie. She drowned."

"How do you know that, little one?"

"I saw her body, in the fields by Dongguan."

Wing smiled brightly, as she'd done in the photo twenty years before, to cover her distress.

"She came home," she said.

28

Mei woke twice in the night. She'd slept for so long during the day and had heard so many secrets that she couldn't settle. The second time, she rose and went to the window in the study, as Wing had done on the night Mei and her sister had been brought to the orphanage. Nothing moved in the courtyard, and the hills were vast and dark. The old woman slept on a thin mattress, her face untroubled. She looked happier at having unburdened herself.

In the morning, Wing bustled about, making Mei's breakfast and taking care of her. A rainstorm pattered on the window.

"Why did you never tell me about Ping?" Mei was lying on a sofa with springs that had long since given out. She wasn't hurt anymore. She just wanted to know. "Not the whole story—that I'd had a sister."

"I thought about it, Mei. When Bai had gone. You were a little girl. The other staff members had left by then. There was no one apart from me who could remember it. But I thought you'd never see her again, and she would never know of you. You'd just stopped asking me who your mother and father had been. I didn't want to hurt you more."

"I understand, Auntie."

They spent the day quietly. Every so often, Mei checked her phone, but there was nothing except for instant messages from Luli: *Where ARE you, girl? Talk to me!!* She ignored them, safe in the cocoon of anonymity. She was enjoying being out of reach, with the old woman coddling her. Wing couldn't walk very far, and not being able to leave felt comfortable. In the late afternoon, she got up to stretch her legs and looked out of the window.

As she did, a green car with tinted windows and army plates came through the gates. It halted in the courtyard below and two soldiers got out—youths with polished boots and eager faces. They opened the doors for a woman officer and a young man in a long coat who yawned as he stepped in a puddle, saying something that made the others laugh.

It was Yao.

Mei stepped back in shock. She had thought she was far away from Guangzhou, but they had come after her.

"What's wrong?"

"Nothing, Auntie. A visitor."

"A visitor?" Wing's face filled with concern, as if any intrusion down the long lane to the Institute was bound to be trouble.

"I'll go and see." She didn't want them marching up, asking her guardian hard questions.

By the time she reached the last flight of the stairs, Yao was starting to climb them with the woman officer. The soldiers were running behind them, while a middle-aged man looked on from the hall with a group of assistants. Mei had never seen him before. The people who managed the Institute came and went often, and Wing was the only constant.

"Mei," Yao said, surprised to find her approaching.

"What are you doing here?" She examined his face, trying to find meaning, but it looked as carefree as usual.

"It's nothing to worry about. They need to ask you some questions, back in Guangzhou."

"What questions?"

The others stood watching and listening silently, as if watching a performance. Yao hesitated, embarrassed at being forced to explain in public.

"We can talk later, Mei."

"No. I want to know now." Mei raised her voice, the words echoing from the tiles. She felt herself starting to panic.

"They found something when they were investigating the Wolf—some evidence. You can explain it, I'm sure."

"Evidence? What evidence?"

"I can't tell you. Not now."

"Why did they send you?"

Yao shook his head, as if he couldn't take her interrogation anymore, and glanced at the officer. She said something that Mei didn't catch and the two soldiers sprang up the stairs, grabbing her by each arm. She tried to pull free, but they held her.

"Tell them to let me go, Yao." She stared at him, willing him to intervene, but he turned away.

"We're going to the station."

"This is stupid. I need my things."

The woman barked at the soldiers, and one let her arm go and ran up the stairs. The other led her down behind Yao. Far above, she heard the soldier marching along a hallway and banging a door open. She was half-led, half-pulled out across the courtyard to the car. Then the soldier placed a hand on her head and pushed her into the passenger seat. After two minutes, his partner ran out with her bag and threw it into the trunk. He sat by her while the second soldier climbed behind the wheel, and Yao got into the front seat.

"Thank you, Major. Your help has been invaluable," Yao said to the woman through the window. She saluted sharply. Despite everything, Mei admired his sense of authority.

She'd hardly formulated the thought before the driver put his foot down and the car squealed forward. Mei looked back for a glimpse of Wing, and the guard abruptly slapped her cheek. The shock of the blow made her cry out.

"Yao. Stop them."

He didn't turn. "Just do what they say, Mei."

At the station, the soldier pushed her sideways and forced her head down onto the seat, with her back to him, then pulled her hands together behind her back and snapped handcuffs on. The metal jammed into her skin. She thought of the cell at the base and the Wolf's gray face as he had been released from the bench. This was how it started, *shuanggui*. Why hadn't she realized that before? She'd believed the Party's powers were used for the good of the people. It was a force for justice, no matter how harsh. Now she was in the trap.

She walked, trying not to look at the faces staring from a crowd of people gathered in the waiting hall for the Guangzhou train. On the platform, they marched to the front of the carriage. A guard waved them on board, unlocking a door at the end.

"Give me the key, then you can go," Yao said.

The guard obeyed and bowed to the soldiers before entering the next carriage. They stepped inside, and Yao locked the door again. They were in a deluxe soft sleeper, with two bunks per cabin—the kind reserved for officials. It was empty.

"You can release her now."

"We shouldn't," one of the soldiers replied.

"You're scared of a girl? Think she might overpower you? Put her in there and I'll deal with her."

A grin spread across the soldier's face, and he punched Yao lightly on the arm. He said something under his breath to his companion, and they both laughed. Unlocking the cuffs, he pushed her into a cabin, where she fell against a sofa. Then he threw in her bag and slid the door closed.

Alone, Mei attempted to calm herself. Dusk was falling, and she couldn't see much from the window. She tried lying on a bed, but she was too anxious to rest. An image of the Wolf's torturer spitting on the window forced itself into her mind, and she shuddered as she imagined his hands on her. The train jerked its way out of the station, on its way to her inquisition.

They were passing through a valley, with mountains on both sides, when the door slid open and Yao came in. He sighed heavily as it closed and then sat beside her, patting her hand.

"Are you okay?"

She tried to stop herself, but she couldn't. Her jaw quivered, and a tear spilled down her cheek.

"How do you *think* I feel?"

"I'm sorry, Mei." He tried to put one arm around her shoulder, but she shook it off and pulled away.

"What's the evidence?"

"I don't know exactly—"

"What is it, Yao? Don't lie to me."

"They found the money in your room. The Swiss francs from the envelope were taped under the bed." He looked unsure whether to trust her. "Mei, you told me you gave it to the Wolf."

Mei stood and leaned against the carriage window, her agitation rising as she absorbed the shock of the accusation. "Yes, I did. I didn't take anything."

"Because it looks like you were working together. You kept the money for him because he was being watched."

"God, Yao. They're setting me up, don't you see?"

"Who would do that?"

"Isn't it obvious? Pan Yue."

Yao frowned. "Don't accuse the deputy secretary of a crime. She helped you when you didn't deserve it."

Mei gasped. She'd given Yao a hard time over his family, but she'd always trusted him. He'd been on her side, against authority and the petty stupidities of their training. This wasn't the Yao she knew—it was the voice of his father, of the Party elite. Her blood rose as she stared at him.

"I didn't deserve it? What do you mean?"

Yao looked disdainful. "You know. You've protected the Wolf, although it was obvious that he was out of control. Pan tried to clean up a mess, and you blocked her. You behaved stupidly, and you ignored my advice."

"So this is my punishment, is it?"

He didn't answer directly. "Tell them everything. They'll believe you if you tell the truth."

She faced the window, feeling the weight of the train push her as it rounded a curve and started to head toward Hunan. Yao was wrong. Pan would do anything she needed to please Chen, to advance her own career. She'd thought they might let her go, but they wouldn't, of course. There was one witness, and she wasn't a reliable one.

"They won't listen, Yao. They've got enough to finish me. I won't be able to escape. The Wolf didn't."

She shuddered, remembering the cells she'd passed by to reach him—the smell of people who'd been locked up and left to rot in limbo. Yao's hand fell on her shoulder, turning her.

"I can help. I just have to call my father. Evidence can be found, and evidence can be lost. It's happened before."

He looked at her, his eyes soft. He stroked her cheek with one palm, and his left arm slipped around her waist. Then he bent forward and kissed her. His lips were warm, and his tongue darted into her mouth. She let it circle hers, the physical pleasure like a balm.

Yao pushed forward, parting her legs with a knee. "I wanted you, but you were too tight," he murmured. "You need me now."

He kept kissing her and took his hand from her cheek, reaching down to her blouse and unbuttoning it. His long fingers slipped inside and caressed her breast, arousing her.

Then Mei realized.

She pushed him back with both palms, surprising him with her force. "It wasn't Pan. It was you."

He smiled, as if she were being silly.

"Come on, Mei. You don't think that, do you?"

He reached forward to stroke her cheek again, but she brushed his arm aside with one hand.

"Tell me you didn't set me up. Plant the evidence and offer to save me. You were the only one who knew. What are you doing here?"

Yao smiled with his perfect teeth and shook his head. He couldn't deny it, and he didn't care.

"Don't be a cock-tease." He put his arms on her shoulders and pinned her to the window, then leaned in to kiss her again. She turned her face away and attempted to wriggle out, but he tightened his grip.

"I'm going to fuck you, Mei. I've waited for it for a long time. The sooner you let me, the better it will be for you."

His face was inches away, and there was a small gap between their bodies. Mei twisted her feet into the character two stance and pushed her knees inward, rooting herself to fight. Yao was too aroused to notice.

"You think I won't resist?" she said.

"Not if you're smart."

She was too tense on her first blow, a *jing cheung* palm strike to his chest, driving the base of her wrist into his floating rib, but she felt it compress. Yao staggered back in pain.

"You bitch," he said, his face flushed. He stepped forward and raised his arm to strike her. But Mei's first blow had settled her into combat, and the turmoil in her brain was gone. Seeing the path of his long, slow roundhouse slap before he even launched it, she darted her left arm to deflect it as she transferred her weight to her right hip and punched him in the throat.

This time, she was fully relaxed, the force traveling up through her knees and hips, through her arm and loosened fingers until, at the last split-second, she turned them into a fist and slammed it into him. His larynx crunched, his eyes bulged, and he drifted on his feet like a tree about to fall.

The *sifu* always said: *Wing Chun is efficient. Defeat your opponent in the shortest time. End it, and be on your way.* As Yao tottered, she pulled her other elbow back and drove the base of her palm powerfully into his open jaw. His teeth crunched as his head snapped back, compressing the nerves in his neck, and he lost consciousness. The fight had lasted four seconds.

As he teetered, she leapt behind to catch him before he hit the floor, so that the crack of his skull would not alert the soldiers in the next cabin. Squatting, she placed a hand over his mouth to prevent any noise emerging and held him around the throat by one arm. It was now his survival or hers. If the guards heard her or if she released Yao, she would soon be in *shuanggui,* strapped to the tiger bench. Mei squeezed until Yao's face turned pink, then kept her vice-like hold until it had turned tomato-colored. She didn't stop, even when his feet started to twitch.

He took a minute to pass out, and two more to die.

29

Yao's head rested in her arms. His tongue, which she'd felt inside her mouth only moments before, lolled to one side of his lips, a livid purple. Mei kept her grip on him after there was nothing left, half-afraid that he'd spring back to life and half-afraid to consider what she had done. Finally, as his body cooled and his face turned waxy white, she let him go. Pulling herself from under him, she got up. Checking that the latch on the door was locked, she sat on the sofa, Yao by her feet. She shook and her teeth chattered. Imagining that the guards might hear her, she clamped her jaw shut. Then she felt a rush of nausea. She scrambled into the toilet—a privilege for the deluxe traveler—and knelt at the bowl, retching liquid with half-digested chunks of the lunch Wing had made.

The train roared on toward Guangzhou.

After she'd washed the vomit off her lips and splashed cold water on her face, she sat down again. Her blouse buttons were undone where Yao had pawed her, and she refastened them. She looked at his lifeless body and, for the first time since he'd attempted to rape her, wanted him back. He'd been her closest friend at the Commission—an irritant, but a constant ally against its stupidities. She had been fonder of him than she'd acknowledged to herself, and his final betrayal had stripped away the precious illusion that she had been different. Not another girl to have his way with, but someone he respected, looked up to for her intelligence, for herself.

But he hadn't. He'd been waiting for the moment that he could possess her as well. She'd had no brother, just a predator in disguise. She shivered, feeling a wave of self-disgust at her stupidity. Would she never grasp that she was alone in this world and had to fend for herself? Others might follow Yao if she gave herself in, force her to submit because she was beyond the law. Some wouldn't have his finesse, or even ask first. She could not let them near her.

A stench rose from the body. The corpse had urinated, a damp patch spreading down one leg of its pants. The smell woke her from paralysis and forced her into action. The soldiers might enter at any moment and find him. She squatted down and pulled off the jacket, tossing it on the sofa. Then she undressed him as rapidly as he'd wanted her to do in life, unbuttoning his shirt, untying his shoes, pulling off his pants from the ankles. She reached onto the bunk and brought down his traveling bag with its Louis Vuitton seal, taking out a set of light-blue cotton pajamas.

When he was naked, she threw his things into the toilet and dressed him again in his pajamas, pulling the pants over his cold buttocks and tying them at the waist. His cock spilled from the front of the pants and she tucked it inside, feeling nothing. Then she buttoned his pajama shirt and paused to observe him. He looked almost peaceful. She pushed her arms under his armpits and maneuvered him so his head pointed toward the bunk, then shoved her feet against the sofa and pulled him up.

The body was stiff, and its legs could not bend. She stood by the bunk and drew the covers over him, propping him on one side with his head facing away from the door and shoving one arm across his chest. It was the best she could do to make him seem asleep. She placed a book from his bag on the bed, and dimmed the cabin lights. Then she went into the toilet and washed the urine off his pants to dull the smell, before spraying some air freshener around the cabin.

Opening her bag, she brought out a T-shirt she sometimes slept in. She stripped to her underwear and put it on, leaving her legs bare. Then she removed her makeup and tousled her hair. She sat as if she'd just climbed out of bed, while she looked through his jacket pockets. One held his wallet, with his Party card inside, the other a phone, with a screenshot of a naked woman scrambling to cover her breasts. The key to the carriage doors, which the guard had given him, was in a side pocket.

She examined his bag. He had a toilet bag of deodorants and aftershave, all in luxury brands. There was a Swiss Army knife and a Poppy tablet with a suede cover. She felt around the bottom of the bag, unzipping a side compartment. It held a thick bundle of dollars and Swiss francs, held tightly in a tube with a rubber band. Unwrapping it, she saw three one-thousand-franc bills, rendering drab the hundred dollar bills with Benjamin Franklin on them.

As she stared at the money, there was a knock on the door—a double rap. Mei jumped and looked at the body, stiff under the covers. She couldn't do any more to conceal it.

"Hold on," she called. She dimmed the lights until the cabin was almost in darkness and switched on a reading light. Then she unlatched the door, pulling it back two inches. The soldier thrust his hand through the gap to widen it, looking at Yao's body.

"He's asleep."

"Wake him."

"No." Her voice was high and loud and she repeated it more softly. "No. Yao must rest. He wouldn't be happy if you woke him up now. He's been hard at work." She smiled, and rested her bare leg in the gap in the door, next to the soldier. "And he's not done yet."

The soldier looked down at her leg. He had a light mustache on his upper lip, and he looked no more than eighteen. He blushed, unable to cope with her fake brazenness. Retreating from the door, he tried to sound stern.

"I'll be back later. Tell him that."

"He won't like you interrupting. He'll be fully occupied until Guangzhou, believe me."

She pushed out her breasts, propelling him back. He scurried back into the next-door cabin, leaving the hallway empty. Mei waited until she heard the click of the door, then exhaled. She sat again and looked up the timetable on her phone. It was half past eleven and Hengyang was next. Four hours to wait.

The night passed dismally slowly. Just before two o'clock, as they pulled into Chenzhou, a storm burst above the hills, casting lightning across the sky. Each boom of thunder made her squirm: She was afraid the soldiers would return. She squealed and then giggled, as if afraid. Then she started to moan, making grunting noises in rhythm, faster and faster. She thumped the side of the bunk and let out two loud moans. The corpse lay on the bed, not knowing what he'd missed.

At three o'clock, she dressed in the dark. The train had crossed into Guangdong and she saw a city in the distance. She stood by the window as the lights grew brighter, her bag in one hand. The train slowed into Shaoguan, passing pink oleander bushes, and sweat ran down her palms. She walked to the door, peering out into the corridor. It was empty, no light under the door of the next cabin. She crept to the end and stood there, waiting for the brakes. As they took hold, she put the key in the carriage lock. It wouldn't turn and she wrenched twice, afraid to look over her shoulder. She calmed herself and tried again. This time it clicked, just as the train came to a halt.

Walking through, she grasped the handle and twisted, then took two steps onto the platform. She stepped away without closing the door and fell in behind a family from the next carriage. Her head down, she saw from the corner of her eye the drawn blinds in the soldiers' cabin, remembering with horror that she hadn't pulled them closed in her own. The moon would be shining down on Yao's blanketed body.

Sitting on a bench a hundred feet away, she waited nervously. A guard walked along the platform slamming doors, not caring whom he woke. At her carriage, he gave the door an extra-hard shove, a small protest against the Party elite who could not be bothered to do it themselves.

One minute, two minutes. A light came on in a carriage next to the soldiers. Then, imperceptibly at first, the train started moving. It crept along the platform, parading the corpse past her. Gradually, it picked up speed until, with a slash of light, it disappeared around a bend.

"What do you want?" Mei jumped. It was a uniformed official, her hair fastened under her cap.

"I'm waiting for a connection."

"Where are you going?"

"Shenzhen."

"Shenzhen West; 3:53. You shouldn't have gotten off. It would have been much simpler at Guangzhou. Platform Four." The official stalked away, her duty done.

Mei hauled her bag through an underground passage and onto the platform. She stood at the edge, her phone in one hand. As long as the screen remained blank and she couldn't hear sirens, she knew that the soldiers hadn't woken and found the body. They were enjoying the last two hours of sleep before their disgrace.

After fifteen minutes, she saw the lights of the Shenzhen train, thundering south toward her.

30

Mei pried herself from her seat at Shenzhen West just before nine o'clock and pushed into the platform melee. The train bearing Yao's body had been due to arrive in Guangzhou three hours earlier, and the soldiers must have discovered him half an hour before that. She was already a fugitive.

At five o'clock, she'd stepped past the blanket-covered heap in the next seat and walked to the end of the carriage. A blast of humidity had rushed in through the window as she'd tossed first her phone, then its battery, and finally its SIM card out. *Let them try to put that back together.* She needed a plan, but as she'd fretted in the hours after leaving Shaoguan she'd rejected each possibility. Returning to Guangzhou wasn't conceivable—she'd been drawn into the Wolf's disgrace, with Yao's blood on her hands. Guilin was no better—she wouldn't get near Wing without being arrested. It was agony to imagine the old woman gazing from her window as Mei had been taken away.

Her only chance lay in her bag, and it would involve abandoning her country and throwing her identity away, like the phone she'd chucked from the train. She hadn't dared look around but, as she left the freight station and walked past garages and warehouses to the Liyumen subway, she paused. She felt safe among the trucks on Taoyan Road and the people heading for the train—they were rushing to work or to deliver their cargo. Nobody cared about her.

She took out the passport of Lizzie Lockhart—the person that Song Ping had become—and leafed through the pages to the yellow-banded departure card tucked by her visa. Mei examined the girl's writing. The cursive in which she'd written her name with a ballpoint pen wasn't so different from Mei's English script. She had entered China at the Futian crossing on July 15 after arriving in Hong Kong. Mei flicked to the girl's photo. They could pass for twins because that was what they'd been.

As she reached the subway, a police car halted on the far side of Taoyan Road. She turned her head away and, when she glanced back, she realized that the cops weren't interested in her. One had lined up by a food cart for breakfast and the other stood smoking by the car. She bought a single ticket and scrambled down the escalator as quickly as she could. By the time the Laojie train left, she had made up her mind.

First, she needed to mimic the woman she'd seen on the Guilin train—one who'd traveled to China and was returning to her western life. One who did not fear being put in detention by the Party. At Laojie, she took the Yongxin Street exit and headed toward Donglong Fashion Street. This was Luli's territory—the place her girlfriend loved to parade on summer evenings. It was a bustle of stores and shops, located on walkways and in warrenlike markets. It was easy to linger all evening, walking arm-in-arm with friends, hopping into cafés for food. Neon signs flashed in garish colors. For Luli it was heaven, but Mei hated the fakery—pink miniskirts, leather jackets, and T-shirts with brazen slogans.

Now it was her sanctuary. As she entered, she disappeared among the shoppers and stallholders—another woman in search of a bargain, maybe spending the money from a factory job to cheer herself up. She marched into a mall and looked on racks for clothes, emerging with two pairs of Levi's jeans, three T-shirts, a hoodie with "Brooklyn Baby" on the front, leather boots, and a trench coat. She bought makeup at a boutique, and a JanSport backpack at a nearby department store, paying for her entire wardrobe with Yao's cash.

Mei forced herself to eat lunch, stuffing noodles into her mouth and fighting the urge to vomit. Then she grabbed a donut from a stall to inject even more sugar into her blood and trotted, laden with clothes, into a hotel. The clerk took away her passport as she checked in under Lizzie's name.

The room was stuffy, and she couldn't force the window open. She threw her stuff on the bed and undressed, stuffing her clothes into one of the plastic bags. Then she made the shower as hot as she could, blasting the traces of the night from her body. Afterward, she put on a robe and stood before the mirror to check her appearance. Her face was pale, her eyes were bloodshot, her cheek was still marked where the soldier had slapped her in Guilin, and the knuckles on her right hand were raw where she'd punched Yao. Despite the food she'd eaten, she looked as lifeless as a dummy. She drew the curtains, set an alarm, and fell asleep.

When the alarm squawked, she sat up in bed, bewildered. It took her a minute or two to remember what had happened. She sat on the edge of the bed, trying not to panic. Her life was ruined, discarded like her clothes. She moaned softly to herself, then louder as she recalled handing the passport to the clerk. That evening, the city's inspectors would come and take a copy for the records. Perhaps they had already arrived and were waiting for her.

"*Stop it,*" Mei said out loud in the empty room. It was just a fantasy—she had to keep her nerve.

She put on a T-shirt and a pair of jeans and took her makeup into the bathroom. As she brushed powder on her cheek and put on pale lipstick—the kind she'd seen on the American girl in the train—her spirits revived. She zipped the hoodie and pinned her hair with a clip, then slung her backpack over one shoulder and sashayed down the hallway in the coat and boots as if she had nothing to fear.

Her confidence lasted the walk to the subway, the two stops south to Luohu, and through the exit to the border crossing. Then, at the sight of the lines in front of the border, it evaporated. She walked without thinking toward the line for Chinese nationals and then veered to the one for foreigners. Her hands were shaking; when she glanced up, an official with gold braid on his blue cap was staring at her. A middle-aged couple joined the line, chatting in a strange language.

As they shuffled forward, she breathed deeply and thought of the American shows she'd watched with Luli, trying to remember how the actors spoke. An official stamped the passport of the woman in front and waved to her. He smiled with a brief flicker of his jaw muscles. Then he opened her passport and stared at the photo. His eyes were blank, absorbing everything and giving away nothing. Mei smiled like a kid who didn't feel the need to be serious. He snapped his eyes down and turned the page, satisfied.

Mei relaxed as he pulled out her departure card and put it to one side. He looked at the visa for a few seconds, then at the card again. His expression didn't alter, but he beckoned with two fingers at the official who'd stared at her. The man walked across, pleased to be summoned.

"Come with me, Miss Lockhart." His English was neutral and polished, nothing like those of the actors.

They reached an office to the side of the barrier, and he indicated a chair opposite his desk. Then he examined the passport in detail, going through the same sequence as the guard. When he'd finished, he looked up and gave her a warmer smile.

"You enjoy being in this country, Miss Lockhart?"

"Oh, yes I do! I've had such a great time here. Chinese people are very welcoming."

"You have traveled widely?"

"I visited many places in Guangdong and I took the train to Hunan and to Sichuan. I love their food. It is very spicy!"

Mei flapped a hand in front of her open mouth and grinned. She was doomed if he made any inquiry—he wouldn't find any trace of Lizzie Lockhart in Hunan or Sichuan—but her American accent felt passable, and she was acting for her life.

"That is why you stayed too long?"

"I did? Let me see."

He leaned across the desk with the passport. "You have a sixty-day visa and you have stayed for seventy-nine. July 15 to today, October 2."

"Oh my God. I'm so sorry. It's all my fault."

"You're right. It is your fault."

"I guess I was having too much fun."

The man stared at her stonily. "Too much fun. I envy you. Take your passport and travel home safely. You are welcome in China, Miss Lockhart, but you must respect our laws."

It was only as Mei crossed over the bridge to the Hong Kong side of the border, above the canal that divided the mainland from the New Territories, that she realized she'd joined a different world.

At elementary school in Guilin, boys had teased her about her name because it sounded like America—*Mei Guo,* the beautiful country. *Mei* was slang for American. *Meirican.* Two of them had weaved around her, putting on accents and calling her a Yankee.

Well, she was an American now.

PART II

31

*W*hen the phone rings, Lockhart is at the window, looking down at the gates of the compound. Two military vehicles have been parked outside for the past three days, their soldiers sweltering in the August heat wave under the green canvas roofs. He feels sorry for them, having to arrive each day to intimidate the residents when a poster of Li Peng, the premier who sent tanks into Tiananmen Square two months before, would do the job just as well. Two of them have already fainted and been taken away.

The heat is intense, and August has been worse than July. It is nearly 100 degrees and humid. People move slowly in the streets, conserving energy. The police posted at Tiananmen to stop anyone making trouble sweat in their caps. The part of the square where the tourist buses park is empty, and Mao's portrait stares across from Tiananmen Gate to the Great Hall of the People. Beijing has a dream-like air, as if June had never happened.

He props one arm on the windowsill, trying to generate a breeze, as he watches Margot pack. She is on her hands and knees on the floor, sorting out papers and pictures, placing them in boxes for the movers. He feels low and irritable, like the city. Political life has ground to a halt while the Party's leaders tussle in Zhongnanhai over the next step. He's been sent home from the embassy with their tickets and passports, booked on a flight to Washington, where a desk job beckons. His adventure is over.

"Is this Tom Lockhart?" The gravelly voice pronounces the vowels in a formal accent.

"It is. Who is this?"

"Economic counselor at the U.S. embassy?"

"Yes. Who is this?"

"Until recently."

Lockhart doesn't say anything. The man has shown too much inside knowledge for comfort—Tom rather than Thomas, his job, the fact that he has been instructed to leave. He looks at his watch. Four o'clock in the afternoon in Beijing, four o'clock in the morning on the east coast of the United States. He likes that he spends his day with his case officer asleep and thus unable to offer guidance. He'll miss Beijing—an unpredictable challenge, with an excuse to do what he wants and justify it to Langley later. Besides, the seventh floor is empty in August. Sedgwick is on Cape Cod with his second wife.

"I want to show you something," the voice says.

In the silence, Margot gazes at him inquiringly. Lockhart raises his eyebrows, as if in bemused exasperation, and tilts an imaginary cup to his lips. She smiles and goes to the kitchen.

"Tell me who you are."

"You're familiar with where I am," the man counters. *"At a siheyuan near Gulou Xi Dajie."*

Lockhart looks around. Margot is still in the kitchen.

"That means nothing to me."

"A lady has been living here, but she does not pay the rent for herself. It comes from the China Postal Savings Bank, which receives a monthly deposit from an account at Wing Hang Bank in Hong Kong. You control this account, on behalf of the Central Intelligence Agency."

"I think you are mistaken. It is the first I have heard of any of this," Lockhart says.

"One hour," the voice says. *"You will not be in danger. I want you to see something."*

When the call ends, Lockhart checks his watch. Sedgwick is out of reach, at least for two hours. *"I'm going out,"* he shouts. *"Won't be long."*

He takes his bicycle from the gate—the good thing about military rule is that he doesn't need a lock—and cycles through the embassy district to Dongzhimen Road, then turns west amid the flow of bicycles. He rests his jacket on the handlebars, enjoying the wind in his shirtsleeves. Passing the red and green edifice of the Drum Tower, he enters the hutong district, its ancient siheyuan courtyard houses tiled in thick terracotta, with carved wood façades.

Two police cars have forced their way up a narrow street and are parked by a gate that leads into an alley. Lockhart gets off the bicycle and rests it on a wall by a clay pipe shop five hundred feet short of them. He has a bad feeling, but something in the voice on the phone pushes him forward. It had an air of disdainful certainty—as if the speaker knows all about Lockhart and isn't impressed.

The police are expecting him when he walks up the street. The officer in charge holds out a hand for his black diplomatic passport and, after flicking through it, points at the gate. Lockhart walks up the alley to a one-story siheyuan at the end. He is curious to see it— he knows the address but has never been to the place, only paid the bills. He pushes open the door and crosses a dingy kitchen, with pots on the walls, to a tiled courtyard.

A tall man stands in the courtyard, his blue Mao tunic unbuttoned and his shirt open at the collar, smoking a cigarette. There are two butts at his feet; as Lockhart enters, he pulls a red-and-gold pack of Chunghwas from a pocket to offer him one.

"I smoke Marlboros," Lockhart says.

The man shrugs. "These are better." He indicates the door that leads to the rest of the house. "Look in there."

There is a wide bed in the first room, facing a silk wall hanging of a crane on the roof of a temple. It is hot, and there is a smell like rotten eggs. Two flies buzz around the bed, on which lies the body of a woman. Another sits in a pool of blood that has collected from a deep wound in her chest. To judge by the smell, she's been dead for some time. She was beautiful, with long, dark hair and a feline face. Lockhart has seen her photo but it didn't do her justice, even dead. He looks at his watch again and then stands by her, closing her dull, sightless eyes with his fingertips.

He goes into the next room, past a screen that hides a basin and shower, toward the sound of crying.

Two babies lie side by side in cots in the darkened room. They are tiny, mirror images, with delicate eyes and tufts of dark hair. One sleeps, but the other's face is red and clenched, bawling in hunger. They wear tiny white embroidered dresses, as if for a visitor.

The man comes into the room.

"You didn't know?" He offers the cigarettes again, and this time Lockhart takes one. It tastes of plums as he inhales.

Lockhart shakes his head. It is a goddamned mess. He can imagine what Sedgwick, who didn't like the plan in the first place, will say. He is on his way out of China, and this is the coup de grâce.

"This is what you got for your dollars. Was it a good investment?" The man leans on the wall, staring at Lockhart. He is in his forties, and it looks like this isn't his first corpse.

"Who are you?"

"I work for the Ministry of State Security."

"You didn't answer the question."

"You didn't answer mine. Look at what your money bought. Silk covers and pretty dresses, an apartment for a mistress near Zhongnanhai. A bloody death. You are responsible for this."

"We didn't pay for it, and we didn't want it."

The little girl still cries, but softer now.

The man shakes his head. "Americans. You think everyone wants to be like you. We also want a society where the rich are indulged and the poor suffer, where addicts and criminals fill the cities. You forget that emperors have ruled China already. The people do not wish to return to that."

"And if they do, you send in the tanks."

The man snaps at him. "China is still finding its way. It is changing, but the Party cannot risk chaos."

"How will the Party deal with this?"

"That is not your affair. It will be handled."

"What about these two?"

"There are facilities to care for them."

Lockhart laughs bitterly. The man is quite convincing in his way, but he knows what his country's orphanages are like. Kids there can scream for food or attention and not be helped for days, like the twins across the courtyard. They will lie in their own dirt, two abandoned girls.

"You'll put them in a Social Welfare Institute? You might as well throw them in the garbage."

"You know about it, do you?"

"I've done some research."

The man smiles. "Ah, your wife. She made inquiries, I believe. Why would a child receive better care from the wife of a CIA spy who bribes and corrupts and is a party to bloodshed, than from the Chinese people?"

Lockhart has heard enough from this self-righteous apparatchik who cares nothing for love and humanity, only for the rule of the Party, at whatever cost in lives. Margot would have made a better mother than anyone he can think of, if nature hadn't denied her.

"Because she'd love her, not treat her as propaganda."

"They will have a better life here than they would in America," the man says, stepping on his cigarette.

The baby has worn herself out and is drifting off to sleep in her cot, by her sister. Lockhart looks at the pair, abandoned in a hutong in Beijing, in a country in turmoil, with their mother dead.

"You want to bet?"

32

Lockhart drove south on Interstate 280, taking the curves south through the hills toward San Jose. He usually felt at peace on this road, savoring the journey to Silicon Valley with the window down and the sun shining, free of the San Francisco fog. Today, he was weary and despairing.

He'd killed Lizzie, or he'd let her die. In his mind, it made no difference. It had been his role to protect her, and he had utterly failed. The truth was, he'd admired what she had wanted to do. He'd made a half-hearted effort to dissuade her, but they had both known his heart wasn't in it. She'd told him he would have done the same in her place and he'd thought: *You are my daughter.* He had worried about her, but deep down, he'd thought of her like himself—that she was charmed.

He had won her in a bet and lost her recklessly. *Don't be so cocky. Luck won't always be on your side,* Sedgwick had warned him years ago, but he'd laughed about it afterward. His talent was to make things work, even if there were bumps along the way. That was why they put him in the field, no matter how much they frowned on him. No one was better at improvising when the book didn't say what to do next. It had worked for him all his life, in Beijing, Kenya, Vietnam.

He'd thought she was the same.

All this time later, he didn't know which one Lizzie had been—the one who had slept or the one who had been crying. When Lang had grasped what Lockhart meant, he'd shaken his head, disgusted at the idea. But it was hard to dismiss. They had been alone, beyond the reach of the law. Lang's task was to cover up the crime, and this was as good a way as any. Lockhart had struck him where he was most vulnerable—his pride. They would be sent to an orphanage as far away from Beijing as possible, down in the south, Lang said. Your wife will receive a call.

For years, Lockhart did not doubt that he'd won his bet, even if he had nobody to tell. Lizzie had had the best life a child could want. She'd won the lottery of life, from a Chinese orphanage to a U.S. sub-urb. He had sometimes wondered what had happened to her twin, feeling a twinge of guilt that she lacked the opportunities Lizzie had. But that had been the deal and, as China grew and became wealthier, he stopped worrying. Lizzie knew a girl at school who'd been adopted from Guangxi, and Lockhart heard that things were getting better there.

Now he'd lost everything. His life no longer felt like a series of lucky events, but stations on the way to an inevitable tragedy. The affair was over, and he would never go back.

He looped slowly through the Los Altos Hills, descending on the far side toward San Jose. At Sunnyvale, he left the freeway and navi-gated a maze of roads, lined with red-roofed houses, each standing on a plot like a Monopoly piece. The sun was high in the sky, behind a streak of cloud. As he crossed an empty highway, the Poppy campus stretched out before him. The image stamped on millions of phones stood by one corner of the road—a gold-leafed statue of a poppy flower.

He knew the story. Henry Martin had been a brilliant, rebellious kid who'd abandoned Stanford in his junior year to take off around the world. In India, studying Hinduism, he'd met a guru who achieved a higher state of consciousness by smoking opium. Martin had be-come a disciple and, when he returned to Palo Alto, had named his startup after the poppy seed. That was the legend. Officially, Poppy's name referenced the golden Californian poppy, a far more innocuous flower.

He was greeted at the gate by the first of the eager black-uniformed helpers who swarmed the campus, doubling as assistants and con-cierges. The young man gave him a pass for Building Seven, halfway around the circle on which the low offices were set, and waved him on

his way. Others appeared inside the entrance to guide him up the wal-
nut stairs to Martin's office, where an assistant fetched chilled water.
He was on a mezzanine with glass panels looking out over rows of
employees sitting at screens, busy designing software for the next
product launch.

"Tom!"

Lockhart jumped. Martin was striding toward him, waving. Another assistant walked by him, trying to draw his attention to a piece
of paper. Martin took it from her and ripped it in half.

"I hate this stuff, I've told you that." Then his face turned solemn
as he approached. "Tom. I'm so sorry for your loss. Let's talk, man."

Poppy's founder was six feet four and two hundred pounds, with
collar-length graying hair. Everyone else was draped in black, but he
wore a gingham suit and vest with a pink tie, like a giant toddler. He
put an arm around Lockhart as he led him into an office, then pulled
two leather Mies van der Rohe chairs to face each other. Martin
squeezed himself into one and sat with his head in his hands, his fingers laced through his hair.

"Tom, I can't even imagine. I'm so sorry, man. I feel terrible. Can
I help in any way?"

Lockhart felt like Mr. Wu, being offered a payoff by Martin to
keep his mouth shut about his lost daughter.

"Thank you, Henry, but no."

"Listen, Tom." Martin stared at him earnestly. "When this is over,
you have to set aside time for yourself. I don't know if you're a man
of faith, but find someone to talk to. You need closure."

"Thanks for the advice." Lockhart ached to leave. He could not
bear to listen to Martin's attempt at therapy. "I came to say goodbye,
Henry. You'll understand that I can't do any more for you."

Martin looked puzzled. "But you have to. Don't you see? You
can't walk away now; you have to carry on. She'd want you to."

Lockhart stood, his temper flaring. "You have no idea what Lizzie
would want. You didn't know her."

Martin heaved out of his chair and put a hand on Lockhart's
shoulder, restraining him. "There's something you don't know, Tom.
We've found a new one. Come on, I'll show you."

On the other side of the engineering floor, Martin waved a hand at a panel and the door slid back, revealing a room. "Neat, huh? Here, look," he said, holding up his watch.

"There's a chip inside. It saves having to keep an identity card clipped to you. The world's moving toward wearables. It's going to be a great business." He looked carefree as he talked, as if he'd already forgotten Lizzie.

The room was flooded with light from floor-to-ceiling windows. Five designers sat at a trestle table, working silently at laptops. White objects were being extruded from a row of 3D printers along one wall. Martin opened a panel and pulled out a tablet. It was silver, with the poppy emblem in gold—the latest model.

"Time for a break, gentlemen," Martin said. The designers rose silently as one and filed out.

When they had gone, Martin put the tablet on the table and walked around it, his face reddening. He picked up an object from a 3D printer and flung in on the floor, then kicked it across the floor, as if reacting to a silent provocation. His mood had changed again, like the weather.

"This is so *fucking* unfair. We're being killed, Tom. There's a piece in the *Times* every day about how badly we treat the workers, and they're not ours. We can't even get inside to find out what's going on. We send you, and look what happens."

Lockhart squeezed one hand into a fist to keep himself under control. He badly wanted to leave. "You're quite safe, Henry."

Martin's shoulders drooped. "Hell, I'm sorry. Forget what I said, will you? I'm sick and tired of it. I feel for all those kids, not just her. You're the only person who can stop it."

"I can give you other names. It's over for me."

Martin shook his head and slid the silver tablet across the table at him. "I told you. You can't go."

Lockhart lifted the tablet and pressed the start button. The black screen lit up in silver and white and a Poppy shimmered in the middle as the software loaded. "It's like the others?" he asked.

"One difference. You'll see."

He watched as the poppy dissolved and a set of icons filled the

screen, each with a title. Instead of the Mandarin characters he'd expected, they were in English. He tapped an application and the dome
of the Capitol appeared. It was the Yahoo weather app for Washington, D.C.

"Whose is this?"

"It was ordered by a young woman for her boyfriend's birthday.
She thought it would be a nice present, so she bought one online. She
was right. It's the most amazing device. This came off the line at Long
Tan, got loaded on a ship at Shenzhen, across the Pacific into Los
Angeles. FedEx to Indianapolis, then BWI. Loaded on a truck to
Washington and a van to Dupont Circle. He was delighted, until a
guy from Langley came to the door."

"How did he know?"

"We told him. He's an old friend of yours, says he's looking forward to seeing you. I couldn't let you go, even if I wanted to."

"Who was the birthday boy?"

"Works in the West Wing, with the National Security Adviser. He
was intending to take his present to work. This isn't only our problem
anymore, Tom. It's out of my hands."

33

Mei left the Metro at Friendship Heights and walked up Western Avenue. Drifting clouds sheltered the sun, and the breeze was cool on her face. She'd used Yao's illicit dollars for a flight from Hong Kong to Washington, changing in Chicago, and booked a cheap hotel off Connecticut Avenue. Now, for the first time in days, the muscle ache in her shoulders had eased. For the moment, she'd escaped the humidity and terror of Guangdong.

This was how freedom felt.

She'd never been to the United States, although it was common among her university friends. The older generation were lost in wonder at how easily people of her age traveled. One graduate of Sun Yat-sen had gone to study at Georgetown, others to Yale and Stanford. Their wealthy parents had paid the fees without blinking— nothing was too much for one child. But Mei had fought so hard to get what she wanted that she would not do anything to risk it. Let others travel the world and return to jobs that had been saved for them. She didn't have that luxury.

Walking off at Reagan National, she'd been met by nothing but an anonymous terminal with a few outlets—Starbucks, Hudson News. The other passengers had hurried past to get through immigration quickly, but she had lingered on the walkway, preparing herself for examination. Lizzie's passport put her in the fast line with the U.S. citizens, leaving the Chinese to wait. The immigration officer, a Latino with a shining pin on his uniform, scanned the passport quickly.

"Welcome home, ma'am," he'd said, his attention already turning to the rest of the line.

The cars went by on Western Avenue with none of the urgency of those in Shenzhen, driven by people shopping for groceries or returning from dropping their kids off at school. Mei passed a school with two buses parked outside. Through the windows, she saw lines of small children sitting at desks, a teacher bending down to check their work. It felt like an idyll—the peaceful streets and the trees with their red and yellow fall leaves. A place where everything was in order.

Half a mile on, she took out a map she'd bought near her hotel, then headed off the highway into a grid of streets lined with clapboard and brick houses with landscaped front lawns and beds of flowers. She was on a sidewalk shaded by trees, hemmed in by Hyundais and Toyotas. To her left, she glimpsed between houses to the backyards, with basketball hoops and trampolines. At the rear of one Colonial, there was a small replica of the house itself, for children to play in. She walked to the end of the street and consulted the map again. Her destination lay a few hundred feet to the left along Perth Street.

As she stood a car passed slowly, with a gray-haired woman driving. Her window was open and, as she paused briefly at the junction, she waved and smiled, displaying a bright row of teeth.

"Lizzie!" she called.

Mei smiled, not replying for fear of being identified as an impostor, and the woman drove on with a wave, leaving her frozen in the spot. Her initial plan, to take a casual look at the house from which Margot Lockhart had written to Zhu Wing twenty-three years before, evaporated. Instead of turning into the street, she kept walking, pulling up her hood as if to shield the glare. She looked left and right for a hiding place, but there was nothing. Broad lawns surrounded her, houses fenced her in from all sides. A police car drove by, Chevy Chase Village in blue on the side. One of the cops glanced at her through dark glasses as it turned two blocks ahead.

Her shoulder muscles tightened, reviving the ache. The idea that she'd escaped being spied upon by leaving China was another illusion. She sped up, walking briskly toward the end of Cedar Parkway, past large houses painted cream and white. The trees became denser here and their branches reached up, hands clutching at the sky. The street ended at a T-junction staked with two signs: red Stop and yellow Dead End. Its arrow pointed to the left, along a spur road.

The road felt like a path of no return. To her left were thick bushes leading into woods, and to her right houses with large windows overlooked her. She didn't glance around but ran quickly, trying to figure out where the Lockharts' house lay, a few hundred feet to her left, through the woods. She bent down, using a parked truck as a screen, and pushed through an old fence that had been crushed and split by the suckers of climbing plants.

On the far side, she found herself in a glade, her hand bleeding from a thorn bush she'd battled through. Trees reached above her, and the glade floor was carpeted with pine needles. The hissing of water intruded from a hundred feet. Looking through the trees, she saw the green fairway of a golf course, bunkers piled with white sand. The course looked immaculate, but no one was playing. A golf cart, painted deep green, was parked by a bunker.

Mei sucked the back of her hand, and a red drop welled up from the scratch. She smeared the blood and started to walk back in the direction she'd come, this time within the woods. After a few minutes, she saw the houses on Perth Street through the fences at the rear. Two gardeners trimmed bushes, one on a ladder. She halted near the house, hidden in the undergrowth.

The Lockharts' house was double-fronted in faded red brick, with shuttered windows and a gray-tiled roof. It had a garage to one side and a lawn leading to a tennis court. Black shutters concealed the rear windows, and there was no sign of life inside. She couldn't get close enough to raise her head above the fence, but the house looked empty. Mei sat on the forest floor and lay back, resting her head on her backpack. Sun spilled through the trees and lit her face. She felt drowsy, jet lag and sleep deprivation catching up with her.

When she woke, the sun had dropped in the sky and she was cold—her skin was pimpled on her arms. She couldn't believe how the heat had waned, not held by clouds or humidity. Shivering, she stood and fastened the zip on her hoodie to hold in the warmth, then pulled the trench coat from her backpack and put it on. It was dim in the woods, and the windows glowed in the house. Mei stepped from the bushes and stood in the glade—invisible and unable to hear anything. She walked forty feet closer, where she could observe the house.

A conservatory at the rear led to a kitchen that looked crammed with appliances and dark oak doors. A woman was sitting by herself, both hands clasped around a mug. She was twenty-three years older than she'd been in the photo, and she looked pale and unhappy, but there was no doubt.

It was Margot Lockhart.

Mei watched her, neither of them moving. She was starting to wonder how long Margot could stay immobile when she pushed back her chair and rose to pace around. As she left the kitchen, Mei saw her climbing the stairs, her face passing a window halfway up. A light came on in the rear bedroom, and Margot's face appeared, staring out of a window.

She was still a handsome woman. Her hair, curled in the photo Mei had seen, had straightened and her shoulders were broader. But she had the same soft features and kind face. Mei wondered if she could be seen—the woman seemed to be staring at her. But Margot didn't shout out or acknowledge Mei. She looked so lost in thought that she noticed nothing.

The lights were on in other houses, but none close enough to be a threat. It felt as if they were joined together, Mei in the woods and Margot in her house. They had missed each other before. When Margot had driven away from Guilin with Ping, Mei had been very close. Perhaps her cries might have been heard.

Mei started to walk.

34

There was a door in the wall along the back of the Lockhart property. It gave to Mei's fingers as she pushed it, allowing her to walk through onto their property easily. A wooden shed had been pitched on the land at the rear, behind the tennis court. The door was open and tools hung on pegs by a rocking horse with a straw mane. It looked like a birthday present for a little girl, long ago.

Red and yellow leaves were scattered on the court. The net was slack and a bucket of balls stood by one baseline. The rear of the house rose before her, through the court's wire fence. Margot had moved from the window, and Mei could no longer see her. She walked across the lawn, not bothering to hide from view, and tried the handle. It was locked, and the kitchen was dark. She twisted the handle again, and then knocked on the window.

Mei felt a vibration in the house and a light went on in the hallway. Margot came into the kitchen and stood by a door twenty-five feet away, staring at her. Mei knocked on the glass and waved, calling out for her to open the sliding door, but Margot didn't appear to hear. She pushed herself against the kitchen wall and turned away, running back into the hallway. Mei banged on the door in desperation, trying to make her come back, but all she could see was the half-lit kitchen. As she waited, starting to panic, a siren went off inside the house, and on her arms and hands she saw reflections of a flashing light from above. She glanced up at an alarm box fixed to the rear of the house, which was now pulsating in blue and white.

The woman must have set off a panic button inside the house, Mei realized. The trees at the rear of the yard were glowing with reflections from the alarm, and she looked around wildly, trying to decide what to do. She could run for the gate in the fence and try to get out of the neighborhood, but she would be stranded in Washington, without any idea of what to do. She couldn't retreat, so she had to get to Margot fast—it was her only hope. She lifted a stone from the border of a flowerbed and hurled it through the pane, reaching inside to turn the key. Inside, the sound of the siren was deafening. Scrambling across the kitchen, she missed her step and sprawled on her hands and knees, then staggered to her feet and ran into the hallway and up the stairs. The first bedroom she found was at the rear of the house, where she'd seen Margot.

A shadow moved on a frosted glass door into a bathroom, and Mei tugged at the door, but it was locked.

"Let me in," she called in English above the screaming of the siren.

"Get out." Margot sounded panicked.

"I have to talk to you, Mrs. Lockhart."

"Just go. My security company is coming."

"She was my sister." Mei put her face to the door, shouting desperately. "Lizzie was my sister. I need to talk to you."

The siren was the only sound she could hear. Margot had gone quiet inside the bathroom. Mei looked around the room. A stone, split in two to expose a polished crystal face, rested on a mantelshelf. She picked it up and walked to the bathroom door, holding it behind her shoulder. Then she stopped. What good would it do to keep on smashing things? She couldn't make the woman engage, inside her own home, by frightening her. She was still grieving for her daughter. Mei let the stone fall and sat on the bed, resting her hand on the silk coverlet and bowing her head. Her arrest would come soon. By tomorrow, she'd be on a flight to China.

Amid the chaos and noise, she wept, holding her face in her hands. As she did, a key turned in the door and the siren stopped. She felt the relief of silence, broken only by the chime of the door. Margot walked past her, not stopping, and went down the stairs to the hall. Mei waited for the sound of guards climbing the stairs to take her away, but all she heard was a murmur of voices. Then a man's shoes crunched along the gravel again, his car started, and he drove away.

Mei was still crying when Margot returned to the room and knelt in front of her, pulling her hands away from her face.

"Oh my God," she said. "I don't believe it."

She sat next to Mei on the bed and stroked her head, looking at her with concern. "Don't be frightened. They're gone," she said. It was the first comfort Mei had felt since she'd been in Wing's room in Guilin, and she started to shake with relief, unable to speak coherently.

After two minutes, Margot got up and went into the bathroom, returning with a handful of Kleenex.

"What are you doing here?" she said.

Mei sniffed. "I've been stupid."

"You really are her sister," Margot said in wonder.

"Her twin."

"This is crazy." Margot sat beside her on the bed, shaking her head. "Why didn't they tell me?"

"You didn't know?"

"If I had, I'd have adopted you too."

"Would you?"

"In a heartbeat. Two cute girls. Are you kidding me?" Margot gulped as if to stop herself from cracking, and stood up. "Come on. I need a drink."

The kitchen was huge, as if Margot were operating a restaurant from her house. There was an eight-burner Viking stove and a double-fronted refrigerator, bigger than the one they'd had for the entire orphanage in Guilin. Margot opened the oak door of a wine chiller lined with bottles. She took out a bottle and took down two glasses from a high cabinet, gesturing at Mei to sit at the island. She poured out white wine and took a gulp. Mei followed, feeling alcohol bubble through her brain.

"So who are you?" Margot said, putting her glass down.

"My name is Song Mei."

"Like my Lizzie. Song Ping. You were in the orphanage in Guilin?"

Mei nodded.

"They never tell you anything in that country if you're *laowai*. Who adopted you?"

"Nobody. Until I went to university, I stayed with Zhu Wing, the woman you met. I saw your photo together."

"I remember her. She was nice. I was such a rookie, she had to show me how to hold Lizzie. But why did she hide you?"

"She was told to keep me secret."

"She was? That's weird."

Mei hesitated. She didn't know whether to say more, but there was a puzzle in her head. "I think your husband knew about me. He thought I was Lizzie at first, but when I explained, he didn't look surprised—not like you. It wasn't a shock."

Margot tensed. "Where did you meet Tom?"

"In Guangdong, where I work."

Margot took another gulp and placed the glass on the countertop, turning the stem in her fingers.

"So he kept you secret from me, what a surprise." Margot's face stiffened and the lines at her mouth became deeper. She sounded bitter. "I don't know if he told you, Mei, but we're not together anymore. We've been separated for some years now. One reason is that I couldn't believe a damn thing he said. He always left a few things out—including women. His job was all about lying, and I guess he kind of slipped into the habit with me."

"He deceived me. I trusted him and then he disappeared."

Margot gave a shout of ironic laughter and said, "That's the man I married." She topped up their glasses.

"Tell me how you found Lizzie," said Mei. She remembered Lockhart in the Dongguan marsh, the quiver in his voice as he'd said: *I can't*. The question hit Margot the same way, and she stretched her lips back tightly, as if trying to fix a smile, and blinked a few times to clear her eyes.

"We lived in Peking. That's what we called it then. It was where we met. I was teaching and he was at the embassy. Small world. Anyway, we got married, tried to have a child. It wasn't working. Something was wrong. . . . The treatment wasn't great. They mostly had the opposite problem. I thought maybe we should adopt, but when I made an application, it got nowhere. Constant delays. Then we had to leave."

"Why?"

"It was 1989. We had no choice."

"Why not?"

"What do you call it there? The June Fourth Incident. Six Four. You were a month old. I wish you had seen it. We lived in a compound in Qi Jia Yuan. Everyone was out on the streets at night, excited. We'd walk around, feeling joyful, like springtime. Then, one night, we heard gunfire. I looked out of our window and saw PLA trucks packed with helmets, on their way to kill people."

"They arrested counterrevolutionaries who were threatening public order. No one died in Tiananmen Square." Mei spoke automatically, not even sure whether she believed it herself.

"Are you serious?"

"I studied history."

"I lived it."

Mei halted before the argument got out of hand—she didn't want to fall out over the past. Bad things happened in the year of her birth, but for twenty-three years, China had recovered, grown prosperous. She hadn't asked too many questions about that time, until now.

"You left Beijing," she prompted.

"President Bush—the father, not the idiot—imposed sanctions, and we were told to go. Tom was . . . Tom was a target. One day, when we were packed and ready to go. I received a call. It was the director of the Guilin home. He said they had a child for me. I hadn't been told because of a mistake with the papers. But she was ready. I could come and get her immediately. It was kind of strange, but I didn't ask questions." Her lip trembled. "That was Lizzie."

"You didn't get a choice?"

"Lizzie was what we were given. She was good enough for me." A tear slid down her cheek. "More than enough." She paused, looking into her wine, as if it told fortunes. "Could I ask you something? It's stupid, I'm afraid."

"Yes, Mrs. Lockhart."

"Call me Margot, please. I wanted to hold you again, if I could. It's like holding her."

Margot opened her arms, and Mei let herself be enfolded in them. Over Margot's shoulders, she saw along the garden to the shed and the woods, the darkness from which she'd entered. She could feel Margot breathing against her and she thought of Lizzie's body in the pond, the water spilling from her mouth and her hair floating on the surface. She was terribly tired, as if she could fall asleep and not wake up. She wondered if this was what life would have felt like, if she'd been chosen.

35

Lockhart was in the back of the van next to Sedgwick, with only a tiny slice of a view through the windshield. They had been sitting in the same position for an hour, waiting.

"I'm too old for this," Sedgwick said.

"Quit whining. You should be happy to be out."

"I'd rather be in a bar."

Sedgwick shifted on the seat, arranging his legs around boxes of equipment. Lockhart had known him for thirty years, but he would have had trouble picking him from a lineup. Sedgwick's mustache was turning white and he'd put on some weight, but he remained featureless—he sat in his London Fog raincoat, fading into the background like a hundred spies. Lockhart leaned forward, peering through the glass at the street. A rain shower had passed, and the leaves were glistening on the trees.

"Nothing yet," he said.

"Maybe she'll cancel," Sedgwick said gloomily.

"She won't. She never does."

"You shouldn't have let Margot go. She was good for you."

"That was a long time ago, Al."

"Yeah, but don't you miss her?"

"Sometimes." Lockhart looked at the squat green fire hydrant on the corner of the block. He remembered Lizzie walking past it in her brown wool coat, when she'd been three years old. They'd just bought a retriever puppy and she'd run up the street after it, squealing with laughter. "More now."

"I'm sorry, Tom." Sedgwick shuffled again. "God, who designed these seats? This is penance. Bless me, Father, for I have sinned. Five Our Fathers, four Hail Marys, and three hours' surveillance."

"It's your operation, not mine."

"Just the same as in the old days."

"Yes, but I retired."

"We don't recognize that concept."

"They're moving," the driver said.

Lockhart looked through the glass, then flattened himself against the side of the van. It was uncanny to see them together. Margot unlocked the car door as the girl waited on the other side. Mei wore one of Lizzie's outfits—black pants and a green jacket—and she looked identical. What strange fantasy were the two of them living out? Margot had seemed almost healthy, nothing like the pale and exhausted figure of recent days. When he'd told her the truth about Lizzie, it was worse than when they'd separated—as if he'd broken her.

"What the hell is going on?"

"I honestly don't know, Al."

"Margot doesn't hate you that much, does she?"

"She might," Lockhart said grimly.

Margot's Lexus started up the street and turned onto Magnolia Parkway, their van following three vehicles behind. They drove along Western Avenue, past the recreation center and into the heart of the village. The driver and the technician in the front looked unhurried, as if they did this every day. The rear of the van was packed, and there was hardly room to move. Sedgwick winced as they swung around the corners, as if feeling his age.

At Friendship Heights, Margot pulled into the underground parking lot by Neiman Marcus. Their driver kept going to the next block, turning into an open-air lot and finding a spot opposite Bloomingdale's. The driver leaned back and retrieved a silver suitcase from Lockhart's feet. He removed a squat telescope, plugging it into an electronic device nestled inside the case. Then he put on a pair of headphones, opened his window a shade and sighted the Capital Grille through the scope. As he did, Margot and Mei emerged from the lot, crossing the road into the restaurant.

"They'll be sitting near the window," Sedgwick said.

"How did you fix that?" Lockhart said.

"We tip well."

Soon the women appeared at the window and sat at a table, taking menus from the waiter. Margot glanced at hers briefly and set it down, leaning forward to talk.

"Is this Mandarin?" The driver gave the headphones to Sedgwick and he held one pad to his ear.

"Sounds like Martian."

He handed them to Lockhart, who put them on. It was like listening to a crowd inside an echo chamber if the sound were passed through soup. He heard scraps of Margot's voice, but her words were mostly lost.

"Is this the best we can do?" Sedgwick said.

The driver shrugged, whispering with the technician over the controls. They tried for another few minutes but it was useless. Eventually, Sedgwick passed the headphones to the front and climbed out of the van on the blind side of the restaurant to catch some air. Lockhart joined him, wanting a cigarette. They stood silently, looking around the streets until, after twenty minutes, the drive spoke.

"Movement." The driver had taken out a pair of binoculars and was gazing at the restaurant. "One's up, the other's at the table. She's going somewhere, can't see."

"Bathroom break," Sedgwick said. "Which one?"

"Mrs. Lockhart."

"Ready, Tom?"

"Let's go," Lockhart said.

He followed Sedgwick onto the sidewalk and across Western Avenue to the restaurant. They went up the stone steps to the side and entered the establishment through the main door. It was dark, with wood paneling and dimmed Art Deco lights, but he saw her at the end of a row of banquettes as clearly as if she were his daughter, sitting alone. Sedgwick waved aside a waiter, and they walked to the table.

"Hello, Song Mei," Lockhart said, sitting in Margot's seat. He had only a minute or two before Margot returned and things became complicated. He wanted to finish the task by then.

Mei looked up, startled. She seemed gentler in Lizzie's outfit, without her suit and the wariness with which she'd entered the VIP room at the Golden Dragon. Her plate of tuna and rice had hardly been touched, and her glass of white wine was still full. She said nothing.

"This is Alan Sedgwick, with the CIA. We need you to come with us now, Mei. We have to leave."

"Mr. Lockhart." She stared at him, not moving.

"Come on, Ms. Song." Sedgwick put his hand on her arm to try to lead her, but she pulled it free.

"Why are you here?" she asked Lockhart.

"The question is, why *you're* here," Sedgwick said. "You entered the U.S. under a false passport."

From the corner of his eye, Lockhart spotted Margot making her way back to the table, along the line of banquettes. He turned to face her, holding both his hands up, as if in surrender. She saw them from a few tables away, and her face narrowed in incredulity and disgust.

"Hello, Margot," Sedgwick said.

"Nice to see you, Al." To Lockhart, from years of marital experience, she sounded dangerously calm.

"Just some agency business. Ms. Song is coming to help us. I'm sorry we have to interrupt."

"We're having dinner. Can't this wait?"

"Do you know who this woman is?"

"It's the first time we've met, in fact. Tom never mentioned her to me, Al. Does that surprise you?"

Lockhart stepped forward. "Margie, let's talk about this—"

"Keep your hands off me," she growled, and the maître d' glanced over from the other side of the room. The men from the van were at the bar, nursing glasses of beer.

"You realize who she is?" Sedgwick said.

"I think it's rather obvious, isn't it?"

"I meant what her job is."

"She was telling me when you interrupted. I'd like to get back to our meal. We're catching up on things."

"You know she's traveling on Lizzie's passport?"

"Is she?" She turned to Mei. "Is that true?"

Mei nodded, and Margot laughed. "God, that's just the sort of stunt she would have pulled."

"Let me do my job, Margot," Sedgwick said. "I have to take her now. This is a matter of national security."

Margot sighed. "It always is. Okay, do what you have to do. I'm used to it. Mei?" Mei stood awkwardly and Margot embraced her. "I'll see you again, okay? Thanks for finding me."

"Great," Sedgwick said. "I'll leave Tom here. You two can have a talk. He'll explain. Guys?" He walked with Mei to the bar, and the van pair escorted her out of the room.

Margot sat and pushed her plate to one side, while Lockhart took Mei's place opposite. "I'm sorry, Margie," he said.

She glared at him. "You're sorry? Did this slip your mind? The fact that Lizzie had a twin? I should add it to the list, should I? I'm waiting, Tom, for a reason ever to speak to you again."

Lockhart could still picture Margot's face from the first time they'd met, when he had found her in the corner at an embassy event, getting quietly drunk. She had a few more lines but the same eyes. He'd betrayed her and she'd been angry with him many times. But even separated, amid tragedy, she was the woman he'd loved.

"I'll try," he said, beckoning the waiter.

36

When Mei woke, she was in a cell. She was wearing a gray jumpsuit, and she lay in bed. It felt as if she had lost consciousness for a long time and had woken from a dreamless sleep. She blinked and looked around, turning her neck to take in her room. The cell was nine feet by fifteen and was painted light gray with a concrete floor. An aluminum toilet and basin fixed to the wall in one corner provided the only contrast to the blankness of the box. She could have stood against any of the walls and blended in like a chameleon.

She blinked again. The air was dry, like the air in a sauna, and her eyes felt scratchy. It was coming through vents fixed around the walls near the floor. The door looked airtight, and the single window—a narrow slot about three feet long and not quite two feet high—was double-glazed and fixed flush with the wall, high up. It felt like being in a Mason jar, put away for storage. She could hear a faint hiss as the air was circulated into the cell and out again. The window was frosted, and the only other light came from a single diode in the ceiling.

A tray was thrust through a slot in the door with a clang, and she twisted around to see. It hung in midair and she heard nothing from the other side of the door. She put her feet on the floor, which felt warm under her soles, and walked over to take it. There was nowhere to sit apart from the bed, and she perched it on her knees, prodding dubiously. The meal looked as hermetically sealed as the room—two tepid and rubbery pancakes, a little tub of maple syrup, a pat of butter in foil, a plastic knife, a container of orange juice, and a cup of pitch-black coffee.

She remembered driving at night, in a convoy of two Escalades, through the lights of Washington and out over a bridge into darkness—suburbs and woods, then a highway, then an expressway. She saw little through the tinted windows, and the two CIA keepers in the front hardly spoke. There was only the faint crackle of a radio, then, some time after midnight, the moan of country music. She had slipped into a doze as they passed highways, sometimes bumping across the meridians on rough tarmac. It was a low-key, efficient journey, with none of the high-speed drama of Guangdong.

It was impossible to tell the time—her watch had been removed, and there was an unchanging light from the window. When she'd eaten what she could of the breakfast and washed her face in the basin, she lay down and stared at the ceiling. Her last glimpse of Lockhart had been through the windows of the Capital Grille, as she'd sat in the Escalade, waiting for the other car to arrive for the journey. She'd watched him sitting with Margot, talking.

A couple of hours seemed to have passed and the light had faded a little when the door opened. A guard came to take her, leading her along a low corridor with his head just inches from the ceiling. He put her in another cell, at a table with two chairs, and left again. There was nothing in it but the furniture and a matte panel on one wall. After a while, the man she'd seen with Lockhart entered and sat opposite. He looked tired, not just of Mei, but of the whole thing, as if she'd just been expelled from an expensive college. He put a file on the desk, unopened.

"What are you doing here?" he said.

"You brought me."

"Don't be clever, Ms. Song. You came into this country two days ago, on a U.S. citizen's passport, and broke into a private home. You work for a government agency in China associated with the Communist Party. Right there, there's enough to detain you for espionage and keep you inside for a very long time. Even if they wanted you back, we'd demand a higher price than they'd pay. So you don't have much on your side, except my goodwill, which has been strained by the games you've played with a bereaved woman who's my friend."

Margot's not your friend, Mei thought.

"Shall we start again?" Sedgwick said.

Mei nodded.

"What are you doing here?"

"I came here to see Margot Lockhart, the mother of my adopted sister. I want to go back to her."

Mei had spent the previous night in Lizzie's bed. After they'd talked, Margot had fetched her some towels and a pair of her daughter's pajamas. They fit exactly, and she lay there, warm and comfortable for the first time in days, looking at the paintings on the walls and a photograph of Lizzie playing soccer for her school, surrounded by her friends. It had been her parallel life, on the far side of the world.

Sedgwick's expression of vague irritation hardened into something more specific. "Well, that's not possible, is it, Ms. Song? I don't think Margot wants to take a murder suspect into her home. The authorities in Guangdong have placed an alert for you on their borders for the killing of"—he paused to consult the file—"Zhang Yao. That means you've committed felonies on two continents, and you belong in jail. You can stay in this one, or we can return you, in which case your life will get worse."

"I don't want to go back," Mei said.

"Then you'd better think of a way to help us," Sedgwick said, picking up the file and leaving.

Two days and nights passed before she saw Sedgwick again. Life slowed to a trickle in her cell. It became a kind of torture, just existing, sometimes using the toilet or putting water on her face, lying down and watching the ceiling, trying and failing to see something through the window. They didn't play loud music or waterboard her. They left her alone.

At dusk, the window darkened, but the rest of the cell remained identical—the same color, the same temperature, the same slight hissing sound. The light turned off later and came on again at dawn, taking its lead from nature but adding little. She slept in fitful bursts, dreamed lurid dreams—a rail journey through red hills, a luminous cavern, the sea beyond the river, black as night.

"What have you got for me?" Sedgwick said. He looked as disenchanted with her as before.

"I can't think of anything." It was true. After so long alone, it felt as if her brain had ceased working.

"Tell me about this man," Sedgwick took a photo from the file and turned it on the table between his fingertips so that it faced her. It was a grainy image of the Wolf, taken from across a street in Guangzhou, near the PLA headquarters. It looked a few years old.

"This is Lang Xiaobo, secretary of the Guangdong Discipline Commission."

"Known as the Wolf. Where is he now?"

"I don't know."

He stared at her and put the photo back into the file, then got up from the seat, as if to leave. She couldn't let him depart—she feared another two days of gray isolation.

"He was arrested," Mei said. "I saw him once—I was taken to see him. He was in a military base somewhere."

"In Guangdong?"

"I think so."

"Tell me about your sister."

"Secretary Lang brought me to the place where she died, near Dongguan. I saw her body. It looked as if she'd drowned."

Sedgwick sighed. "The problem is, I already know these things, and I know more than you've told me. She worked at Long Tan and she wasn't the only one to die. Twenty others have too. We know that he was investigating and that you helped him. Now, he is in *shuang-gui,* and so would you be if you had not killed the man they sent to fetch you. None of this is hard to discover."

"If you know it all, what do you want from me?"

"Make me an offer," Sedgwick said, leaving.

When Lockhart came, they let her outside. The guard gave her a pair of boots and a jacket and led her through the hallway to the end of the block, where he opened a door and she saw the sky. It was like the lid of a box had been removed, letting light flood in. He stood thirty feet away, on an expanse of green lawn, waiting for her to adjust to the glare.

"Come on, let's walk," he said.

It was a bright fall day. The sun was high in the sky, glinting off the foliage on the birch forest that stretched around them on all sides. She looked at her prison. It was a low block, finished in cedar wood and shingle, like a summer house without windows, at the edge of a wide lawn that led into the trees. It didn't look threatening.

"Where are we?" she said.

"Virginia. Camp Peary."

Her legs felt shaky from lack of exercise, and he slowed to let her catch up to him as they walked toward the woods. The lawn was mown, and the path between the trees was cut precisely and strewn with wood chips, maintained with rigor. The undergrowth had been cleared, leaving a yellow and brown carpet of fall leaves amid the trunks. They walked down a slope past a tennis court; the path ended at a lake. There was no one in sight, but Mei heard a faint echo of vehicles, as from another territory.

"How do you feel?" Lockhart asked.

Mei shrugged. They reached the edge of the lake and stood by the water. Two canoes rested on the shore, overturned for shelter. There weren't any boats on the water, only a view of trees.

The answer was: She was lost. No matter how imperfect her sister's life and its brutal end, she'd gained parents, family, identity. Mei was stateless and rootless, a child alone. She was in *shuanggui,* locked away anonymously beyond the reach of law, and it was oddly familiar. As a child, she'd been dumped in an orphanage, a nonperson in a nonplace.

Now, she was there again.

37

Lockhart returned the next day, and the guard gave her a raincoat to walk with him. He was in the same place on the lawn, water dripping off the hood of his jacket and his hands in his pockets. She'd been awake most of the night, wondering if she'd ever get out. When she walked up, he offered her an awkward hug, their coats rustling together. His face was pale, and it didn't look as if he had shaved that morning. They made a fine pair, she thought.

The lawn was soggy, and when they reached the end of the prepared path, by the side of the lake, he turned onto a narrow, muddy section by the water's edge and started to walk around it. She followed him in silence. The coat they'd given her was military—green camouflage, too long in the sleeves.

"How are you?" he asked.

"I'm okay."

"They're not mistreating you?"

"The food is horrible."

Lockhart gave a brief laugh. "It's the only torture they're allowed."

They reached a wooden hut, filled with rods and fishing nets, and he walked to a bench by the water. Mei waited for him to ask some more questions, but he just sat on it, staring at the lake. His body was clenched as the rain fell; he exuded misery. She felt sorry for him.

"Tom," she said. "Where did I come from?"

His hood rustled as he angled his face toward her, but she could only see the tip of his nose. "I don't know. It's an enormous country. Hundreds of millions of kids, lots of them in orphanages."

"You knew I was her sister."

Lockhart sighed and shook his head. "That's not a mystery, is it? You look the same."

"It was more than that."

"Was it?" He turned and stared into the distance, where a patrol boat skidded across the water, leaving a white trail.

"Margot said they didn't tell her about me in Guilin. They gave her my sister. Why did they hide me?"

"Look, Mei, it's your country," Lockhart snapped. "You work for the Party. You know more about how they do things than I do. I lived there for five years, and I never figured it out."

She'd expected to be interrogated, but she was asking questions and he hadn't stopped her yet.

"Tell me about Lizzie," she said.

"Lizzie? She was wonderful. It's hard to say that. 'Was,' not 'is.' I can't make sense of it. You know, you hear of kids in those orphanages having something wrong with them." He paused. "I'm sorry—"

She shook her head, not wanting him to stop.

"Anyway, she was perfect. Smart as a whip, very funny. She loved the U.S.—her life, I mean. I don't feel as if she missed China. She always wanted to go back, that's natural, but she did well here. Scholarships at school, a place at Princeton, she was terrific. Margot was great, like I knew she'd be. I was the problem."

She let her eyes ask the question.

"Margot must have told you. We'd had a great time together in Beijing, then we came home. She was happy here, but they stuck me on a desk in Langley, made me a case officer. I had to sit while the ops officers did the interesting stuff in the field. It wasn't a good time. I was drinking too much, and I had an affair." He grimaced. "Lizzie gave me such a hard time about it when she grew up—worse than Margot. I went abroad, I was in Nairobi and Hanoi for her teens. I was a poor excuse for a father. You didn't miss much."

"I would have had a sister. And a mother."

Lockhart patted his knee. "You're right. And it didn't hurt Lizzie.

She did fine. She was interested in international relations, and she spent a year in London at graduate school. I was so proud, even though I didn't have much to do with it. I used to visit her, in a cold apartment on the Pentonville Road."

"She was like you."

"I thought so. I took pride in it, stupidly, as if she was her father's daughter, despite my fuckups." The rain had eased, and Lockhart pushed his hood back and ran a hand through his hair. "One of her projects was on migrant workers in China. She wanted to go back, to make a difference. She had perfect Mandarin, and she joined a work- ers' rights NGO in Hong Kong. I thought that was a great idea, I didn't think she'd be in danger, except. . . ."

He stopped talking and, when she looked across, Mei saw a tear on his cheek. He didn't feel to her like her interrogator or the man who'd deceived her in the marsh, not anymore. He was the man who would have been her father, if Wing had made another choice.

His hand was still on his knee, and she put hers upon it. "Except for what?" she said.

"I'd left—" His voice croaked and he coughed. "I'd left the agency and become a consultant. There's so much work for people in my line now, you wouldn't believe. I was on contract with a company that paid off the Saudis on a weapons deal and got hit by the DOJ. They'd just settled when a lawyer called me. Poppy was going crazy over what was going on at Long Tan and needed someone. These kids were throwing themselves off buildings. It was bad publicity.

"I spoke Mandarin, I'd worked in Beijing, I knew people there. I was a good fit. I went to visit with Henry Martin, and he said he'd do anything to stop the deaths, but it was beyond his control. His phones and tablets were built there, but he didn't run the place. A Hong Kong guy called Cao Fu owned it. He'd told them he'd handle it, but he didn't do anything.

"I liked the project. I'd spend time with Lizzie, and we'd work on the same thing. I didn't realize that she'd become obsessed. She'd cross the border and spend hours talking to the workers by the gates. It upset her how they were treated. 'It could have been me,' she told me. She was angry that I was working for Martin. We'd bought her a

Poppy phone when she was a teenager, but she threw it away. She said she wouldn't be a Poppy fan girl anymore. I said Martin was trying to help, but she laughed.

"She was right about Long Tan. They took me on the sanitized tour, with workers all smiling happily in a six-bed dormitory, with lots of space. They introduced a psychologist they'd hired to counsel the workers and showed us the fields where they played soccer. But it all felt fake—the place was like a country where they could close the border at will. Lizzie introduced me to some of the workers, and they told me more. They had to work hard, but that wasn't the problem. It was secretive. They were split into teams, with different uniforms, separated from the others. None of them had met the kids who'd died.

"I couldn't get inside, so I paid a couple of them to be my agents. I asked them to let me know if they saw anything. I was in the Peninsula one night, and Lizzie arrived. She'd found out what I'd done, and she was really mad. She said it was typical of me—that I was exploiting them, they could lose their jobs. I told her there was nothing to worry about, and she said if I meant that, she'd do it herself. She'd go inside there and find out what was going on. It would be easy to get a job—they recruited all the time because so many had left. All she'd need was an identity.

"When I thought about it, I realized it could work. She was smarter and more inventive than any of them. She could find out what was wrong in there, and then I could get Poppy to fix it. It would be easy to buy an identity in Shenzhen—it was full of clubs where girls took money for favors. I needed one who would misplace it for a few weeks and hide at home. Lizzie and I planned the thing. Her identity, how long she'd stay inside, how we'd keep in touch. We had a great time.

"In July, she went in. She had no problem getting recruited—she just walked in and that was it. They put her on the Poppy line, which was perfect. The shifts were long and she was tired, but it was okay. It wasn't as bad as she'd feared. She'd call me from a café by the gate, so no one could overhear. The last time we spoke, she said she'd heard something. She missed the next two calls and I started to worry, but there was nothing I could do."

Lockhart clenched his jaw, remembering.

"Then the two girls I had been paying died—I was told they jumped off buildings. I hadn't heard from them in a while, and I'd thought something was wrong. Martin got me to visit the parents of the victims and offer them money to keep quiet. He wanted to keep it out of the press. Their parents both told me the same story—the kids had gotten new jobs and stopped calling, then turned up dead. I panicked. I tried to get back inside but they cut me off."

He took a stone, casting it across the lake, and faced her. "That's when Madame Zhou called me at the hotel," he said. "When they'd killed Lizzie, like they killed the rest."

"Why would they kill them? It makes no sense."

"Not then. But Martin called me at the Peninsula just after Lizzie vanished. He said they'd discovered something."

38

Poppy had built its flagship DC store in a former Postal Service building on Farragut Square. The company had bought the structure and stripped it out, lofting away the safe by crane, restoring the 1930s tiles, and installing a glass staircase that led to a mezzanine. The limestone façade was blasted to gleaming white, and sunlight shone through polished windows. It looked as glamorous as one of the city's monuments as they sat in the Escalade.

"Why should we trust her?" Sedgwick said. He was in the front seat, looking back at Lockhart.

"She can help," Lockhart said.

"Is that true, Ms. Song?"

Mei nodded. It was enough for her to be out of Camp Peary, even if she didn't know what would happen next. She wanted to stick with Lockhart—she'd found herself trusting him, if only because he seemed to be hurting as much as she was. After five days alone in a cell, she needed a companion.

The store was nearly empty as they stepped through the door. Outside, some late commuters rushed along the street to nearby offices in suits and sneakers. Inside, a pair of tourists held a Poppy tablet, leaning close to admire it. The curved edges were beveled, and the familiar logo glowed on the screen. An assistant, wearing the store uniform of jeans and a white T-shirt with the pink Poppy logo, waited, smiling. Sedgwick led the way up the staircase.

"Alan? I'm David. Welcome." A lanky man, sporting stubble and black-framed glasses, put a hand on Sedgwick's arm at the top, making him flinch. "I'll show you to Henry."

He walked them behind a counter and through a white oak door to a workshop, where engineers were stripping the faces from phones and tablets and delving inside. At the end, he held up his pass to the entry plate. A second door pulled back, revealing another room with a long oak table.

Henry Martin was standing at the end, nodding intently at a young man who was talking to him in a low voice. The man had a thin frame and a scrubbed, pink face: an eager student.

"Tom!" Martin bounded across the room and slapped Lockhart on the back. Mei took two steps back, overwhelmed. She had watched videos of Martin unveiling new products, praising the little miracles as he paced the stage.

"You must be Mei. *Ni hao*," he said, turning to her. "This is an honor for me." He bowed and presented a card, holding it with both hands. On it were a Poppy logo and two words:

HENRY MARTIN

"I'm sorry. I do not have my card," she said.

"No problem," Martin said, smiling like a spotlight. He placed an arm around her shoulder and drew her into the room. "I'm fascinated by your life. I would love you to meet Jade, my daughter. She's from Sichuan."

"That would be nice." She spoke faintly, feeling overwhelmed.

"Okay, here we are." Sedgwick looked irritated by the effusiveness of Martin's welcome, which hadn't included him. He stood by the door with Lockhart, separated from his prisoner.

"It's great that you came." Martin's attention was still on Mei. He sat at the head of the table and pointed to the chairs nearby. "Mei, you sit there. Tom, Al, there. Joe—" He waved at the man he'd been talking to. "Take a place. Okay, we're set."

The man who had led them in placed a metal case on the table and took out two boxes. One was filled with small screwdrivers and other tools, set in individual slots under a Perspex lid. The other was a white cardboard container with a silver Poppy logo from which Martin extracted a tablet.

"Want to hold it?" He passed it to her and she saw the petals of the Poppy logo grow and sparkle on the screen, like an improved version of nature. "This is our new one, out last week. It's twice as fast, with five times the graphics capability. It's so beautiful. It's blowing people's minds." He pressed the button to switch it off.

"Why don't you show us, Henry?" Lockhart said.

"Okay. It's pretty remarkable. If they weren't screwing with my business, I'd be impressed."

Martin lifted the Perspex lid and took two tools from the box. Then he pushed them into two tiny side-slots and twisted. The aluminum plate clicked and slid free. Putting it on the desk, he took a screwdriver, unfastening six screws from the frame inside. The interior of the plate was intricately ridged, like a coastal shelf. He unclipped a few more components and then the device lay on the table, reduced to pieces of aluminum, silicon, and glass.

The logic board held several chips around a square semiconductor, an inch wide, printed with a Poppy. He tapped each in turn. "Flash, flash, I/O controller, and this is the master chip. Most of these are commodities—it's the way we combine them that matters. But this is the brain."

"So tell us what's wrong," Lockhart said.

"We design the chips, then they're made in Taiwan and shipped to Long Tan, where the tablets are built. The problem is, this isn't our chip. It looks like it, works the same, the same specs, but it's fake."

"How do you know?"

"The serial number doesn't match anything from our facilities. It's come from nowhere."

"Why?" Mei stared at the tiny chip. It looked as if it belonged there, with its pink logo on black silicon. It had found its way into the heart of the device, like a cuckoo in a nest.

Martin laughed. "That's the question. They do knockoffs of our products in China all the time, but this is inside our own device. We pay for the chip, and it's assembled at Long Tan. They've gone to a lot of trouble for nothing."

"I doubt it," Sedgwick said.

"So do I, but I haven't solved it," said the young man Martin had been talking to when they'd arrived. His voice was low, and he stared at the floor as he spoke. "It needs more time."

"Is this the only American one?" Sedgwick asked Martin.

"So far, but they've only just been launched and we were lucky to find it so fast. There have to be others."

Mei picked up the tablet's box. It was creamy white, with a pink line around the edge, and a rainbow-colored anti-forgery hologram in the shape of a poppy stamped on the bottom.

"I think I saw one of these," she said.

Lockhart's apartment was a walk-up in a limestone on S Street with bay windows at the front and a fire escape at the rear. He'd bought it after his marriage broke up and, at first, it had felt small and empty without his family. He'd come to appreciate his freedom and the solitude, but Lizzie's death had brought the loneliness back.

His visits to Mei at the Farm had been the only thing he'd looked forward to in a long time. He had driven south, taking his time across Virginia, as the radio played. With Lizzie gone, she was the closest he had to a daughter. When she emerged from her cell in her oversized coat, jogging a few paces for exercise, it almost made him smile. For all the pressure Sedgwick was piling on her, he knew that someday they would let her go, and he feared what her life would become.

He brought out his French press, grinding beans and heaping powder into it, then placed it on a tray with three cups and cookies from the corner store. He didn't know the etiquette for a Party official who'd been in custody, but Sedgwick was talking politely to Mei in the other room about the China of the 1970s. He'd had a change of heart about her since she'd volunteered her tidbit in the Poppy store. "Let's find somewhere to talk," he'd said as they left.

"Mei's telling me about the Four Seasons in Guangzhou," Sedgwick said as Lockhart brought in the tray. "I had no idea."

"It's quite something." Lockhart looked at Mei, perched on a sofa he'd bought at Crate & Barrel, picking it at random to fill the place.

"You want to know what I saw." She cut through the pause as Lockhart poured coffee.

"We do," Sedgwick said.

"If I tell you, will you help me?"

"I'll try," Lockhart said. They weren't just words, an interrogator's promise to keep a subject talking. He meant it.

"You talked about Secretary Lang," she said to Sedgwick. "I went to see him one night in his home. When I was there, I saw a box in his sitting room, like the one Mr. Martin showed us today. I noticed it because I thought it was odd. He isn't the kind who would buy one. I thought it was a gift."

"Did you see the device?" Lockhart asked.

"The box was sealed. He hadn't opened it."

She was formidable, Lockhart thought. Getting off the Farm and back into her clothes—Lizzie's, really—had restored her. He believed her story, although it was the flimsiest of evidence, and there was no way to be sure.

"Why should we trust you?" Sedgwick asked, expressing Lockhart's unspoken question.

For the first time since Lockhart had encountered her at the Golden Dragon, Mei smiled. "I'll prove it," she said.

39

As Lockhart walked over the little bridge to Shamian Island, he saw the first of the wedding couples. The woman was perched by a flowerbed in a meringue-like dress and the photographer was arranging her husband by her side, instructing him to gaze at her lovingly. They weren't the only couple there—two more were posing nearby, under the colonial buildings. He could see why photographers were drawn to this spot. It was like stepping from twenty-first-century Guangzhou into Canton, the nineteenth-century trading post of the British Empire.

He'd been in the Nanfang International Electronic building near the banks of the Pearl River, and his pockets clanked with the contraband he'd bought for a few dollars at the stalls—the plate of a Poppy phone, a pair of headphones, a replica Samsung Galaxy with an operating system that looked like a Japanese video game. All fake, despite the sign above the entrance warning of the city's crackdown on piracy. Nobody seemed to care.

Two men who had been lounging on a glass-topped display case when they entered had ushered him back when he'd shown interest in the parts. He'd traced a finger along the grooves of a pirated case. Yes, they could do more—a dollar a part for orders of a thousand or more. They had a supplier in Longhua. The cops couldn't find him—he moved around every few weeks, and they could be bribed. Anyway, there was no need to worry. There were plenty of other places—Guangdong was full of ghost factories. They'd set up their equipment one night and be gone the next.

The local mania for commerce amazed him. Apart from food, it was the only thing that counted for the Cantonese. In Beijing, people wanted to know your family, what province you came from. In Guangzhou, nobody cared. The older generation was already well off. People who had land built apartments and rented them out, living easily. They had enough money to pay the taxes on a second child if they wanted one. They paid lip service to the Party, but only for the connections it offered.

He went into the Starbucks store along the promenade and took a cappuccino to a table. The place was empty save for an American couple drinking and reading. He instantly recognized their looks of nervousness and longing. They were here to adopt a baby. They would be staying in the White Swan Hotel, in a group of eager parents-to-be, waiting for a call. Lately, he'd found himself wishing he'd gone with Margot to Guilin. After he'd made his bet with Lang, he had wanted to keep clear of the venture. He had felt guilty, fearing that someone at the orphanage who knew what he'd done would catch his eye. When Margot had returned with Lizzie, it had been a relief—she had displayed no sign of knowing. Now he regretted not being with her at that moment.

A young woman entered the café and stood at the counter. Her black hair was tied in a topknot and she gripped her backpack between her knees as she counted the change for her espresso. Her face was pale, with only a dab of red lipstick. Mei's description had been accurate, Lockhart noted approvingly. The woman carried her coffee to his table.

"Hello, Mr. Lockhart. I'm pleased to meet you. I feel as if we know each other," she said.

"Ms. Lai."

"And how is Song Mei?"

"She is well, thank you."

"I'm sorry about your daughter." She lifted her eyes and gazed at him. Lockhart liked that she did not look away or behave awkwardly—he found it easier.

"Thank you."

"I got your message." She blew on her cup and took a sip. "It was unusual, I must say, but interesting. We can talk about that, but I want to ask you something. Who do you represent?"

"I'm employed by Poppy."

"Not the CIA?"

"The agency is taking an interest."

"You worked there, am I right?"

"Some years ago."

"You see, the Ministry of State Security does not usually cooperate with the CIA. It's just not what we do. We don't regard it as an ally. Not like the Democratic People's Republic of Korea, for example."

"The suspicion is mutual."

"I imagine so." Feng smiled.

"But I thought you would be interested in my information. It might help to foster understanding."

Feng nodded and sipped her espresso, leaving some dark foam on her lips. Then she bent over to lift her backpack. She unzipped it and lifted out a white cardboard package with a Poppy emblem on the side.

"We *were* interested," she said. "It came as a surprise, I have to admit. Nobody had informed us."

"Nobody?" Lockhart said.

He was starting to like this young woman. She'd even smiled faintly when she'd mentioned North Korea, as if they both knew what kind of ally it was. He wondered if she was telling the truth. If so, it was astonishing. He was used to one agency not telling another one what was going on—it was harder to get information out of the FBI than out of a teenager. But it was dangerous for any Chinese official to try to starve the MSS of evidence.

"Nobody." Feng zipped the tablet back into her bag.

"So it might be useful to talk further?"

"It might."

They left the Starbucks, Feng with her backpack on her shoulder, and walked over the promenade to the Customs Hotel. Lockhart looked around him, but he could not see anyone except for tourists, photographers, and wedding couples.

"Did you bring an escort?"

"They allow me out alone," Feng said, walking through the entrance as he held the door open for her. They ascended stairs to the second-floor balcony that looked out on the terrace. Lockhart knocked at a room and a pair of eyes appeared at the edge of the door as it opened a crack.

"This is a raid. Open up," Feng said.

Mei opened the door fully and stood, dressed in Lizzie's clothes—jeans and a T-shirt.

"Look at you," Feng said, throwing her backpack on one of the beds, then hugging her. "Welcome back, Miss America. I missed you."

Mei looked questioningly over her shoulder at Lockhart, who nodded. She had been pacing the room fretfully for an hour, worrying about the risk she was taking. Feng's voice was the best sound she'd heard for weeks.

"I missed you too," she said.

"Okay, love-in over," Feng said, detaching herself. "Tom told me you thought of this. It was smart. I can't make promises, but I know people who would forgive you a lot for it. There's a lot for them to forgive."

"I had no choice, Feng. He was going to—"

"Forget it. He was asking for trouble, that boy. I'd have done it myself. Now then—" Feng sat cross-legged on the floor and took out the Poppy tablet and a file of papers.

Lockhart twisted himself onto the floor next to her, unable to cross his legs like her. He propped himself on one hand instead while Mei arranged her limbs gracefully by his side.

"Okay," Feng said, tapping the tablet. "We found this in Secretary Lang's house, at the back of a drawer. The cops missed it, of course. Who knows why we pay them? It was like you said. We stripped it and found the chip. Someone went to a lot of trouble to put it in there, but we don't know why."

"Nor do we," Lockhart said.

"I thought the NSA could crack anything."

"I thought *you* could," Lockhart jousted in return.

"So we're stuck."

"I've got a suggestion. You're the government. Why don't you walk into Long Tan and raid the place? Send in the PLA. They wouldn't let me in, but they can't stop you, can they?"

"Yes, they can. This is Guangdong."

"So what?"

"Guangdong isn't run by Beijing. The local Party controls it. Everything goes through Chen. If we want to get inside Long Tan, we need permission from him, and we won't get that. This is his kingdom, and that place is his biggest asset. Nobody in Beijing likes it. They don't like him acting like he's Mao and singing red songs. They don't want him on the standing committee. They'd love to topple him. But they need evidence, and there isn't any."

Mei remembered Chen's voice on the roof, taking the Wolf away. It all came back to Chen. He could not be investigated; he prevented anyone getting into the factory. Pan had been following his orders when she had sent Yao to arrest Mei. The people who had killed Lizzie were too. As long as he was in power, they were playing around the edges, finding clues as to what was going on, but remaining in the darkness. There was only one way to get through.

"Do you think Lizzie found it?" she said.

"She might have. We'll never know."

"I want to try."

"No way." Lockhart shook his head.

"That's crazy," Feng said.

Mei had waited for so long. Since she'd seen her sister for the first time. In the cell in Virginia, as she'd pined for release. When she'd flown to Hong Kong, under guard in the CIA plane. She had searched for the chance to rescue Lizzie's life, to make things better again. Despite their protests, she saw them wondering. They were professionals, after all. It might be reckless, but it was their only hope. If she didn't want to carry on living in limbo, trapped between China and America without a home in either place, it was the only chance for her, too.

40

The minibus drove through the gates at seven-thirty in the morning, with the heat coming. The sun was rising over the campus, poking through stray clouds. It was a hot day—could be in the nineties, the driver said, turning up the air-conditioning—and the old women picking through the street markets had hoisted their parasols. The morning catch from the Dongguan employment agency amounted to three: two Shenzhen students and Jiang Jia, the twenty-five-year-old daughter of a tungsten miner from Heyuan.

Outside the single-story recruitment center inside the campus, the guard took Jia's identity card. She stretched her arms in the sunshine as she waited for him to copy down her details.

"Stand still!" he said sharply, moving to the students.

Jia obeyed, shifting into the shade cast by the building only when he had turned away. Her brown hair was shorn to the collar—not the fashionable cut she could find in the city, and soon would. She wore a cotton jacket, T-shirt, jeans, and Rocky sneakers. Her belongings—clothes, toiletries, a stuffed panda with black eyes like hers, family photos, and a sticker-covered radio—were in a canvas bag.

She stood for two hours, wanting a drink of water but unable to leave her spot. The building faced south and the concrete wall radiated heat. At ten o'clock, they were taken inside and allowed to sit while they waited to be screened by an official. Three characters were marked on the wall above her head: "Love, Respect, Discipline." There was still no food or drink, and a guard confiscated a carton of apple juice as one student took it from her bag.

The official looked up when Jia was finally called at two o'clock. "Identity card." She studied it. "What's your birthdate?"

"September 12, 1988."

"Ethnicity?"

"Hakka."

"Why are you here?"

"I moved to Shenzhen two months ago. I worked in a restaurant, but I don't have residency, and it is expensive to live. A friend says this is a good place. They take care of you."

"The best, as long as you work hard." The woman appraised her. "You want to work, you're not a slacker?"

"I'm a hard worker."

"Good." She glanced down at the card. "Jiang Jia. There are many opportunities to prosper, if you prove yourself. You have chosen a lucky time to come. We are very busy. Plenty of overtime."

"I want it. My brother is joining the Army. We need money for his place, and my father cannot work. He has lung disease."

"What are your ambitions?"

Jia stared at her hands, folded together in her lap and smiled shyly. She was embarrassed.

"I love Poppy phones—they are cool. I heard you make them here. I would like to do that."

The woman smiled. "So you don't want to be a fashion designer or an artist, like other girls here."

"Oh, no. I couldn't do that. I'm not that smart. My brother is the clever one of our family."

"Well, maybe you'll get your ambition, Jiang Jia. Who knows? I want you to sign this paper and this one, too. It's for voluntary overtime, so you will be first in line to help your brother. The nurse will check you, and we'll take your photograph. We'll find you a job to do."

By four o'clock, they were on their way. One of the pair of students was still with Jia. The other hadn't made it through, but her companion wasn't worried—she was too busy gazing at the new world she'd entered. As the bus drove along an avenue toward the dormitories, the shift changed and the side streets filled with bodies.

Some rushed toward a supermarket to beat the lines, others sat down in the shade. Jia could not see anyone who looked as old as thirty. Even the uniformed guards, patrolling in pairs in electric vehicles, were kids.

They were passing a soccer field when two men, both in jeans and tunics, ran by. One chased the other and, as the first reached the edge of the field, his pursuer leapt on him, dragging him to the ground and punching him on the head. The bus sped on, and Jia turned to watch through the back window. They rolled on the ground, and one man landed a punch before two guards ran from a building. As they reached the fighters, one guard drew a nightstick and thrashed the bodies, while his partner kicked at them from the other side. The bus turned a corner, cutting off the view.

The driver shook his head at the man sitting beside him—another recruit—and they laughed.

"Those Uighurs are always making trouble," the driver said.

"They should be sent back to terrorist-land."

"When the guards are done with them, they'll throw them out. If they can still walk, after a good beating."

They halted at an old building with high brick walls, and a supervisor led them inside in a group.

"Women here, men there," she called.

The old warehouse smelled sweet—it must have been used to store a fragrant crop once. Now, it had been split up into boxlike rooms leading off a corridor. The supervisor collected their identity cards and led them along the passage, pointing them to the rooms where they would sleep.

Jia's dormitory came second. The supervisor handed her a tag with a number and pointed inside. It was on the first floor, with windows that had been draped with cloths to dim the light. The room was crammed with triple-decked bunks, like a night train, and women were dozing or reading or flicking phones in about half the beds—the others were empty. Jia walked slowly through, searching for her bunk.

She found it in the corner, on the bottom of a stack of three. The upper bunks were taken, but no one was in them. Setting down her bag, she took out most of her things, laying the clothes in a box next to the bunk. She unfolded the sheet and blankets on the bed and made it. Then she tucked her panda by the pillow and sat, hearing whispers and faint music. She still hadn't eaten.

At seven-fifteen, the other bunks started to stir, their occupants climbing down and putting on shoes. They drifted out of the room in a crowd, emptying it. Two walked past Jia without pausing. For a while, she was by herself. Then she heard noises, and ten women entered the room, laughing and joking. Two came to the bunks above her but did not acknowledge her, changing clothes before wandering out again. Picking up her card, she followed them.

Outside, she joined the crowd walking across a courtyard to another building. It wasn't like the eruption of the afternoon—there was no urgency in the progress. Some paused to smoke, and others strolled, their arms entwined. She smelled the destination from fifty feet away—a canteen. She walked past women washing at a trough and entered a dining hall packed with trestle tables. The intense warmth and the odor of the cooking tempted her to pile a tray with food, but her card was empty.

There was nothing for her here. She walked back to the dormitory and reached into her bag, retrieving her radio. Then she took a jacket and went out into the night, which was still humid. Four men in tracksuits were taking wild kicks at a soccer ball on the field that stretched in front of her, lofting it high into the air. She headed for a bench on the far side and sat alone, tuning her radio.

She knew this place—the dormitory blocks deep inside the campus and the smoking chimneys. The glow of the furnaces about half a mile away, closer to the river. She was familiar with its nighttime presence—the shapes that loomed in the dark sky and the whine of electric carts.

She took the badge and looked at her photo, cursing the haircut she'd suffered. The badge was like the other one, but, with another name—not Tang Liu, but Jiang Jia. They were flags of convenience, identities stolen or borrowed. She didn't know if Feng had found this one or concocted it. It had come with everything she'd needed—a *hukou* resident permit, a high school card, a story. She had practiced for two days as Lockhart quizzed her about Jia's family, the place they lived, and her father's illness from the tungsten mine.

Mei turned on the radio, with the volume low. It was a Han opera, the high voices swooping like birds. When she plugged in earphones, the music died and she could hear only a hiss.

She spoke quietly. "Hello?"

"Where are you, Song Mei?" Lockhart asked.

"Inside. No problems."

"Are you okay?"

"Hungry, but okay."

"Be careful."

The hiss resumed and, when she extracted the cord, the voices declaimed their love again. Mei walked back to the dormitory slowly, hoping to find a cake or even fruit—any scrap of comfort.

41

"Love. Respect. Discipline."

The instructor intoned the words slowly and solemnly from the front of the training room. It was eight o'clock in the morning, the start of the day shift, and Mei sat with ten others behind Formica desks, trying to look eager. There was no air-conditioning and the room smelled of sweat, but she was at least doing something, rather than roaming around, fearing discovery.

The man pointed to the girl beside Mei. "You. What are our values?"

The girl was nervous, and faltered as she repeated the words. "Respect. Discipline. . . . Love."

"Wrong. You?" He turned to Mei. She tried to appear eager, but he looked like a time-server of the kind the Party seemed to attract to positions of petty authority. His stomach bulged over the belt of his regulation pants, and he'd greased a lick of black hair to his head.

"Love. Respect. Discipline."

"Correct. Love comes first. Love always comes first at Long Tan. How many of you know our founder's story?"

No hands were raised, and he pursed his lips sullenly, as if the class had already proved itself unworthy. Mei kept her eyes fixed on him. Every official was a door to be unlocked.

"Cao Fu was born in Hubei in 1949, the year of the revolutionary victory. His parents were peasants, but they loved their son, and they taught him that he could be great. Cao fulfilled their love by building a business that is the envy of the world. It shows other nations what our people can achieve when they have unity born of love. Love of the family and of others. Long Tan is a family. We eat together, we sleep in the same house, and we work as a team. We are building a new world."

He nodded several times. "This is a good way to work, isn't it? With love for others. Isn't it?"

"Yes. Very good," Mei said firmly, and the others joined in, murmuring the word obediently.

"Respect." The instructor was now on a roll. "We respect each other. Cao trusts you to join his workplace. Weaklings are turned away. Everyone in this room already has our respect. You will be paid very well, you will eat good food. There are many things on our campus. Feel free, we want you to enjoy them. But treat our instructions with respect. We know what is best for you."

"We are honored." This time, the student next to Mei was the fastest to respond, earning a nod from the instructor.

"Discipline. Cao was taught discipline by his loving parents. Without discipline, he could not have created this company. He would not be a billionaire and own a private jet. He could not show his love by building a mansion for his mother. He was hungry, but he never wavered. You will have a far easier time than Cao Fu did. Ten hours a day? No! He worked fourteen. Six days a week? No, seven days! He wasn't paid for overtime work. He wasn't pampered."

The whole class murmured approvingly before anyone could grab the lead, and the instructor beamed. Mei nodded, smiling the way that Pan did, to lend her own authority to others.

"Now, to show you respect, we will have a break. Stretch your legs! Enjoy our tea, made with our own Long Tan leaves, prepared especially for us. Welcome to our happy family."

Outside, the ground was wet with rain from an earlier shower and it steamed in the sunshine. The girl who'd messed up her reply to the instructor smiled shyly at her as she sipped tea.

"He was friendly. I've heard stories about how unhappy people are here. But I feel better now. I am Han Jun. What is your name?"

"Jiang Jia," Mei said. She envied the girl for being so easily pleased by a free cup of tea. She'd been as trusting herself not long ago, but that innocence had been snatched from her, leaving distrust and doubt.

"I'm from Guizhou," Jun said. "I came to Guangdong to study but I need to earn money. The courses are very expensive."

When they were called back, the instructor was grinning as if he couldn't believe their luck.

"I have exciting news. Our plan for the day has changed. We usually spend time practicing the tasks you must master. But we are so busy, we have so much to do, that you will go to your new positions to allow you to learn faster. It is an amazing privilege. Our finest workers will teach you. I will take two of you, and supervisors will escort the others."

He consulted a list. "Jiang Jia and Han Jun. Come with me."

A golf cart waited outside, and the instructor turned to address them as it bumped up the avenue.

"This is a special day, and you are luckiest of all. Guess which line you have been chosen to join?"

Looking at his glowing face, Mei wondered if he could be as much of an idiot as he appeared. Had he been brainwashed into this state of euphoria at everything that Long Tan did, or was he a fraud?

"Might it be Poppy?" She was able to slip into the voice of Jia easily—that naive wonder was how she'd felt on her first morning in Guangzhou when she had arrived in the city from Guilin, forever ago.

"Yes!" He slapped the seat delightedly. "You are so lucky, girls. You will build these magical devices."

The plant was in the newest part of the complex, a fifteen-minute drive away. From a distance, it looked like a hangar by the side of a runway—a white structure with an arched roof, punctuated by a line of windows about a hundred feet in the air. The walls below were solid, offering no clue as to what was happening inside. To penetrate it, Mei, Jun, and the instructor had to pass through two sets of electronic doors, separated by a hallway. The second door opened with a pop, as if the vacuum inside had been punctured.

In the changing rooms, a woman supervisor gave them each a set of slip-on rubber shoes, white overalls, and cotton caps. She mimed how to fold their hair under the cap, and tie it at the back. Mei looked into the mirror and a gowned technician stared back at her, one disguise layered upon another.

The instructor clapped his hands as they walked out. "Excellent. Let's take a look. You have never seen anything like it."

He led them into an elevator, and the doors opened two levels up, onto a walkway high above the factory floor. Mei pressed her back to the rear wall of the elevator as the instructor walked out, oblivious to the height. She saw tiny, white figures through the slats and felt faint.

"Come on!" He waved to Mei, with Jun by him. "This is your only chance to see the view!"

Fixing a smile on her face, Mei grasped the handrail on both sides of the walkway and strode toward him, fixing her eyes on his face. She didn't like looking at him, but it was better than gazing down. As she reached him, trying not to tremble, he gestured expansively at the view.

"Wow!" Jun cried.

Mei pulled one arm over and clamped it to the rail on the open side, then dragged her stare from him to the far side of the facility, a few hundred feet away. In the canyon below, at the bottom of her field of vision, white shapes twitched and moved. She kept her focus blurred.

"There. One billion dollars of investment. The finest factory in all of China—that's where you will work. Now let's go and try."

"Wonderful," Mei said, already scurrying to the elevator.

Even on the ground, the scale of the plant was stunning. Hundreds of workers were packed like worker bees, each with an allocated task. Mei saw eight assembly lines, each several hundred feet long, along which frames were slowly passing, with parts being clipped into place and screws fastened. The hum of the conveyor belt was the only sound. Some workers sat silently on stools and others stood, taking parts from plastic bins with one movement and fixing them with a second. Supervisors watched nearby, in case of errors. It was a giant, human machine.

"This is assembly. The parts are delivered over there." The instructor pointed to bays on the far side of the hangar, where forklift trucks were unloading boxes from huge trucks. They were scanned by teams of workers and unpacked into bins, ready to be digested.

"This is amazing," Jun said.

"Isn't it? Now we'll go to work."

They found a space by the end of the line, where the audio port was clipped on the frame and the structure folded, like metal origami, into its final shape. A team of six was finishing the job—fastening four tiny screws into the frame with miniature electric tools. Mei stood by a girl with bitten fingernails and strands of hair snaking from her cap. She watched as the worker held each frame, fixed her screws, and with two prods of a tool—*zzzp, zzzp*—sealed one side. Then the boy opposite her fixed the other side.

They did the same again, and again. It was hypnotic to watch. After an hour of it, Mei's feet were sore and she was bored, but she couldn't move. A supervisor watched the other workers while the smiling instructor observed her and Jun. Everyone was locked in position until, at four-thirty, a buzzer sounded. The line stopped, and the girl by Mei put down her tools as chatter replaced the electronic hum.

The other workers walked off the line, leaving only Mei and Jun standing there with two supervisors and the instructor.

"One hour until overtime starts. Now we can start welcoming you into Long Tan's family. Would you like that?"

"I am eager for the opportunity," Mei said quickly.

They stood at the line, trying to fix the screws in place as supervisors passed them tablets. It was far harder than Mei had imagined. The tiny screws slipped in her long fingers, and twice she stabbed herself with the sharp tool.

"Faster! Faster!" the instructor cried happily. "Now you can respect yourself. Now you learn to work."

Fuck eight generations of your ancestors, thought Mei.

"I love my job," she said.

42

Mei found him on her fourth evening, after the buzzer had signaled the end of the overtime shift. She had been moved to the start of the line, where her task was to clip a spring into the frame as it started its journey through many pairs of hands. The sound of the buzzer jolted her, so deep was the trance she'd trained herself to enter.

Her fingers were raw, but she'd learned to place the screw in the slot silently and efficiently, to avoid getting caught by the spring. She did her task as it had been designed, and the supervisors looked past her, on the hunt for other miscreants. A public apology to Long Tan, written by the woman who'd stood in her place before, was taped nearby. The offender had left, and in a few days, Mei had seen many faces come and go. The turnover was so rapid that she could hardly remember the faces of the departed—it was a shifting, fleeting community.

Nobody wanted to stay. They'd come there because it was easy to get a job, and it gave them a start in the city. But they all hoped for a better life: model, pop star, fashion designer—their dreams were impossibly big. She'd stopped worrying that somebody who had known Lizzie would recognize her, despite her tinted contact lenses, shorn hair, and makeup. She realized that being identified at Long Tan was as likely as being spotted in the street in Guangzhou.

Mei limped down the line to where Jun was gathering her things. Her feet and legs did not trouble her as long as she was concentrating on her assembly tasks. But at the end of the shift, they started to complain. She longed to soak her muscles in a hot shower, but anyone who lingered provoked angry shouts from the crowd in the hallway. She sat by Jun on the golf cart to the dormitory, both silent until they'd had their food. They were in a line of buses and electric buggies whipping along the avenue. Mei was resting her eyes on the horizon at the day's last light when she saw him.

It was a snapshot from the corner of her eye as he passed, but she knew it was him from his bearing. He sat erect in the front of a golf cart, by the driver, his hand wrapped around the handle of his cane.

"Stop!" Mei called to the driver.

"What?" Jun murmured. She was half-asleep, jolting awake only when they hit a bump.

"See you later." Mei tripped in her rush to abandon the vehicle as it halted, running across the avenue to another vehicle that was heading back the way they had come. He'd disappeared into the distance and she pressed her foot to the floor, willing the driver to accelerate after him. His cart had passed out of sight beyond a row of trees, but she saw him as they caught up. He'd stepped from the vehicle and was walking into an apartment block.

The man had vanished again by the time she got inside. She stood in the lobby, listening to a ping-pong game echoing from a recreation room along a hallway. Then she heard the clicking of a cane in the distance. She circled the lobby to isolate the sound and found a corridor leading to a hall. As she ran along it, the door at the end closed behind him, the tip of his cane darting through.

It was a canteen, but not the kind she was used to, where hundreds of workers crammed around serving stations for meat and vegetables. Even as they ate, they were watched. Last night, an official had stopped Jun as she tipped her remains into a bin and told her to finish her rice. It was poor discipline to leave it because it was plentiful, he warned; Cao had gone hungry when he was a child.

There were no spies in this restaurant. It was for managers, who were allowed to eat in peace. Mei waited until he'd collected his food and settled at a table alone. Then she took her chance. When she sat opposite, he stared at her in shock as she took out a contact lens to show him one green eye. His jaw fell open, showing a maw of half-chewed food. His face was as delicate as a butterfly, his eyelashes long and fine. He gulped in shock.

"They said you were dead." As he spoke, he half-rose in his seat and Mei placed her hand on his to reassure him and hold him in his place. She looked around at the other seats, but nobody had noticed.

"I'm not dead. I'm here."

"Who are you?" He reached across and plucked her badge. "Jiang Jia. This is crazy. This doesn't make sense. You're a spirit." Panicked, he tried to stand again and she grasped his wrist.

"Listen to me. You wanted to talk after you rescued me. I had to go, but I'm here now. I'll tell you everything."

"Give me your badge."

"Will you let me explain?"

He nodded, and she unclipped the badge and handed it across the table, studying him carefully in case he panicked. As he looked at it, he mouthed the words of her alias and stared at her.

"I knew it was wrong. I said it was those stupid strips—they couldn't even get the date right. They said you'd died on the Monday night, but I'd seen you that week. I saved your life."

"Liu was your friend, wasn't she?"

"She was my dear friend. You're not her."

Mei saw his brain working slowly, piecing together evidence. "I'm a relative of hers. A close relative. I need you to come with me. There's something very important I have to tell you. If you were Liu's friend, if you loved her, you must do it in her memory. She would want you to."

"I burned money at the temple. I prayed for her." He talked to himself like an automaton.

"Thank you. Let's take a walk."

He nodded silently and, walking over to the bin, tipped his remaining food in. Nobody told him off for wasting it, and he was still chewing on his last mouthful in a trance as Mei led him out. She got him onto an electric cart and sat at the back, holding his hand. He gripped it blankly, as if his brain no longer understood but his body was set on cooperating. They stayed on board until the last stop, by the compound gates, where she led him through to the street. It was nine o'clock, and a crowd of workers stood, chatting and smoking.

The *Hui Chun* poster was still in the apartment entrance opposite the Internet café, one corner flapping down. She ignored the elevator and climbed the stairs, with the man following her. On the second floor, she knocked on an apartment door, raising her face to a spy hole. An elderly caretaker with a long beard opened the door, nodded at Mei, and led them through to a room.

Lockhart was there, sitting at a desk by a window with a view of a dingy interior courtyard. The desk was piled up with electronics—a desktop computer, a laptop, and two hard drives—but he was not using them. Instead, he scribbled on a pad of paper. When he noticed them, he walked over to lock the door and then hugged Mei. It was the first time she'd emerged from Long Tan since entering the factory.

"This is him," she said in English.

"Are you okay?" he asked, holding her by the shoulders. She nodded.

"Great work, Mei. You're good at this."

"Wait," the man said, rattling the handle of the door. "I should not be here. Let me leave."

Lockhart stood in front of him. "You'll be here a few minutes and then you can go. You're not in danger."

"If they catch me, I am," the man said. He wrestled with the handle and opened the door, then stopped. Feng stood on the other side, in a dark coat and beret. She stared at him so fiercely that he retreated to the desk, sitting mutely with his eyes on her as she unbuckled her coat.

"Sorry. Traffic," she said to Lockhart, pulling another chair from the corner and sitting astride it, her hands resting on the back. She was just two or three feet away from the cowering captive.

"Name?"

"I can't. I can't—" He stammered the words, glancing piteously at Mei as if she'd betrayed him.

Feng flourished her identity card. "I work for the Ministry of State Security. I asked your name."

"Ma Tung."

"Okay, Ma Tung. We're going to talk, and then you'll go back across the road and forget about our conversation. You will not mention it to anyone. It never happened. Is that understood?"

Ma gulped like a fish, wide-eyed.

"You understand?"

"I do."

"We don't want to hurt you. I'm grateful to you for saving me. I know you helped Tang Liu," Mei said.

"We don't want to, but we will, if you say anything. You will disappear. You will be forgotten." Feng put on a slow, stupid voice. " 'What happened to Ma Tung?' 'I don't know. He vanished.' We can do it easily. We have the power. You know that, don't you?"

Ma trembled. "Yes."

"We want to know one thing. Then you can go. Okay?"

Ma nodded, his trance-like state returning, as if he'd seen so many strange things that he'd slipped into a dream.

"Where did Tang Liu go?"

"I don't know. She disappeared."

"No," Feng said with exaggerated patience, as if talking to an idiot. "Before. When you saw Jia, in the crowd near the boy who died. You said she'd 'made it out.' Where was she?"

"She—I don't—"

Feng rocked forward on the chair and slapped Ma on the face, leaving a red mark on his cheek. He stroked it in shock.

"Don't waste my time. Don't lie."

"The—I—"

"Where was she? Tell me *now*."

"The ghost shift," he said.

43

Mei saw the glow of the Internet café from beneath the window—the strip-light sodium and the liquid crystal of computer screens. She looked down into the alley's darkness nervously.

"We don't have long," she said in English.

"How much time?" Lockhart said.

"They lock the dormitories at eleven-thirty and the lights go out at midnight. It's after ten."

Ma still sat at the desk, head down, resting on the hard surface. He'd started moaning after answering Feng's question, as if he had injured himself. Feng ignored him, getting up from the chair and throwing her beret onto the desk by his head. She picked up his cane and examined it, running a painted nail over its glossy surface.

"This is nice. Malacca, with a sterling silver handle. Monogrammed. How old? Nineteenth century?"

Ma moaned again.

"I bet you picked it up in Hong Kong. How much?"

"It was my great-grandfather's. He was a trader in Canton."

"That's quite a family. Tell me about the ghost shift."

Ma pulled himself upright and groaned, louder and with more resentment. "You said I could go," he sulked.

"When we're finished, I said."

"I answered your question. That's all you said you wanted."

"Explain what you meant."

Ma looked tired, Lockhart thought. The excitement of being kidnapped was fading, and he was becoming irritable. Lockhart knew it was the time in an interrogation when the subject could go silent and refuse to cooperate—not because it made sense but out of obstinacy, the urge to prove that he still had autonomy and had not been entirely crushed.

"Come, Ma Tung," he said. "Then it will be over."

Ma raised his eyes balefully. "There are five teams in Long Tan—white, yellow, green, blue, and purple. Everyone's a member of one of the teams—it identifies where they work and sleep. Then there's one more, red. We don't talk about it much. I don't know what they do, nobody does. They work in the north of the complex, factory P-1 and dormitory P-2. They're sealed off from the rest. They call it the ghost shift."

"What do they make there?" Feng asked.

Ma shrugged.

"Is it tablets? Poppy tablets?"

"Maybe."

"How do you know about it?"

"I work in the management office. We arrange all the shifts for the facilities, even the break times. We choose the sports teams, who is allowed to take their holidays. I've got a lot of responsibility. Everything must run smoothly. They trust me." Ma looked panicky again. "I took a very big risk for you. I saved your life," he said to Mei. "Aren't you grateful?"

"I really am." She leaned forward to touch his arm.

"It sounds like an important job," Lockhart said.

"It is." Ma puffed up in his seat. "You know what it's like. There are good jobs and bad ones, nice shifts and nasty ones. I can reward those who deserve it and make things easier for them."

"In exchange for money? For a red envelope?" Feng asked.

Ma looked insulted. "I'm not greedy. People want to bribe or threaten me, but that won't work. I'm kind to my friends. I put the ones I liked on the ghost shift, if they asked me."

"Did they want to go?"

"They used to. The shifts are shorter, and they have four beds to a dormitory room. It was the best assignment, but it was hard to get in. Only people with good ratings, who didn't gossip."

"You said they used to. Did it change?"

"When the deaths started, so did the rumors. People got scared. They said that people who went on the ghost shift disappeared."

"Did they?"

Ma nodded, avoiding Feng's stare. "When they were assigned, we had to take them off the database, as if they'd left. There aren't any records, but I still remember them. All of them." He looked at Lockhart, appealing to him. "It wasn't my fault. I couldn't have known."

"Was Wu Ning one of them?" Lockhart asked.

Ma hung his head again. "I miss Ning almost as much as Liu. Liu was the best. We used to hang out together. She was sweet."

The mention of his daughter jolted Lockhart. He felt sorry for Ma. He didn't have friends, only people who had wanted a favor that wasn't really a favor at all—to be put on the ghost shift. He thought of Lizzie, tracking the man down and getting her way, as she'd always done with him.

"Tang Liu wanted to be on the ghost shift?"

"I warned her, but she insisted."

Lizzie hadn't told Lockhart that—she'd kept it from him. She hadn't wanted him to stop her, he knew, so she hadn't confessed everything. She had inherited his belief in not telling the desk officer too much. He looked at Mei, standing silently by Feng, and wondered if she had the same trait.

"You can go now," Feng said. "Thank you for your cooperation. We will not harm you—if you do one thing."

Mei moved two days later. The women in the bunks above, who had hardly talked to her, were on overtime when she left the dormitory. Jun was in the recreation room, playing ping-pong with a boy who'd caught her eye, and Mei didn't interrupt. She took her bag and walked.

A guard stood under an umbrella, waiting. It was raining so hard that drops bounced off the canvas roof of an electric cart he'd parked by the dormitory. Lightning lit his face, and thunder boomed over the Long Tan complex, rolling across the delta. The storm had washed the other people from the streets—she and the guard were alone as they rolled along the main avenue, swerving around ponds of rainwater. They passed the plant where she worked, driving into the deeper reaches of the compound. After a few hundred yards, the streetlights ran out and she began to feel as if she'd been kidnapped. The only illumination came from shards of lightning as the storm moved west. She waited for the next bolt, staring to see what it might reveal, but all she could see were the rods of rain in the headlights.

There was a glow ahead. As they got closer, she made out a strand of light across her field of vision. It was a fence, leading to a sentry post. They had come so far that, looking back, she could hardly see the buildings in the rest of the compound. It felt as if they'd passed into a foreign country.

At the sentry post, she saw a twenty-foot-high fence. It was rooted in a strip of dirt forming a no-man's-land, with lights every thirty feet. Made of mesh, topped with a line of razor wire, it curved into the distance, creating a compound. A hundred yards away, a guard was patrolling the boundary with a retriever. The dog bounded along, sniffing the line of the fence.

The driver pulled an envelope out of a bag and handed it to the sentry, who shone a flashlight on the sheaf of papers inside, glancing at Mei. He nodded them through, along a driveway leading to the heart of the compound. The rain was easing, and Mei saw a five-story building, long and narrow—a dormitory block.

This was P-2.

Two people stood at the door as they arrived—a woman holding a bundle of clothes and the instructor. She hadn't seen him since her first day, but he beamed at her like a long-lost friend.

"Jiang Jia! I saw your name on the manifest, and I came to make you feel at home. I'm pleased to see you. Some people have the right attitude from the start—the spirit of Long Tan. I sensed it in you. This is my true home, although I am found in many places. I always seek recruits to the best team. Not many are good enough."

He wore similar pants as before, with his belt drawn around his belly, this time with a striped tie. It was topped with a red zippered jacket, the same color as the tunic of the woman next to him, who bowed to Mei as she handed her a red stack of tunics and white towels.

"We dress in comfort here, Jiang Jia. Truly, you are lucky. This young lady will take you to where you sleep. Rest well, refresh yourself! There is so much to learn here, so much to enjoy."

The woman led Mei to an elevator, and they rose to the fourth floor. They walked along a corridor, a soft light beside each closed door. Halfway along, she knocked, then placed a card in a slot and opened the door. It was pitch-dark inside the room for a few seconds, then a bright light switched on and Mei heard laughter and clapping.

"Surprise! Surprise!"

Three young women crowded around her, one holding flowers and another a frosted cake. The third lifted the stack of clothes from Mei and set them down on a bed before hugging her.

"Jiang Jia. Welcome to our home!" she cried.

"Go now. We'll take care of our new friend. Away!" another said, leading the supervisor out. She was dark-skinned, with crooked teeth and a smile that twisted on one side. Cutting slices from the cake, she offered the largest to Mei and took a small one for herself.

"I have to watch my weight. We eat too well in this place—so many pastries," she said. "Here, let's sit on your bed to talk. It's right by the window. I hope you like it."

Mei examined the room. Instead of bunks, there were four single beds pushed against the wall, each with a set of shelves above. A door at the end led out to a balcony. It was more like being back in her room in the Party compound than in her old Long Tan dormitory.

"Tell us all about yourself, Jia," the girl said. "Where do you come from, what are your dreams? Tell us about your family. I miss my family, but I am so happy to be here. I do not want to leave."

Sitting on the bed opposite, the others giggled.

"Don't smother her, Ling. Let her relax," one said.

"You're right. She must settle in. I know! Take a warm shower! We have one here. It will calm you."

"Maybe later," Mei said.

"You must do it now!" Ling cried. "Your clothes are damp from your journey. Take this bathrobe. You'll feel better."

Mei didn't want to, but her new roommates were so insistent and so merry that she had no choice. She undressed and stepped into the shower. It was as luxurious as they had said. The water pummeled her, filling the cubicle with steam, and she soaped her body. The women stood nearby, asking her how she felt and laughing.

The curtain drew back, and there was Ling, naked. She stepped into the shower before Mei could protest and stood there, her eyes dark and fragile. Ling wrapped her arms around her and put her mouth to Mei's ear. Beneath the shower's hissing noise, she whispered.

"They listen to everything."

44

It was her best breakfast in weeks, another universe from the fare at Camp Peary. A chef cooked scallion pancakes, and she could choose among six types of tea set out in small pots stamped with the Long Tan logo. Instead of the rice and noodles of her old canteen, there were bowls of warm soymilk, slices of turnip cake, steaming baskets of dumplings.

She ate and drank while her roommates nibbled on pancakes and prawn dumplings, keeping up the cheerful banter of the night. They seemed to have mastered it so completely that they could hide their feelings without effort. They had developed a language, a way of communicating in code and giving warnings while seeming carefree. Mei was learning to speak like that herself—to say one thing and mean the opposite. They sat at a four-person table, not one of the trestles of her old canteen. Light glowed through the hall's high, frosted windows: There was no outside view, but it felt warm and comfortable. The place was filled with cheerful-sounding hubbub, everyone smiling at the new day.

"This morning," said Ling, "you'll see the psychologist, Dr. He. They want to be sure you are happy and have no worries. She is a nice woman. She listens carefully to all your feelings."

"Oh, yes. You must tell her everything," said another roommate. Her name was Shu, and she wore thick glasses. Of the three, she seemed the least anxious about being spied on.

"It shows how much they care for us that they have hired a psychologist to know our emotions. She wants the best for you."

"I understand," Mei said.

The instructor arrived at their table. "Come along, ladies. I am here to take Jia for her induction. If all goes well, she will be back with you soon."

The others left, and he led Mei through long corridors to an office, where a woman was waiting for them. She looked little older than Mei and wore a white coat one size too big, the sleeves rolled up to keep them off her wrists. Her office was colorfully decorated, with a large armchair opposite her desk and a vase of flowers.

"You came last night, Jiang Jia? I hope you are settling in. This place is quite different, isn't it?"

"I like my room," she said. "My roommates are nice and the bed is comfortable. I slept well."

Dr. He smiled and pushed her thick-framed glasses up her nose. "Some of our new arrivals are surprised. But we want you to feel at home. You will be here for some time. Are there things you want to ask? Do you have worries?"

"I don't think so."

"You haven't heard bad rumors? I know that some people are scared to be here. I don't blame them. I look at the guards and the fences. They scare me too, although they are necessary. You asked to be brought here, didn't you? Why was that?"

"I heard it was nice. They said I would make friends and that it was a good place to work."

"Yes, we do vital work. There are some things that we cannot explain, which is frustrating, but they have a purpose." The psychologist examined her papers. "So you come from Heyuan?"

"My parents still live there."

"I was born in Zijin, but I love the city. We must know many of the same places. I would love to gossip."

"So would I." Mei smiled politely. Her hands felt clammy and she squeezed the chair's fabric. She'd thought her worst risk was to be recognized, not a coincidence like this.

"I'm sorry we can't do it now. We are so busy at the moment that it must wait a day or two. But I won't forget. Good luck on your first day, and remember, this is vital work."

. . .

Building P-1 was much smaller than the hangar where she had worked before. It was divided internally by a high wall running the length of the building. There was only one assembly line in sight and it moved more slowly, with fewer supervisors. She saw two red-uniformed women carrying out the task she'd been responsible for, applying electric tools to Poppy tablets.

The instructor strode toward her, his arms in the air, amused.

"When did you come to Long Tan, Jiang Jia? Only a few days ago. And already you have been promoted. Does this look familiar?"

Mei nodded. "Yes, very familiar."

"There are fewer people here, only the best. You are already well trained, so we are happy to welcome you. There are only a few things to learn, and then you will fit in here. Let us take a tour."

He strode along the line, with Mei following. Halfway along, she saw Ling and Shu bent over tablets. They were handling the battery frames for the devices, placing parts in trays. They smiled as she approached, then watched for the next tablets in line to arrive. The line moved far slower than in her old facility, and there were fewer tablets to deal with.

"Will you work with us? You'll love it here," Shu said.

"Perhaps she will. But first, I have to show her around," the instructor said. "She must see everything."

They reached the start of the line, close to the delivery bays, and looked back. Two guards stood on a walkway above the floor, looking down on both sides of the wall. The operation was small enough to be monitored without binoculars.

"So, Jiang Jia. All familiar, yes?"

"Yes, except—" Mei hesitated, not knowing whether to be honest. She trusted him even less than before.

"Tell me! Don't be frightened. Is there something unusual, something you don't understand? Speak up."

"They aren't making tablets. They are taking them apart."

"Yes!" The instructor clapped his hands and laughed. "You're right, of course. You wouldn't miss that."

It was the strangest assembly line she had seen, one that ran backward from the delivery bays to the end. Instead of parts coming from trucks into the bays, workers were unloading pallets stacked with finished tablets in boxes, shrink-wrapped and ready to be sent along the Pearl River to the world. Each box had on it the Poppy logo, a photograph of the device, and a hologram. They were identical to the one Feng had recovered from the Wolf's house.

The workers stripped the packaging and brought each one to the start of the line, where they were unpacked and placed on the belt. The empty boxes were put to the side. Mei watched as the line rolled into action on each tablet, starting with the final screws being taken out, the frame unhinged. The tablet passed down the line, each component being stripped and placed in a slot on a tray. The tray was wheeled down the line by the matching device until the frame was removed from the rear plate and laid in with the other parts.

Within twenty minutes, the operation of assembling the Poppy tablet had been reversed. It was back in pieces.

"Here, take a look." They walked to the end of the line, and the instructor pointed to one of the trays.

It was a marvel of precision. Every screw, every spring, every chip and battery had a place in the tray's rubber inset. Even the box in which the tablet had been wrapped stood nearby.

Other workers in red tunics hoisted the trays and stacked them twelve-high on a cart, then pushed them in a long line to the edge of the hangar, and out of the building through sliding doors.

"Do you have a question?" The instructor smiled mischievously.

"Why are they doing this?"

"Can you guess?"

"I don't know. I can't think."

"What is the third value of Long Tan?"

"Discipline," she said.

"Which means quality. The highest quality in the world, that is what Cao requires. We have quality checks, but we cannot see *inside* our devices. Sometimes, we must take them apart." He laughed. "To go to all that trouble to build them, and then do this. It is a tribute to his discipline."

"I see."

He looked at her. "Come on, Jiang Jia. I see you have another question. What did I tell you? Speak up!"

"Why are there so many? Why do you have to open all of these devices to check on them?"

The instructor shook his head. "Cao Fu has very high standards, he does not take chances. If you were the boss, we would check one or two. He checks many thousands. Could you run the best factory in the world?"

Mei tried to look humble. "I couldn't."

"No, you couldn't. Cao Fu is the only one who can. That is why we should not question him."

The instructor fixed his customary grin in place and clapped as if he'd taught Mei a useful lesson. But he strode back up the line with a touch of impatience. He wasn't happy.

45

Taking apart the tablets was trickier than putting them together. Mei had a place halfway along the line, in sight of her roommates but far enough that she couldn't talk. Her task was to unscrew the logic board from the panel, lifting the bar that held it down after removing two screws. Then she took a scalpel and slit the black rubber encasing the board—it had been heat-sealed on the other line, and there was no way to open it. She put the bar in a foam rubber slot, next to the parts that had been removed up the line, and the tablet moved onward.

The problem was the screws that fastened the board. Most were easy to take out; she slotted the bit into the star-shaped screw head and, as she applied torque, they lifted. But some were so stiff that the tool slipped, and she had to wrench it to make it turn. It made her hand ache and spoiled the screw, which she would then discard in a bin. When it was impossible to shift, she had to alert a supervisor, who took the tablet to a workstation near the line for a remedial crew to work on. It felt like a failure every time—she was mangling the job.

Mei cursed those who had made her job so hard, until she recalled that she'd been one of them, rushing to fix the thing together on the other line, not knowing that all her work was for nothing. The tablet would be loaded on a truck and taken to P-1 to be ripped apart again. It was her second morning on the line and, although the work was frustrating, it was less tiring than in the original Poppy facility. The pace was slower, and she had time to pause, even rub her feet between jobs. Many fewer tablets passed by. Things moved so slowly that she was able to look around the facility, staring into the rafters until a guard met her stare. Mei dropped her gaze to the wall that divided the building. She couldn't see through it, but she heard the hum of machines.

It was then, standing at the line, that she noticed something. The workers in red who wheeled the trolleys full of trays passed through a sliding door to her rear about a hundred feet away. The door closed behind each one. But half an hour later, the same worker would return through another door, this one in the central wall behind her, to pick up another cart. The whole circuit took twenty minutes from exiting to entering again. After a while, she could predict exactly when the next one would arrive. They were in a permanent loop—taking a cart, delivering it, returning it empty.

Mei wanted to see where the sliding door led, but it was impossible from where she stood. She started to flex one leg as if suffering from a cramp and pace around between tasks. She slowly lengthened her circuit until she could peep through the door briefly as it opened into a long, curved hallway.

"Jia, are you ill?" The instructor's voice boomed in her ear, making her jump.

"It's just a pulled muscle."

"Carry on, then. But you can always see the doctor. We take good care of our family."

She fixed a smile on her face and caught the eye of Ling, who frowned, warning her of danger.

Supper was fish steamed in ginger, *choi sum* greens, and yellow bean tofu. Here, they could leave their dishes on the table, with plates unfinished and rice to spare, and the kitchen staff would collect them. Ling had been talking to a friend at another table, but as Mei finished her food, she came across.

"Let's take an evening stroll. You haven't seen everything."

"I'll come." Shu rose from her seat.

"Please do," Ling said, and Shu sat again, obeying the coded command.

Ling led her from the back of the building to the recreation field.

It was empty—Mei hadn't seen anyone playing sports on it since she'd arrived—and they stood out in the night. It was a thousand feet to the perimeter fence and, beneath the moon, she saw a dog leaping playfully as his guard led him along the fence. The guard's flashlight swept the dark ground inside the fence.

"You're curious," Ling said.

"Am I?"

"That's not good." Ling took her arm. "They don't like anyone to be so interested. Don't worry, they can't hear us here, I think. But you should be careful. He saw you looking."

They were on a soccer field, its lines glistening in the moonlight. The outline of P-1 lay ahead—the assembly building and a smaller square attached to one side by two tubes. One of them must be the hallway she'd seen on the other side of the sliding door. They were windowless, but skylights glowed on their roofs.

"How long have you been here?"

"A year," Ling said. "I'll never get out."

"Why don't you go?"

"They won't let us. If you ask, they say you're disloyal. You're putting your ego above the collective. We can't speak to our families. They won't allow us home for the New Year holiday."

"Does nobody leave?"

"A few do. That's a big deal. We have a party for them to celebrate. Wu Ning, the girl who was in our room before you? She did. She complained, and they let her leave. They made a cake."

Ling smiled as if encouraged by the example—that she might be lucky. She didn't know what had happened to Wu Ning, Mei realized. They were kept sealed away, not knowing that death was the only way out.

"Can't you escape?" Mei pointed toward the border fence.

Ling's eyelids fluttered. "*Someone* did."

"When?"

"About a month ago. There was an alarm one night—the lights flashing and the sirens going. They came to our rooms and searched them. They wouldn't say why, but I heard a girl had disappeared."

Mei's heart felt as if it had stopped and she heard herself breathing loudly in the night air. "Who was it?"

"A girl on the trolleys. She hadn't been here long. I saw her a few times. She looked like you." Ling's voice was guileless.

"She got out?"

"That's what they said."

The lights were on in the dormitory building, and they stood on a wide-open space, exposed to view from all sides, encircled by fence. The only other buildings were the two that formed P-1. It was perfectly designed to encircle its occupants, with nowhere to hide. Mei turned in a circle, trying to see how Lizzie might have done it. The sniffer dog barked to her left and, as she looked toward it, she noticed one weakness—a tiny flaw.

"We should go," Ling said.

As they walked, Mei thought of Lizzie. She imagined her sister out in this field, gazing around; on the assembly line, figuring out how to unlock P-1's secrets and to take them with her. She'd suspected Lizzie of being foolish, of behaving recklessly to impress Lockhart, but now she saw how clever she had been. She'd had a plan, and it had almost worked.

46

It was eleven o'clock, nearing the end of the morning shift, when the girl who did the task opposite slipped away to the restroom, leaving Mei alone. She looked over her shoulder. The supervisor had drifted along the line to ensure that the flow of tablets would not be held up by a jam of trolleys. Mei had just taken both screws from the securing arm and placed it in the tray. There wouldn't be a better moment.

She took the scalpel in her right hand and bent her shoulders so she could not be seen. Then she placed her left hand against the tablet and, with a swift, deep stroke, slashed the tips of three fingers. Blood spurted, covering the tablet, and she reeled away from the line, clutching her wrist and crying in pain. This part she didn't have to pretend: It hurt like hell. She'd tried a light slash—the most blood for the least injury—but she'd cut down to the bone.

There was a commotion, and a klaxon sounded as the line halted. Ling rang to her and wrapped a cloth around her hand, but the blood would not stop. The white cloth turned red and blood dripped down her uniform. A supervisor brought a chair and she sat, shaking and feeling faint.

"I'm sorry," she said. "I'm so stupid."

"How did it happen?" Ling asked.

"I looked the wrong way as I cut."

A gurney came, pushed by two nurses. They strapped her hand and helped her onto it, then wheeled her the length of the line, with the workers gazing at her as she went. She lay facing up, observing the ceiling of the factory. Even the guards on the walkway peered at her.

In the medical room, near Dr. He's office, a doctor placed strips on the cuts and bandaged up each finger separately. She was given a tetanus shot, a painkiller, and, finally, a cup of *Longjing* tea. It was the most efficient emergency care she'd experienced in her life.

Mei was dozing when the instructor came.

"Jia! The last person I'd expect to have such an accident on the line. You are always precise." He sat by the gurney, bending forward to look at her bandaged fingers.

"I'm upset to have let you down. I don't know what happened. I feel so ashamed of myself."

"You mustn't. Cao Fu says in his book: 'If someone attacks us, we strike him harder. If they are troubled, we help them.' What did I tell you on the day you arrived? Love comes first at Long Tan. You will rest until you are recovered. Only then will you need to work again."

"But I feel terrible lying here. Even if I cannot work on the line, I want to contribute. There must be other things I can do, without using these fingers." She paused. "I could push the trolleys, like some of the others do. That wouldn't hurt. Allow me to do that."

The instructor's face split into a grin. "Jiang Jia, I congratulate you. You have the unbending spirit that exists inside the truest of our workers. Yes! If the doctor agrees, tomorrow we will find you a new job."

He stalked out again. Mei put her head back in the sunlight and nodded when the nurse asked if she wanted more tea. It was a gilded cage, full of rewards for those who remained obedient.

The caretaker had shuffled off, and Lockhart was reading the final chapter of Deng Xiaoping's biography. He felt restless and impatient, but all he could do was wait. He could not even walk out into the alley, for fear of being noticed. Feng had driven him to the building in the early morning a few days before, with a suitcase of clothes, a couple of books, and some sheets for the bed. Since then, the farthest he had walked was between the bedroom and the toilet. The courtyard prevented anyone from looking in.

This silence gave him the same feeling he'd experienced before—

the dread of what was happening inside, with no ability to control it. He wondered how he could cope if it happened again. She wasn't his daughter, but he'd grown attached to her, and he admired her bravery. If he could have shielded her, he would have done it, but Lizzie's death had proved to him that he was neither as powerful nor as lucky as he'd imagined. He felt fragile, a vessel that could break.

Since Feng's last visit, he'd received a few cryptic emails—they were making progress, there might be something to see soon—but nothing that showed she really trusted him. Sedgwick was impatient for information, and Henry Martin's temper was fraying. He was in limbo, with nothing to do but hope that Mei could succeed where Lizzie had failed.

He heard steps on the stairwell and a knock on the door.

"Okay, I've got something," Feng said, as he opened it. She had a suede messenger bag slung over one shoulder and carried two cups of coffee from the Internet café in the alley.

"Come in," he said to her back, as she walked past him and dumped her bag on his desk.

"I shouldn't show you. I shouldn't even tell you I'm not showing you." Feng removed a laptop from her bag and placed it on the desk. It was the latest Poppy—a fifteen-inch, high-resolution screen that glowed with information. She pulled up an Ethernet cable and plugged it in.

"Nice gear," Lockhart said.

"What download speed are you getting?"

"Sixty-five megabits. Pretty fast."

"That should work. Comcast will catch up sometime next century. Wait there, would you? National security."

He watched from the corner as she made a connection and entered a series of codes. She opened a window: a satellite view of the Long Tan complex, showing the buildings from above.

"That's terrific, but I can use Google."

"Come closer."

Lockhart stood behind Feng as she zoomed in, making it larger and more precise than any satellite view. He could see a line of trucks next to what looked like an aircraft hangar. Then, as he tried to make

sense of the image, one of the trucks moved. It drove along the side of
the building and then reversed so that its rear door was close.

"Shit. This thing's live."

Feng said nothing, but shifted the magnification higher. Lockhart
saw a pale square extend from the rear of the truck and two red dots
move slowly around it. He couldn't believe the evidence of his eyes.
He was watching people.

"Chengdu Pterosaur drone, at forty thousand feet. This is ad-
vanced Chinese technology. The images are clear, aren't they?"

"Almost as good as a Predator."

"We watch people from the sky, like the CIA. The difference is, we
don't blow them up. It's more harmonious."

"What is this?"

"It's part of the complex, in the northeast quadrant, away from
the rest. There are two buildings with a fence a little less than a mile
in diameter. One entrance here. Trucks go in and out in the day, load-
ing and unloading. Building P-1, Building P-2. Mei is in there. This is
the ghost shift."

Feng pulled the magnification back to a panorama of the complex. It was eleven-thirty in the morning, and clusters of red dots
spilled from one of the buildings onto a green expanse. The glossy
line of the fence encircled them, and two trucks were lined up at the
entry point. From aloft, without sound to go with the images, it was
peaceful.

"Can you go closer?"

Feng enlarged the image until it filled the screen. The camera was
pointing down on a barnlike building, with two tubes extending from
it to a square structure a hundred feet away. Both tubes were bent
in the middle: It looked like the larger building was embracing the
smaller one.

"What's that?"

"That's P-1."

"Why is it divided like that?"

"Don't know. This is the dormitory. She must be sleeping there."
Feng moved the image to P-2, and they looked at it in silence for two
minutes. The red dots swarmed it like an ant's nest.

"You're full of surprises," Lockhart said, leaning on the desk. "I didn't know the MSS had drones. I thought that was the PLA."

"The CIA had them, and we got jealous. There was turf warfare, but we struck a deal. Does it matter? I'm lending it to you, which is nice of me. You can watch this all night. Remember, you get a fine view until the weather turns bad. Then all you'll see is clouds."

After she left, Lockhart sat at the desk, mesmerized by the images. He moved the camera from one building to another, then along the perimeter fence, watching the dots and wondering which one was Mei.

47

As Mei stacked the cart with trays, the cut on one finger opened and blood oozed through her bandage. The nurse had fitted a new one after breakfast, strapping her fingers together and placing a mitten over them, which made her look like a white-gloved traffic cop. The bandage turned pink, but the color didn't get darker. She was safe for now, and she returned to stacking the trays. Wedging the left side of each into her palm, she took the weight with her right hand to avoid injuring herself more. The trays weren't heavy—the parts of each tablet, extracted on the line, weighed no more in pieces than when she'd held it in the Poppy store. Two nights before, they had shown the workers a video of Martin onstage in San Francisco, showing off the latest devices, with the instructor leading the applause.

Mei looked at the supervisor, to check if it was okay to move, and he waved her forward. The worker in front was passing through the doors. She followed, crossing the floor and glancing above her to the guards. Nobody seemed to be watching—she had regained her status as an invisible cog in the Long Tan machine. She maneuvered the cart around a corner at the edge of the building, using her hips to keep it in line, then the doors slid open ahead of her and she passed out of the hangar.

She was in the walkway now. It had a low ceiling, with glass panels in the roof that filled it with light. Mei's sneakers squeaked on the concrete floor as she shoved the cart. The boy ahead was out of sight and she couldn't hear anyone behind her. She was alone in the tube for a minute before another door loomed, sliding back to admit her to the other building.

Her first sight was a tall kid in jeans and a T-shirt, who stood at the door with a handheld scanner attached to a tablet. Smiling, he scanned the codes on each tray, then checked his tablet to ensure that each had registered. He grinned again, holding her gaze as if he would like to know her better, and waved her along a trail marked in green paint. As she moved forward, Mei looked around. She was in the smaller building she'd seen from the field.

A hundred feet ahead, a conveyor belt ran along the first floor, where two workers loaded it with trays, then snaked in an S-shape up to a mezzanine. That floor was filled with workstations staffed by pairs of employees. One half of each was a programmer, dressed like the boy who'd greeted Mei at the door. Mei saw one—a woman with a mop of hair—tracing lines of figures on a screen, then breaking off to tap a Poppy tablet. The other half of each pair was a technician, wearing safety glasses. This one took a long metal probe and bent over the workstation. Mei couldn't quite see what he doing, but his safety glasses reflected an intense, flickering light. It was the same pattern at each station: a programmer and a technician, lines of data and the blue-white pulse of something being soldered.

Then it made sense. She didn't have to see what they were doing— she knew. It explained the ghost shift, why the tablets were being taken apart, how one had arrived in Washington with a chip inside that nobody recognized. This was where they made the rogue tablets.

Mei was gazing so intently that she almost bumped her cart as she reached her spot. She parked it by a worker who unstacked the trays, putting them on the belt that carried them toward the mezzanine. This part of her job was complete—the path beneath her feet switched to a painted line of footsteps to the left of the conveyor belt. Mei followed and entered a hallway, emerging at the end of the building.

It was the turning point, where the sequence that had started in Building P-1 reversed. The belt curved down from the mezzanine floor, bringing the trays back down. Two workers stacked them into trolleys again, and Mei stepped forward to take hold of one. She saw the porter in front pushing his cart through another set of sliding doors, and she followed. Another kid with a scanner, with a less committed smile, checked her into a second walkway.

It was similar to the first, starting out straight before turning a long semicircle. As she reached the apex, Mei heard only the cart ahead and nothing behind.

She halted.

Sliding one tray out, she held it with her injured left hand and explored the slots in the tray. Each one contained a part from the original tablet, as before. It took her a minute and a half, glancing in both directions down the curve and listening for footsteps, to find it.

She pulled out the part she'd identified. It was the tablet's logic board, with each of its chips in place. She touched each, until she reached the main processor, with the Poppy logo etched on its face. It was still warm from being soldered in place.

After resting her finger for a second, she stuffed the logic board back into its slot and returned the tray. Using her shoulder, she pushed it back into motion and guided it around the curve.

Past the door at the far end of the walkway, she emerged into the main part of the building. This time she was on the far side of the dividing wall—the mirror of the one she knew—looking along another line of red-uniformed workers. They were working in groups, as their counterparts. But Mei was back through the looking glass. Instead of taking tablets apart, they were putting them together—it was a line to reassemble the tablets.

A supervisor beckoned her to a bay at the head of the line, where the trays were lifted from the cart. They were slotted into frames on wheels, and Mei was allocated one. As she pushed it along the line, workers reached behind their bodies to take pieces and fix them together. The tablet was remade in front of her eyes. She passed the places she had worked, watching the frame fixed to the shell, the board reinserted, batteries and audio clipped in place. At the end of the line, the restored tablets were put back in boxes and shrink-wrapped.

As good as new.

. . .

Mei was walking to the factory for the overtime shift at twenty past five when she felt a tap on one shoulder.

"Jia, what a nice surprise," said Dr. He. Her face was flushed. "We never had a chance to talk about the old days in Heyuan before. Do you have time now?"

"I'm due back on shift, I'm afraid." Mei edged away from the psychologist, smiling earnestly.

"I'm sure they can spare you. I will let them know. Don't worry— you won't suffer for telling me about home and family. Discipline is vital at Long Tan, but what comes first?"

"Love," Mei said.

In her room, Dr. He walked to a cupboard at the side of the room and took out a box and some cups. "Would you like tea?"

"Thank you, no. I have just eaten."

"I hope you don't mind if I do. At this time of day, I try to relax and remember the day. It is a discipline. The things that I did right and I am proud of. The things of which I am ashamed."

"I will remember that."

"Let's try now. What made you proud today?"

The psychologist poured water onto leaves and steam rose. The left sleeve of her coat dangled, making her look like a teenager.

"I was proud to learn new skills and not to be prevented from working by my foolish injury."

"Ah, yes, your injury. Let me look." Dr. He carried her cup to the desk and set it down, examining Mei's hand.

"Such a terrible thing to happen, so soon after you arrived. Injuries are rare here. I was shocked when I heard. I hope we will analyze this incident and correct our failures."

"It was my fault, Dr. He. I was being clumsy."

"And today? Did anything make you ashamed?" The psychologist sipped tea, peering at Mei through her bangs.

"Sometimes I fell behind. I need to get faster."

"Nothing more?"

"I am sure there are others for me to reflect upon."

"Tell me about your parents, Mei."

"My mother is very kind and has a great spirit. She was born in

Guangzhou and she trained as a nurse. She works in the Chang'an Hospital in Heyuan. But she looks after my father now. Sometimes, he says he is just a burden on her. It distresses her."

Dr. He smiled and broke into a dialect that Mei didn't understand. "天不生無用之人地不長無根之草."

Mei smiled uncertainly and shrugged.

" 'God does not produce useless men. The earth would not allow rootless grass to grow.' I'm surprised you haven't heard that, Jia. It is one of the first Hakka sayings that my father taught me."

"My parents are from Guangzhou. They moved for work before I was born. I wasn't taught Hakka, I'm afraid."

"Not at all? It must have been tough when you were at school. Which one did you attend?"

"I went to Heyuan Number Three Elementary."

"Do you still have friends from there?"

Mei shifted in her chair, trying to keep her eyes on Dr. He.

"Some, yes."

"When did you arrive in Shenzhen?"

"After the New Year. I wanted a new life."

"Were you in Heyuan for the earthquake?"

Mei froze. She'd been in Guangzhou, the only cadre with no family to visit for New Year. She had a split second to choose.

"No, I'd left. My parents felt it, but they weren't hurt."

"Mine too. It was bad around the Xinfengjiang Reservoir. I hope it isn't worse next time."

Mei couldn't risk it any longer. She squeezed her left hand into a fist, crying out as her cuts opened.

"Oh no." She held her hand out, showing blood seeping through the bandage. "I'm sorry. I don't know what happened."

"Jia, you need treatment. What a shame. I was enjoying our talk very much. It was enlightening."

Dr. He led Mei to the medical center, where the nurse repaired her hand. She felt no pain as the bandage strips were snipped off and replaced—the sensation was drowned out by fear.

48

The next day, Mei was ready.

She didn't return to the dormitory at the end of the afternoon shift in case Dr. He caught her. Instead, she walked in the field with Ling, taking another chance to scan the landscape. The heat was intense. It had built up all day as if it were still high summer, although the rainy season was coming to an end. She could feel the breeze starting to blow in gusts.

"How is your poor hand, Jia?"

"Better, thank you."

"I was worried about you."

Mei stopped and took Ling's hand.

"Ling, they will let you leave. I'm sure of it."

"I want to see my mother again."

Mei gazed across the field at P-1, trying to gauge the distance from the building to the fence. It looked a long way, in blazing sunshine, with heat rising from the field. The flat fields shimmered like an oasis.

"Let's go," Ling said. "I can't stand any more of this." She was dripping with sweat and wiped her neck with a tissue.

At her station, Mei waited for the overtime shift to start and the last of the trays to be stacked on her cart so that she could make the round again. She had two and a half hours to go—seven complete circuits from the assembly line through to the other building and back again. She looked at her watch as she pushed the cart through the door for the first time, timing it.

At eight o'clock, she came to the end of the assembly line on the other side of the wall for the sixth time, and pushed the tray—now emptied of parts—through the door in the wall to her starting point. She was ten minutes early. If she set off again, she'd be stuck with her cart in the other building when the klaxon sounded for the end of the shift. As she reached for the first tray to stack the cart, she clutched her hand and called to the supervisor.

"Can I sit for a minute? My hand hurts."

"Yes, sit here. Shall I call the nurse?"

"No, I'll be all right. I'll use the restroom."

Mei gazed into the bathroom mirror as she splashed water on her neck. Her hair was growing out at the neck, where it had been shaved close, and the contact lenses that made her eyes black felt gritty. She didn't recognize herself. She had started to shake, and she pressed her hands by the side of the sink to stay calm. The pretense would soon be finished.

She stood and walked back to the line, smiling at the supervisor as she grabbed a cart and started to stack it with trays. It was the right time, and she didn't want to be delayed. She put her shoulder to the frame and pushed, setting off on her circuit for the last time. The doors slid open and she was in the first walkway, out of sight of the worker in front, her sneakers squeaking on the floor. She looked through the panels above her head. Black clouds were massing in the sky, which had turned violet.

The boy at the entrance smiled when he saw her and gave her a wink as he bent to scan the trays. She did her best to respond, before pushing the cart on toward the mezzanine. At the far end, she glanced at her watch as she waited for a new one. It was 8:26. The beauty of Long Tan was its predictability. There was no slacking as the end of the shift approached, no winding down or drifting away. The line worked at full speed until the moment the klaxon sounded and then it stopped, abruptly and completely.

Mei watched the girl ahead of her push through the door onto the return walkway. It was 8:27. As she took her cart, she stepped discreetly on the brake of the next one to delay the worker behind. She pushed it toward the exit as fast as she could—she needed to get through the door.

Looking ahead, she saw trouble. The smiling boy had switched places and was holding his scanner as if saluting her. She gave a grimace, as if complaining about the weight, as she reached him.

It was 8:28.

"What's your name?" he said, bending to scan the trays.

"Jiang Jia." Mei found herself whispering. Her voice had cracked and she could not speak.

"What do you do in the evenings?"

"I read. I watch television."

He stood with his hand on her cart. "I'd like to see you."

8:29.

She smiled. "I'll think about it."

The cart felt like a dead weight. She grunted with effort, edging the wheels onto the pad in front of the door. It slid back and she wheeled past his hopeful smile. As the door shut behind her, she let the cart slip forward and pushed with all her might, leaning at a forty-five degree angle to thrust her weight against it, her left hand throbbing in protest. She heard the splash of raindrops from the dark sky above her as she galloped along the hallway, the cart weaving from side to side with speed, almost hitting the wall.

8:30.

The klaxon sounded, echoing along the bend from both ends.

Mei kept running until she reached the apex, where she'd stopped the previous day. The lines in the hangar would have halted, and her friends would be drifting off to relax. The protocol was to push the cart to the end of the walkway and into the assembly plant when the klaxon sounded, but nobody could see her. With luck, she'd have a few minutes before they noticed that she hadn't emerged. She was more worried about the scanner boy. What if he followed her?

Mei couldn't do anything about it now—she'd cast her lot. She reached into the trays and felt for the slots in which the logic boards had been placed. Extracting one, she stuffed it into her pocket, brushing her finger past the warm chip. Then she took another, pulling a tool from her pocket and levering the chip from the board. Reaching into one pocket, she removed a foil packet and twisted it open. When she was finished, she looked above her head, seeing fat raindrops starting to splash on the glass panel, and pulled the cart against one wall. She reached up and thrust her left hand over the top tray. She was past caring about the pain as she gripped the metal and, raising her knee, wedged one sneaker into the gap above the third tray and heaved herself up.

The cart tipped, its front wheels lifting from the ground, and she placed her foot on the fifth tray, shifting her weight across the top of the cart. The maneuver trapped her left hand and she felt the skin rip but she ignored the pain, reaching out to grasp the top rail and pull herself forward.

She crouched, ten feet above the ground, and reached into one pocket for the assembly tool again. Then she stood gingerly, feeling the trays buckle under her but hold, and touched the window. Rain was starting to spatter loudly on the glass. She leaned across, wedging her useless left hand against the frame and putting her weight on it. Taking the tool, she slotted it into the first of four latch screws and twisted. It was stiff, but she laced her whole body behind it and felt it turn—she'd had plenty of practice. The second came out and then the third, dropping to the floor with tinkling sounds. The fourth was the hardest but she willed it free.

Banging the frame, she pushed upward, but she couldn't force it free from her angle. She hooked the cart away from the wall with her feet, so that it was directly under the panel, and tried again. It creaked loudly and lifted to a thirty-degree angle, where two folding struts locked it. That was as far as she could force it. She placed her hands on the edge of the frame, by the open end. Pushing up, she squeezed her shoulders through the gap and onto the roof. Her left hand felt dead as she clawed the smooth surface, trying to get a hold.

Inch by inch, she pulled forward, feeling the rain flood down her neck. There was more light than she'd imagined—it glowed from the hallway onto the open window. Her shoulders wedged in the gap between frame and window, but she kept tugging, feeling her uniform tunic catch on the metal and pull down her body. Finally, she scrambled out, blood pouring from her hand and a fresh cut on her neck. She looked at the angry sky, seeing the first crack of lighting unleash a torrent of rain, and laughed, letting the water run into her mouth.

The clouds had opened and she could hardly see, which meant she was hardly visible.

The drop was twelve feet, but she didn't have time to worry. Lowering herself over the edge, she gripped the ledge with her good hand and, swinging awkwardly, fell to the ground. Spilling backward, she banged her shoulders and scrambled to her feet. She was more than a thousand feet from her target—an open sewer that crossed the field, draining water on nights like this. Seeing it as she walked with Ling, she had realized how Lizzie had escaped this prison.

Pointing herself toward it, she ran.

49

ockhart had nothing to do but sit and watch the screen. Every few hours, one drone would pull away for refueling and the image on the laptop would go blank. But, within a few minutes, another would arrive on station and the pictures would flicker back to life. Somewhere, the ministry's controllers kept their machines floating in the atmosphere. At dusk, it became harder to see the buildings, but the people stood out. The blobs of the workers' tunics faded, but the infrared cameras showed their body heat as a red glow.

It was a factory, with shift patterns that matched those in the main Long Tan compound, but he couldn't see how everything fit together. They lived and ate in P-2, that was obvious. At mealtimes and at the end of the day, people walked there and disappeared inside. After breakfast, they spilled out toward P-1, the assembly plant. The building that intrigued him was the annex attached to P-1 by two tubes. Lockhart was sure they were hallways—he'd enlarged the image when the skies were clear and had seen heads passing under panels. Inside the annex itself, the infrared image showed heat spots.

The operation was connected to the Long Tan complex. One set of trucks drove from plants in the outer compound, entering along the access road and unloading at P-1. Workers loaded another set of trucks, which left the compound and drove to the exit, bound for the expressway. When he was bored, Lockhart counted the trucks arriving at P-1, noting the numbers on a piece of paper. It was only a small fraction of Poppy's output—P-1 wasn't self-sufficient, nor was it a finishing plant for every Poppy tablet. It was a puzzle.

At eight-thirty, Lockhart heard the caretaker open the apartment door. Feng came into the room, putting her bag on the table, and looked over his shoulder at the screen of the laptop.

"Anything happening?"

"Nothing much."

"There's a storm coming, so the drone may back off for a while. They don't like turbulence."

Lockhart nodded. When he looked back, he noticed something odd—like nothing he'd seen before. The camera was locked on the walkways linked to P-1, and a red dot had appeared against the white of the roof, by one of the panels. He checked the time in the upper right of the screen. It was 8:36—late for anyone to repair the roof. Lockhart switched the image back to a normal camera, and the reds, greens, and oranges were replaced by a gloom in which little was visible.

Lightning flashed at the window, followed almost immediately by an enormous clap of thunder. A sheet of light filled the laptop screen and he saw a shape on it where the red dot had been.

"It's her," he said.

Feng stood by him. "What is?"

The image was so poor that he switched it back to infrared and pointed at the red dot. As they looked, it shifted slightly, moving from the curve of the roof to the ground next to it.

"That's your evidence?" Feng said.

As Lockhart pulled the focus back to show a panorama of the compound, the image shook. The rainfall outside the window grew louder, and lightning flashed as the storm broke.

"Wait." Feng seemed to be appealing to the drone's controllers, not to him. She bent her face up to the screen.

They had three seconds before the drone pulled away, and the image went with it. The buildings loomed at the bottom of the screen, and between them and the fence lay a dark expanse of field. As they watched, the red dot detached from the walkway and moved diagonally.

The screen went black.

"It's her," Feng said.

. . .

Mei ran blind, the rain pelting her face. She felt the light of the buildings recede but didn't look back. She was by herself on the field, and she watched wet earth and grass passing beneath her. She glimpsed a white line on the pitch, and then it went by. The field filled with water as she ran, pooling and splashing. Once her front foot slid from under her and she almost fell.

The ground hardened, and she felt the gravel of the running track around the field. She stopped, crouching to keep her profile low as she tried to recalculate her course. The walkway was far behind her—five hundred feet or so, she reckoned. Rain would be pouring through the panel, flooding onto the floor and toward the doors at either end. She hoped that nobody had followed her and that she would have time before a breach was found—she desperately needed it. She was at the far side of the soccer field, near the storm sewer. A dog barked, not far away.

Mei walked a few steps, her head low, and then broke into a run, keeping on the alert for guards. If they were at the perimeter fence, they should still be another five hundred feet away, but the dog had sounded closer. Feeling the rain on her face let up, she saw a patch of sky, dotted with stars, emerge among the clouds. The storm was passing westward, taking with it the downpour that had hidden her. Soon she would stand out on the landscape.

Suddenly, missing her footing, she tumbled and grazed her knee. Hearing water in front of her, she reached out and splashed a hand in a muddy stream. She was perched on the downward slope of the open drain. The sewer was doing its work, taking water off the field and toward the border of the complex, where it would flow out through channels toward the river. Without it, the compound would turn into a swamp.

The dog barked again, and she pitched forward, slithering into the stream. It was a couple of feet deep—too shallow to float but deep enough to keep herself hidden. The water, which had bucketed from the receding clouds, was fresh, but the bottom of the drain was slimy with mud. She slid her hands along, trying to crawl on her hands and knees. It was slow progress, and the sky was clearing, exposing her to the sight of anybody close to the lip of the open sewer, or anyone gazing along its length. She was best protected from the side.

Something like safety lay a hundred feet ahead—an open pipe into which the sewer water flowed. She half-crawled, half-scrambled toward it, waiting for the sound of the guards, and flung herself the last few feet. The pipe was three feet wide, and the water from the sewer welled up as it forced into the gap, rising to about half the pipe's diameter. It would leave her little room to breathe, and she couldn't see far down its length. But that wasn't her immediate problem.

The end of the pipe was sealed with a grate.

Mei felt under the water's surface. The grate was fastened to a wooden frame, and she could not unbolt it. She ran her fingers along the wood, feeling its splinters, and pulled the bars with her good hand, trying to pull it free. It shook at the bottom, where the wood had bloated. She couldn't do more with one hand, so she turned around and lay flat in the water, feet to the grate. Pulling back her knees, she kicked as hard as she could with her heels. The metal shifted in the frame, making what sounded to her like a huge noise, but didn't move.

Mei kicked again, and again. She was broadcasting her presence, but she had no choice. On the third kick, she felt the bottom of the grate give slightly. She kicked wildly a fourth time, and then a fifth. On the sixth, the bars at the bottom broke free. Turning, she wrestled at them with her hand, trying to force a bigger hole. She was half-submerged, water flowing around her neck, as she worked. After a minute, she dipped her head through the gap and kicked against the sewer's sides to get her shoulders through. Waggling her body, she eased through, holding her breath underwater.

As her feet cleared, she came to the surface and shot along the pipe. She was floating, carried on the stream of water that gushed down the narrow channel. She struggled to avoid drowning as the water tumbled her over and frothed in the pipe, not knowing which way was up as she flowed downstream in darkness. Whenever her face surfaced, she tried to catch a breath. It was happening too fast to think—all of her attention was focused on snatching oxygen.

The pipe turned a bend and became wider, the water level falling as the internal pressure eased. Mei was dumped on her back, water flowing around her. She sat, coughing and retching. A hundred feet ahead, water cascaded from the end of the pipe in a waterfall, and the night sky was visible—the world beyond Long Tan's borders.

This was how her sister had escaped. She knew it.

The waterfall shone as if illuminated, and she crawled toward it. The closer she got, the brighter the light became, until she poked her head into a dazzling glare. The headlights of three Jeeps were shining on her; next to one of them stood a man with a self-satisfied smile.

"Jiang Jia," the instructor said. "We must teach you discipline."

50

Two guards took Mei by both shoulders, extracting her from the pipe. She'd lost a shoe, and the bandage on her hand hung down in strips. Dragging her, scraping her along the sewer floor, they stood her up by the vehicles. Water dripped down her face, and a contact lens had lodged in the back of one eye.

"You are soaking wet. We must get you dry. Take off your clothes," the instructor said.

Mei looked at him in disbelief. She was standing in the open air, surrounded by men.

"Remove her clothes."

The guards stepped toward her, and one reached down to unzip her pants. As she struggled with his hand, the other slapped her, cutting the inside of one cheek on a tooth. He stepped behind her and gripped her by both shoulders while his partner got on with his task. He pulled off her shoe and then reached around her waist to strip off her pants and underwear. Then he lifted her tunic and ripped off her bra, taking his time to run his hands over her breasts. She stood naked, trying to cover herself, as the instructor inspected her body. He searched the pockets of her soaking tunic, pulling out the logic board.

"Here."

The instructor handed her a towel, and she wiped herself down, leaving smears of mud down her body. She felt utterly degraded as she struggled to pull on a fresh uniform, still barefoot.

"Now," he said. "Let's talk."

He opened the rear door of one of the Jeeps, then sat in the front himself. As she dipped her head to enter, the other passenger looked at her as if she were a student who'd broken the school's rules. It was Dr. He.

"I was puzzled by your answer, Jia. I wondered how you could have forgotten. The Year of the Dragon started on January 23, and you were in Heyuan on February 16, when the earthquake struck. You did not register in Guangzhou until later in the month. A Heyuan girl who does not know any Hakka dialect? You are a mystery."

Mei kept silent—there was nothing to say. She kept her head down, staring at a crushed cigar butt in the Jeep's ashtray. The door clicked open, and the seat shifted as Dr. He climbed out. The instructor hummed tunelessly. As the door opened, a pair of polished shoes appeared in her line of sight, and she smelled fabric infused with cigar smoke.

The instructor clapped his hands. "Show respect, Jia. You are in the presence of a great man whose hospitality you have abused. Not many people have this privilege. This is Cao Fu."

Everything about Cao was angular—the line of his jaw, his cheeks, his nose. His cigar was twice the diameter of his long fingers, on which the knuckles stood out. When Mei raised her head, he stared at her for a moment before resting his cigar in the tray by his last stub.

"Open your eye." Her held Mei's jaw in one hand and gazed into them, then held open one eyelid and with his finger and thumb gently rubbed her eyeball, plucking out a dark contact lens.

"There, that's better." He discarded it on the floor and picked up his cigar again. "A girl with one green eye and one black eye. I've never seen that before. Your face is familiar. Who are you?"

"My name is Jiang Jia."

"I don't think so. It is unlikely." His voice was light and resonant; he spoke as if he'd experienced so much deception that it didn't bother him. "What is the second of the precepts that everyone at Long Tan learns?"

"I don't know."

Fu grunted and took a puff of his cigar, blowing a swirl of smoke around the interior of the Jeep. "Was she not taught, instructor? Is that the reason for her bad behavior?"

"It is the first thing we teach, Dr. Cao. I taught her the precepts myself, on the day she arrived." The instructor stared at Mei indignantly, as if she had let him down in front of his boss.

"What is it, young woman?"

"Respect." Mei mumbled the word, sick of the game the members of Cao's cult played for each other.

"Yes, respect. By your behavior, by lying even about your identity, you show us no respect. Do you think we're stupid? Do you think we don't understand this game? Who are you?"

"Jiang Jia."

"All right. Let's see how long you will stick with that story. We can be on our way."

The instructor nodded, rapping furiously on the window to summon a guard. He hopped from the Jeep and crossed to the passenger seat before he could be forced into the indignity of driving. A Jeep pulled out ahead, and the driver tucked in behind it, the third forming a convoy. It sped along the perimeter road by the drain, passing a checkpoint with a raised barrier. They were outside the compound, but Cao's command reached beyond his territory.

The Jeeps hurtled around a shallow bend. The storm had drifted across the delta, visible now only by the flickering of far-off lightning on the horizon. They swung left, past another checkpoint and over a bridge, and then entered the complex through a gate that Mei had not seen before. Two buildings lay in their path, both of them half-empty—they had a dozen stories, but only a few were lit. It was a long ride from the main streets of the complex. There was an oddity about them that Mei couldn't identify at first. As she was pulled out of the Jeep by a guard, she realized what it was: They had no nets.

Cao strode ahead, his cigar glowing in the night, followed by the instructor, chattering at his shoulder. Mei walked behind, handcuffed to the guard who'd pawed her. He'd pushed away another guard, as if his violation had turned Mei into his chattel. She didn't look at him or register disgust—she was too scared by the dark buildings. Her nightmare had returned.

They took her most of the way by elevator, and got out on the eleventh floor, leaving only one flight of stairs to the roof. She stood with the guard on a landing while Cao and the others climbed the last steps and swung open the door. Then he led the way, tugging on the handcuff so that it bit into her wrist. She felt faint just looking at the roof, glistening with water from the storm. Cao was striding across it, toward the far edge.

"Bring her," the instructor commanded.

The guard pulled her out, tugging her across the threshold. The sky was wide and black, the last of the storm clouds breaking. It was brilliantly clear—stars shone and aircraft sped south toward Hong Kong. To the north lay the bend of the Pearl River and Guangzhou. After the exhilaration of her near-escape, she knew her fate. She let herself be pulled toward Cao—there was nothing she could do. He had halted near the side, looking at the twin building a hundred feet across the void.

As they neared, he tossed his cigar into the chasm between the roofs, where it plunged like a doomed firefly.

"Who are you?"

"Jiang Jia."

The instructor clapped once. "Where is your respect? You must—"

"Quiet, idiot."

Mei was terrified, almost broken, but if she could have laughed, she would have. Cao had treated the instructor as she'd wanted to since the first time they'd met. She smiled at him, but his face was frozen and rigid.

"Show her what we do to liars," he said.

The guard unlocked the cuff from his hand and pulled her free arm in front of her. He cuffed her wrists together and pushed her toward the edge. Her patina of calm cracked as she saw the drop—made worse by the facing building, which formed a tunnel to the ground. Her head spun, and she tried to scramble back, but the guard shoved her with his knee. Another held her cuffs on a metal hook attached to a wooden pole. They had done this before.

"Kneel," the instructor said.

Mei obeyed, her back to the roof's edge and her toes waggling in space, as if praying to Cao.

"You know happens next," he said.

"I—"

Before she spoke, the guard kicked her legs from under her and they dropped off the roof. Her wrists snapped agonizingly against the cuffs, which the second guard held with the hook, leaving her half-on and half-off the roof. The metal bit into her wrists, and she couldn't breathe.

"Further," Cao said.

The guard walked slowly, lowering her over the side. She was in agony. Her body shook, and she could feel gravity tugging at her feet. She would be swallowed up, she knew. An image came to her of the bracelet-like weal on her sister's wrist as the body had turned in the pond.

"My name is Elizabeth Lockhart," she said in English.

Cao looked down at her as if, for the first time, she had said something that interested him.

"Bring her up," he said.

The pain in her wrists was so intense that she thought they might break as the guard walked backward, dragging her onto the roof. When he was done, she lay there shaking.

"Where do you come from?"

He spoke English with a crisp, hard accent—the kind he might have acquired at a boarding school.

"I'm American." She turned her head to one side to speak, feeling the damp grime of the roof on her cheek.

"You're a spy?"

"No. No." She would do anything not to be dropped back over the roof. "I work with an NGO. In Hong Kong."

Cao put back his head and laughed.

"You're a do-gooder? Trying to save the world? Why are you bothering Long Tan, where people are happy? Why aren't you in Af-ri-ca?" He elongated the syllables with disdain.

"Your workers are badly treated. I wanted to help."

"Nonsense. You know nothing, Elizabeth. Don't try to colonize us with your sophomore ideas."

She raised her head to speak. "I'm an American citizen. My family knows where I am. So does the U.S. Consulate."

"That was in another country. You've joined Long Tan's family. Why did you steal that logic board? A souvenir? Enough of your lies."

Fu knelt by Mei and gestured to the guard to roll her over on her back. He held a badge with her photo on it and clipped it to her tunic. Then he got to his feet, wiped his knees, and walked away.

"Get rid of her," he said.

51

The guards pulled Mei to her feet, with her wrist bleeding from the handcuffs. Cao had vanished through the door on the other side of the roof, and she was alone with them and the instructor. The man had puffed up—pleased that, with Cao gone, he was the boss.

He pointed to the handcuffs. "Take those off her."

The guard who'd groped her did so, then took a cloth and wiped away the blood. He wasn't showing solicitude; he was eliminating evidence.

"Jiang Jia," the instructor said. He addressed her as if he hadn't listened to her last words, or as if he preferred to go by her badge. "We gave you our trust, and you let us down. You have betrayed the spirit of Long Tan and put our workers in peril. That disappoints me—"

"Fuck your grandfather." Despite everything, saying it felt good.

His face stiffened. "Put her there," he said.

Two guards stood by Mei's side and grasped her by her upper arms, pulling her to the edge of the roof. She held her eyes away from the precipice, looking at Guangdong—the cities and the river that carried the world's goods. In the last moments of life, she wouldn't let him see her terror.

"Wait."

The instructor walked up to Mei and faced her, as if he couldn't bear to let her have the last word. He opened his lips to talk but didn't speak as, with a splattering sound like a melon bursting, blood drenched his face.

Mei felt the grip on her arm slacken as the guard to her left twisted and sagged to his knees. His skull had blown apart in a spray of red; he was already dead. Mei and the instructor watched open-mouthed as the man's body tipped backward, plunging off the roof. As it did, the guard on her right also fell to the ground with blood spurting from his leg.

Time slowed down. A mere second had passed, and Mei didn't know what was happening, except that they were under fire. She saw the instructor's face clear as his brain came back to life. They were standing three feet from the edge of the roof and he had the stronger position—facing her, her back to the edge. There was only one move for an untrained fighter with the advantage of weight and he took it instinctively, pushing his arms toward her, palms out.

It was nothing—she'd trained for such a moment, and he had given her far too long to react. She thrust her hands up to his arms, so as to sense which one would push harder. It was the right, and she brushed his left arm away while her left hand encircled his right wrist, pulling. *Use your opponent's weight to your advantage,* the *sifu* always said. The instructor was off balance and she dragged him forward, darting aside to let him pass, almost like a matador. He stumbled two steps, mouth opening as he recognized his fate.

Then he fell into the chasm.

Mei crouched, scanning the roof. The shots had stopped, but she had to get down somehow. She rolled toward the exit and raised her head. It was a hundred yards away, and she couldn't get there by rolling. She crawled ten or twenty feet, waiting for a shot, and then got to her feet and ran a few paces with her head low. No response. She scrambled to her feet again. Nothing. Taking a deep breath, she ran for her life.

A few feet from the exit, the door opened, and a man stepped onto the roof with a gun in his hand. It was Lockhart.

"Get down!" he shouted.

He shot, the explosions booming across the roof as a body fell behind her. The wounded guard had limped after her, but now he was dead. Lockhart went to check on his body, then ran back to her.

"Are you hurt?" he asked.

"Not badly."

He knelt, checking her. Her hands were bloody and limp, and her legs and feet were lacerated. Blood leaked from her wrists where the cuffs had bitten her flesh.

"Don't move."

Mei was too weak to question him. She lay her head on the roof as he placed his jacket over her. Her body shook and her teeth chattered. She saw a light in the sky, which grew as it hovered above Long Tan toward them. In the last seconds, as it floated across the roof, she heard thundering. It landed fifty feet away, rotors spinning—a Harbin Dolphin helicopter in green camouflage, with the red star of the People's Liberation Army.

A soldier in overalls climbed out as the blades slowed, pulling a stretcher with him. Another joined him, and they ran across the roof to Mei. Slipping webbing bands under her body, they lifted her onto the stretcher and covered her with a foil blanket. Lockhart walked alongside as they carried her back and slid the stretcher into the rear cabin. It was locked in place by a third crew member as Lockhart took a seat. The soldiers secured the doors, and the craft started to lift as soon as the latches clicked.

Mei saw only the sky twisting across windows as they climbed across the compound.

"Where are we going?"

"Somewhere safe," he shouted above the roar.

When they'd reached a stable altitude, a nurse came to the front to examine her. She worked rapidly, bandaging her wrists and applying dressings to the wounds on her leg. Giving Mei an injection, the woman tucked a container of pills in her pocket, tapping the label. Mei nodded—she would have to dose herself.

Before long, they descended. The helicopter bumped through turbulence on its way down and described a lazy circle, lingering before landing as if the pilot had to pick his spot carefully. The touchdown was so gentle that Mei wasn't sure the flight had finished until the soldiers removed their harnesses, the rotor whine softened, and a door slid back. The nurse loosened Mei's bindings and placed an arm beneath her shoulders to lift her.

As Mei sat, she got her first view of the outside world. She'd expected to see an airport or a PLA base, but they were resting at the edge of a marsh. The pilot doused his lights and lit a cigarette.

"That guy can fly," Lockhart observed, and a soldier nodded.

He unbuckled his harness and took off his helmet, then climbed out and turned to Mei. She clambered to her feet, every muscle aching, and he lifted her down. When they'd walked some distance, the engines pounded and the rotor blades screamed. The helicopter lifted, as delicately as it had arrived.

The only light on the marsh was from a pair of nearby headlights, and he held Mei's arm as she limped across to a stationary SUV and they climbed in. Feng sat behind the wheel.

"Unbelievable. You made it."

She punched the wheel, then reached back and held Mei's bandaged hand. Mei put her head in her other hand, trying to recover from the shock. After a while, Lockhart gave her a tissue to wipe her nose.

"What are we doing here?" she asked.

"It's as far as we can go."

"Feng has a fleet of PLA aircraft at her disposal," Lockhart said. "Helicopters, aerial drones."

"I know how to ask nicely. Tom will handle it from now on. Now, I don't want to rush you, but did you find anything?"

"A logic board, but they took it."

"Anything else?"

"A master chip."

"Where is it?"

Mei opened her mouth, pointing a finger down her throat.

"You're joking." Feng laughed as Mei shook her head. "Just clean it up before you show it to me, okay?"

"Come on," Lockhart said.

They got out and Feng bumped the SUV across the field to the road, waving as she drove. They were in the marsh, perhaps fifteen hundred feet from the Jinggang'ao Expressway. Lockhart stepped into the field, beckoning her to follow, as he had before, and she limped behind him.

The marshes deepened on both sides of the path into rice fields. A boat had been abandoned in one field, its slats rotted, sunk halfway beneath the surface. They headed toward two lights, suspended off the ground; as they approached, Mei saw lanterns on poles. They marked the jetty where she had stood before, where she'd seen Lockhart standing in the beam before he escaped. Mei was exhausted— she couldn't stay upright much longer. She sat on the wooden slats until the waterway echoed with the sound of an engine chugging through the delta—a fishing boat with masts jutting in a V shape. It came to a halt by the jetty, the tires that hung from its side bumping and squeezing against it. Lockhart climbed up and flipped onto the deck, then reached for Mei. She clasped his hand, and he hauled her on board and led her to a tar-faced captain under a rickety awning, surrounded by trash.

The old man grunted an acknowledgment as they climbed below, then steered his boat toward the Pearl River.

52

The cabin was as cluttered as the captain's nook. It was stuffed with plastic fuel cans, wooden crates, wire cables, and half-broken chairs. A pile of old videocassettes occupied a corner, from before the days of the DVD. It stank of diesel oil, fish, and marsh water, some of which was sloshing around in a dirty bucket. Two crew members lay on narrow bunks, one snoring and the other reading the celebrity pages of a Hong Kong tabloid. Lockhart kept walking through a passageway to another cabin that was emptier and unoccupied.

"You should rest," he said.

Mei nodded—she didn't have the energy to reply—and lay on the thin mattress on one of the bunks. The bulkhead by her side sloped inward, following the line of the hull. Lockhart rummaged through a compartment under the bunk and pulled out a rough blanket that smelled of oil; she pulled it up around her neck, closing her eyes. She'd experienced terrible things, and she tried to think of something nice instead—wearing a tiger-head hat with Wing on the fifteenth day of the spring festival, when she'd been six.

She dozed off to the throbbing of the diesel, waking several hours later. The cabin light was dimmed, and Lockhart lay in the bunk above. The engine was working harder than before, and the boat was being rocked by waves as it pushed forward. Water slapped against the outside of the porthole near her knees, but she couldn't see anything out of it but darkness.

When she woke again, Lockhart stood by her, shaking her arm. She heard voices from the captain's deck. The porthole shone with the lights of another boat, which had drawn alongside. Lockhart took a tool, like a screwdriver with a T-shaped end, and poked it through two holes in a bulkhead panel on the other side of the cabin, at floor level. The panel was about three feet high by six feet wide, and he twisted the tool twice to unlock it. Pulling it free, he pointed— *get inside.* Mei was groggy, but she climbed down and pushed her body into the gap, feet first. She heard Lockhart tidying up behind him, then he climbed in beside her and secured the panel behind him.

It was pitch-black, and it felt like being buried alive in a sarcoph-agus, a fellow slave beside her. She heard Lockhart's breathing, low and steady, and the creak of the boat shifting in the water. They lay on cold metal with a stamped metal panel inches above their noses. Lockhart said nothing, but he took her left hand, giving it a squeeze that was painful but comforting. Straining her ears, Mei heard the echoes of voices, then a motor's whir and the sound of creaking. Boots descended a ladder and then, without any warning, there was a deafening bang. Someone had jumped onto the roof panel.

Another person climbed down more gently, while the owner of the metal-tipped boots paraded up and down, stamping the panel by Mei's head, as if testing it. It felt as if they were being crushed under-foot, as if a boot might break through at any moment, kicking their bodies. Then the banging stopped, and a conversation broke out be-tween two men, starting with murmurs and then getting louder. Mei couldn't make out the words. One man laughed, then footsteps as-cended the ladder. After two minutes, the vessel's engine roared and waves rocked the boat.

"We're out," Lockhart said.

He unlocked the panel and pushed it, letting air and light back into the hole. Mei pulled herself backward and climbed out, kneeling on the bunk and gazing through the porthole. She saw lines of lights and the hulking shapes of container ships. The boat was moving again, rocking through the Pearl River estuary toward the sea. Lock-hart sat by her on the bunk, as if nothing untoward had just hap-pened.

"We can go up," he said, looking at his watch.

Both crew members were asleep as they passed back through the other cabin. It didn't look as if they planned much fishing. Mei breathed the air gratefully as they surfaced. The captain was still at the helm, but with one hand on the wheel now—it was a simple matter to navigate the reaches of the Pearl River estuary. The aircraft in line to land at Chek Lap Kok formed a string of lights as they sailed toward the clustered islands between Hong Kong and Macau. It was an hour before dawn.

"What did the customs want?"

"Money."

"How much?"

"The usual."

Lockhart pulled a wad of notes from a pocket and handed some to the captain, as the man changed course to skirt Lantau Island, along the route of the Macau ferries. Mei sat on a grimy bench, looking out at the cluttered South China Sea, dotted with rocky outcrops, boats, and ferries. A fat container ship, stacked high with the output of factories, inched across the horizon, which was glowing with the approach of the sun. It was five-thirty—twelve hours since she'd started her last shift—when they squeezed past Cheung Chau and headed across the West Lamma Channel toward Hong Kong.

They chugged into Aberdeen Harbor on the island's south side as dawn broke, between Aberdeen promenade and the triple-towered apartment blocks on Ap Lei Chau. The captain steered past gaudy junks and floating restaurants to the row of lashed-together boats and swung his vessel in line. As soon as they'd stopped, a boat pulled up beside the cabin—a flat-bottomed sampan with a roof of green canvas strung on hoops, red and yellow flags fluttering in the breeze. A man tending an outboard engine shouted in Cantonese for them to hurry, and the captain turned his back, his business done.

The sampan puttered across the water, past the Jumbo Kingdom restaurant, as if they were tourists taking a view of the Aberdeen Harbor before breakfast. Cars flitted past on Aberdeen Praya Road, up early to be the first through the tunnel to Central. The sampan moored at the harbor side near the Tennis and Squash Club, where a red and white taxi waited. When they climbed in, the driver didn't wait to be told a destination. He headed east along the highway connecting Hong Kong's dormitory bays, driving on the left-hand side of the road under the road signs with English names.

They drove along a beach strip, then turned up Deep Water Bay Road, a winding climb past narrow bends, with a steep rock face on one side and the Hong Kong Golf Club on the other. The lush fairways were spread at the bottom of the valley, with a few players on an early round. They climbed higher, clouds above the valley, the sea shining in the bay behind them. The farther they went, the more sculpted and protected the mansions looked. A gray battleship of a villa loomed at the top of one bend. There were no signs of life, and Mei wondered if it was a home or merely an investment—a place for some tycoon to stash millions in Hong Kong dollars in case he had to flee.

The taxi darted off the road, down a cobbled driveway to a house propped above the valley, and Lockhart paid the driver while Mei climbed up stone steps cut into the rock. She emerged on a wide marble terrace with a swimming pool. A table and chairs had been placed at the end, with a priceless view over Deep Water Bay. Past sliding doors, cushions sat plumped on sofas in a wide living room, and the kitchen surfaces gleamed. Nothing moved.

"I wonder who owns this," said Lockhart.

"You don't know?"

"I didn't fix it. Feng gave me the keys."

Mei couldn't make sense of it, and she didn't try. She went through the kitchen and upstairs to a bedroom. A closet lined one wall, filled with expensive dresses—Prada, Alberta Ferretti, Gucci. She took off her uniform and kicked the clothes to the side of the bathroom, stepping into a white marble shower. Afterward, she dressed in silk pajamas from the drawer and stood by the window. Below her, a gardener was skimming leaves from the swimming pool with a net. She felt like an heiress.

53

Lockhart rested on the terrace until noon, letting his body heal in the sun. He hadn't used a gun outside a firing range for a long time, and he'd been lucky to take down the guard in two shots. He'd realized as he ran up the stairs to the roof how frantic he was to save her; desperation had helped his aim.

When he rose from the lounger, he was alone. The gardener had left for the day, and the maid had disappeared. She'd laid out sandwiches on a plate on the kitchen island, with a bowl of chips for the expatriates. He poured a Coke into a long glass and sat by the island to eat. Then he went upstairs to check on Mei, poking his head into the shaded bedroom. She was asleep on the surface of the quilt, her hands flung back from her head, defenseless. He went into the next bedroom and lay down himself, but it took him a very long time to get to sleep.

At six o'clock, he was woken by a sound in the basement of the house. By the time he reached the kitchen, Feng was there, having climbed the stairs that led from a garage below. She carried two cases and was trailed by a man like a cable guy, in overalls, with a belt of tools and a case. They looked as if they had brought enough to move in for a few weeks.

"How do you like the place, Tom?"

"I'm impressed."

"It belongs to a friend. He doesn't use it much."

"If he has a house on Deep Water Bay, he's doing well."

"Family money." Feng patted her companion on the shoulder and pointed along a corridor. "There's a room there to set up."

Lockhart heard footsteps on the stairs, and Mei walked in. Barefoot, wearing a silk tunic and pants, she'd regained some color in her cheeks and looked more human. He pulled out a stool from the island and poured her a glass of water from the fridge. As she drank deeply, he saw that the bruises on her hands and wrists were turning purple.

"How are you, darling?" Feng asked.

"I have something for you."

Mei pulled a tiny square from her pocket and laid it on the kitchen counter—a master chip engraved with the Poppy logo. Feng prodded it suspiciously, as if it might be infectious.

"You swallowed this?"

"Don't worry, it's clean."

"That's not the problem. You're not supposed to get water on it, never mind store it in your stomach."

"I sealed it in a rubber."

"Where did you get *that* from?"

"A girl in the dormitory gave it to me."

"God, Mei. You're quite an operator."

Lockhart rested a hand on Mei's shoulder, which felt thin through the fabric. "You did it."

"We'd better check before we celebrate," Feng said.

Feng's companion had stuffed one of the rooms at the rear of the house with his equipment. He'd put a computer on one desk, linked by cables to two Poppy tablets, and placed a soldering iron on another table close by. It looked like a crude version of the workstations Mei had seen in the factory. The technician had started to take one of the tablets apart, prying open the face, exposing the insides and going through the sequence of unscrewing parts and pulling them out. He paused when he reached the inner frame, stumped for a moment. Standing behind him with Feng, Mei pointed at the next screw. Finally, he had the parts on the table, and the logic board was exposed to view.

Feng gave him the chip Mei had smuggled out, and he placed the logic board under a jeweler's loupe and held a heat gun to the back of the board, melting the solder. Brushing away the soldering flux, he pried the master chip off the board with pliers. He cleaned the face and then lined up the replacement chip, soldering it in place with the incandescent prods of the soldering iron. Once he was happy with it, he reassembled the tablet, as rapidly and deftly as Mei had seen it done, and slotted it back in the dock. Then he pressed the button to start the device. They watched nervously as a counter whirled on the black screen, then the tinkle of a Poppy tablet booting sounded, and the pink branches appeared. It worked.

"I need an hour," he said.

They spent it on the terrace. Feng found a bathing suit upstairs and lay on an inflatable raft in the pool, waving her arms in the water, while Lockhart and Mei sat on chairs. Mei scanned the Deep Water Bay beach in the sun with binoculars, watching a couple with kids bouncing in the shallows of the ocean. The technician appeared right on schedule an hour later, tapping on the sliding doors to get everyone's attention. Feng maneuvered herself to the side of the pool by scooping the water and put on a robe.

By the time she emerged, the sun was setting and she had gotten dressed. She crossed the terrace and sat in front of them.

"Congratulations, Mei."

"The same chip?" Lockhart said.

"Identical."

"But you don't know what it does." Mei said.

"We do now. We found out while you were inside Long Tan. The NSA sent over a helpful young man to work with us. You met him in Washington, I think. He's called Joe, or that is what it says in his passport. Not good at eye contact but very clever. We enjoyed the cooperation."

"We ought to do it again," Lockhart said.

"Maybe. I shouldn't tell you this, but you earned it."

Mei nodded. She didn't care what they said—it was forgiveness. She had brought herself back from the ghost shift, and they had stopped talking about Yao, or breaches of discipline, or traveling on a false passport. She was not locked in a PLA camp or Camp Peary. She was at liberty.

"I'll keep it simple," Feng said. "Everything sent over the Internet is scrambled so that nobody can read them except the person they're intended for. Every document, every file. They're encrypted on the sender's computer using a number called a public key. The key is exchanged with the other computer to decrypt the message, but it doesn't matter if the number is intercepted on the way because possessing the public key isn't enough. You need to know the private keys—the two numbers the computer has multiplied to create it."

"Can't you work out the private keys from the public key?" Mei was no cryptographer, but she had factored numbers.

"That's the clever part of it. The computers use two very large prime numbers for the private keys and it's extremely hard to factor large primes. It's impossible, actually, unless you have a very powerful computer and a lot of time—months, perhaps years. As long as you use random prime numbers, it's safe. The only thing is, they must be random. If someone knows one of them, or even what it might be, they can unscramble the public key and your message. They can unlock everything."

"And this has something to do with the chip?"

"The encryption is built into the master chip. It generates random primes to create the public key. But if the chip has a security flaw and selects numbers that appear random but actually aren't, the encryption is breakable. That's what they call a trapdoor. If somebody has fixed the chip, they can factor the public key easily. It means that nothing on the device is safe. No emails, no documents, nothing. That's what they've done with these tablets. They can read everything on them, anytime they like."

"You might as well put your emails on a poster and hang it in Tiananmen Square for the tourists," Lockhart said. "It's cute. You're sent your tablet, wrapped in its original box. You think it's okay because it's come straight from the factory. It can't have been tampered with. But they fixed the factory. Think about it. The ability to know everything that was being said in Zhongnanhai or the West Wing. That would be worth plenty. Worth building a ghost factory for."

Mei thought of the tablets being packed in boxes, ready to be loaded onto the trucks outside P-1. "Where have they gone?"

"They were gifts to officials, sent anonymously with compliments from Poppy," said Feng. "We've found sixteen with Politburo members, six with the Politburo standing committee, five with PLA generals. Those are the ones we've retrieved, but there's a list of others. It's spreading."

"They've sent some to the U.S. now," Lockhart said. "To the White House, the Pentagon, the CIA. The U.S. ambassador to Berlin got one last week. Everyone wants the latest Poppy tablet, and they don't ask questions."

"Let's take a walk," Feng said.

She led Mei and Lockhart down the stone steps to the exit and walked a hundred yards along the driveway. They stood by a slope covered in trees and bushes, with a set of steel stairs leading down fifty feet to a platform underneath the driveway. Feng descended, holding the handrail, and they followed. They passed knotted banyan trees and ficuses, leaning out over the gorge but rooted on the hillside.

"All the utilities come down here. It's remarkable," Feng said.

"Great infrastructure." Lockhart said.

They halted on the platform, the endpoint for the staircases that reached down into the gorge from the rear of the other properties. In front of them stood a padlocked metal gate with a turquoise sign reading No Unauthorized Entry. It would be easy to ignore the gate and slip over the handrails, Lockhart thought. The path beyond it led through greenery to a property commanding the hillside—a white stucco villa behind a balustrade, half shielded by palm trees.

"That's Cao Fu's house," Feng said.

54

Mei stepped onto Deep Water Bay Road, wearing a Gucci dress in pink with a dahlia print she'd taken from the closet. Viscose clung to her hips, and the racer back exposed her shoulders. In her twenty-three years, it was the most glamorous thing she'd ever worn.

A mistress's wardrobe rather than a wife's, she'd thought as she'd rippled her fingers along the clothes, trying to picture their owner. She was as tall as Mei and had a similar figure. All the hemlines were short, and the shoes stacked in boxes all had high heels. Mei had taken a glossy pink pair to go with the dress and a matching wallet. The owner didn't do casual. She seemed to spend most of her time going out at night, looking pretty. It wasn't easy to walk in the shoes, which were half a size too big. Mei fastened the ankle strap tightly, ignoring her bruises. Her heels broke the night's silence.

She buzzed the entry phone at Cao's property, stirring a guard from his post. The man opened the gate, looking at her appreciatively, and Mei smiled brightly.

"I'm here to see Cao Fu."

"Is he expecting you?"

"I know him well. My name is Jiang Jia."

"Wait here."

The guard strolled up the driveway, and she looked at the front of the house. Two black Mercedes were parked near the door, a driver waiting in one. She couldn't see guards, except for the one who was now walking back toward her. He opened the gate to admit her, then led her to the front door. A maid took her into the hallway, where a middle-aged woman stood, bristling with suspicion.

"What do you want? My husband is busy."

The woman was dressed in a silk tunic and pants and had a beautiful face—a fine nose and high cheekbones. She'd reached an age at which she didn't display her legs the way she had done once, and she regarded the pink dress as if Mei were wearing explosives.

"I have to speak to him."

"You must leave. Now."

A mahogany door opened onto the hall, and Cao appeared behind his wife in a smoking jacket.

"I'll handle this."

His wife whipped around to face him, pointing a finger. "You told me—"

"I said I'd handle it. You—" The guard stiffened. "Come."

Cao's study was large and comfortably arranged. Aside from his mahogany desk, it held three sofas, and shelves weighted with books, ornaments, and photographs of him with Hong Kong celebrities and mainland politicians. In one, a young Cao stood by Deng Xiaoping, showing the Great Leader a crude production line in a small factory. It sat on the desk, by a panorama of the concourse at Long Tan, lined with workers applauding. Sliding doors looked onto the monumental terrace.

"I'm surprised to see you here, Miss Lockhart." He sat on one sofa and gestured at her to put herself opposite. The guard, who had halted inside the door, was doing his best impression of a statue.

"You thought I was dead?"

"I wasn't sure. You brought an army with you."

"It wasn't my army."

"And this time? Are you alone?"

"Yes."

"Then you're brave. Naive and reckless, like many Americans, but brave, I admit that. What do you want?"

Mei opened her wallet and brought out the old Long Tan card with Lizzie's photo on it.

"You said I was familiar. Look at this badge. It belonged to a woman called Tang Liu, and it was found in a field in Dongguan. Your thugs killed her a month ago, and they left it there. That was stupid of them."

Cao stared at the badge and scrutinized Mei. "So, you make a habit of coming back from the dead," he said.

Lockhart grasped the pipe forming the handrail to the steps and pulled himself under. He wore a tracksuit and sneakers and carried a canvas bag. Above, Cao's house looked like a wedding cake, set on the glowing terrace. Lockhart stood under a banyan tree, watching for activity. After five minutes, a guard walked along the terrace, gazing across the valley from the balustrade.

Lockhart ran up the steps while the guard was still at the far side of the terrace, pausing by the top. When he raised his head, his eyes were at ground level between two pillars, and he saw across the terrace to the guard. The man stopped to light a cigarette and walked back, first crossing the terrace, then turning back toward the house. Lockhart took a syringe, holding it in his fist with his thumb on the plunger, and waited. The man drew on the cigarette as his left leg passed Lockhart's nose.

Reaching up, Lockhart thrust it deep into the man's thigh, through his uniform pants, as his lungs took a last shot of nicotine. He spluttered, ejecting the cigarette like a missile, and dropped to the ground. Lockhart swung himself over the ledge and sat on the body. After a couple of seconds, feeling no movement, he rolled off, lifting the gun from his bag and crouching by the side of the terrace. He was in shadow, and he had a clear view through the glass doors into Cao's study. One of them was ajar, and he ran directly for it, afraid of stopping in case another guard appeared.

He had a view of three people as he pushed open the door. Neither the guard, immobile on the far side of the room, nor Mei on a sofa thirty feet away saw him. The guard stared at a wall to his left, and Mei was looking at something else in the room. The only pair of eyes to lock on his was Cao's—Lockhart had walked straight into his line of sight.

Before Lockhart could lift his gun, Cao leapt toward Mei, reaching for her with his hands. He'd gotten halfway there when she rolled her body with astonishing speed, bringing her left arm high in the air and punching him on the side of the neck. An instant later, her left foot thudded into his groin.

Lockhart swung his gun toward the guard, who hadn't moved. The man raised his arms in surrender, and they looked at Mei, who was on top of the semiconscious Cao with an elbow around his throat. Her fashionable dress was all ruffled up. Lockhart averted his eyes, but the guard didn't.

"Don't talk or move," Lockhart said to the man. Then, to Mei: "Jesus, where did you learn to fight like that?"

"Syringe," she replied.

He threw the bag to her and walked across to the guard, gesturing at him with the gun to sit. By the time he'd taped the man's mouth and locked the mahogany door, Mei had injected Cao in the leg; he was now unconscious. She lifted herself off and smoothed her dress. Then she sat and extracted a pair of women's sneakers, unlacing her heels and placing them in the bag with the syringe before zipping it.

"Let's go," she said.

Lockhart pulled the tape from the guard's mouth and pointed the gun at his head. "You won't be hurt as long as you do what we say. Carry him," he said.

The guard nodded and walked over to Cao, hoisting him on his back with his arms supporting Cao's legs. Cao's neck lolled to one side, and Lockhart taped his wrists in front of the guard's body so he wouldn't tip backward. He didn't hear any sound from behind as they crossed the terrace, with Mei in the lead, to where the other guard was stretched. The loudest noise was Cao's hoarse breathing. Lockhart's gun wasn't needed—the guard lurched a few times as he struggled with Cao's dead weight, but he was an obedient mule.

The gate to the stairs was unlocked, and they descended, with the glow fading behind them. Once, the guard pitched forward as he caught his foot, and Lockhart grabbed his arm to prevent him tumbling down the slope. At the bottom, they silently arranged Cao's limbs on the handrail so that the guard could climb over and hoist him on his shoulders again, and then started the ascent. The guard's breath grew louder as he labored up the slope, and Lockhart handed Mei his gun so he could heave from behind.

Feng stood on the terrace laughing as they dragged Cao up the steps. Lockhart cut his arms free and lowered him to the ground, letting the guard sprawl by the pool, exhausted but grinning. He seemed to like being on their side. When they'd regained their breath, the men each took one of Cao's arms, pulling his body across the terrace and along the corridor to a rear bedroom. They got him onto the bed in three shoves, and then Lockhart handcuffed his wrists to the frame.

By the time they returned to the kitchen, the women were having a party. Feng was drinking from a bottle of Louis Roederer Cristal, and Mei was swaying to a Justin Timberlake song that was being piped through the ceiling. The guard gazed, his mouth open, as if he'd discovered goddesses.

He had done his job so well that Lockhart poured him a glass of champagne.

55

They ate breakfast around the pool, while Cao stayed in his room. When they had gone to bed, the guard had taken the overnight shift outside his door. The guard was now asleep, so they had replaced him with the gardener. The window was sealed, the door was locked, and Cao was cooperating sullenly; the risk of him breaking out of his room was low. The water was shining blue and green, and the maid had prepared a five-star spread, ferrying it out on trays.

"Won't the Hong Kong Police search the neighborhood?" Lockhart asked.

"You're kidding," said Feng. "Too many important people to upset. They won't come to this house."

"You're sure?"

"Absolutely certain."

Hearing a rumble of vehicles by the house, Feng dropped her toast and stood. It was the first time that Lockhart had ever seen her agitated. She piled her things on a tray, gulping down what was in her mouth and waving at them to follow. Running toward the house, she pulled back the door and shouted for the maid. There was a flurry of boots on the stone steps, and two soldiers strode onto the terrace, ahead of a green-uniformed officer.

Feng hurried over to meet him, as he looked at Mei. He had dark circles under his eyes and dyed black hair. His eyebrows were set so high on his temple that they lent him an expression of permanent surprise.

"Major General Sun, this is Song Mei and Thomas Lockhart."
Feng pointed at them. "The general is political commissar of the
PLA's Hong Kong Garrison, and he offered us his house for this oper-
ation," she explained.

The general pinched his lips, looking at Mei's robe as if he'd seen
it somewhere before. He wore six rows of ribbons above the pocket
on his green uniform and the gold stars of the PLA on his epaulettes.
His shirt collar was tinged with sweat in the morning sun.

"He's ready, General. This way," Feng said.

"Shouldn't you change?" Lockhart asked Mei, after Feng had
taken the general inside. "He saw the robe."

"I don't have anything to wear except a torn Poppy uniform. Everything else belongs to his girlfriend."

She went to find something less obvious from the collection, picking a pair of pants and a pale blouse. They waited for an hour before
Major General Sun emerged, still with his baffled expression. Feng
led him toward the steps, but he stopped in front of Lockhart, offering his hand.

"Mr. Lockhart, I would like to talk to you."

He wandered across the terrace and stood at the edge by the pool,
extracting a packet of cigarettes and offering one to Lockhart. He
tore the filter off his own, and propped it in the corner of his mouth,
the smoke wreathing around him, before affably putting his hand on
Lockhart's arm.

"My condolences," he said. "Losing a child is a terrible thing. We
who have not done so can only imagine the pain."

"Thank you," Lockhart said. He thought of Cao, locked up in
the house just a few feet away, and wished the man had been on the
roof when they'd arrived, so he could have killed him. It didn't seem
like justice to hand him back to the people who had let him grow
wealthy.

"You know Henry Martin?" the general said, still puffing. "He is
a remarkable man—an original, a brilliant innovator. We need more
men like him in China. I'm sorry that he was embarrassed in this way.
It was inhospitable."

"I will pass on your message. I'm sure he will appreciate it."

"I would like to meet Mr. Martin. Tell him that." The general patted Lockhart on the back and left, his soldiers following.

"Would you raid his house if you were the Hong Kong Police?" Feng came and sat, calmer now that the general was gone.

"I don't think so," Lockhart said. "Why is the PLA so fascinated by Henry Martin?"

"The PLA has interests in lots of enterprises. They probably think he could teach them a few things. Shall we go in?"

Cao sat at a desk with his back to them, writing on a sheet of paper. His face looked pale from his abduction and unsettled sleep, but his clothes were neatly pressed. The guard had found him a set of fatigues, and he'd showered in the bathroom. His eyes passed briefly over Feng and Mei before settling on Lockhart.

"Who *are* you?"

"I'm the man who would have killed you if she hadn't kicked you in the balls. You're a big man when you've got an army behind you, but she beat your ass bare-handed."

Cao stood. "I'd like to leave now," he told Feng.

Lockhart hit Cao as he got close, crunching his fist against the man's angular jaw. Cao slumped, striking his head on a chair and tumbling to the floor, his split lip oozing. Lockhart flapped his hand in pain—his knuckles had struck Cao's bone and were already swelling. He didn't regret it.

"How many did you kill?" he said.

Cao dabbed his wound with one finger. "No one who obeyed the rules was in danger. And why do you care?"

"You asked my name. It's Lockhart."

Cao looked at him appraisingly.

"Was that girl a relative?"

"She was my daughter."

He nodded at Mei. "Is that one too? They both made trouble. This one is a fighter, and the other one. . . . I remember. She ran a long way before they caught her. She nearly got away."

Lockhart clenched his fist, but the twinge of pain forced him to restrain himself. "The sentence for murder is death, Cao. It's what you'll get."

Cao climbed to his feet and sat by the desk again, wiping away the blood so that it wouldn't stain his clothes. "That's not what the general told me. I'm not under police arrest. I haven't been charged."

"You're in *shuanggui*," Mei said.

He shrugged. "We'll see for how long. I told him I would cooperate with your investigation as a demonstration of my loyalty. Those who are self-interested might have led me astray. I am prepared to criticize myself and rededicate myself to the Party's work."

They were standing in a semicircle around him, with the guard hovering by the door. Cao was the only one seated. He'd somehow taken a place at the center of things, without being asked.

"You've forgotten," Feng said. "General Sun has departed. We're the only ones here, and the rules of *shuanggui* are hazy. People have a habit of turning up dead, like in your factories. We might not notice if something hits you. This room's not suitable for conversation. Let's continue downstairs."

The guard shackled Cao again, and they went through the kitchen to the stairs that led to the cellar. It was a dank space, smelling of gasoline. Car tires lay on the concrete. One wall was lined with tools—a power drill, saws, spades, hoes, a lawnmower, a rack of screws. There was barely any light, just the glow under the door.

"Remove your clothes," Feng said.

"Who are you to tell me that?"

"Do it," Mei said.

Cao's eyes narrowed slightly, as if imagining what he'd do to her if the tables were turned, and unbuttoned his military shirt. He bent to untie his laces and pull off his pants and underpants. His body was smooth and unlined, with a small belly and thin legs.

Feng walked to the tools and selected a tire iron. "Hold him," she said to the guard, who gripped his former boss by the shoulders from behind without hesitation. She swung the tool through the air in one quick motion, and smacked it up through his ribs, into his liver. Cao screamed and fell to his knees on the concrete, clutching his midriff.

"Smart people do stupid things," she said. "I saw the list of those tablets you sent. They went to the most powerful people in the country—provincial governors, the Army, the Navy, Beijing ministries, the Politburo, the Standing Committee. Everyone in a senior position was on it, except for one person. He didn't receive one—because he was the one giving them out."

Cao was bent over the floor. Racked with pain, his body looked old and frail. He'd stopped protesting and was silent. Feng reached out a foot and rolled him on his back, like a cockroach.

"Chen Longwei. He's your best friend, isn't he? Your mentor. The man who let you make a fortune in return for a few million yuan and some favors."

Cao was still trying to catch his breath, his legs splayed on the floor. He tried to speak a couple of times before managing it. "Let me get dressed. I'll tell you what you want."

The guard looked at Feng, who nodded. He handed Cao his clothes, and the man buttoned the shirt. He couldn't stretch to put on his pants, but he laid them over his groin. He was still gasping in pain.

"I don't know what they make in there. I don't ask them. That was the deal. I made sure no one talked and no one got out of there. All I know is that he wanted to use the factory, and he said he'd shut the whole place down if I didn't help."

"So you killed your workers for him?"

"Does it shock you? It wasn't hard. There's a wall around Long Tan, and we have our own police force. Twenty bodies? It's nothing. Millions died in the Great Famine. Did that make Mao a criminal?"

The images of Lenin and Stalin had vanished from Tiananmen Square since he'd lived in Beijing, but Mao was still lying in state in his mausoleum. Lockhart looked across at Feng to see how she would answer, but she turned away, ignoring the question.

56

They left at five, two soldiers in the leading Mercedes, Cao in the rear sedan with Mei. The guard was in a driver's uniform, having held the door open for her as Cao stalked to the other side. It wasn't easy to swing her legs in an Alexander McQueen dress with a gold dragonfly wing pattern that finished just below the knee. Its cap sleeves and tight silhouette made it look like a catwalk *qipao* dress. She paired it with black Dior pumps—savoring her last fling with the wardrobe of the general's mistress.

Cao wore an open-necked silk shirt and a dinner suit, which the guard had brought from his house. Both the Hong Kong police and Cao's wife had been told to stop looking for him. Mei stared from the window as they drove down Deep Water Bay Road, not engaging Cao. It had taken him two days to make the arrangements, and she had said nothing to him in that time. He'd tried to kill her and he'd murdered her sister. Even if he was useful, even if they did have a mission for the night, she had no intention of offering him any humanity.

A motor launch with a maroon hull and cream leather seats waited by a jetty at the Victoria Recreation Club, and four people climbed on board—one soldier, the guard, and the wealthy-looking couple, out for the evening. Mei sat in the stern as it zipped to Cao's yacht—a giant version of the same color scheme, with a sleek two-decked cabin and a radar antenna. The crew looked as if they were happy to be sailing, even if it was just a night out in Macau, rather than an oceangoing voyage. The engines hummed without the rough diesel of the fishing boat—more like the Mercedes.

They dawdled through the East Lamma channel, then the captain opened the throttle, the bow lifted, and they left the Hong Kong ferries behind, surfing across open water and dropping anchor in the Cotai marina. In another limousine, on the Ponte de Sai Van Bridge across the harbor, Mei watched Macau light up in the dusk. Neon pulsated up the tulip bulb of the Grand Lisboa casino, a pink and orange temple to luck. The Wynn Macau sat opposite, a restrained wave amid the brashness of the old Portuguese colony. Macau was Las Vegas on the water—bolder, bigger, and wealthier.

"Are you sure he'll come?" Mei broke her silence.

"He can't resist Macau."

In the Grand Lisboa's lobby, Mei paused to look at a glass-encased Qing sculpture of a horse's head, while a manager bowed to Cao, offering an escort to the upper stories. It had cost Stanley Ho nine million dollars to reclaim the piece, looted from a Zodiac fountain in the Old Summer Palace in Beijing by French and British soldiers in 1860. The punters streaming into his casino hardly noticed—they were interested only in their own fortunes.

The party ascended through the floors of the Grand Lisboa, from the *sic bo* tables by the lobby to the main gaming floor, dominated by a giant blue egg on a gold stand. The Crazy Paris floor show played as they walked beside a balcony, with half-naked women in glitter costumes dancing the can-can for the men who'd risen from the tables to stand. Mei had to walk rapidly behind Cao to keep up—he was already on the escalator to the upper floor, where the gaming halls gave way to the VIP rooms.

The manager opened the last door on the curved corridor, ushering them through. As they entered, Mei saw that she'd entered another world—a casino of its own. Instead of bawdy entertainment and players cursing their luck on the public tables, this was a hushed place where millions could be placed in side bets on a single coup. A month before, an official had given a talk at the Commission on money laundering in Macau—how bribes and kickbacks could be funneled out of China through credit accounts with the junkets, into casino chips and then into Hong Kong dollars.

A Buddha statue sat in the middle of the room, between two bac-

carat tables. A squat dark-skinned man in a crumpled suit played at
the first, while at the other, six players were arrayed around a gambler
with a stash of chips. The gambler creased his card and peered under
it, letting the tension build. The Player's box contained a queen and
an ace. He flipped the card—a three; the crowd deflated. The banker
had a jack and a seven, and the dealer scooped the chips from around
the table.

The partner in Cao's junket was a young man with a thin mustache and shaky hands. He led them to a side room with an ornate
bar, where a waiter brought Coca-Cola and trays of snacks.

"Welcome to Macau, Jia." Cao held his glass to hers, forcing her
to respond. She did it, hating him as much as the moment when he'd
left her to die, then pushed it to the back of her mind.

"Darling," she said. "Teach me to play."

"Of course, my dear."

Five piles of chips were stacked at his seat, opposite the figure
eight, at the emptier table. Mei sat to Cao's left, in the ninth place, as
the dealer stuffed fresh decks into her shoe. Ten seats were arrayed
around the kidney-shaped table, but she'd been dealing only for the
squat man. His pile of chips was low, and he looked as if he'd lost
pleasure in the game.

"Give me good fortune." Cao took a pile of chips, each worth a
thousand Hong Kong dollars, and slid them to Mei.

"Wait." She delved into her clutch bag, palming an identical chip
as she reached inside. She made a show of applying her lipstick, then
took half of the chips he had passed her, blowing on them and sliding
them back. Her own was on top of the pile. He put it by his right
elbow.

"I'll keep these." She pointed at the remaining chips massed in
front of her, the demanding mistress accustomed to getting her way.
"When will your friend arrive? I want to have fun."

"He'll be here soon—"

As he spoke, the door opened and a group of plainclothes security
men came in, fanning out through the space. Two stood by their
table, one at her left side, the other by the lone gambler. Cao whispered in the security man's ear, and the man lifted his jacket from the

back of his chair and walked away. The same was happening at the other table—the game ceased and the players dispersed. A couple wandered toward the bar and then, finding it closed off, headed off back into the casino. The room emptied, leaving just Cao, his junket partner, the guards, and the dealer.

A minute passed, with the dealer sorting her chips silently, before Chen walked in. He stood by the door, soaking in the atmosphere, as if home after a long journey. His suit was finer than on the stage in Revolutionary Martyrs Park and in the compound, when he'd urged the cadres not to deceive the Party. This was the Chen of Macau and Hong Kong, not the People's Republic. He stepped toward the Buddha between the tables, stroking one hand down its side to appreciate it.

"How is your luck, Cao Fu? Are you ready to play?" His voice had the rich timbre she knew.

Chen took the seventh seat, and the barman placed a tumbler of whiskey, stacked with ice, by his elbow. He took one sip, then glanced past Cao toward Mei. As he smiled, she felt a terrifying sense of isolation. She was alone with both of them in a sealed room—two men she knew for certain would not hesitate to kill her.

"Introduce us, Cao Fu." He showed no sign of having recognized her from his lecture in the auditorium.

"This is my friend, Jiang Jia."

"I envy you in discovering such a beauty. Can she be trusted? We have things to talk about, and I wouldn't want to subject her to the indignity of being searched. Not in that dress."

"I find her discreet."

"Then she is welcome. A beautiful woman will bring us luck." Chen rose and walked around Cao's chair to Mei, kissing her hand. She felt his warm breath. "Let us trust one another, as always. Our friendship has brought you wealth."

"It has many benefits for you, as well."

"We both gain. Why would we spoil it?"

He turned his eyes to the dealer and nodded, placing ten thousand Hong Kong dollar chips on Player. The $1,300 bet was his official monthly salary. Cao beckoned to the junket partner, and the man hurried over.

"A side bet. Ten times every chip. Can you handle that?"

"Of course, sir. We have no worries, when it's you."

"Very well." Cao slid ten thousand-dollar chips onto Player, matching Chen, plus an invisible side bet of one hundred thousand.

The dealer dealt him the Player cards. Cao squeezed back the top corners, then turned them to peer under the edges. His face didn't change as he threw them across the table to be flipped. A king and a nine—a natural coup. Mei squeaked excitedly and clapped her hands.

"I brought you good fortune, like you said."

"I want you at my side," Chen said to Mei.

Cao clipped a cigar and lit it, placing a hand on Mei's back. "You can't have everything."

"I will, soon. Don't bet against me."

"Are you a powerful man?" asked Mei innocently.

"Very."

The two men repeated their bets. The dealer slid the cards to Cao and placed two more on the Banker's square. Cao creased both cards, looking at them as impassively as before. He slid them to the dealer, and she exposed them. An ace and an eight—another natural.

"This is a lucky night, Cao. It is the Year of the Dragon, the year of good fortune and prosperity." Chen turned to Mei, cradling the extra chips the dealer had passed. "You asked if I was powerful. In one month's time, the Party holds its National Congress in Beijing. I shall join the Politburo Standing Committee. It has been agreed. Does that sound powerful enough for you?"

"I like men who are unafraid, who seize their chances and take risks. Cao is just such a man. That's why he pleases me." She placed her hand on Cao's, as he rested it on the table, fighting back her revulsion.

"I would please you more," Chen said.

She stared back into his copper eyes and smiled.

"Then play for me."

57

Lockhart was in the back, behind the Army officers, the Macau Public Security Police, and a woman from the Guangdong Commission for Discipline Inspection, who seemed—amid the bundle of security forces—to have the best claim to authority. He didn't have a prime view of the screens in the security center of the Grand Lisboa, but he'd found his way in. Feng had stood up for him, despite the grunts of protest.

Tension crackled as they watched the video from the camera high up in one corner of the VIP room, its view partly obscured by the Buddha's head. They could hear more clearly—the microphones in the baccarat table and the chip were working well. As Mei made her challenge to Chen, the woman put a hand up to her mouth. Lockhart couldn't tell, watching her from behind, if she was scandalized or impressed.

The security room was black and enclosed, the banks of screens producing the only light. They could see every part of the casino, from the treasures in the lobby to the gambling floor and behind the scenes in the kitchens and changing rooms. One camera even displayed the Crazy Paris dancers in their dressing rooms, for security or late-night amusement. They'd left two security officials in place to cover the rest of the building and were focused on this one contest.

On the screen, the dealer pushed a pair of cards to Chen, who had taken on the Player's role. He beckoned to Mei to sit with him, to touch his cards for luck. Cao tried to look jealous, but he was a bad actor, glancing at the camera as if willing the charade to end. Chen was too absorbed by Mei to take any notice.

"How much longer will it take?" Cao said suddenly.

"Will what take?" Chen was looking at Mei.

"The ghost shift. When will it end?"

The silence in the room thickened, and Lockhart leaned forward in his chair. It was a delicate thing, inserting the hook, and Cao lacked subtlety. Lockhart felt the inquiry dangle in the air.

"Don't talk business, silly melon," Mei said. She took one of Chen's hands and folded his fingers over a chip. "Put that in a good spot for me. I want to play along with you."

Chen took his cards and squeezed them from the table, displaying them to Mei while keeping them from Cao. A ten and a three. He nodded to the dealer, and she slipped a third from the shoe.

"We'll be done soon. Why, Cao Fu? Have you lost your nerve? Are you panicking? That won't please Jia. You see—" The dealer turned over a five, giving him the coup. "She's lucky."

"I'm under investigation. The news is full of stories about bodies at Long Tan. People are asking questions in Zhongnanhai. I was called by a member of the Politburo. They want it to stop."

"The mountain is high, and the emperor is far away. Ignore them."

Cao slammed a hand on the table. "I can't ignore them. I killed people for you. This isn't a game, Chen Longwei."

"Some weaklings fell off buildings because they caused trouble. Why are you so scared? She's braver than you." Chen turned to her. "A little death for a good cause. Are you shocked?"

Mei fingered his lapel. "Can I confess something? I'm a little ashamed." She leaned in to whisper. "It excites me."

Chen slipped his arm around her waist. "Listen to her, Cao Fu. She is a patriot. Was the Cultural Revolution easy? It was tough and painful, as I saw with my own eyes, but the Party emerged stronger. Zhongnanhai is weak, and the people yearn to be led. That's why they want me. That's why this girl desires me more than she desires you, Cao Fu. I know what these idiots write, everything they think. I know their inner thoughts, not the words they utter in public for the masses. How corrupt they are, how contemptible. The people will be told."

A red machine sat on the desk next to Pan. It was like a telephone without buttons, just a handset and a light. Two technicians had brought it into the room with them, connecting it to a box with a thick cable. When Chen stopped speaking, the device flashed. Pan listened for thirty seconds before replacing the receiver.

"Now," she said.

Mei had opened her mouth to say she was going to the restroom, when the door blew out of its frame, batting a guard across the room into the Buddha. His body fell limply as soldiers fired canisters of gas into the space. Another guard tried to pull his gun but was blown backward by two bursts of automatic fire.

Mei couldn't raise her arms in surrender because her hands were covering her mouth and nose, trying to block the gas. She dropped to her knees and rolled under the table, where she found the dealer. Soldiers ran across the room and pulled Cao and Chen to the ground at gunpoint, fastening their hands behind their backs with cuffs. She'd opened one eye when another soldier reached under the table and dragged her out, burning her knee on the carpet. He rolled her over and tied her, barefoot and breathless.

She was in that position five minutes later when the gas cleared and Pan entered. All Mei could see of the woman were her shoes and black pants, until she crouched by her.

"Find her a chair," Pan told a soldier.

Two of them hauled her up and propped her in one of the armchairs from the bar. Her hands were fastened at her back, and Pan tucked down Mei's dress, now ripped at the knee.

"If I had my way, I'd put you in detention for the killing of Zhang Yao and other breaches of Party discipline. Why didn't you take my advice?"

"You set me up," Mei said, still coughing.

"Don't listen to her—it's bullshit. I'd bust you out, even if I needed a tank. Take the handcuffs off her." Feng stood by Pan, holding a pair of sneakers and a coat for Mei.

Pan glared at her and then gestured to the soldier to cut her free. "Remember what I told you, Song Mei. We cross the river by groping stones. You found a stone that was hidden. I commend you."

Feng gave her the sneakers, and she laced them as she watched Pan walk up to Chen. He was on the floor, his arms cuffed behind his back, his expensive suit stained with blood.

"Chen Longwei, I place you in detention for serious violations of discipline and abuses of power. You have committed mistakes that have endangered the Party." Mei noticed that even Pan's voice wavered slightly at the gravity of arresting one of the Party's leaders.

"This is forbidden," Chen said indignantly. "I did not give permission for any such inquiry."

"I am authorized by the Politburo Standing Committee. A direct order came from Beijing this evening."

Two soldiers took Chen by the arms, marching him out of the VIP room and along the corridor, with a guard walking ahead of them. The others formed a parade, with Pan at the head—a fifty-foot-long cavalcade of Army, police, and plainclothes security.

"Come on. We can't miss this. Beijing said to make a big display. They're going out through the casino," Feng took a hundred-dollar chip from the table and threw it to Mei. "Have a souvenir."

The soldiers' boots echoed down the VIP corridor and, when they got to the escalator, the column was marching along the balcony above the main floor. As they descended, the floor had come to a halt. The Crazy Paris dancers stood on the blue-lit stage, staring at the night's best entertainment. Cards were no longer being dealt at the tables—everyone had risen to witness Chen's disgrace.

Feng and Mei broke into a run to keep up, as applause started to ripple across the floor. They walked through the lobby into the night, the neon on the casinos outshone by the lights of police cars, Army vehicles, and mobile phones and cameras. A crowd had gathered outside the Grand Lisboa to watch—even the rickshaw drivers had halted. Two lines of police were holding the crowd, clearing a line to the official cars, but Pan halted by the doors for thirty seconds, allowing the passersby time to take photos of Chen with their phones.

Lockhart stood at the front of the crowd as they led Chen past. Then Feng grabbed Mei's hand and pulled her, chasing down the path so they would not be left behind. They clambered into an Audi at the rear of the convoy just before it took off, streaming out of Cathedral Parish toward Zhongshan, lights flashing. Motorcycles pushed other vehicles from its path, clearing the way to the mainland. Mei sat by the window as they hurtled along the roads, hardly noticing as they crossed the border at Gongbei. She had come home under her own name, a return she had feared might never happen, but she was occupied by something else—the sight of Chen's and Lockhart's faces as the police had paraded Chen out of the casino.

She could swear they knew each other.

58

It was midnight. Mei knew the place by smell as she stepped from the car—it was country air, a long way from Guangzhou. The convoy had thinned along the way, losing the Macau police and outriders at the border. It comprised six Army vehicles and three Audis. They'd halted by a line of green-painted hangars that were vivid in her memory. She'd seen them behind the Wolf's interrogator, as he'd spat at her, on the night of her detention.

A committee of welcome waited by the detention center—a squad of soldiers and, standing in front of them by himself, the Wolf. Pan was occupied at the Army truck that held Chen, ensuring that everything was in order for his transfer, and Feng was asleep. Mei didn't wait. She opened her door and walked toward him. It reminded her of the night in the marsh, when she'd seen him out there, smoking a cigarette. Officials massed nearby, but he remained a lone beast.

"How are you, Song Mei?" The Wolf was showing symptoms of his detention—he moved more stiffly and was wearing a cheap cotton suit.

"I am honored, Lang Xiaobo." She took his hand in hers and bent her head. She'd thought she might never see him again and he'd be banished to the far north, a broken and discredited man.

"They tell me you saved me." The Wolf chuckled. "Six o'clock and all I had on my calendar was another session in the cellar with those animals. Then everything stops, and suddenly I'm an honored guest. A hot shower, fresh towels, and new clothes—" He plucked at the suit. "A dinner of delicacies. They couldn't do enough to make me happy. The Party always reaches the correct conclusion, I find, but it can take time. You have rehabilitated me."

"I only did my duty."

"That's not what I heard."

"I found her father, as you asked me to."

He nodded. "I knew you would."

They were interrupted by the sound of marching as the soldiers brought Chen across the tarmac toward the detention block. He had been stripped of his suit and was dressed in Army fatigues, still handcuffed. Pan walked next to him with a thick file. She halted by the Wolf, smiling.

"I am pleased that justice has been done, Lang Xiaobo."

"A painful form of justice, Pan Yue, as you know, since you were in charge of torturing me."

"It was a mistake. The Party has exonerated you of all charges. We will find the truth from the guilty man."

"You're sure he's guilty, are you?"

"We have irrefutable evidence of Chen's betrayal of the Party. Do not worry. There is no error."

The Wolf pulled out a pack of Chunghwas and lit one, breathing out two blue streams through his nostrils. He held up the cigarette, smiling.

"They gave me this tonight. I've had to make do with some terrible shit from Qinghai. I thought it was a life sentence."

"You shouldn't be smoking at all," Mei said.

"Allow an old man a little bit of pleasure." He turned his smile onto Pan, letting it chill. "I'm not worried about your error, since I am taking over responsibility for this inquiry. Since Chen is in *shuanggui,* I am in charge. You will work under my command until we find you another assignment, perhaps somewhere challenging. I spent a long winter in Heilongjiang once. It was good for my character."

The Wolf took Mei's arm and walked to where Chen stood, handcuffed to two soldiers. Chen looked at them both contemptuously and spat on the tarmac, but the Wolf ignored him.

"Chen Longwei, you've met Song Mei, a cadre in the Discipline Inspection Commission. She is already establishing a strong record of bringing criminals to justice, starting with you. I believe that this feat will soon be recorded in the *People's Daily*, and she will be rewarded."

"She's a whore, and you're a weakling, Lang Xiaobo. You've always been jealous, chasing after me for scraps from my table. I could make you do anything I wanted, all our lives. Is this your revenge?"

The Wolf took a last drag of his cigarette and flicked it into the dark. "You don't recognize her, do you? When I tell you, maybe you'll change your mind. You're right about me, though. I was weak. I should have done it much sooner. Do you know when I first wanted to? Three decades ago. You're not the heir of Mao and Deng, Chen. You're a worthless fool who cared only for yourself. What does it say for our Party that you could have ended up in charge?" He turned to a soldier. "Put him in the detention cells."

"What should I do?" Mei asked.

The Wolf looked at her, taking in her appearance for the first time. The coat Feng had brought only just covered her knees, and the laces on one of her sneakers trailed on the ground.

"We'll find you a room, and you can rest. I'll take you. Pan Yue can set things up here."

He took Mei toward the hangars, pausing on the way to instruct Pan, who was awaiting orders.

"We start tomorrow. I have a list of people for you to bring in for questioning. The first is Thomas Lockhart."

The Harbin Dolphin helicopter lifted from Shek Kong, with Lockhart strapped in the same seat as before, watching the New Territories recede as they climbed over the towers of Shenzhen and flew north. They'd sent a Jeep to the Peninsula at dawn, breaking what he'd hoped would be a long sleep. But he couldn't complain. The PLA was treating him like a VIP, driving him out of Hong Kong at high speed and laying on breakfast at Shek Kong. The pilot had leaned around as Lockhart donned his flying helmet and put one thumb up.

It was a short flight—twenty minutes door-to-door from the Shek Kong terminal to the airbase—with a fine view of the Pearl River, snaking through Guangzhou. By nine o'clock he had been driven across the tarmac, shown to an interview room with padded walls, and given a cup of coffee in a porcelain cup and saucer. He sat without being told what would happen, but knowing it. It had been twenty-three years since he had been summoned without warning from his Beijing apartment. People have habits, he'd learned. No matter how hard they try to break them, they leave a pattern. This was how it had started, and this was how it would end.

The Wolf entered the room ten minutes later, with a file under his arm. Lockhart scanned his face. He was thinner than before, and his hair had turned gray. He looked a little fragile, as beaten up by life as Lockhart felt. He realized that he was pleased to see him again—they had only met once, for half an hour, yet he was the only person who understood.

"Hello, Lang Xiaobo," he said, standing.

"Tom." The Wolf put the file on the table and shook Lockhart's hand, resting the other on his shoulder. "It has been a long time. I thought of you often. You have not aged. You look the same."

"So do you," Lockhart lied.

"Would you like one?" The Wolf pulled out a pack of Chunghwas and offered it to Lockhart.

"I'm trying to give them up."

The Wolf smiled. "One every two decades. That's not so bad. I still prefer them to Marlboros. Sit." He sat opposite, holding the pack of Chunghwas in front of him and turning it in one hand, like a Rubik's Cube he was trying to solve.

"I am very saddened by her death. It was a terrible thing. I wish I could have stopped it. I feel guilty that I did not."

Lockhart sighed. He had been dreading this moment, facing the man who had won the bet they should never have made. But now it felt like a relief to be there, to confront it.

"You were right. I couldn't take care of her properly. I should have left her here, with Mei."

"Do not say that. She was a fine young woman. She died honorably. You should be very proud of her. She did extraordinary things with her life. She was like her sister, I think."

Lockhart blinked. "I think so, yes."

The Wolf puffed his cigarette and opened the file, reading the top sheet to relieve the tension. "Tom Lockhart, economic counselor to the U.S. embassy in Beijing between 1986 and 1989. Officer of the Central Intelligence Agency. Required to leave China for breaches of national security. Subsequently posted by the CIA to Vietnam and Kenya. His wife did not accompany him on these trips and they later divorced. Working as a consultant, mainly for U.S. corporations."

Lockhart sipped his coffee. "That's accurate."

"Would you like to know more about me?" The Wolf stood and leaned against the wall, eyes on Lockhart. "Lang Xiaobo, a member of the fifth generation, born in Beijing in 1952, son of a teacher and a lawyer. I happened to go to the same school as a boy called Chen Longwei—Beijing Number Six Middle School, near Zhongnanhai. We were twelve when we met. He was likable, then. Impish, with a rebellious streak. He provoked the teachers, but he had impeccable connections. His father had fought alongside Mao and had worked in the Foreign Ministry. Mao declared the Cultural Revolution two years later, and suddenly Chen was a Red Guard. You know those kinds of kids at school. Imagine if they could do anything they wanted. Chen turned into a vicious bully. His gang beat and tortured the teachers they called 'capitalist-roaders,' and they painted 'Long Live the Red Terror' on the wall in their blood.

"It was a dangerous time. My parents were 'blacks'—suspected of being bourgeois and counterrevolutionary because of their jobs. I knew that, at any minute, a gang might put them in dunce caps and parade them in the streets. I stuck close to Chen so that they would be left alone. It worked. In 1968, they sent us to the countryside to learn from the peasants. Chen and I went to the same farm in Hubei. Those people had been through the Great Famine. They knew more life than he ever would. He was sixteen. But he formed a village committee to purge them. I try not to think too much about what happened there. Men died, women were raped and discarded. I knew of two peasant women who were thrown off a roof. I thought of those days when he was up on that stage, singing his red songs about Mao."

"I thought you admired the Party," Lockhart said.

"It is always a work in progress. It has made mistakes." Lang tipped ash from his cigarette to the floor and glanced down as he spoke. He looked sad, Lockhart thought. "The last time we met, we talked about the June Fourth Incident. I remember I lost my temper with you. I'll tell you why. That year, we all were in Beijing. You, Chen, and me. He was at the Ministry of Civil Affairs and I had joined the Ministry of State Security. I was a spy, like you. But that wasn't the important thing in my life—it was my wife, Xiaoli. She was an artist I had met at a gallery. My life had been so drab, and she was so beautiful. They were my happiest days."

"I met Margot at that time."

"Then you understand. You know what it was like in Beijing then, the talk was of freedom and reform. Xiaoli had friends who supported the ideas of Fang Lizhi and got caught up by it. I loved her, but I told her not to go too far. I knew things could change fast. She wouldn't listen, and she went to the Square on the night of June Fourth. I stayed up waiting for her, but she never returned. They were caught by an army unit in a side street, and Xiaoli died. She was thirty-two."

"I'm sorry."

That was what the whole affair had been about, Lockhart realized. The Wolf had taken his stupid bet because it had struck a nerve. He'd sent Lizzie to America to prove something that he doubted himself.

59

The Wolf lit another cigarette.

"Two days later, Chen called. He said they were asking questions about me at the Ministry of Civil Affairs—*Did Lang Xiaobo share her views? Should he be investigated?* 'You don't, do you?' he said. 'No,' I told him. Xiaoli had been dead two days, and I betrayed her to save myself. He said he would deal with it. It was like being back at school with him again. I didn't realize that he was a traitor."

"Was he?" Lockhart said.

"You recruited him."

"Not exactly. He volunteered."

The Wolf walked back to the table, took a blank sheet of paper from the file, and inscribed the characters of Chen's name at the top. "Would you mind if I took notes?" he said.

"This is classified information." Lockhart leaned across and took one of the Wolf's cigarettes. The aroma of the smoke was like being back in Beijing with him, in the *siheyuan* with Chen's dead mistress.

"You must want justice."

Lockhart nodded. It was a fair bargain. An old piece of information on a single discredited agent in return for revenge. "I knew Chen. He found me at a reception in the Great Hall of the People, after a trade mission. It was a year before June Fourth, and he was my easiest recruit. He said he'd give us information in return for a passport. I thought he was a Party hack without a conscience—he was less of a Communist than I was. But you don't pick your friends in that business, and Langley loved him. I was a hero—Beijing was in chaos, and I had a source in Zhongnanhai. He had expensive tastes, and I did what I needed to keep him happy. We set up a Hong Kong account for him. We found a place for his mistress."

"It was a beautiful *siheyuan*."

"She liked it, he liked it. We were happy." Lockhart inhaled the tobacco. "Until he got her pregnant. Then it fell apart."

The Wolf nodded. "That's when Chen called me. He sounded panicky, which wasn't like him. Even when he was beating people until they bled, he was calm. He said he had a woman who had been causing trouble. Things had gotten out of control, and he needed me to deal with it. He had known that he would need a favor—his mistress for my wife. I didn't understand how he could keep a mistress in Gulou Xi Dajie on his salary, so I did some digging. I turned up the accounts and the link to you. I should have reported him as a traitor, but I was in his grip. So I did what he asked."

The Wolf passed his palm across the table, wiping an invisible layer of dust. His fingertips were yellow, but his hands were mottled. *Bad circulation,* Lockhart thought. Years of sitting in meetings, drinking toasts at Party banquets, biding his time to make amends.

"Twin girls, in a basket by the bed. They were hungry and crying, but so small that no one heard. He'd killed their mother and left them there. That was his last act as a father. If I'd smothered them in their baskets, he wouldn't have cared. He disgusted me, and I hated the Party for producing him. But I convinced myself that you were the villain—it was easier that way. I wanted to teach you a lesson, but I should have learned one myself. No one had ever stopped Chen, so he thought he couldn't be stopped. If I had kept my temper, those girls would have gone to an orphanage together. That would have been better."

"It wouldn't have," Lockhart said. "We loved Lizzie, although it was for a short time. I've often thought about us in that *siheyuan*. We fought over the twins like objects. We didn't know how precious they were."

The Wolf shrugged. "We were young men."

"How did you find Lizzie?"

"I followed them, over the years, I knew where they were, what they were doing. It wasn't difficult."

"You wanted to win the bet?"

The Wolf grimaced. "It started out like that. But as they grew, it changed. I visited Guilin when Mei was six years old. She won't remember. I was in a party of officials and I saw her, playing in the courtyard. Xiaoli had wanted children, but she died too young. I asked myself what she would have done. I got Sun Yat-sen University to take her and, when she graduated, I recruited her."

"And Lizzie?"

"I knew when she came to Hong Kong, and when you followed. I wondered what had brought you back, and it led me to Long Tan. You may not believe it, but I respected you. I had seen what you could do, and I believed that if you were interested in something, it had to be interesting. I read the files, and I started to ask myself why so many of them were dying. I knew I was putting myself at risk by inquiring, but I didn't care. I was too old, too tired to keep on protecting him. When I saw your daughter, I knew. It had his mark."

"Why did you show Mei? Wasn't that cruel?"

"She had to fight. I gave her a reason to."

Feng held Mei's hand as she sat on a narrow utility bed in a room painted a drab olive green. Lockhart had told her who her father was after she had woken up. The Wolf had come with him to talk about the past, and they had taken her to a PLA officer's room with a mahogany desk and a fading map of Guangdong pinned on the wall. She had noticed their shame as they talked about their past.

When Mei was young, she'd imagined her parents. Villagers, she thought, who were too poor to bring up more than one child. Maybe, she'd even admitted to herself, they had wanted a boy. It wasn't such a terrible crime. She looked around the orphanage at all the girls, left on the street. But she dreamed that they had loved her, that they had wanted to keep her, if it had been possible. It had been a difficult time, tough enough for peasants to feed themselves, without an extra mouth. That was what she'd told herself when she was small.

"I want to see Chen," she said.

"Are you sure about that, treasured one?"

"He should know what he did."

"He won't care. It makes no difference to him if he had his daughter killed. He stabbed your mother and left you behind." Feng knelt and stroked her arm. "You know what he is. Forget him."

"I want to go."

A Jeep was waiting, but Mei set off across the tarmac on foot, walking past the landing lights with Feng beside her. Two fighters had left at dawn with a roar, but since then the only activity had come from the detention center. Vehicles crossed back and forth, and a parade of officials had entered and left the building—Chen was already a Party attraction. They waited outside for half an hour before the Wolf emerged to take them through.

The Wolf led them to a room with a two-way mirror, where Mei stood with her face so close to the glass that it misted with her breath. Chen was in a padded room, reading the *People's Daily*. It had nothing about his arrest and wouldn't for several days, while Zhongnanhai pondered what signal to send. But one story had made it to Weibo—a few paragraphs about an arrest in Macau—and the social network was buzzing with the news.

She stared at him, scanning for a likeness. They'd taken his suit, and he hadn't shaved. His hair was unkempt, and his stubble was gray. He already looked older, face crumpled by his fall. She remembered him in Revolutionary Martyrs Park, bursting with the power of high office. Now, he looked like a petty gangster, plucked off the streets of Kowloon.

Mei turned and stood with her back to him and her palms against the cold glass. Feng was still glued to the view.

"I don't want to talk to him. Let him rot."

"You're so right, baby."

"He's not my father," she said as she left.

60

"Are these limes fresh-squeezed? Like, this evening?"

Reassured by the waiter, Henry Martin relaxed in his bucket armchair and sipped his drink. He was sitting with Lockhart in the Atrium bar of the Four Seasons, seventy stories above Guangzhou, with a floor-to-ceiling view of the Pearl River. The curved roof and sides of the Haixinsha Island stadium were lit in white bars, making it grin like a shark, and the Canton TV Tower was pulsing through a light show, turning blue, red, green, orange, and finally multicolored in stripes and bars.

"You should see the Zaha Hadid opera house. It's over that side," Martin said, twisting his body to point across the bar. "Man, she's a genius—she's got vision. She didn't get anything built until she was forty-five, and it was a fire station in Germany. Nobody wanted her stuff. Can you believe it? If you try to make something original, idiots get in your way."

Martin was in a three-piece lilac-colored linen suit that matched the carpet of the bar perfectly. Lockhart wondered if he'd chosen it intentionally and would change again to fit with his dinner reservation. Martin put down his vodka and lime and waved his arm across the city, taking in the perfect needle arch of the Liede Bridge, lit up in yellow and orange.

"These guys don't mess around, do they? Don't get me wrong— I'm a capitalist. But they've got something going here. As an American, doesn't it scare you? Six hundred million people taken out of poverty. Whatever you say, they get stuff done. They built the

Shanghai-to-Nanjing bullet train in the time it took to fix the broken elevator in the Delta terminal at JFK. I checked every time I went through there. I told the president the other day. He was really pissed."

"They've got problems, too. Corruption, one-party rule, human rights," Lockhart said.

"For sure. But sometimes I wonder about moving over here. California's finished. It's got a terminal case of democracy. We're allowed to vote on everything, so nothing gets done."

"*This* hasn't put you off?"

"I'm glad it's over. Cao was hard to deal with. He wouldn't let us inside, and now I know why. He said the workers were happy, the media was exaggerating. He didn't mention that he'd been killing them. We're lucky most of the story didn't get out. That's another thing they do well—control the flow of information. They'd be great at product launches. Anyway, I don't have to deal with Cao anymore. They've put him in a labor camp, I heard."

"Will you stay in Guangdong?"

"I'm not going to lie. I thought hard about leaving. There are plenty of other places we could go—Bangladesh, Indonesia. China's not as cheap as it used to be, and Chen screwed me. I didn't know whom to trust. But here's the thing. I went to Beijing to thrash it out. Those guys talk a lot of bullshit for public consumption, but they don't smoke their own dope. They want Poppy to stay, and they said they'd fix it so I don't face any trouble. I'll be a friend of China. Having seen what they do to their enemies, I prefer that."

Martin drained his vodka and lime and popped a rice cracker into his mouth as he stood.

"They offered me a new partner. Old-school good technology, here to stay. The People's Liberation Army of Guangdong. Their commercial operation needs an upgrade, and we can learn from each other. I'm having dinner with the guy who fixed the deal—Major General Sun."

Lizzie's procession set out late the next morning. Wing had resisted Mei's efforts to tone it down, and it stretched down the Li River promenade by the Jiefang Bridge. Two marshals lined them up under the palm trees—a snake of children from the Social Welfare Institute with banners, mourners for hire in white suits, pallbearers carrying a scarlet papier-mâché house for the ghosts of the dead, a marching band.

The limestone hills were circled in mist, and Guilin was going about its business. Under the promenade, two women stood up to their ankles in the river, washing clothes. Lockhart and Margot took the lead, wearing sashes and carrying incense sticks, with Mei and Wing behind, holding photos of Lizzie. As they crossed the promenade, heading up Yiren Road, the band's cymbals clashing, bicycles swerved and the women at the Milk Tea One stand offered drinks. It was a fine procession, and it lengthened as passersby joined the throng.

It had been Wing's idea, and Lockhart had wondered if it wasn't a mistake, on top of Lizzie's funeral at a Unitarian church in Chevy Chase. Margot had been somber on the flight and hadn't spoken as they drove through Guilin to the orphanage. But Wing waited for them in the courtyard as they passed through the barrier, and Margot had leapt out of the car to hold her close. She had even asked him to photograph the two of them in the same place as before.

Now, as they crossed the red suspension bridge over Xiqing Lake, it was hard not to enjoy the spectacle. Wing looked triumphant as women under parasols waved at them from motorcycles. The sun broke through the mist to reflect off the lake and the Nengren Temple's yellow walls stood on the other bank, two stone snakes slithering along its tiled roof.

"I'm glad we came," Margot said.

"I'd do anything to bring her back," Lockhart said.

"I know you would." She touched his hand.

As they reached the temple, the band peeled off for drinks, and Wing led them into the inner area, past an altar lined with candles and a stall selling money. Lockhart bought a five-tiered tower of red and gold paper and put it amid the ashes in a brick oven. As he lit the paper, smoke billowed from the chimney, and Margot clutched Wing, her eyes streaming.

The temple Buddhas were brightly polished, and the altar shone with red lacquer. The three largest sat cross-legged on their ornamental thrones behind the altar, their arms outstretched and their eyes closed. Wing took an apple from her pocket and placed it on the altar as an offering. Lockhart thought of Mr. and Mrs. Wu, grieving for their daughter as he'd tried to pay them off. He remembered Lizzie as a child, throwing snowballs in the yard. An image gripped his heart, of her fleeing across the Dongguan fields, looking for him.

He walked out of the temple and stood by the gate, gazing across the bridge to the lake. Two of the orphanage kids went past, heading for the supermarket at the end of the block with a crisp banknote. When he looked up, Mei was standing by him. He hadn't heard her approach.

Lizzie was my fortune and I squandered her, he thought. He wanted to say it out loud, to confess, but all he managed was: "I miss her."

Mei put her arm through his and they stood together, watching the children run back with candy to sweeten the bitterness of death.

Acknowledgments

I first saw China twenty years ago and it has fascinated me ever since. On my visits since then, government and Party officials, academics, business leaders, workers, and citizens have shown me everything from the Central Party School in Beijing to factories in the Pearl River delta, and talked openly about their country and their lives. I thank them all. I was helped by many people who know China, the world of corporate intelligence, and the technology industry in Guangdong and Hong Kong. They include: An Ping, Alison Bradley, Jack Clode, Leo Fang, Rana Foroohar, Julia Grindell, Tommy Helsby, Kathrin Hille, Rahul Jacob, James Kynge, Chris Leahy, Ian McCredie, Richard McGregor, Mark Nicholson, Jim Ohlson, Euan Rellie, Shang Lin, Zhang Lifen, Zhou Ping, and my fearless Guilin taxi driver. I drew on books and research by Leslie Chang, Rania Huntington, Li Ling, Flora Sapio, and Ezra Vogel. Garry McKenzie introduced me to Wing Chun on a winter night in Hackney. My agents David Kuhn, Becky Sweren, and Gill Coleridge were unfailingly supportive and I owe a debt to Mark Tavani, a great editor. Thanks above all for their forbearance and love to Rosie, Yasmin, and Rachel.

About the Author

JOHN GAPPER is an associate editor and business columnist of the *Financial Times,* and the author of several books including the novel *A Fatal Debt*. He lives in London with his wife and daughters.

About the Type

This book was set in Sabon, a typeface designed by the well-known German typographer Jan Tschichold (1902–74). Sabon's design is based upon the original letter forms of sixteenth-century French type designer Claude Garamond and was created specifically to be used for three sources: foundry type for hand composition, Linotype, and Monotype. Tschichold named his typeface for the famous Frankfurt typefounder Jacques Sabon (c. 1520–80).